Testament Hill

This is a work of fiction. Names, characters, places and events are a product of the author's imagination or used fictitiously. Any resemblance to real persons either living or dead is coincidental and not intended by the author.

Copyright © 2015 Philip J. Kadwell

All rights reserved. No part of this book may be reproduced in any form whatsoever without written permission from the author.

Published by Liberty Street Publications
P.O.665, South Lyon, MI 48178
Design by P.J.Kadwell

ISBN: 978-0-692-69674-3

Acknowledgements

Many thanks to all those who graciously gave their time and effort to review this book. Special thanks to Lauren Kadwell, Cindy Livesay and Stephanie Harrigan.

This book is dedicated to my wife, Deborah, for her patience and encouragement during the often arduous process of writing and editing a novel.

It is the greatest art of the devil
To convince us he does not exist
-Baudelaire

Chapter 1

Friday Morning

The blue and grey Volvo station wagon snaked down the dark, twisting blacktop of County Road 23. In the rear view mirror, Doctor Claire Brannigan could see the eastern horizon brightening with daybreak. She lifted her hand off the steering wheel and checked her wristwatch: 7:45.

The endless ribbon of highway rushing by and the monotonous drone of the engine was luring her to sleep. She rolled down her window. Sharp autumn air whistled in and tousled her short-cropped auburn hair. Claire Brannigan shivered and brought the window back up.

Up ahead, a road sign:

> Incorporation Limit
> Testament Hill, Missouri
> Population 623

Claire sighed. *Almost there. Thank God.*
Then a hundred yards further, a billboard:

> Prester John
> Tent Revival, Saturday, Oct 28, 1962
> Boone County Fair Grounds

Claire squinted at the sign and pulled over onto the shoulder in front of the billboard. The Volvo's tires ground to a stop on the bone dry gravel. She turned off the engine and set the parking brake. Then she leaned over, popped open the glove box, took out a couple of tissues and jammed them in her blouse pocket. For a moment, Claire considered the stub-nosed .38 caliber revolver partially concealed behind a map of Missouri, then reached back in and pulled the revolver out of its holster.

She climbed slowly out of the car, stiff from the two hour drive from the University of Eastern Missouri. The professor of geology clasped her arms over her head and stretched out her lithe, five foot nine frame, casually dangling the .38 from her thumb.

She brought her arms down, and with practiced ease, clicked open the .38's cylinder and checked that the hammer rested on the one empty chamber. It was a safety measure that prevented the firing pin from slapping a bullet if the hammer was accidently jarred, as from a fall on a hard surface. The gun may have looked small, but Claire knew that a .38 inch diameter lead slug flying willy-nilly at 1200 feet per second could have tragic consequences.

Claire closed the revolver back up with a snap of her wrist and slipped it into the pocket of her jeans.

She stepped behind the billboard, slid down her pants and crouched to take a pee.

A blue jay called out a warning. Claire looked up. Perched on top of the sign, the bird was outlined by the rising morning light. It tilted its head and scrutinized her.

"What are you looking at?" Claire whispered.

The sky lit up with a blue flash accompanied by a dull boom. Squawking loudly, the Jay flew off. Claire could have sworn she felt the ground shake a couple seconds later - a vibration as if a loaded semi was driving by. But the road was empty of traffic.

Must be lightning and thunder in the distance.

Finishing her business, Claire pulled her jeans up off her well-worn hiking boots, tucked in her white linen blouse and got back in the car. After stowing the Smith & Wesson, she flipped on the interior light and checked her appearance in the rearview mirror. Her slate blue eyes under her high forehead returned the cool assessment. She looked tired from the long drive from Springfield. She forced a grin and examined her teeth for residue of that morning's rushed breakfast of toast smeared with peanut butter and rubbed her forefinger vigorously across her gums. For a self-conscious second, Claire regarded the deep dimples that formed with the smile, then turned off the light, sat back in the seat and turned on the engine.

A State Highway Patrol car startled her as it zoomed past, heading towards the dawn, emergency lights flashing furiously. She watched until the red blinking faded, then pulled the Volvo back on to the road and drove into the western darkness.

A few minutes later, the sun came up behind her, igniting the landscape in the fiery hues of the fall. Ahead, the road curved to meet a railroad crossing at right angles. A dark figure was standing at the side of the road. Claire only got a half-second glimpse: A man - very tall. His face was hidden in the shadows, but she thought she saw the glint of teeth. The man was either smiling broadly or snarling. His arm was extended, and he had his thumb out as if to hitch a ride.

No way.

But as Claire flew by, she saw he merely had his palm open, more like signaling a greeting.

How strange.

A Sinclair gas station, glowing under sulfurous yellow lights, materialized out of the dark.

Thirsty and in need of a pick-me-up, Claire slowed and drove in. Next to the gas station office she spotted a Coca-Cola Vendo machine. She parked the car and strode over to the machine, fished a dime out of her pocket, dropped it in the coin slot. She opened the dispensing door, and grabbed the neck of the eight ounce, blue-green bottle. It was stuck. She pulled harder and the bottle broke loose and her hand jerked back from the release of tension. There was a sharp pain, and Claire looked down to see a jagged scratch across the knuckle of her forefinger. Dark crimson blood oozed out.

"Are you okay, ma'am?" The attendant had come out of the booth and was holding a rag. He looked to be about 17, tall and gangly, wearing grimy striped overalls and a greasy forage cap. He stepped closer and offered her the rag.

Claire said, "Thanks but, I have some bandages in my car."

The attendant grinned, revealing one missing upper incisor and bottom teeth crowded together in a jumble.

"Couldn't help but notice what happened," he said. "I'm really sorry." He bent down and examined the vending machine. "Don't know how it could've cut you…" He fumbled around, running his hand around the dispensing door.

"Ah!"

He pulled out shiny object, and held it up. "It's a piece of jewelry…looks like a crucifix or something. Must of got torn off somebody leaning over the machine. Your hand probably caught on it."

He held it out for Claire to examine.

Claire saw that it was not a true crucifix, which would have an image of Christ on the cross. It was more like an Apostles' Cross with three lobes on the end of the four arms, representing the twelve apostles. It was crude and the cross oddly angled and distorted, so that it almost looked like a stick figure. It had the verdigris patina of aged copper. Embedded in the axis was a quarter-sized, roughly cut yellow crystal. A citrine - or perhaps a yellow zircon, Claire guessed. The cross was surrounded by a circle of metal attached at the foot of the cross. It looked cheap - just a tarnished trinket. Some kind of good luck amulet.

"It's yours if you want," The attendant was saying.

"No, that's okay…" Claire took a closer look and noticed tiny letters roughly engraved on the circle: *VRS*. The letters were vaguely familiar, but the memory was elusive, something far in the past.

"All right, I'll take it, thanks. I guess I earned it." Claire took the cross gingerly from the attendant's hand and slipped it in her pants pocket. There was something about the inscription and the serendipity of its discovery that made her feel she should have it.

I can put it on my necklace later, she thought- *can't hurt.*

The attendant was saying "…sure I can't give you something for your hand?"

"I'm good." Claire tried to smile. She turned and walked briskly back to her car.

"Hey, you forgot your soda," The attendant called out.

Claire waved her hand over her head. "Not thirsty anymore. You can have it."

She suddenly was eager to get out of there, away from the station and the creepy attendant.

Police Chief Owen Childress cursed as he tried to keep his coffee from spilling when his Ford Interceptor patrol car bounced over some potholes. He had some news to tell Karl Beamer and knew that the well driller was out at the Jackson farm. Since that old fool Cal Jackson was too cheap to have a telephone, Chief Childress had decided to drive out.

Childress became aware that he was chewing his lip again, and put his hand up to his jaw to remind himself to stop. As he ran his fingers along his grizzled and almost double chin, he realized he had neglected to shave that morning.

I must take better care of myself. If I don't, I'll end up just like those old farts who sit around in front of the town hardware store, wearing baggy overalls and making idiotic conversation about the good ol' days and passing along rumors about who was sneaking off to the woodshed with whom.

Not me, he thought fiercely. *I'm going to hold off going out to pasture as long as I can.*

The contemplation of old age and mortality caused a chill to pass though Chief Childress like an icy shadow. He wasn't a spring chicken anymore: Fifty-eight. Someday, he would have to take off his badge and hang up his holster for the last time.

He reached for his coffee and took a swallow of the bitter lukewarm brew, regretting now that he hadn't put a dollop of Old Crow in it.

The trip to Jackson's farm gave Childress the opportunity to get out of his claustrophobic office - and away from Edith, his talkative dispatcher and Frank Hooper, his creepy deputy, whose behavior had recently become odder than usual, if that was possible.

The image of Deputy Hooper flashed in Childress' mind.

With his elongated gaunt face, thin lips and ever shifting beady black eyes, the deputy's features worked together to give Hooper the uncanny semblance of a Doberman Pinscher.

Childress spit out the window.

He wished he could get rid of Hooper, but he followed the rules and did his job...marginally. Chief Childress couldn't justify firing him just because he was creepy. Eventually, Childress figured, Hooper would act totally out of line, and he could let him go. Hopefully, it wouldn't be something too awful - that innocents wouldn't be involved. Maybe his deputy would just shoot himself in the head while cleaning his precious nine millimeter automatic. Childress smiled at the thought.

He turned up the drive to the Jackson farm and parked his cruiser in front a mustard colored Ford F6 truck. Karl Beamer, the owner of Acme Well Services, was standing at the back of his truck, operating the Speedstar drilling rig that was raised from its pivot mount on the chassis.

Childress thought: *Ol' Karl's probably happier than a possum in a corn crib, with all the business the dry spell was bringing in.*

The spell was causing the area's water wells to dry up. The first was at Amos Doyle's farm in mid-summer. As the season wore on, the phenomenon expanded to other farmsteads. Now it was at Jackson's.

It was the damnedest thing. Childress had witnessed a few droughts in all his years in the county, but never one that caused this many wells to run dry.

He watched for a minute from his cruiser as the Speedstar's spudder beam hoisted its drill bit with the groan of rusted and tired metal. The percussion drill had seen better days, but kept doing its job.

Just like me, Childress mused.

Karl Beamer lifted a canvas gloved hand off a handle on the rig and pulled up his tattered baseball cap up to swipe his forehead, leaving a streak of grey mud. He was focused on the drill's operation and hadn't yet noticed the Chief. His hand returned to the lever that controlled the rising and falling of the bit, while his other loosely gripped the cable. The beam came down and the twisting cable slipped back down into the well hole, pulled by the weight of the heavy chisel-like bit.

Childress knew Beamer's years of experience enabled the well driller to judge the type of geology the bit was chipping through by the reaction of the cable as the bit stuck. A dullness in the impact indicated it was time to insert the bailer and pull out the slurry of muddy water and crushed debris that was accumulating at the bottom of the hole.

"Let's get you out of the abyss," Childress heard Beamer say as he pulled again on the lever and the spudder beam rocked back up. Then he noticed the Childress's cruiser and lifted a hand in greeting.

As Claire exited from the gas station, she caught a glimpse of a black and white Plymouth police cruiser nosing out from a large white cedar tree.

"Oh, crap."

She was driving a bit too fast, and guessed she probably hadn't come to a complete stop before going out into the street. She eased up on the accelerator and glanced down at her speedometer to make sure the Volvo was now a little under the speed limit. She checked her rearview mirror. The cruiser had pulled onto the road and was following her. For a moment it just kept pace, staying about 20 yards behind.

Then the red bubble light started blinking, and the cruiser accelerated up to her rear bumper.

Claire slowed, drove to the side of the road and stopped.

Deputy Frank Hooper smiled. He finally got somebody. There had been complaints about truckers blowing through town at daybreak, and even though he usually worked the afternoon shift, Hooper was happy to occasionally set up an early morning speed trap for a couple hours. He hadn't been sleeping well lately, so he figured he might as well make some overtime. He was beginning to think he wouldn't nick anyone that morning. Until now.

He grabbed his ticket pad and climbed out of his patrol car, leaving the engine running and the flasher on. As he smoothed out his uniform, he caught a glimpse of himself in the driver's side window. He adjusted his eight point garrison hat and pushed up his aviator-style sunglasses, grunting in satisfaction.

He took his time walking over to the odd-looking foreign car. He was going for a dignified gait as he thought befitting a law enforcement officer. As he got closer, Hooper got a better look at the driver, and wetted his lips in anticipation. It was a red-haired woman, and she looked attractive. Very attractive. This would be a good end to his boring midnight shift.

Hot damn.

He got to the car window and tipped his hat at the driver. "Driver's license and vehicle registration, miss," he said, attempting to sound nonchalant but with an air of command.

Claire looked up, momentarily startled by the deputy's wolf-like grin. She put on a smile. "Of course, officer. Is there a problem?"

"Driver's license and registration, miss."

While Claire leaned over and rummaged through the glove box, Hooper took the opportunity to eye the driver. He was disappointed to see she was wearing pants rather than a skirt, and some type of clunky man-like boots instead of heels. His fantasy began to deflate.

As Claire searched for her documents, she carefully slid her .38 back out of sight. Then she surreptitiously undid the top button of her blouse.

"Ah, here we go." She handed the papers to Hooper.

The deputy took the papers and illuminated them with his flashlight. He pretended to study them but his attention was more on ogling the driver. His pulse accelerated as he noticed Claire's partly exposed sheer lacy bra.

"You know, miss, you did not come to a complete stop

when you pulled out of the gas station back there."

His distraction was not lost on Claire. She smiled again, and raised her eyes, opening them wide. "Really, officer…" Claire studied his name tag. "…Hooper. I thought I did come to a complete stop just for a second."

"No, you did not." The deputy frowned at her. "You're not from around here, are you?"

This bumpkins's detective skills are incredible, Claire thought. *And what moron wears sunglasses when the sun is barely up?*

She pulled out her trump card. "I'm here in town to meet with Chief Childress."

That obviously knocked some of the wind out of the deputy. He'd better be careful how he handled this. Maybe this woman was some highfalutin' bureaucrat from the State.

"Well, then." Hooper handed Claire back her papers. "I am just giving you a warning today. Just make sure next time, you come to a full stop before pulling out onto the highway…" He hesitated for a split second. "Ma'am."

Claire reached down to the ignition, started her car and revved the engine.

The deputy touched the brim of his hat. "Have a good day."

Claire hit the gas and pulled out, her tires kicking up gravel.

Hooper turned on his heel and sauntered back to his cruiser.

"Bitch," he said under his breath.

Chief Childress returned Karl Beamer's wave. As he climbed laboriously out of the cruiser, Childress grimaced at the sharp pain in his arthritic hip and thought longingly of the bottle of bourbon in the bottom drawer of his desk.

He made his way over to the rig and raised his voice over the sound of its engine. "How's it going, Karl?"

"Just give me a minute to secure the drill, Chief." Karl Beamer said. The cable went taut and the chisel bit jerked up out of the hole. It was dripping with slate-colored sludge.

Then he turned to Childress. "Same old story." He pointed at the well hole. "This drought has everybody drying up. Just got to drill deeper to get down to the table."

"It's the Curse," Childress said half-jokingly.

Beamer frowned and turned his attention back to the rig. "That's all bullshit, and you know it, Chief."

There had been lots of talk around town about what was causing the wells to go dry. Some people blamed the so-called Curse of Testament Hill. The same curse that caused weird lights on the ground in the dead of night, freak accidents, children being born with abnormalities and some with strange powers. Any misfortune in Testament Hill was likely to be attributed to the "Curse".

Chief Childress's opinion was the drought was probably a quirk of the weather.

Still, he found his eyes wandering over to Beamer's twelve year old son, Gilbert, sitting on the fender of the drill truck. The boy was already tall as a man but still had the petulant, impish face of a child. He was smoking a cigarette, seemingly watching the men through his dark, round wire-rim sunglasses. Of course, Gilbert couldn't see them, but Childress always got the eerie feeling that he could somehow sense a scene before him.

The doctors had told Beamer and his wife that their son's blindness was due to something called optic nerve hypoplasia, or de Morsier syndrome. It was caused by a hormone deficiency. Gilbert's mother, however, was certain the Testament Hill Curse was to blame.

Karl Beamer once confided to Childress that he suspected his son's affliction was a result of experimental fertilizer the federal government tested back in '52, using the land next to the Doyle farm. God knows what nasty chemicals might have been involved.

Some of the locals in Testament Hill thought Gilbert had been touched by angels and believed him to be a "healer". They would ask Karl's permission for his son to perform a laying on of hands to cure them of various afflictions, ranging from the cancer to corns. Most of the time, Gilbert's attentions didn't help, but the occasions when someone got better stuck in the minds of folks. People have selective memories, Karl Beamer one time observed to Childress. His son Gilbert's failures were forgotten, his "successes" became legend

"I'm his father," Beamer had told Childress, without much conviction, "I know better."

Chief Childress figured that Gilbert's laying on of hands didn't cause any harm. Karl Beamer would only allow his son to go in when traditional medicine had failed to affect a cure. He wouldn't let anybody pay for Gilbert's attention. If they wanted to bring an apple pie or a smoked ham by the house, that was alright, but no cash would be accepted.

Childress watched as Gilbert tilted his head and slowly rotated it back and forth. A monarch butterfly flitted by. In a flash, the boy's left hand shot out and closed into a fist. Then he brought his fist to his face as if he was going to examine what it had captured and opened it. With his other hand, he snatched the monarch from his palm, holding it between his forefinger and thumb. Smiling benignly, his buckteeth hanging over his lower lip, he rubbed his fingers together. The orange and black insect fluttered on frayed wings to the ground.

"Jesus, Mary and Joseph." Childress murmured.

Childress turned back to the rig when the drilling bit clanged to a stop on top of the tower. Karl Beamer locked down the cable and looked over at the Chief. "Now, what can I do for ya, Owen?"

"Just wanted to let you know, Karl," Childress stepped closer, "I got a call from the university. The geology department is sending out some kind of expert to look into our situation."

"Is that so?" Beamer said suspiciously.

"A friend of mine in security at the school is on the same bowling team as the head of the geology department. My friend told him about our water problem here. The department head said he would ask their expert hydrologist give me a call. Sure enough, she called the next day said she'd be happy to come and investigate. Should be arriving today. Apparently it would help her with some of her research. Doing it for free. Her name is Doctor Claire Brannigan."

Beamer grunted. "Lotta good that's going to do. Is she going to conjure up some rain so the water table rises? I swear, it's like the pits of Hell have opened up and drained off all the water around here."

"We'll take any help we can get." Childress rubbed his nose. "Karl, I expect she will be wanting to talk with you, being the well-driller around here. If she comes around asking questions, try to be polite."

Beamer nodded.

"Another thing… " Childress looked back towards Beamer's son, who was now slowly turning in circles in front of the cruiser. "Do you think Gilbert might visit Widow Wheeler? She's been poorly lately. Doctors can't find anything with their probing and poking. Think it may be mental. Maybe your son could get her feeling better."

"I guess so," Beamer said. He narrowed his eyes. "You know how I feel about the whole thing, Chief."

"It sure would be appreciated."

"I'll arrange it, then."

Childress nodded. "Well, I got to get going." He turned and headed back to his car. "Remember to be nice to Miss Brannigan," he said over his shoulder.

Chapter 2

January 10, 1952
Rapid City Air Force Base, South Dakota

In spite of its enormous size, the Convair B-36 Peacemaker was barely visible through the driving blizzard.

It materialized on the tarmac like a ghostly apparition as Johnny Preskovics walked towards the aircraft with the rest of the thirteen man crew of Flight 2122.

Bombardier Preskovics pulled the collar of his flight jacket tighter around his neck and tried not to think of the flight ahead. The B-36 heavy bomber, attached to the USAF 28th bomber wing, was scheduled that morning for takeoff at 500 hours for a routine crew readiness flight. Preskovics knew better. Flights aboard the B-36 were never routine.

The previous evening, Preskovics and the crew had spent a few hours ribbing and toasting the ground chief who was setting off on a five day pass to get married. Tumbling out of his cot at four a.m. that morning, Johnny "Pres" tried easing his hangover by drinking a glass of tomato juice and then orange juice, along with popping three aspirins. He still felt like shit on a stick, but as the icy wind slicing across the airstrip bit into his face, it numbed some of the throbbing in his head. The raucous banter that usually ping-ponged among the crew before a mission was subdued, dampened by the aftereffects of the bachelor party and the prospect of flying into the fierce weather.

Preskovics followed the other members of the crew up the access ladder into the gigantic aircraft. He always was the last on board, and as he reached down to close the hatch, in a secret ritual, rapped his knuckles three times on the thin aluminum hull and murmured *via con dios*. Then he took his seat in the canvas chair at the bombardier's station and dozed off and on as the crew went through the six hundred item check-off list.

Finally, the engines ran up with a roar like a hundred Harley Davidsons at full throttle and the largest bomber ever built accelerated down the runway, the bumps and swaying enough to make an experienced sailor seasick. The pilot pulled back on the yoke and the B-36 nosed up and left the earth, slowly rising into the sky. Climbing through snow to 45,000 feet, the aircraft turned to a south-eastward heading, cruising above the cloud tops of the Midwest. Its destination was Barksdale AFB in Louisiana. The mission was to simulate a bombing run over downtown St. Louis, Missouri.

Prior to getting ready for the practice run, Preskovics had little to do except focus on his misery. He groaned and held his head as the aircraft bounced through thermals. Even in normal circumstances the flight would have been uncomfortable. With a hangover, it was particularly nauseating.

The bomber finally settled into smooth flight, and Preskovics decided it was safe to stow away the airsickness bag sitting preemptively at his feet. As his stomach calmed and his headache notched down to a dull ache, he leaned back and stared out a porthole as the sky cleared. Below the plane, a carpet of corn and wheat fields rolled out, ornamented with green patches of alfalfa, tiny red barns and white farmhouses, ribbons of blacktop and oases of trees.

Even after three years of constant flying, the experience never ceased to amaze Preskovics. It was so unnatural. Man had evolved to tread the earth. To be so high up, cruising through the air, was god-like. This is what angels must see, he mused.

Not that Preskovics really believed in angels - or God, for that matter. There was too much pointless tragedy and evil in the world to reconcile with the idea of a benevolent, omnipotent being. At least not any kind of being that Preskovics would worship. If any supreme being existed, he figured, He would be more like the God of the Old Testament: demanding, vengeful, bloodthirsty. More like a brutal father.

His interest in the problem of Good and Evil led the

bombardier to the ancient teachings of Zoroastrians and Manicheans, which advocated a dualistic concept of higher powers: there were good gods and evil gods, locked in eternal combat. That was logical. That's why good and bad things happen. It depended on who had the upper hand at the moment. It made sense.

In truth, the Preskovics was pretty sure that there was no god or gods. He had never witnessed firsthand any undisputable evidence of a higher power. But if these supernatural beings were real, he reflected, the evil gods had the edge.

With that thought, he glanced down at the access hatch to the bomb bay. Inside the bay were two of the most lethal weapons made by humankind.

The B-36 was carrying two Mark IV atomic bombs. The Mark IV was an improved version of the Mark III "Fat Man" that was dropped on Nagasaki, Japan in 1945. Its yield was 31 kilotons: when it exploded, it was like blowing up thirty-one thousand tons of TNT at once. Or, as Preskovics would say, to give a more impressive perspective, sixty-two *million* pounds of TNT exploding instantaneously.

As he contemplated the bombs, a strange darkness arose in the center of the bombardier's brain and bloomed outward to his eyes until the scene before him was cast in shadow.

Preskovics took a deep breath. At least in their present state, he reminded himself, the weapons could not go off.

The standard procedure was that a segment of the bomb's plutonium core was kept separate during flight to prevent an accidental nuclear explosion. The protocol was called "IFI" for *In Flight Insertion*. Years later, Preskovics would joke that IFI was code for initiation into the mile high club.

Without that missing plutonium segment, there was not enough fissionable material in the core to cause the nuclear chain reaction that was the source of the A-bomb's destructive power. When the aircraft neared its target, that critical component would be inserted into the bomb to arm it.

The threat of unimaginable annihilation represented by the bombs was supposed to make war obsolete. It was MAD - *Mutual Assured Destruction*. The theory of nuclear deterrence had been drilled into Preskovics' head: the existence of the bombs, the B-36s and their highly trained flight crews were designed to prevent war by making its consequences unacceptable.

Preskovics was skeptical of that train of logic. Human beings, from his experience, were often illogical and driven to act more by baser emotional needs then by cool-headed evaluation of consequences. People were quite susceptible to madness.

He turned away and gazed again out the porthole at the Iowa farmland sweeping beneath the bomber. He prayed silently to whatever higher powers there may be, that he was wrong.

A slight change in the sound of the six Pratt and Whitney radial engines shook him out of his reverie. The engines had a reputation for breakdowns, and Preskovics had a very keen interest in their performance, as did the rest of the crew.

In addition to the six piston engines, the B-36 had a pair of General Electric jet engines tacked on the end of each wing to give it added thrust for takeoff. The saying was: *six turning and four burning*.

Preskovics' opinion was that unreliability of the B-36 Peacemaker was due more to its complexity than the quality of it components. With so much crap going on, *something* was bound to fail.

Each twenty-eight cylinder radial engine turned a nineteen foot diameter propeller mounted in a "pusher" configuration. Preskovics could never get used to the appearance: the props were on the back side of the wing behind the engine. This reduced propeller turbulence in the airflow over the wing. The "backwards" pusher design also placed the carburetors in front of the warming effect of the engines as in a common "props forward" position. Without this heat, the bombardier knew only too well, carburetor intakes were prone to ice buildup. The buildup of ice blocked air flow, resulting in a mixture that was too rich in fuel. Unburned fuel entering the exhaust could have catastrophic consequences.

"I got fire." Preskovics heard a flight engineer announce calmly over the communications link. "Number one and four."

In response to the fire warnings, the engineer shut off fuel to the two engines, activated their bromide fire bottles and feathered the props, rotating the angle of the blades pitch to reduce air resistance. Five minutes later, the B-36 lost the number three engine due to an oil leak that sent clods of frozen oil flying back and pummeling the elevator in the tail, threatening its operation.

With the B-36 rapidly losing altitude, the flight commander informed the crew over the 'com that they were going to lighten the load by salving the pair of eleven thousand pound nuclear weapons. Because the aircraft was over a sparsely inhabited area of Missouri, the commander assured them, it was unlikely the jettisoned bombs would cause any casualties. Releasing them would allow the bomber to recover enough altitude to attempt an emergency landing at Blytheville AFB in Arkansas. The commander reminded the crew that there was no possibility of a nuclear explosion because the weapons weren't armed.

The commander cleared his throat. "Preskovics, you know the drill."

"Aye, aye." Preskovics responded. Then, with his mike turned off: "Aw shit, double shit!"

To drop the bombs, it was Preskovics' job as the bombardier to enter the bomb bays and manually pull the retaining pins on the release mechanism that prevented unintended release of the weapons. To say it was a difficult and hazardous job was an understatement.

Preskovics had to wait until the pilot brought the aircraft down to 10,000 feet to make the unheated, unpressurized bomb bay survivable.

"Go," came the command.

Preskovics opened the access hatch, climbed into the bay, straddled the weapons and started pulling out the pins.

The pin for the number one bomb came out without incident, but as Preskovics struggled with the pin for the second bomb, the plane hit a pocket of turbulent air. The severe bouncing caused the first bomb to partially release from its sling. It swung down and slammed into the bomb bay doors, pushing them open. Frigid air screamed in.

"Son of a bitch!" Preskovics' voice was lost in the roar.

He struggled to hang on. The whirlwind pummeled his body and threatened to throw him out of the aircraft. With extreme effort, Preskovics reached out for the retaining pin of the second bomb and pulled. It hung up with just the tip remaining in the bracket. He squinted at it through his fogging goggles. There was another violent lurch of the aircraft, and the bay doors yawned wider. Preskovics stared in horror at the ground rushing up to meet the airplane, now only five hundred feet away. In that split second, he imagined that the cornfield below was flashing with an eerie electric blue light.

"Fuck this!"

Preskovics scrambled back through the bay hatch into the forward pressure compartment and gave a frantic thumbs up to the flight commander, praying that he had done enough. They were now seconds from catastrophic contact with the ground.

"Bombs away." came a voice over the com.

Suddenly Preskovics felt his body gain weight as if he was traveling in a rapidly rising elevator. After the salvo, the B-36 immediately jumped up a hundred feet and began to climb.

Falling at three hundred miles per hour, one of the Mark IV A-bombs hit the ground in a fallow field west of New Madrid, Missouri. The impact triggered backup fuses in its nose which in turn detonated the explosive lens wrapped around the bombs spherical plutonium core. The explosives were designed to compress the plutonium at near instantaneous speed to critical mass.

There was no nuclear reaction because of the missing core segment, but the blast from the five thousand pounds of conventional explosives in the lens created a crater ten feet deep, thirty feet in diameter, and rattled windows of farmsteads four miles away. The only casualty was a swayback horse that had been put out to pasture nearby and was in the wrong place at the wrong time.

The U.S. Air Force promptly cordoned off the impact zone and moved in to recover the wreckage and clean up the radioactive debris from the shattered plutonium core. After examination, it was determined that only one of the two bombs had crashed at the site. A subsequent interrogation of the crew revealed that there was an initial increase in climb rate immediately after the jettisoning procedure, and then a second increase some five minutes later, indicating that one bomb may have been delayed in jettisoning due to a temporary malfunction of the release mechanism. At the aircraft speed of approximately 300 mph, that left a potential impact area twenty-five miles long and two miles wide for the second bomb. An extensive, covertly conducted search could not locate it, and it was assumed to have buried itself deep into large bog and was unrecoverable. No mention of this incident was ever revealed to the public.

After the aircraft made an emergency landing at Blytheville AFB in Arkansas, Johnny Preskovics was grateful to have some downtime to catch forty winks while B-36 was being repaired and the crew headed back to Rapid City.

Ten years later, he still had nightmares of clinging to the Mark IV while the icy slipstream threatened to peel him off and send him plummeting to the farm fields far below.

Chapter 3

The Sleep-Tite Motel in Testament Hill looked much as Claire had imagined.

It was located about two blocks from the center of the town, off Liberty Street, which became County Road 23 once the city limit had been crossed. Claire pulled into the driveway next to the motel's red "no vacancy" neon sign with the "no" part unlit, and did a quick survey by driving in a circle around the parking lot. It was a simple red bricked row of rooms, numbered 1 through 12. The place was definitely not new, yet it looked tidy and well maintained. The first unit was next to a modest ranch style house, with an "office" sign above the door of what obviously once had been the attached garage.

It could be worse, Claire thought, a lot worse. She parked the Volvo by the office, and as she walked to the door, was surprised to see that it had an outdoor pool. There was a small patio and modest cabana all surrounded by a hedge of juniper. Amazingly, it looked to be still open in October.

She checked in with the slightly disheveled proprietor who was standing behind a scratched up yellow Formica counter. He was a rail thin man in a cowboy shirt with thinning mouse-brown hair and parchment skin, probably in his mid-fifties. He wore a dog-eared name tag that proclaimed his name was Mr. Baranowski.

"I keep a clean, respectable place here, miss," the man said, his beady eyes narrow with suspicion.

Claire didn't look up as she signed the registration, "That's good to hear."

"Will you be staying long?"

"I'm not sure how long, Mr. Baranowski." Claire made an effort to sound friendly. She looked up. "I'm Claire Brannigan, the hydrologist requested by Police Chief Childress. You may remember: I called earlier."

The man's eyes softened. "Oh, yes, we've been expecting you, miss. That's 15 dollars a night. And you can call me "Mr. B." Everyone does."

"Is it too early to check in, Mr. B.?"

"Normally it would be, but we're slow this time of year, so it's okay."

Claire fished out ten and five out of her small purse and held them out. Without a word, the man snatched up the bills and hurriedly squirreled them away underneath the counter.

"Will there be any more of you? I mean from the university?" he said. "I recall something on the phone …"

"That's right, my graduate student, Michael Wilson. I expect him to arrive tomorrow morning."

The eyes narrowed again. "Will you be requiring adjoining rooms?"

"That won't be necessary."

The man looked relieved. He took a key off a board and handed it to Claire. "Number 8, right across from the pool."

"The pool… It's open?"

Mr. B. shrugged. "Strangest thing. For some reason or another, it's staying pretty warm. It's been a balmy fall, but still. Normally, the water would be way too cold this time of year, and we'd shut the pool down. The missus thinks there's something going on underground, a hot spring or something, keeping it warm. You're welcome to use it, just remember it's closed after dark."

After parking in front of number 8, Claire carried her lone suitcase into the room, flicked on a light switch and looked around. There was a double bed flanked by an end table. On it was a lamp with a yellowed shade and an avocado green alarm clock and telephone. There was a luggage rack in one corner and a chair with no cushion pulled up to a small writing desk by the window. Claire walked to the back and peeked into the bathroom. It was in need of an update. The sink had separate faucets for cold and hot water. Claire hadn't seen one like that since her grandmother's house. The bath tub had an exposed pipe running up to the showerhead. It least the bathroom looked and smelled clean.

Claire went to the bed, lay down and shifted her weight around. The bed was stiff, but that was better than sinking into a canyon.

Hell, this will work.

Anyway, she didn't expect to be spending much time in the room. She sat up, reached for the phone and dialed "0".

"Front desk." It was Mr. B.'s tobacco rasped voice.

"This is room number 8. Could you connect me to the Testament Hill police station, please?"

"One moment."

There was a couple of clicks, the sound of ringing.

"Testament Hill police station."

Shit.

Claire recognized Deputy Hooper's voice. "Chief Childress, please."

"The Chief is not available. May I ask your business?" If the deputy recognized her voice, Claire couldn't tell from his tone.

"This is Claire Brannigan from the university. Can you leave him a message? I have arrived in town, and am staying ..." she hesitated, suddenly leery of telling him where she was, "at the Sleep-Tite Motel. He asked me to contact him when I arrived."

"Yes, he's expecting you, Miss Brannigan. He's out of the office at the moment He was wondering if you could come down to the station around noon today." The deputy responded in a cool, clipped voice.

"I'll be there."

"Excellent. I will pass that along."

"Thank you." Claire got the satisfaction of hanging up first.

On the way back to town from Cal Jackson's farm, Chief Childress decided to make a quick stop by the county fairgrounds to see how things were going for the coming revival. He wanted to make sure the setup was in line with codes and regulations. He also wanted to check out this "Prester

John" fellow and make a judgment on his character. Revivals were less worrisome than circuses with all the dicey carnies, but you still had to watch out for hucksters and criminal types.

He drove his cruiser into the fairgrounds. There were five trailers parked neatly in a row, ranging from a tatty old Roycraft to a shiny new Airstream. Nearby, several men in dungarees were busy stretching out a large green canvas tent on the ground. A tall man with long blond hair and crossed arms stood apart watching them.

John Preston hated this part.

Setting up for the revival was a tedium he could do without. First, he had to negotiate the fee for using the property. Next, he had to acquire all the permissions and permits, then put ads in the local papers, maybe some on billboards on the highways near the town. Finally, the huge tent, the stage, bleachers, lighting, and sound system had to be put up. He had his crew, of course, but they required constant supervision and cajoling.

He scanned the fairground and saw that they were busy doing their jobs in a halfway competent way. He wiped his damp brow with a sleeve, cursing the unseasonably warm weather. *Wait*, he thought, *this weather's good- this drought around Testament Hill could be serendipitous. Makes for better pickings at the revivals when people are having troubles.*

He ran his hand through his blond, almost white hair. It was thick and wavy, long enough so that it flowed over his collar in the back. John Preston considered his hair an asset. Along with his six foot two frame, it gave him an air of mystery and authority.

He could be one of the prophets.

"Prester John," one of the crew called out, referring to John Preston by his stage name. The scrawny young man was standing with an impossible tangle of speaker wires in his arms.

"You can do it, Howard." The preacher told him. "Just

take your time."

What an idiot, Preston thought. *The guy even looks stupid.*

He chuckled to himself. Actually, most people in Missouri looked to him like half-wits. As a matter of fact, so did people everywhere he traveled in the country. Born suckers.

They all had fantasies that the world is something other than harsh, uncaring and pointless. That tragedy didn't strike without rhyme or reason. That everything is part of God's plan. They want to be deceived that there is something more than what is experienced in their dull, tedious lives.

They deserved to be fleeced.

A sudden chill went through him and he jammed his hands into the pockets of his black leather jacket.

The preacher realized that he was trying to convince himself what he did was simply a job - making a living. A pretty good living as a matter of fact. Still, a nagging doubt about his profession had been dogging him lately. He laughed aloud. *Maybe I'm starting to believe my own bullshit.*

He was startled out of his revelry by a low rumbling voice at his back.

"Might you be Prester John?"

Preston spun around, his hands reflexively up in a defensive stance.

A big man in a police uniform raised his hand. "Easy, now." He pointed to the patch on his sleeve. "I'm Owen Childress, Police Chief of Testament Hill. "

Preston lowered his hands and casually put them back in his pockets. "I'm Prester John, officer. What can I do for you?"

The preacher sized up the Chief. He knew it was always smart to be polite to the local police. In these small towns they set down the law. There was little recourse. They were usually tight with the county judges. Some were stereotypes - acting like petty dictators in their near absolute power, getting their kicks by making outsiders squirm in their presence. On the other hand, some were easygoing, even friendly, happy to see some new activity in their domain.

"Welcome to our little village, preacher." Chief Childress smiled. The smile was a little cautious but genuine.

This one seems to be the latter, Preston thought. Although - he decided, sizing up the man's confident carriage, sturdy bulk, and penetrating gaze- not a man to be crossed.

"Thank you, Chief Childress. How can I be of assistance?" At that moment, Preston went on auto-pilot. The preacher had been through this little routine a hundred times before, in a hundred different Podunk towns in the Midwest.

Born in 1928, near Big Spring, Howard County, Texas, Preston had been an only child.

His parents lost their small ranch during the depths of the Depression when Preston was eight. It was a dusty cattle ranch that demanded long hours with little return. Still, losing it to the bank broke his mother's heart, and she died soon afterwards. That's when his father took to the bottle.

When he wasn't on a binge, Preston's father found work in the oil fields. During the heyday years of the East Texas oil boom, father and son constantly moved from job site to job site.

Once they stayed in place long enough for Preston play football at the local high school. His tall stature, rifle arm and ability to read the defense soon earned him the starting quarterback position. Then Preston had to leave in his junior year to follow his father to the next job. He never got the perks of being the senior star quarterback of a small Texan town. It was years before the resentment wore off.

Although exempted from military service during WWII because of his essential work, Preston's old man got drunk one afternoon and joined the Marines. He was sent to the Pacific theater and was killed during the assault on Okinawa in June, 1945. Preston, then seventeen, tried to enlist after his father's death, but the recruiter told him to come back after his birthday in October. That August, two atomic bombs were dropped on Japan, and in September the country surrendered unconditionally and the war was over.

Preston changed his mind about enlisting.

Two years later, on a scorching summer day, a traveling evangelist came to the Oklahoma town where Preston was living in a beat up Nomad trailer while working for an oil wildcatter. The evangelist was staging a tent revival.

Preston decided to go to the revival out of curiosity and for some diversion from his dull and grueling routine.

The preacher's name was Wesley Clapp.

"Well," Chief Childress said, raising his voice, bringing Preston back to the present. "You know the curfew limits, I'm sure. Got to be done with your revival Saturday by nine PM."

"Yes, sir. We don't want to cause any problems."

Owen Childress looked the preacher up and down with his experienced eye. Prester John was tall and broad shouldered, meeting his gaze evenly, with an air of easy confidence and a twinkle of humor in his eyes.

This guy has been around the block a few times, Childress thought.

Prester John was saying "We appreciate you letting us bring our revival to your fine town."

Childress looked around one more time. "I'll be seeing you, Preacher." He turned abruptly, walked back to his cruiser, eased himself in the driver's seat and drove off.

With a couple of hours to kill before meeting the police chief, Claire decided to get a bite to eat. After a recommendation from Mr. B. at the front desk, Claire strolled down to the Sunbeam Café, a diner one block from the motel towards the center of town. She sat at the counter and ordered a lunch of a hot turkey sandwich with mashed potatoes and coffee. The meal was tasty, and Claire wolfed it down, surprised at how famished she was.

While she drank her coffee and contemplated the wisdom of ordering a slice of homemade pecan pie, she entertained herself by eavesdropping on the locals.

Two couples sat together in a nearby booth. Claire estimated one couple to be in their late fifties, and the pair that sat across from them in their early thirties. Claire figured they were either mom and pop with their son and daughter or perhaps with a married child and his or her spouse.

The home cooked meal and the banter of the family's chatter made her a little nostalgic for her own childhood: family dinners, gathering around the TV in the evening. Of course, home life wasn't storybook. She recalled feeling that there was something wrong with her family because it didn't mirror what she saw on the television. As she grew older, Claire came to the realization no family did. There was always some dysfunction: obsessions, selfishness and even dark secrets roiling every household.

"I can't wait for the revival Saturday night." The older woman was saying with enthusiasm with a particularly flat Midwestern inflection. The group had finished their meal and were dawdling over coffee.

She raised her spoon. "I saw Prester John once before, when I was visiting my sister in Ames. He's wonderful. He baptizes people so they can be born-again, start fresh, live in Christ. I did it, and it changed my life."

"Oh, Ma," said the young man across from her. "How did it change your life?" He waved his hand in the air. "Here you are, same old Testament Hill, same old day in, day out, boring, tedious routine."

"It's what's inside that changes," the woman said. "The spiritual life."

"Really?" The boy sneered "*Prester John?* What a joke."

"Now Jacob," the older man said, "You've never seen the man. How would you know?"

"I don't have to, Dad. Those evangelicals are all the same: fire and brimstone. Repent. Give generously to keep the word alive."

"It's not like that at all," the mother said. She leaned forward. "You should come see for yourself, Jacob. You and Sarah. You'll change your mind, I'm sure of it. The man is special."

"Special good at fleecing people." Jacob smirked.

Claire found herself nodding.

"All I can say is you can't talk about Prester John until you've seen him." The mother looked to the father. "Isn't that right, Peter?"

The man shrugged. "I suppose so."

The mother turned to the girl. "Sarah, you get your husband to go with you. And you both should think about being baptized again. I guarantee you will find it quite inspirational."

The girl demurred.

"I'm not stupid," the mother continued. "I know that some of the stuff Prester John does is hokum. But God as my witness, that man has got the power of the Spirit."

Claire was impressed by the woman's ardor.

I might have to see this for myself. Nothing else to do around here.

Claire tucked a tip under her saucer, then glanced around to locate the register to pay her tab. She noticed a tall young boy in sunglasses sitting by himself at a table by the entrance. He was staring at her. Claire looked down for a moment, pretending to study her bill, then lifted her eyes. The boy still appeared to be watching her. Ignoring him, she got up and paid the cashier and headed for the door. Just as she was about to pass by, the boy stood up, blocking her way. He was holding a knarled oak staff.

He's blind, Claire realized. *He couldn't have been looking at me.*

"Excuse me," She said, expecting him to step away.

Instead the boy stepped closer. "You're not from around here, are you?" he said in a surprisingly low, resonating voice.

Even though he spoke in a fairly friendly tone, Claire felt strangely threatened by the question. "Excuse me, I'm on my way out the door."

The boy didn't move. "My name is Gilbert."

Claire thought, *Is this kid the official town greeter?*

"Hello," Claire mumbled, carefully skirting by him and

reaching for the exit door handle. As she stepped out into the street, he called after her.

"Welcome to Testament Hill, Doctor Brannigan. We've been expecting you."

Chief Childress got to the station at eleven. Doctor Claire Brannigan was expected at noon and Childress wanted to take care of a few odds and ends before she arrived. He got the coffee percolator going and reminded himself to ask Edith, the dispatcher, to pick up a couple of cans of Eight O'Clock coffee on her way to work. He also needed to call Claude Wiggins, the local car mechanic, about checking out the deputy's Plymouth cruiser. It had developed a squeak in the brakes.

He sat at his desk and shuffled papers until the sound of perking sent him to the coffee maker. He waited a minute until the water splashing inside the glass cap was the color of maple syrup, turned the percolator to "warm", then poured some brew in his favorite glass mug, leaving some room at the top. Hesitating for a moment, he reached into the bottom drawer of his desk, pulled out a pint of Old Crow bourbon and dumped a generous shot into the mug.

Childress went to the window holding his coffee. The midday sun was washing the town with a soft light. The station was two doors down from the crossroads that marked the center of Testament Hill, so the window gave a good view of the heart of the town.

Next door was the local newspaper office, then on the corner was the sandstone edifice of the Union State Bank. Across the street was Norm's barber shop, Testament Hill Hardware and Norquist Drug and Soda Shoppe. Except for a young woman walking by holding the hand of a small child and the odd vehicle passing through, the street was unusually quiet.

Childress lifted the mug to his mouth and blew on it gently, testing the temperature of the water vapor as it rose to his face. He took a sip, and sighed in satisfaction.

"Ah, now that's the ticket."

He was startled when a great horned owl swooped down over the street.

"Hey, little buddy, what are you doing out in the daylight this fine day?"

The owl banked and dove towards the police station. For a moment it appeared as if it was going to smash into the station window. Childress instinctively shut his eyes and ducked his head, and when he looked back up, the bird had turned and disappeared into the glowing dome of the sky.

He knew there was no way the owl could have heard him, but it did give him a turn.

He took another sip of coffee. His eyes wandered up and down the street. The town had changed little through the years. The scene outside could have easily been out of his teens when he would stop in after high school to get a soda or malt at Norquist's before walking the mile out of town to his family's small dairy farm. Testament Hill looked peaceful and serene - a picture of the ideal Midwestern town.

But Childress knew that the appearance was deceptive and the facade hid a dark side.

Sometimes he swore he could actually see the evil if he looked hard enough. If he peered into the black spaces under porches, along unlit alleyways between buildings, in fruit cellars and spring houses, in the gloomy foliage of the woods at the edge of town - it was there: a lurking shadow.

He had mentioned it once to his wife Flo.

"What do you mean you see it?" she had asked him one evening while they relaxed on Adirondack chairs on their front porch drinking iced tea. (His with a secret shot of bourbon).

"I don't know, Flo, it's hard to explain."

"Well, what does it look like?"

"It doesn't *look* like anything. Just black shadows, like a black bear at the edge of a wood."

"You mean they look like bears?"

"Never mind, Flo."

He never brought it up to her, or anyone, again. Except

once, to Edith, one day in the office.

She gave him a knowing look. "Not everyone can see or hear it. Only those of us who are familiar with evil and have experienced it in our lives." She made the sign of the cross, and leaned in close. "What, exactly, have you seen, Owen Childress?"

Childress was sorry he mentioned it. He didn't really want to think about it. It was probably just his imagination, or he thought darkly, maybe because of his drinking. It could do things to the brain.

He really needed to cut back.

But then, how would he relax? How would he take the edge off? He laughed to himself. It was a vicious circle: he drank to forget things, and the drinking made him see even more.

A Volvo pulled up in front of the station.

Must be the girl from the university, Childress figured. Who else would be driving a foreign car around here? He finished his coffee, took out a piece of Doublemint gum from his top pocket, popped it in his mouth, and opened the door.

A tall, slim red-haired girl wearing a pair of faded Levi's and matching jacket stood in the door way. She smiled. "Hello," she said. "I'm Claire Brannigan, the geologist you asked for."

For a second, Childress was taken aback. Claire did not fit his notion of a university professor. She was strikingly pretty.

"Good morning. I'm Chief Owen Childress." He motioned with his hand. "Please, come right in."

He stepped aside and waited until Claire stepped in, then closed the door. "Would you like some coffee? Just made a fresh pot."

"Sounds great."

"Help yourself, then have a seat." Childress pointed to the coffee pot then waved his hand at the chair in front of his desk. He watched as Claire got her coffee. The geologist was slim but the width of her shoulders, ramrod posture and strident gait gave the impression of an athlete.

Childress sat down at his desk. He waited until Claire was settled in a chair and briefly met her eyes over the rim of his coffee mug as he took a sip. He placed the mug carefully on the desk. "I want to thank you for coming to Testament Hill to help with our problem," he said.

"I hope I can be of some assistance, Chief." Claire tried the coffee. It was strong enough to take rust off a car.

"How are your accommodations? You are at the Sleep-Tite Motel?"

Claire nodded. "Only place in town."

Chief Childress chuckled. "That's right."

"Actually, it's fine."

"Good."

Childress proceeded to tell her about the situation in Testament Hill: Farmer Doyle's place out west on County Road 23 was the first well to dry up. Then, one by one, other wells went dry, the phenomenon spreading out like a plague from Doyle's place.

Claire said, "What happens when they drill?"

"Get water again after going down twenty feet or so. But now, some of the new or re-drilled wells are drying up. It's like the water table keeps dropping. Way too fast, in my opinion, even with the dry spell we've been having."

Claire frowned. "You don't think it's because of the lack of rainfall?"

"I've lived here all my life, seen a few dry spells, but none that affected the wells like this." Childress rubbed his chin. "To tell you the truth, wells around here have been coming up dry for a few years, just that lately, it seems to have accelerated."

The phone on the desk rang. Childress reached for it. "Excuse me," he said to Claire, then into the phone: "Testament Hill police, Chief Childress speaking."

Claire couldn't help but overhear snatches of the conversation. Apparently it was the Highway Patrol on the other end of the line. There was something about a trooper and his car going missing the morning before. Claire recalled the flash of light and boom driving into town and the speeding police car, but decided there probably wasn't a connection.

Chief Childress hung up the phone. "Sorry about the interruption."

"No problem." Claire sipped her coffee then said, "Seems like Mr. Doyle's farm is the place to start my investigation."

"I agree," Childress said. "I have to warn you, old man Doyle doesn't like people poking around his farm."

"I'll tread lightly."

Childress picked up his mug, his thoughts going to the bottle in his bottom drawer. "How about I pick you up tomorrow, say about nine? Take you out to Doyle's and get you introduced?"

"Sounds good." Claire stood up. "I'll be ready."

As she stepped to the door, it opened. An older woman stood at the threshold. She was maybe mid-sixties, grey streaked hair tied tightly back in a bun, wearing a printed frock dress with a threadbare black sweater draped around her shoulders. "Oh." She looked Claire up and down.

"Hello. I'm Claire Brannigan."

"Edith Brown, meet Doctor Claire Brannigan," Childress said from his desk. "She's the geologist lady from the university come to investigate the groundwater situation."

Edith entered the room, closing the door carefully behind her, her eyes never leaving Claire. She put the bag she was carrying on a desk in the corner of the office.

"Edith's our dispatcher," Childress explained. "She takes phone calls when we're not here or busy. She coordinates with the Sheriff and the Highway Patrol. And, of course, helps with administrative stuff."

The woman studied Claire through wire rimmed glasses. She brightened and smiled. "I do the busy work the boys just can't seem to do.... or do correctly."

"Men." Claire smiled, shaking her head.

Edith reached out and took Claire's hand in hers. "Is your family from around these parts, dear? The name Brannigan sounds familiar."

"No, not really. My father used to tell me we had some ancestors on his side that were from the Ioway tribe."

Edith gave her a quizzical look.

Claire laughed. "I take after my mom in the looks department. Her people are from Ireland originally."

"Ah, yes," Edith blinked. "Welcome to Testament Hill. God bless you for coming." Her shimmering hazel eyes roamed over Claire's face for a moment. Then she stepped back and made the sign of the cross with her free hand. "Revelation 12:9," she said. *"'And the great dragon was cast out, that old serpent called the Devil, and Satan, which deceiveth the whole world: he was cast out into the earth, and his angels were cast out with him.'"*

Claire let Edith's hand drop from hers.

Chief Childress said from across the room, "Don't take no never mind. Edith's always Bible quoting something or other."

Chapter 4

Satisfied that everything was going smoothly, John Preston walked to his Airstream trailer with the intention of fixing a glass of iced tea and going over his notes for the revival the next evening. When he got inside, he changed his mind and grabbed a cold beer out of the tiny refrigerator. He sat back on the bench at the fold out table and watched clouds float lazily over the tall blue spruces at the end of the fair grounds.

He didn't need to go over any notes. He knew his routine front to back, back to front, as second nature. It was what he did, who he was - a preacher. That's what he was cut out to be.

He realized that the first time he witnessed Wesley Clapp perform.

Preston remembered it like it was yesterday, even though it was back in 1947 and he was just nineteen. The revival took place in a ramshackle, dust-blown Oklahoma oil boom town, where he was working as a roustabout for a wildcatter. He sat in the back row on a crude pine bench inside the revival tent. He wanted to be able to slip out inconspicuously when he had enough. The tent was packed with men, women and children of all ages. In the stifling heat the children fidgeted and the women leaned towards each other and chatted while the men sat back, legs spread out, many working on wads of tobacco, some puffing away on a corncob pipe.

Then Wesley Clapp walked in and stepped to the stage. The crowd hushed. Preston was not impressed. The man was older, maybe sixty, around five foot five, wearing baggy hound's tooth dress pants held up by red suspenders. His white, sweat-stained linen shirt was rolled up at the sleeves, one tail hanging out. What was left of his hair had grown long and was plastered across his damp forehead.

It was Wesley Clapp's eyes though, that got Preston's attention. They were large, black and fierce. Preston sensed the crowd tensing as those eyes searched over them.

Then Clapp began to speak. His voice boomed and commanded like Moses come down from Mount Sinai.

In spite of the preacher's forceful presence, the preacher's Biblical tirades passed through Preston with little effect. The young man's upbringing in the rough oil fields of the Southwest had left him a jaded cynic.

Preston was, however, impressed by the amount of cash that he witnessed being piled up on the offering plate that passed through the audience after the sermon. In addition to the offerings, Clapp got more money by selling small vials of "healing water" that he had supposedly brought back from a secret well in the Holy Land.

Preston decided to get in on the action. After the show, he shared a few beers with the preacher's crew and found out they were always looking for more hands. He thought about leaving a note for the oil wildcatter's pretty red-haired daughter that he had been secretly seeing, but couldn't think of anything to write. He left with the Wesley Clapp's troupe at dawn and never looked back.

At first he earned his way by doing errands and helping with the setup. His gift for gab and reading people got him shilling for Clapp - masquerading as a member of the audience, drumming up enthusiasm and sometimes feigning an affliction that the Reverend Clapp would then miraculously cure.

Preston's thespian skills steadily honed and eventually his work became vital to the success of the act. He decided to demand more of the action. Clapp refused to give him more of the take. It led to increasingly heated arguments.

Preston eventually became disgusted about the whole enterprise - the lack of remuneration, the deception and the scamming. He consoled himself with the thought that *sometimes* the revivals actually did cure someone, or at least gave them hope and faith. And perhaps, if there was a God, which Preston secretly seriously doubted, that faith would somehow move the divine into action.

In the end, Preston told Clapp to stick it. On a whim, he

joined the Air Force, where he spent four years bouncing around bases in the U.S., England and Germany. After the service, he went back working the oil fields as a roustabout and then eventually took a job as a patrol officer in the small town of Marjorie, Louisiana. There, as luck would have it, his life would take another fateful turn.

After returning to the motel, Claire grabbed a pair of pliers from the tool kit she carried in her Volvo and took them into her room. Then she fished the amulet from the gas station out of her pocket. Sitting on the side of the bed, she turned it over in her hands, examining it. She peered closely at the stone in the center. It was transparent wine red, with no obvious occlusions. Its surface was highly polished, but it was very irregularly and crudely shaped. Claire speculated that it could have been a broken fragment from a larger stone. Then she studied the inscription. It certainly looked familiar, but she couldn't place it.

"VRS" she said to herself, hoping the sound might trigger a memory. "VRS."

Nothing.

She slipped the thin gold chain she always wore around her neck over her head, then used the pliers to open up the split ring at the top of the cross to attach it to the chain. When she was satisfied it was secure, she bowed her head and put the necklace back on. The amulet rested on the hollow at the beginning of her cleavage. It felt pleasantly warm against her bare flesh.

The room phone rang. It was her post-doc assistant, Mike Wilson, on the line.

"Hey Claire, I guess you got to your motel okay. How's it going?" he said in his boyish voice.

"So far so good. I'm just getting started. I met the police chief, Owen Childress, and he's taking me to some farm where he says the first wells dried up"

"You don't think it's just because of lack of rainfall in the area?"

"Not according to Childress. He says he's lived here all

his life, but nothing like this has ever happened."

Claire could visualize Wilson shrugging. "I was looking at the geology maps for the area," she continued. "Testament Hill's not far from the river, and with its relatively low average elevation, the water table shouldn't go down much," she said.

"Hmm, sounds barely interesting."

"Yeah, I know, Wilson, but it gives me an opportunity to get away from all the university bullshit, you know?"

"I do."

"Are you still coming up? I wish I brought more gear. I guess I just wasn't thinking."

"I could drive up tomorrow."

"Great."

"And, Claire, I got nothing scheduled until end of next week, if things get interesting up there," Wilson added.

"Super. University's picking up the expenses. I already got a room reserved for you at the fabulous Sleep-Tite Motel on Highway 23 just east of town."

"You mean we're not sharing a room?"

Claire knew Wilson was joking, but she detected a slightly wistful undertone in his voice. She suspected he had a slight crush on her. It was kind of flattering, but nothing was ever going to happen between them.

"In your dreams," she said.

"Aw Shucks." Wilson feigned disappointment.

Her assistant fancied himself a beatnik with his scraggy beard, trendy tortoise shell glasses, and penchant for berets and sandals. Wilson often had a paperback copy of the *Bhagavad Gita* or Kerouac's *Dharma Bums* stuffed into his back pocket. He had also recently taken up rock climbing, because, as he explained to Claire, some rocks simply needed climbing.

Claire guessed his non-conformity was a way to postpone facing the harsh realities of the world. She also knew that Wilson's youthful posturing belied his expertise in geology, his intelligence, and the work ethic of the farm boy that had grown up in the prairie of western Nebraska.

Wilson was a generally sweet, cute guy, but not her type. Besides, she was already in a personal relationship with Benjamin Trask.

"Okay, what do we need?" Wilson was saying.

"We'll need the cable tool drill rig, the seismograph, a couple of picks and shovels, some flashlights." Claire ticked off items on her fingers. "And, of course, USGS topographic maps of the area."

"Got it."

"And Wilson…"

"Yeah?"

"Don't forget the dynamite."

Chapter 5

After her phone conversation with Wilson, Claire thought about giving Ben Trask a call.

Doctor Benjamin Trask had been her doctoral advisor at the University. He was young for a professor with tenure, only five years her senior. He was considered brilliant in his field of Earth tectonics and seismology. With his encyclopedic knowledge and skill at negotiating the Machiavellian maze of university politics, Benjamin Trask had rapidly ascended the academia hierarchy.

Ben was divorced from an unhappy, childless marriage, and after Claire received her doctorate and the taboo against teacher-student intimacy was no longer an issue, their relationship casually evolved into a romance. Marriage engagement became the next logical step.

Intelligent, pleasant looking, with a good sense of humor and a kind heart, Ben seemed like a good fit to Claire. He, in turn, was attracted by her rebellious, non-conformist personality and even though he denied it, Claire was sure her not bad looking face and body had a lot to do with his attraction to her.

On the flip side, Claire thought Ben was a little lacking in imagination and creativity, which sometimes made him pedantic and a bit stiff. Occasionally, Claire witnessed flashes of spontaneity and held out the hope that eventually some of her devil-may-care attitude would rub off on him.

She started reaching for the phone on the night stand, then stopped. She really didn't feel up to talking to Ben. Instead, she slid down on the bed and closed her eyes, drifting in and out of sleep until the sound of a car backfiring in front of the motel roused her. Claire glanced at the clock. It was six-thirty, and the light was glowing in sunset hues through her room window.

She suddenly felt fidgety. The walls were closing in. She got up, put on her shoes and denim jacket, and stepped out into the cool twilight air. The sky was clear, and a russet three-quarter moon was rising in the east.

Acting on impulse, she stepped into the motel lobby. Mr. B. was stooped behind the reception counter, his head down as if he was reading. A cigarette dangled from his lips. He looked up when Claire entered, and snatched the cigarette from his mouth. He smiled tentatively, his face creasing into a thousand crisscrossing wrinkles like a patch of dried up mud.

"Good evening, miss. How may I help you?" Mr. B. smiled, exposing a set of peg-like, nicotine-stained teeth.

Claire approached the desk. "I was wondering…" she paused, slightly embarrassed. She glanced down to see that the proprietor had been reading *The Black Cloud* by Fred Hoyle. "Is there a tavern somewhere nearby?"

For a moment, Mr. B. appeared perplexed. He lifted his cigarette and took a quick puff. "Well, Doctor Brannigan, there's nothing fancy around here like a nightclub or anything."

"No, I'm not interested in that. Just somewhere where I might get a drink and a bite to eat. Somewhere reputable, if you know what I mean."

"Of course." Mr. B bobbed his head. "There's Annie Duggan's bar and grill, just around the corner from the café. It's kind of a landmark around here. It's a respectable enough place. Annie doesn't allow no shenanigans. Families even go there for dinner sometimes. She makes a shepherd's pie that'll have you coming back for more."

"Sounds perfect." Claire nodded. "Just around the corner?"

"That's right."

Claire headed for the door.

"And miss..?"

Claire turned.

"I'd appreciate you not mentioning to the wife that you saw me smoking. She thinks I gave it up."

Chapter 6

Deputy Frank Hooper was in the middle of his afternoon shift. His patrol began at four-thirty in the afternoon and ended at one in the morning. He was looking forward to a good evening. The sky was clear, and there was no moon. For the time of the year, it was mild.

People might have their windows open and blinds up.

He stopped at Cagney's pub located in the seedy side of town, and bought a fresh pack of Pall Malls out of the machine. He didn't want to run out of cigarettes at a crucial time.

The bar was practically empty, just three or four regulars that nodded absently at him and turned back to their drinks. Old Man Cagney wanted to chat, but Hooper was anxious to get back on patrol. He didn't want to miss anything.

The deputy got back in his patrol car, lit up a cigarette and mused over his options. He checked the clock on the dash. Nine o'clock. He took a long drag, closed his eyes and let the smoke out slowly through his nostrils.

Tonight, Ida Wagner would be his *target*, as he named them in his personal secret code.

She lived at the end of Mill Street. Her property backed up to the railroad tracks. There was a gravel service road that ran beside the tracks that Hooper could pull his car onto and park. A large empty field bordered one side of the house and on the other side, the nearest neighbor's view was blocked by an old storage shed. It was a pretty good setup.

One downside - Hooper mused, as he leisurely pulled out of the parking lot and began patrolling randomly around the town - if a freight train came down the track, the engine's headlight would illuminate the area and his cruiser would be starkly outlined.

There wasn't much of an excuse for Hooper to be sitting there in the dark. It would be hard to explain his presence if anyone (especially widow Wagner) happened to be looking out the window, say, or letting out the cat and spotted him when a train came by.

That would be an unlikely coincidence. But just in case, Hooper had come up with a story: He had caught sight of what looked like a hobo in the rail yard and gone out to investigate. It was plausible. He would be safe.

The deputy pulled his cruiser onto the service road and crept along to minimize the sound of tires on the gravel. The signal light where the tracks headed east was glowing red. That meant no train was expected from that direction anytime soon. Hooper knew that that the signal would go green well in advance of an incoming freight, giving him plenty of time to drive out before getting spotted. The signal for westward heading trains was not visible because it faced away, but that wasn't a concern. From experience, he knew that trains coming from that direction were rare at that time of night.

When he was directly behind Ida Wagner's house, lined up with the back bathroom window, deputy Hooper stopped, shut off the Plymouth's engine and turned his head gradually towards the house, savoring the anticipation, his heart rate increasing. He took a deep breath and released it slowly with a low whistle.

The house was dark. Perhaps he was too late - Ida Wagner had already turned in. Maybe she wasn't even home, but that was unlikely. The clock on the dash read 9:15. Should be just the right time.

Hooper sat there for a few minutes, smoking a Pall Mall, shielding its glow when he inhaled with a cupped hand.

A light flared through Ida Wagner's bathroom window and the venetian blind flew up. There was the pinkish beige glow of bare flesh. Hooper's heart thumped.

Ida Wagner stood at the window pulling it open. She had taken off her clothes in preparation for taking her bedtime bath. Her full breasts rose and fell as she struggled with the sticky window.

Hooper flicked his cigarette butt out of the car and while his eyes remained fixed on the window in order not to miss anything, he groped for his 8x50 Zeiss binoculars under his seat. He put them to his eyes and tweaked the focus.

Ida was no youngster. *Mature* was the word that came to mind. But her body was still quite stimulating to Deputy Hooper. She was certainly sexually experienced. She would know how to please a man. She would be uninhibited in her desire. Hooper fantasized Ida running her fingernails down his back and clutching at his buttocks. Moaning and breathing in hard, hot breaths. Her ankles crossing over his neck as he ...

Hooper hadn't noticed the signal light going green.

The train horn cut the still night air and the bells at the highway crossing a quarter mile down began clanging, shattering the stillness of the night air.

The headlight of the Rock Island Alco locomotive came around the bend to the West, and flashed over the police cruiser.

"Christ!" Hooper brought down his binoculars and jammed them back under his seat. At the same instant, the blinds to Ida Wagner's bathroom came down.

She must have heard it, too.

Waiting ten seconds to make sure the blind wasn't coming back up, Hooper started the engine, crept backwards and got on to Mill Street before the coal drag freight from Ames blasted through.

As he idled down the street, a fantasy ran through Hooper's mind: knocking on widow Wagner's back door. Her peeking cautiously out the curtain, then, seeing that it was the deputy, swinging the door wide open, her nakedness unabashedly exposed.

"Why, Deputy Hooper, I was wondering when you would come," she would say. "I've seen you watching me, hoping you would come to the door."

Hooper felt a burning begin at the base of his skull, rise up and blossom in his brain. For a brief second, his field of vision was filled with a sparkling blue light, like a thousand static arcs. He instinctively shut his eyes, but the light was still there.

Then it went dark.

It wasn't the first time that had happened, but the episodes were getting more powerful, more overwhelming.

I wonder if I should go to the doctor and get checked out.

Then the idea faded and new one came to mind:

One of these days, Deputy Hooper promised himself, *one of these days, I'm gonna just go up to that door and knock.*

Duggan's was bustling when Claire walked in. A couple of customers gave her notice with curious but friendly looks. The place looked clean and cozy. There was the faint smell of cigarette smoke and stale beer, but it was overwhelmed by the tantalizing odor of home cooked food. She was pleased to see some tables seated with family groups enjoying a meal. The pub was just what Claire was hoping for.

Spotting the bar at the back, she walked over and sat down. She thought about ordering her favorite, a dry martini, a habit she'd picked up from her father, but after glancing around the bar again, decided against it. She studied the row of beer taps. "I'll have a Schlitz, please," she told the bartender, a tired-looking bleached blond in a turquoise sweater that was stretched too tight.

The bartender gave her a phony smile, her bright red lipstick giving Claire the momentary impression her mouth was a horrible knife slash across her face. The bartender's nametag informed Claire that her name was *Sherrie*.

"Coming up, sweetheart," Sherrie said without enthusiasm. She stepped away, and a moment later returned with an overflowing frosted mug. She set down on the counter in front of Claire and wordlessly moved down the bar to another customer.

The beer hit the spot. After savoring a couple mouthfuls, Claire rotated idly on the stool and was gazing around the room when a tall man with in a cowboy hat strode in through the entrance and stopped. He was obviously checking out the pub. He wore faded Levis and a denim jacket not unlike her own. A pair of aviator sunglasses was perched on his long nose. His square jaw was clean shaven, set under a wide mouth.

His head swiveled. With his dark glasses, Claire couldn't be sure if he was looking at her or not. Then he smiled, showing a set of perfect, dazzling teeth, and walked straight towards her.

Plunking down on the next stool, he raised a finger to the barmaid who was now busy ogling him. "Schlitz, please," he said in a low, resonant voice. "And a shot of Jim Beam."

He stared straight ahead while his drinks were being prepared. Claire tried hard to ignore him, detecting the faint smell of Monsieur de Givenchy cologne. She recognized it because it was her favorite, and one her fiancé refused to wear, saying it was too "European" for his tastes. Ben Trask preferred to wear ubiquitous Aqua Velva.

The man's drinks arrived, and the barmaid attempted to flirt with him. He reacted with polite disinterest and she finally gave up and moved away. He took a taste of his whiskey, and apparently satisfied, upended it.

There was a barely audible sigh. The man turned abruptly to Claire. He reached up, pulled off his sunglasses and stuffed them into his jacket pocket.

"Hello," he said, touching the brim of his hat. His eyes were startling - a bright amber color that Claire had only ever witnessed in a cat. Again the impressive smile.

Claire couldn't help but smile back. "Hello."

A long wisp of white-blond hair escaped from the back of his hat and brushed his collar. "So, miss, what brings you to God's little acre?"

"Geology."

"Are you the professor from the university I heard about?"

"Guilty."

"I'm John Preston, by the way. People call me Preston" He picked up his beer mug and took a long drink while gazing at her over the rim.

"I'm Claire...by the way."

Claire, trying to be nonchalant, finished off her Schlitz and signaled the barmaid for a refill.

"Claire. What a beautiful sounding name."

"I bet you say that to all the girls."

"Only the ones named Claire."

For a brief moment they stared into each other's eyes. Then the man said, "Geology, eh? Very intriguing."

"Yeah, geology is everyone's favorite topic, along with the Kinsey Report and Wilt Chamberlain."

The man raised his mug. "A hundred points in one game. Unbelievable. A record that will probably never be broken."

Claire nodded. "Amazing."

Sherrie brought Claire's refill. The bartender gave her a dirty look and looked hopefully at John Preston.

"I'm good," he said dismissively.

The barmaid left in a huff.

Claire tilted her head. "I think she's got a thing for you,"

"It's the hat."

"Of course. What else could it be?" Claire thought: *It wouldn't be because of your handsome face, lean and tall physique, low melodic voice or confident, commanding presence.*

Preston laughed. "No, I believe she's jealous of the pretty woman I am sitting next to."

He leaned his body closer. Claire was going to pull away, but she found the intimacy subtly intoxicating.

"So what brings you to this Midwestern paradise?" Claire said, trying to break the spell.

He straightened. "Just business, really...I'm kind of salesman."

"And what do you sell?"

The man's eyes narrowed in thought. "Dreams," he answered after a long second. "That's what every salesman peddles...ultimately."

"I see," Claire said carefully.

"Dreams of a better life. Dreams of escaping from the dull, dreary life of the common man." He touched the brim of his Stetson again. "Or woman."

"By buying a new and improved vacuum cleaner?"

Preston chuckled. "Why, yes... Are you interested?"

Claire shook her head. "I could lead you on, but actually, I'm not at all interested."

"I mean, it's a super atomic, new and improved machine." Preston grinned. "It really sucks. What more do I need to say?"

Claire rotated her beer mug. "You don't really sell vacuum cleaners."

"Vacuum cleaners, encyclopedias, used cars - what's the difference. It's the dream that counts."

Claire nodded. "*The mass of men lead lives of quiet desperation.*"

"Thoreau, *Walden Pond*. So, Claire, if I can offer a tiny ray of hope, a little sunshine, what's the harm?"

"Aren't you profiting from telling lies?"

"What is a lie?"

"Saying something that is not true."

"Ah ha!" Preston said. "Now we come to the nub. The Gospel of John, chapter eighteen, verse thirty-eight, Pilate to Jesus: *What is truth?*"

Claire peered closely at the man in the cowboy hat. "That's funny, you don't strike me as a religious type."

Preston smiled again and Claire found herself captivated by his deep dimples.

"Because I quote the Bible?" he asked. "There's a lot of wisdom in that book."

"Amen."

"You know, the Bible is basically about the struggle of mankind to overcome evil."

"That may be a little simplistic, don't you think?"

"I hear what you're saying," Preston nodded. "But if there was no role of evil in the Bible, there wouldn't be much going on, would there?"

Claire pondered his question for a minute, closing her eyes so as not to be distracted by the closeness of Preston's face. She opened them. "It depends on what you would define as evil, I guess."

"Come on, Claire, you know evil when you encounter it. Of course you do."

"Maybe."

"Some things are unequivocally evil. It exists. It is real."

"It's in the eye of the beholder…"

"Bullshit." Preston took a long drink from his mug and carefully set it down on the bar. "Don't kid a kidder. You think by admitting the existence of evil that you are lowering your intellect to the level of superstition. But in your heart, in your soul, you know the truth."

Claire was slightly irritated at the man's presumption. "You don't know me well enough, nor are you qualified to be psychoanalyzing me, thank you," she said, half seriously, half in jest.

Preston nodded. "Perhaps you're right. My apologies. I'd like to know you better, if you allow me." He raised his glass. "Another round?"

Chapter 7

September 20, 1952:

The beacon on the roof of the '49 Ford police cruiser cycled endlessly. Its red light bounced off Amos Doyle's large white clapboard farmhouse, then swept across the glazed-tile silo, the timber framed barn, streaked out across dark rows of standing corn and circled back to the house. The play of the beam gave the scene a bizarre carnival atmosphere.

A carnival from hell, thought Chief Owen Childress as he sat behind the wheel of his cruiser. He was reluctant to get out. He looked at his watch and noted the time in his logbook: 5:45 a.m.

He had been on the job just four months after taking over for the previous police chief of Testament Hill, Sean Murphy.

One day the previous spring, Murphy was inexplicitly struck by an irresistible hankering for sun and surf. So he sold his house and most of its contents, packed up the family in the Studebaker Commander station wagon and was last seen headed to California on US Route 30.

Childress had wished them luck.

Right now the new Chief was apprehensive. He had seen dead bodies before, of course. He was a deputy for two years before becoming chief, and had served as a combat infantryman in WWII and Korea.

His first DB as a police officer was Mrs. Olsen. Forty-six years old, she fell dead as a stone while hanging up clothes in her yard. Hadn't been sick a day in her life. Her sixteen year old daughter found her face down on the lawn when she came home from school. The State Highway patrol dispatcher notified then *Deputy* Childress that since Chief Murphy was in court that afternoon in the county seat, Childress would have to take the call.

Mrs. Olsen wasn't too bad. It was a little awkward flipping her over because rigor had set in and her arms were flayed out to her sides as if she was going to take flight. As Childress struggled to flip the body, he was acutely aware of Mrs. Olsen's daughter, Astrid, standing to the side, her trembling hands covering her mouth. For her sake he tried to be as graceful and professional as possible.

Mrs. Olsen's long blond hair, greying at the temples, lay across her face. Childress brushed it gently away with hand. She looked peaceful, as if she was just sleeping. *I'll just take a quick nap here on the grass before hanging up the rest of the socks.*

Pressed into the ground by the weight of her head, the face was slightly distorted by rictus into an enigmatic Mona Lisa expression. It was also purpled from lividity, but that was barely noticeable. Childress had been thankful for that, at least.

Then there was his first fatal automobile accident: Ollie Nelson driving into a massive beech tree off Highway 23. The Oldsmobile 98 slammed dead center into the trunk as if Ollie had aimed his car. The Olds accordioned, thrusting the engine into the passenger compartment and the dashboard deep into the seats. If Ollie had been sitting there, he'd have been crushed like a bug. As it was, the force of the collision had catapulted him through the windshield. Ollie was stopped short by the tree trunk, the impact popping his skull open like a watermelon and spattering his brain over the bark.

Childress lost his lunch shortly after arriving on the scene. Luckily, the ambulance had not shown up yet, so there were no witnesses to embarrass him.

Childress's experiences with death had led him to the opinion that the Grim Reaper generally worked in a frivolous, cavalier fashion. There was no rhyme, reason, or justice to the sweep of his scythe. He also suspected that the Reaper took a perverse delight in the totally arbitrary fruits of his harvest.

The memory of those experiences crawled through his head as Childress got out of his cruiser, took a deep breath and walked over to Amos Doyle's old hand-dug well. Two people stood around its raised cobblestone rim, illuminated in a cone of yellow light from a kerosene lantern hung on the roof over the windlass.

As he got closer, Childress could make out Ralph Jaeger, the pig farmer from down the road, and Albert Klug, Amos Doyle's handyman. Klug had both hands on the windlass crank, while Jaeger was leaning over the well, looking into its depths. Standing about ten yards back, with her elongated shadow flickering like a phantasm on the barn wall, was Jaeger's wife, holding Doyle's one year old granddaughter, Ivy, in her arms.

Jaeger stepped up to intercept Childress. "Damn it," he said, "I told Amos he needed to fill in that old well years ago. He would always say he might need it someday."

Childress looked around. "Where is Amos?"

"Went to Riverton to buy a new blower motor for the silo, be back tomorrow," Jaeger said. He pointed to the well. "Klug went to reuse the rope from the windlass, then he noticed the stench."

Childress ignored him and walked up to the well. He was holding a long police issue flashlight.

Klug looked up at Childress, his face pale. "It's Rachel, Deputy. I'm sure it is."

Rachel, Ivy's mother, had gone missing June 22. Some whispered that she had abandoned her child just as her child's father had done.

Almost three months had gone by.

An icy cold slithered up Childress's spine

He leaned over and shone his flashlight down the well. A cold, moist draft rose up out of its depths. The odor it carried was overpowering. Childress choked down bile. He turned towards Jaeger's wife. "Mabel," he said making an effort to keep his voice steady. "Why don't you take Ivy into the house and get her something to drink?"

He waited until the pair were in the house. "Okay, bring it up."

The windlass groaned as Klug struggled with the crank.

"I hooked up a grappling hook on the end of the rope."

he said, his voice choking. "I didn't know what else to do."

"That's alright, Al," Childress said. "She's dead. We can't hurt her anymore."

The grappling hook appeared at the rim of the well. There was a shape dangling from it: a tangle of ragged cloth, bones and blackened flesh, not much bigger than a sack of potatoes. Some dark oily liquid dripped from it. Childress recognized the shape of a head. Long, coal black hair hung from it. It was Rachel Doyle's remains.

Klug looked anxiously at Childress. The deputy nodded. Klug cranked the windlass. The body caught on the edge of the stone and before Klug could stop, thick slabs of putrid flesh sloughed off and slid slowly to the dirt. It reminded Childress of scrapping mud off his boot on the bumper of his cruiser.

"For God's sake!" said Jaeger, who had been watching a few cautious steps back. "Stop!"

Klug bent over, retching. His hands slipped from the crank and the windlass whirled. There was a wet thud from the bottom of the well.

"Gott in himmel!" Jaeger said, reverting to his Pennsylvania Dutch roots. "Gott in himmel!"

The two men stared wide-eyed at Childress.

"I've got to call the county coroner." Deputy Owen Childress turned away and walked on rubbery legs to his cruiser. He said over his shoulder to Jaeger and Klug, "Just leave it be."

He opened the door to the car, got one leg in, and glanced back towards the well. For an instant, a pulses of blue light flashed up out of the well. As he watched, it dimmed and was gone.

"Did you see that?" Childress asked the two men, who were busy rinsing their hands in the water trough.

"See what?" they asked in unison.

"Never mind." Childress finished climbing into the car and made the call to the coroner.

Chapter 8

Oct 28, 1962

Saturday morning

Claire drove with Chief Childress in his police cruiser to the truck farm of Amos Doyle. The day was overcast with a pale light filtering through the clouds. They drove by seemingly endless fields of grey-brown feed corn, their stalks slowly waving in the wind. Claire found the image forlorn and strangely menacing.

On the way, Childress filled her in about the situation at the Doyle farm while taking frequent sips from his coffee mug. Claire was pretty sure she detected the smell of whiskey along with the coffee, but pretended not to notice.

Amos Doyle was taking care of his twelve-year old granddaughter, Ivy, Childress told Claire. Ivy's father, a shiftless, violent drunk named Clyde Deacon, abandoned her and her mother, Rachel, shortly after Ivy was born. The mother and daughter went to live with Rachel's parents, Amos and Fern Doyle, after Rachel lost her home. Then, when Ivy was one year old, her mother died tragically.

Chief Childress reached for his mug. Since he didn't offer any details about Ivy's mother's death, Claire thought it polite not to ask.

"After Rachel died," Childress continued, "Amos and his wife raised Ivy. Two years ago, Fern passed, and Ivy and Amos have been carrying on at the farm."

He glanced at Claire. "Ivy's a little reserved. Don't take it personally if she doesn't respond to you. She's a good girl, mind you. She's just in her own world."

It struck Claire that description sounded like herself as a young girl. "I understand," she said.

"And..." he hesitated. "Ivy... sort of has a special gift."

"I see..."

"You'll see for yourself. It's hard to explain."

To the east, a half-mile or so away, Claire noticed a solitary conical hill, topped by three gigantic oaks.

"That's interesting." Claire pointed. "That's quite a hill, unusual for the topography around here."

"What do you mean?" Childress glanced at her.

"It just stands out, compared to the relatively flat land around here." Claire swept her hand out the window. "This area of Missouri is part of the Mississippi Embayment, the mostly flat floodplain of the river that extends from the confluence of the Mississippi and Ohio Rivers down to the Louisiana delta."

"Hmm, I never knew that," said Childress, politely feigning interest.

"Melt water from the glaciers during the end of the last Ice age widened the river and left silt deposits three hundred feet thick," Claire explained.

"So that hill is unusual?"

"It's just a little too steep and symmetrical to be a natural formation. I wonder if it could possibly a Indian mound."

Childress nodded. "I think some archeologists came out one time, thinking the same thing. They wanted to dig into the hill, but Amos Doyle wouldn't give them permission - it's on the edge of his property. Amos didn't think it was a good idea to be disturbing things. He told them to leave well enough alone, and chased them off with a shotgun, if my memory serves me right."

He pointed out the window. "You know, that's the original Testament Hill."

"The original Testament Hill?"

"Yep. The town's named after that hill."

"Really? That's strange."

"Not when you know the history," Childress said. "The town was first settled at the bottom of that hill, around 1810."

"Interesting."

"I guess, if you like that kind of history stuff. To me, the past is past, you know? It's the future that's important."

Claire couldn't disagree more, but thought it was prudent not to argue the point.

"Anyway," Chief Childress continued. "The settlers were some evangelical sect. Called the place 'Testament'."

"Curious name."

"Yep." Childress took another gulp of his coffee. "Apparently the group was starting westward across Missouri in wagons. They came upon the hill and found out that the local Indians shunned the area, so they figured it might be a safe place to settle. Called the place 'Testament'. Somewhere along the way, name got changed to Testament Hill."

"I see."

"Why they called it Testament, I don't have a clue."

Claire said, "The word 'testament' could be in reference to a *covenant*, like the one between the Israelites and their God, as found in the Bible."

When Childress gave her a quizzical glance, she explained, "I read that somewhere, just kind of stuck in my mind." She looked out the windshield. "But the town's not very close to the mound."

"Not anymore," Childress said. "The whole settlement supposedly burned down not long after it was founded. Some stories say the fire originated at the blacksmith's. Another tale is that it was ignited by lightning during a terrible storm. Then there's one that claims it was set fire by some Indians." He lifted his shoulders. "Who knows? The settlement was rebuilt where the town is now. Closer to the river and the old Holsom Trail. Makes more sense."

"And the sect? Is it still around?"

"Naw. "Nobody knows what exactly happened to them. The area was pretty much wilderness back then. Maybe most were killed or taken up by the Indians, or maybe the survivors, or whatever, just moved on."

The car slowed and turned up a long dirt driveway. At the end, Claire could see a large white wood-sided house situated on a low rise. Behind the house was a barn with ceramic brick silo, two outbuildings and a fenced paddock.

A stooped old man wearing overalls and a ragged straw hat was walking out of the barn, wiping his hands with a rag. He laconically raised a hand in greeting. A young, dark-haired girl wearing a plaid shirt, jeans and cowboy boots bounced out of the back door and ran over to the old man, who rested his hand gently on her shoulder.

"That's them," Childress said. He parked the car and they got out and walked up the drive.

"Amos, here's that lady from the university I was telling you about," Chief Childress said as they approached. "Doctor Claire Brannigan, meet Amos Doyle."

Claire stepped forward and held out her hand. The farmer cautiously reached out and shook Claire's hand. The grip of his roughly calloused hand was very light. "How'd ya do." He searched Claire's face with chicory-flower blue eyes.

"Glad to meet you," Claire said.

"We've been expecting you." He smiled shyly and gently tightened his grip.

Claire returned his gaze evenly for two heartbeats then gently pulled her hand away. "Well, I certainly hope I can be of some help."

The young girl was looking up at Claire with huge dark brown eyes.

Amos Doyle looked down at the girl with obvious affection. "This is my granddaughter, Ivy. Ivy, say hello to Doctor Claire."

Ivy had a heart-shaped face with perfect, almost translucent skin, a delicate nose and a button chin with a cleft. Her shiny, coal-black hair was parted in the middle, and ran down to her shoulders and over her back.

The girl smiled shyly and stared curiously at Claire.

"Ivy, you're such a beautiful girl," Claire said before thinking.

Amos Doyle smiled. "Yes," he said. "She's like an angel."

"Oh!" Claire was alarmed when a large crow whisked in and landed on Ivy's shoulder.

Amos Doyle raised his hand. "It's okay. This is Ivy's friend, Raven. Ivy's raised him since he was a hatchling when his mother was killed by an owl."

"It just spooked me for a minute." Claire said, thinking it was odd that Doyle said *friend* instead of *pet*.

"Crows are very intelligent and can be quite affectionate in their own way." Chief Childress remarked. He had been observing the scene with an expression of mild concern, but now seemed relieved.

The bird turned its head to the side and regarded Claire with a black marble eye. With one flap of its wings, it leapt off Ivy and landed on Claire's shoulder, its sharp claws pricking though her blouse. Before Claire could react, the crow abruptly spread its wings and took flight. With a few powerful beats, it ascended over the house, and flew towards the road.

Ivy's face lit up. She snickered and smiled at Claire. "Raven likes you," she said in a clear, adult-like voice. Chief Childress and Amos exchanged glances.

Claire blinked. "Well, Raven is an exquisite creature."

"He's my best friend."

"How wonderful is that?"

"Real wonderful." Ivy turned and pranced towards the house. "See you later, Miss Doctor Claire," she called over her shoulder.

For a moment the three gazed in silence after Ivy.

Childress coughed. "Where would you like to begin, Doctor Brannigan?"

"Please - just 'Claire' is fine."

Claire looked around the farmyard. "Now, where is the well that first dried up?"

Childress pointed to a windmill whose top was just visible over the barn roof. "I believe it was that one there, am I right, Amos?"

Doyle nodded. "Yep. That's a hand dug well. Dried up a while back. Then, about a month ago," he pointed to small outbuilding by the silo, "my other well started going dry. That one has an electric pump that takes water to the house and barn."

"How deep are they?"

"One on the windmill is down I reckon twenty-five, thirty feet. It's old, dug by my pappy and me. The one in the pump house is forty feet deep. Put that one in about ten years ago."

"What about this over here?" Claire pointed and walked towards a circle of mortared cobblestones near the back of the house. "This looks like an old well too."

"There's nothing there, you don't need to bother," Amos Doyle called out.

Claire got to the circle and looked down. It certainly looked like a well. It was filled to the top with fieldstone.

Claire felt a firm hand on her shoulder. She turned. It was Doyle. Something unfathomable stirred in the depths of his eyes. "Hasn't been used for years. No need to fuss about this one. "

"Of course."

"I think we should start with the one by the windmill," he pointed and walked off.

"Whatever you say."

Before turning away, Claire glanced once more at the pile of stones in the well, idly wondering what types of rocks they were. They glittered if the sun was reflecting off blue crystals. Claire looked skyward. The sky was grey. She looked back down. The glitter had disappeared. *Must be chips of fluorite in the schist,* she decided. Still, she felt the hair on the back of her neck prickle.

"You two go on," Childress told them. "I gotta check in with the office on the radio."

Claire and Doyle walked behind the barn and Doyle stepped under the windmill and removed a couple of boulders off a sheet of rusted corrugated steel covering the well.

"There you go, miss. Not much to see, I reckon."

Taking a flashlight out of her pocket, Claire slipped between the legs of the windmill, leaned over and shone the light down the center of the well. It looked as she expected: a stone-lined pit going down about twenty-five feet and ending in a sandy pebble strewn bottom.

"You're right, not much to learn…" she started to

straighten up when a dark patch on the side at the bottom caught her eyes. She bent back down and leaned way in, stretching her arm with the flashlight down into the well.

Doyle was saying, "Be careful, miss. We wouldn't want you tumbling in head first."

"It almost looks like there's a passage at the bottom." Claire's voice echoed down the shaft. She pulled up.

Doyle blinked. "Don't recall anything like that."

Claire said, "It almost looks like the well broke into a cave."

"Probably just some soil washed away when it was full of water."

Claire frowned. "That's probably it."

"Like I said," Doyle pulled the corrugated sheet back over the well and replaced the boulders that held it down. "Like I said, this well came up dry first. Quite a while ago - maybe seven, eight years. I wasn't too concerned, since I don't keep cattle anymore, and don't need to fill the stock tank. Just use the one in the well house now." Amos waved his hand towards the barn, and started walking.

"Okay." Claire nodded and followed Doyle down a shallow slope to a small wooden building next to the silo. It was about the size of an outhouse. A power line raised on a pole ran overhead back to an electric meter on the barn. Doyle opened the simple latch and swung open the door.

Inside was a steel pipe rising out of the ground and attached to an electric pump. The pump fed a holding tank through a pipe mounted with a pressure switch that turned the pump on when the tank got low.

"This one's downhill from the one behind the barn. If the water table dropped, it would hold out longer," Claire observed. "How is it performing?"

"This well supplies the house," Amos told her. "Even with the holding tank, we have to be very miserly in our use. Probably getting about half a gallon a minute. When it first slowed up, I had Karl Beamer, our local well digger, come and re-drill. He got good water flow ten feet deeper, went another ten for good measure. Worked good for few months, then dried up. I had Karl come and renew it just three weeks ago. Now it's drying up again."

"And it went dry in three weeks?" Claire was surprised - a water table shouldn't drop that fast. "Are you sure your driller got all the way down to the water table, and didn't just hit a clay pocket?"

Doyle pursed his lips. "Karl knows his business."

Claire contemplated what the old farmer was saying. She turned to Childress who had come up and was standing a few feet away listening to their conversation. "Have you seen this before? In years past?"

"People been having problems with wells around here for... probably the last ten years," he said. "But now, like I was telling you, never had them dry up this fast. The drought really hasn't been that bad."

Claire had no easy answer. She'd have to wait and investigate further.

"So, Mr. Doyle," she turned to the old farmer. "I'd like to conduct a few tests, if you don't mind. I have a colleague coming up with some equipment that we'll need."

"What kind of tests?" There was a suspicious edge to Doyle's voice.

"Just a seismic test: drill a few bore holes to get an idea of what's going on underground." Claire tried to sound casual.

"How's drilling some holes going to help?"

"Well," Claire said hesitantly. "We actually set little explosives in the holes to shake up the ground, and study the vibrations to help determine what's going on down there."

Doyle turned without a word and walked back toward the house. He was shaking his head.

Childress sided up to Claire. "Don't worry, he'll come around. He's sometimes a little cantankerous." He lowered his voice. "I'll talk to him. It will be okay to do your tests, I'm sure."

They headed back to the car. Ivy was waiting for them. The crow, Raven, was back on her shoulder. "Does your friend drive an army car?" Ivy said.

Claire stopped in her tracks and stared at Ivy. "Why, yes. He drives an old Jeep, if that's what you mean."

"He's coming up the road right now."

Claire looked down the driveway scanned left and right. She could see the road for about a mile in each direction until it disappeared behind low hills. There was nothing moving. Then movement caught her eye. "Is that..?"

A blob heading up the road resolved into an older red pickup. Claire released her breath. "No, that's not Wilson."

Ivy giggled. "Of course not, that's Old Man Jenson."

Claire raised her shoulders. "Well then..."

Another blob appeared coming from the direction of town. As Claire watched, it developed into a Jeep. It slowed, turned into the Doyle's driveway, rumbled up to the house, and stopped.

Mike Wilson stuck his head out the window. He had a big grin on his face. "Hello!" he said. "The lady at the police station, Edith, told me you'd be out here. I thought I'd just head out."

Chapter 9

Claude Wiggins sat on a homemade stool at his desk talking to himself. He shifted his weight around, trying to get his substantial bulk comfortable. The seat was narrow, and Wiggins' buttocks bulged out and hung over the edge of the seat. It didn't help that his hemorrhoids had been flaring up lately.

"Judas Priest!" he said to the air. "I shouldn't have had those hot peppers in my stew last night. God Almighty!"

He stared out the dingy window of his garage, looking first one direction then the other, hoping to see a potential customer appear down the road. There was nothing. He sighed and hunched over the newspaper crossword and pondered a clue.

" 'Morning star fallen from heaven,' " he said aloud.

He scratched his head. "Venus? No - need seven letters."

He glanced down at the fat tabby basking in the sun coming through the window. "What do you think, Wally?"

The cat blinked at him a couple times and then rested its head between its paws and closed its eyes.

Wiggins turned back to the paper. "Ah ha... Lucifer." He scribbled in the answer with a stubby, well-chewed pencil, and smiled in satisfaction.

Claude Wiggins used to own and run Testament Hill Auto Service in town. For twenty-five years, it provided him and his wife with a decent living. But when a company-owned Sinclair station came into town, he couldn't compete with their gas prices. A few faithful customers kept coming to get gas even though it was a few cents more. After a while, economics won over loyalty. Wiggins shut down the pumps and took down the "Gasoline for Sale" sign.

He was able to get by doing repairs, until a Chevrolet and then a Ford dealership opened up in the county seat, eight miles south of Testament Hill. They undercut his cost for parts, so Wiggins had to lower his labor charges to keep business. After expenses, he was barely in the black.

After a couple years of struggling to make ends meet, he shuttered the shop, sold the property and relocated his repair business to the old family farm.

He and his wife had moved there after his parents passed. His two siblings, having migrated to the city years earlier, had no interest in the homestead. Wiggins never had much enthusiasm for farming either. He figured it was a whole lot of work for a living barely one notch above subsistence.

He built a bare concrete block building for a shop on the property alongside the road. It saved him from paying rent, so his prices could be competitive again.

Business recovered for a while, but as Wiggins grew older and slower, his increasing turnaround time drove more customers away. Nowadays, he was lucky to get the odd flat tire repair, emergency battery replacement, or an occasional towing job. Still, he would walk down to the shop from the house every morning, (except Sundays) sit and wait. And do crossword puzzles.

Since his wife, Gladys, went to be with the Lord a year ago Christmas, Wiggins had trouble getting motivated to do much else. The Farmall tractor needed winterizing, the septic field needed pumping and falling-down eave troughs needed to be re-hung. But Wiggins just couldn't get up the gumption to get going on any of those chores. Some days, he even had trouble going through the motions of getting dressed and eating a meal.

At seventy-two years old, Wiggins understood that his life was pretty much over. Going down to the shop in the morning used to give him some sense of purpose, but now it was more a mindless habit.

Wiggins had another reason to head for the front of the property: he felt easier with more distance between himself and the *thing*. The *thing* that dwelled under the hay silo behind the house.

He first saw *it* in the spring, when raking out the last of the old molding silage at the bottom of the silo. He had half-decided to buy a couple of calves to fatten for market, and thought he might plant a little hay, so he'd need the silo to store and ferment the feed. Cleaning it out was a smelly, messy job. Generations of varmints had taken up burrowing into the decaying compost, and the refuse at the bottom of the silo was a mixture of rotting silage, animal droppings, bat guano and owl pellets. After sixty years or so of exposure to the acidic silage, the concrete floor had deteriorated into loose gravel.

After getting most of the debris cleared, Wiggins stopped working after his arms began to tingle. He assumed it was some kind of tendonitis on his worn-out elbows.

Later that evening, while he was walking by the silo, he noticed a blue light seeping out around the edges of its unloading door. When he peered inside, he was shocked to see electric-like sparks dancing along the floor of the silo where he'd been raking earlier. Wiggins stuck his leg through the door, and without thinking, kicked at the gravel with the heel of his boot. The sparks grew brighter and more frenzied, and Wiggins felt his foot felt get warm. A tingling sensation moved up his leg and into his groin. He pulled his leg back in alarm, and the light faded.

He took pains to avoid the silo the next few days. The light frightened him, but he felt drawn to it like a moth to the flame. A week or so later, Wiggins could no longer resist and went back to the silo. It was early morning. The blue light began blinking from the gap under the door. Like a man in a trance, he walked over and slowly swung the silo door open. Tendrils of dancing sparks covered the ground, looking like hundreds of writhing, glowing blue snakes. In spite of his horror, Wiggins could not resist. He stepped inside.

The dancing became more furious and the snakes of light slithered over his boots and started climbing up his overalls. A tingling rose up into his groin, and crept to his stomach and chest. It entered his head. A wave of euphoria flowed over him, and he felt thirty years of wear and weariness evaporate. From somewhere in the center of his brain, a whispering began. It was not loud enough to make out, and sounded to be in some foreign tongue.

His elation abruptly turned to fear and revulsion as he was struck by an intense unfixed desire. It was like a sexual desire, but it was more, a lust for something that Wiggins could not put a name to, could not bring to focus.

But he knew it was evil.

With an effort of extreme will, the old mechanic yanked his legs from the gravel and fell out of the silo into the dirt. He struggled to get up onto his knees.

Squeezing his eyes shut, Wiggins prayed aloud. *"Ye though I walk through the valley of the shadow of death, I will fear no evil: for thou art with me; thy rod and thy staff they comfort me."*

He knew there was more to the 23rd Psalm, but that was all he could recall. After a while, he cautiously opened his eyes, and without looking back at the silo, stumbled into barn. He reached for his jug of corn whiskey hung on the wall, gulped until he choked and collapsed on a pile of straw.

Wiggins came to as the sun rose higher, and its light filtered through gaps in the barn siding. He got unsteadily to his feet and lurched to the house, promising himself never to go near the silo again.

Now, that Saturday, as he sat in his shop, Claude Wiggins could feel the pull of the light. Every day was a struggle to stay away from the silo. At least down by the road it wasn't so bad.

He didn't know how much longer he could resist.

Claire and Wilson returned to town from Amos Doyle's farm, and after getting Wilson checked in to the Sleep-Tite Motel, they walked down to catch the Saturday chicken dinner special at the Sunbeam Café. After a leisurely meal, they strolled back to the motel, the sun was settling down to the horizon and the sky was a luminous gold and orange streaked with purple and white ribbons of clouds. The temperature hovered at sixty degrees. Wilson brought out a six pack of Pabst that he had cooling in a sink full of ice in his motel room and the pair sat in lawn chairs by the pool, drinking beer and watching the complex play of light on the water.

"Test the water with your hand," Claire said.

Wilson sniffed. "Colder than a witch's tit, I suppose."

"Seriously, check it out."

Wilson unfolded his long frame out of the chair, and carrying his beer by its neck, stooped down at the pools edge and swept his free hand across the top of the water.

"Hey. Wilson looked back at Claire. "It's really warm. This dump has a heated pool? That's nuts."

Claire nodded. "The owner told me it's naturally heated by the ground underneath the pool."

"Geothermal?" Wilson came back and plunked down in his chair. "In Missouri? I don't think so."

Claire waved her hand towards the pool. "Something's heating it, that's a fact."

"I can't imagine what." Wilson took a swig of his beer. "I bet the owner's pulling your leg. Trying to get one over on the city slicker."

"I wonder if there is a connection to the water table situation." Claire absently scratched with a fingernail on the label on her beer. She looked at Wilson, her forehead creased in thought. "Maybe some kind of seismic event is occurring around here, altering the level of the water table, and we could be the ones to uncover it. That would be, as you would say, Wilson, *cool*."

"Speaking about cool." Wilson dug something out of his shirt that looked like a twisted piece of tissue paper.

Claire made a face. "You're not going to smoke that here, are you?"

Wilson looked around. There was no one in sight in the motel lot. The sun had slipped down under the horizon and night was rapidly cloaking them in darkness.

"Don't go ape, Claire." Wilson slipped the joint back in his pocket, finished off his beer and reached for another. "This is some really boss Mary Jane. I got this from a friend doing some work for an oil company in Mexico. You should try some. It will open you up to new worlds, Claire."

"It just gives you that illusion."

Wilson pushed his tortoise shell glasses up on the bridge of his nose, closed his eyes and recited:

> "Row, row, row your boat
> Gently down the stream
> Merrily, merrily, merrily, merrily
> Life is but a dream."

Claire frowned. "What's that supposed to mean?"

Wilson laughed. "Claire, you're so literal. I mean: one person's illusion is another's reality. Reality is fluid."

"No offense, but that's hogwash, Wilson. Drugs deceive the brain; generate false impressions of reality. I don't know how many times I've been approached by a man who's had one beer too many and thinks that he is charming, witty and brilliant, but in reality, is just being an ass. There is only one reality."

Wilson smiled condescendingly. "Claire, you really need to get out more often. Let me ask you this: how would you define *reality*?"

"A rock that stubs your toe."

"Cute. But very narrow. How would things such as love, faith, good and evil, fit into your paradigm of reality?"

Claire thought for a moment. "Let me put it this way: reality is what is generally believed to be true."

Wilson laughed. "Jeez, that agreement is as holey as Swiss cheese. By that definition, the Earth magically transformed from flat to spherical as soon as it was generally accepted to be round."

"Wilson," Claire reached down for her Pabst and took a last sip. "Just…please, be careful. Don't do anything to mess up that wonderful mind of yours."

"I promise, Mom."

"Besides, what if you get caught?"

Wilson chuckled. "By 'The Man' in Testament Hill?

They wouldn't know reefer from a Red Man hand-rolled cigarette."

Wilson retrieved the joint from his pocket along with a Zippo lighter and lit up. He inhaled deeply, held the smoke in and let it out slowly. "Ah, good shit."

Claire shook her head resignedly. She was not happy with Wilson's penchant for pharmaceutical adventure, but she tolerated it and kept his secret. On the job, he was always straight. He had a comprehensive knowledge of geology and a talent for creative solutions. Coupled with an almost uncanny ability to distill a complicated situation down to it essence, Wilson was definitely an asset. If smoking dope in moderation was his only vice, Claire was could live with it.

However, she did worry sometimes about his naiveté. Wilson was too easily swayed by the latest fad or ready to jump undiscerning with both feet into the newest craze.

Oh well, she thought, *he'll become a jaded skeptic soon enough: life will do that to you.*

Wilson's voice was now slightly slurred "What's our first move doc?"

"I'd like to do the seismic exploration," Claire said. "We need that data before we can even make any speculations about what's going on."

"So, back out to Doyle's farmstead? Blow up some worms?"

"Right. Amos Doyle's a little reserved, but he warmed up to me when I connected with his granddaughter Ivy."

Wilson blew out a ring of smoke at the fading sky. "What's going on with that pet crow of hers? What little girls have pet crows?"

You don't know the half of it, Claire thought.

She turned to Wilson. "I'd also like to see if the owners here, Mr. B and the Missus, will let us do a test hole. This heated pool thing is weird."

Wilson closed his eyes. "Forget it. I think they're spoofing us. They got a water heater." He spoke in that particular strained voice of a pot user trying to hold in a lungful of smoke.

"You're probably right."

The two watched silently as the last light faded in the west.

"Wilson, what are you doing this evening?"

"What did you have in mind?" Wilson sat up straight in his chair.

"I was thinking of going to a tent revival I heard about."

Wilson affected a disappointed expression. "Oh, I thought you were going to ask me in for a nightcap."

"Dream on." Claire laughed. "Really, this Prester John guy - I've read about him in a magazine or somewhere. He's sort of famous."

"No thanks," Wilson said. "Not my cup of tea. Actually, I'll see if I can get anything on the TV, then hit the sack. I'm beat from the ride down. Plus, I was up late last night at a frat party."

Chapter 10

The Boone County Fairground looked pretty much as Claire had imagined. It was a large rectangular field of flattened brown grass with four peeling, olive drab Quonset huts clustered at one end. Two pair of plywood outhouses bracketed the huts. Around the periphery, a row of creosoted poles carrying power lines and fitted with floodlights lit the fairground in pale yellow light. In the center of the grounds, a huge marquee tent had been erected.

When Claire arrived, she had to circle the chalk marked parking area twice to find a free space for her Volvo. Knots of people were making their way across the battered turf to the tent.

She parked and walked to the line where people were filing into the tent entrance. The night cool and clear, the stars were stark pinpricks of blue white light overhead. She returned the many smiles of those who made eye contract. The crowd was mostly adults, chattering eagerly. A few grownups had children in tow.

While Claire waited to pass through the turnstile at the tent entrance, she was surprised when she began to share in the enthusiasm. There was electricity in the air.

An angelic-faced teenaged girl with a corona of fine blond hair stood at the turnstile. At first Claire thought she might be collecting entrance fees, but the girl was just handing out a pamphlet. It was titled *The Mission of Prester John.* Claire folded the tract and slipped it into the pocket of her jacket, then made her way to the stands. They were arranged in a half oval around the interior of the tent. A small wooden stage and podium had been placed in the center. On the ground in front of the podium was what looked like a yellowed stone birdbath on a fluted pillar.

After finding a seat, (on the aisle - Claire abhorred the confinement of the middle of an row) she absently scanned the audience and recognized Edith, from the police station, sitting in the front row with her hands clasped together, her face lit with anticipation.

When Claire got bored with rubbernecking, she thumbed through the handout. It was basically an autobiography of *Prester John*.

According to the pamphlet, Prester John was chosen by God in an extraordinary and unexpected way. One night in 1954, a man strode out of a brothel in Cowpunch, Texas. A column of cold white light emanating from the ground enveloped him as he drunkenly stumbled in the dusty street towards his Harley Davidson motorcycle. At first, he felt as if he was going to burn up in the fire of Hell, and prepared to meet the Devil himself. Thrashing and yelling, he fell on his back into the dirt. The burning sensation abruptly changed to a soothing coolness and he was surrounded by an impenetrable golden fog. A feeling of profound peace came over the man, and he lay contently spread-eagled on the ground.

A bearded figure with long hair, wearing a brilliant white robe emerged from the mist. The figure was holding his right arm out, palm held upwards, his bare feet floating a few inches from the ground. The figure smiled at the man, and the man got up on his knees. Although the figure's mouth did not move, the man could hear in his head words from the mysterious presence.

It told him that he had been chosen to spread the True Word amongst the people, and he should name himself after a mythical holy king of the Middle Ages.

The figure bid him to stand, and then placed his hand upon the man's forehead. At that instant, the man's mind was filled with the Wisdom of the Ages in order that he may go forth to spread the Word.

And so it came to be that the man traveled the country for the past eight years, preaching to the people. Obeying the command of God.

That man was Prester John.

The pamphlet went on to state that while there is no charge to hear the word, the Mission greatly appreciated any donation that would help in their task, and would certainly send blessings to the giver.

What a bunch of bullshit, Claire thought.

She put the tract in her lap and resumed surveying the crowd. She estimated that there were at least four hundred adults sitting in the bleachers, now filled to capacity, and perhaps another two hundred standing below.

Let's see, she thought: *if each person gave, say, five dollars in the hat or whatever, that would be six hundred times five...about three grand. Not bad for an honest day's work.*

Claire began to feel a uncomfortable. She never did like crowds - the close proximity of strangers; the restriction of movement; the loss of individuality. Even the odors bothered her. She began to regret her decision to come.

Besides religion wasn't her cup of tea. Born and raised a Catholic, Claire used to fool herself that she was a believer when she was a young and was awed by Catholicism's elaborate, mysterious rituals. But as soon as she grew old enough to think for herself, she drifted away from the Church. There were too many leaps of faith required to be a true Christian, or as she would say, believing required too much suspension of reality.

Then, in college, Claire learned about the world's other religions. She appreciated the creativity and deep thought invested in the amazing variety of religious ideas in the world, and suspected that many had roots in profound truths. That they had millions of followers for hundreds or thousands of years attested to that. However, in spite of what some apologists asserted, Claire realized some religions' basic tenets conflicted with each other. Logically, they could not all be true. Some just had to be *wrong*.

As far as religion's premises were concerned, Claire applied an empirical scientific approach: if a hypothesis cannot be tested for validity and reproduced, it was a dead end. If she had to put a label on it, she considered herself an agnostic: neither believing nor denying the existence of God or some supreme metaphysical being or beings. The truth, at least for her, was simply unknowable.

Claire's train of thought was interrupted as the bare

lightbulbs strung overhead slowly dimmed and multicolored spotlights came on, illuminating the stage in an oval of light. Organ music piped through speakers overhead. Claire recognized Bach's Fugue in D Minor. At a dramatic point in the work, the lights brightened and a figure appeared behind the podium.

It was a tall man, dressed all in black - shirt, pants and a long tailed morning coat. His light blond, shoulder-length hair shone halo-like in the lights. The crowd hushed at the impressive sight. The music faded, and the man raised his hands into the air and leaned forward to the microphone on the podium.

The voice was deep and commanding:

"Ask, and it shall be given to you; seek and ye shall find; knock and it shall be opened unto you."

The man turned his head, his eyes searching over the audience. For a split second, they met Claire's. With a jolt, Claire recognized John Preston, the 'salesman' she had met at Duggan's.

Claire thought she saw a smile briefly cross his face and his head nod slightly. Then he looked upward.

"He who hath ears to hear, let him hear."

From the audience, a few murmured "Amen".

He lowered his hands. "Peace be unto you."

"And to you," replied some in the crowd.

The house lights turned up a bit, and now Prester John's voice was softer. "Welcome people of Testament Hill. Welcome. Jesus said: '*For where two or three are gathered together in my name, there am I in the midst of them.*'" He stepped forward. "Can I get an Amen?"

"Amen!" This time the crowd's response was louder.

Claire looked around. All faces in the audience were raised, enthralled by the man at the podium. *Well, he certainly knows how to work a crowd,* she thought.

"I am not here tonight to tell you how to be right with God." Prester John continued, his voice rising again. "You already know in your hearts what you need to do! You just need to tell that Satan to get behind thee!"

"Amen!"

"I am Prester John and I am here to tell you to kick that devil out of your hearts!"

"Amen!"

Prester John raised his hands again. "Who am I?"

"Prester John!"

"Who am I?"

"Prester John!"

The preacher bowed his head and closed his eyes. For long moments he said nothing. Claire could sense the crowd becoming restless. Then his head came up, but his eyes stayed closed.

"People of Testament Hill! I know you have been troubled as of late. I know your tribulations. I see the land has dried up. The blessing of rain from the heavens has passed Testament Hill by."

Now, the preacher's arms spread out at his sides. "*'If I shut up heaven that there be no rain, or if I command the locusts to devour the land, or if I send pestilence among my people;*

If my people, which are called by my name, shall humble themselves, and pray and seek my face and turn away from their wicked ways; then I will hear from heaven, and will forgive their sin, and will heal the land': Second Chronicles, Chapter seven, verse thirteen. Can I get an Amen?"

"Amen!"

"Will you turn away from your wicked ways? Each of you..." Prester John slowly looked over the audience, making eye contact. "...know what I am talking about." His head stopped, and he focused on one spot in the crowd. Claire followed his gaze and was surprised to see Deputy Hooper meeting Prester John's stare with wide eyes. The preacher then continued to search out the audience. He turned towards Claire and she had no doubt he was looking directly at her. Even at a distance his amber eyes were mesmerizing.

His somber expression softened and he smiled. "If you pray and seek his face, God will heal."

Claire looked down, and pretended to be examining the pamphlet. When she looked up again, she was relieved the preacher's attention had moved on.

Prester John clasped his hands behind his back and stepped away from the podium. He began pacing in a circle on the stage, his head bent. After a long minute, he brought his head back up.

"I'm here to warn you: the power of Satan is all around us, my friends. He came as the serpent to whisper in the ear of Adam and Eve. Beguiled them so that they ate of the forbidden tree in the midst of the garden. *'And the Lord God said, Behold the man is become one of us, to know good and evil.'*"

Prester John jabbed a finger in the air. "Adam and Eve's innocence was destroyed: they now knew sin. For disobeying God's command, they were cast out of the Garden of Eden."

Prester John stepped back to the podium, extended his arms and grasped its corners. "Let me tell you how it is, my friends: Samyaza was one of God's archangels. He was jealous of the attention God gave to Man, so Samyaza, and those angels who had come under his influence rebelled against God. Tempted by Earthly pleasures, Samyaza and his followers incarnated, that is, became embodied in flesh, and came down to dwell among mankind. These are the Fallen Angels, and their leader, Samyaza, we call Satan."

The preacher moved in front of the podium.

"Here, they saw the daughters of men and that they were fair, and took them for wives. The offspring of this blasphemous union were Nephilim, the giants of Genesis. The Fallen and the Nephilim spread unspeakable depravity, so the wickedness of man was great.

"And so God tasked righteous angels led by the Archangel Michael to destroy the Fallen. Thus transpired the War in Heaven. The rebellious angels were defeated and those few that survived fled back to Earth."

Then God declared that *'the end of all flesh has come before me.'* and brought forth the Deluge, so that the waters would destroy the Fallen angels and the Nephilim and cleanse the Earth of corrupted mankind. Only Noah and his family, whom God found to be *pure* were spared.

Prester John closed his eyes. Claire guessed he was collecting his thoughts or perhaps letting the impact of what he was saying settle over his audience. More likely, she decided, it was just for dramatic effect. He brought his hands down, clasped together, fingers pointing to the ground.

"But ten of Fallen angels escaped by going into the underworld. God allowed them to survive that they may tempt men to do evil. But he trapped them in their refuge, *Sheol* - a place of darkness.

"The Bible says: '*And the angels which kept not their first habitation, he hath reserved in everlasting chains under darkness unto the judgment of the great day.*' "

Prester John stared upward for a moment, then resumed.

"Samyaza and his followers, though trapped in the underworld, try to seduce us. These Fallen angels work hard to tempt us, to drive us to do evil things. To give in to our darkest desires. Understand this: they get their energy from evil, as a tree receives its energy from the sun. The more evil in the land, the stronger they become and the more they can spread their poison. "

The preacher raised his hands, pointing and sweeping them across the grandstands, "Know that The Fallen are physically trapped in Sheol, and can only work as spirits, whispering in your ear, like the serpent. And my friends… they work among us every day causing grief and tribulations. Know also that these demons cannot *make* you do anything, because God has given you all *free will*. The freedom to do good or evil. The only way to defeat them is to be strong and righteous."

He paused for effect. Then he called out loudly, "Amen!"

The audience rejoined. "Amen!"

Claire looked around. Prester John's speech was causing a varied reaction. Some people were frowning, perhaps skeptical or disbelieving. Others, with eyebrows knitted, gave the impression of being slightly baffled by what he was saying. But most appeared enraptured, caught up not so much as the message as the medium: the powerful presence of Prester John.

Prester John stepped back from the podium, and, taking his time, drank from a glass of clear liquid.

Claire had to admit that she was a little mystified herself by Prester John's message. She vaguely recalled hearing of the Nephilim, perhaps from one of Wilson's ramblings about religion and ancient myths.

It seemed every month her assistant would turn to something new. One month, Wilson would be into Hindu traditions, another Zen Buddhism. For a while he was enthusiastic about Kabbalistic Judaism, then on to Native American belief systems. His latest, if she remembered correctly, was Manichaeism. Claire recognized Wilson's behavior as the typical exploratory forays of a young, inquisitive mind. She had gone through similar phases herself.

Prester John returned to the podium once again.

He began talking about the drought, quoting the Bible again: *"When heaven is shut up, and there is no rain, because they have sinned against thee; if they pray toward this place, and confess thy name, and turn away from their sin, when thou afflictest them:*

"Then hear thou in heaven, and forgive the sin of thy servants, and of thy people Israel, that thou teach them the good way wherein they should walk, and give them rain upon thy land. Amen."

"Amen!" now the crowd was reacting enthusiastically.

Claire's mind began to drift. The preacher's words got her thinking about evil.

From personal experience, it seemed to her that terrible events were either caused by acts of Nature or the behavior of mentality deranged individuals. Natural disasters occurred without malicious purpose. Volcanos and tornados weren't evil. Animals that attacked each other for dominance or sustenance weren't evil. Only human beings could do evil things - senseless behavior that caused pain and suffering for its own sake. Claire figured people alone were the source of evil. No external forces needed to be input into the equation.

Prester John's raising voice brought back her attention.

"I will pray for relief from this curse of drought, and I bid you to join with me so that we will be united in the power of earnest prayer," He said, putting his palms together.

After a rather lengthy, and what Claire thought was a somewhat rambling prayer, Prester John raised his hands once more.

"Jesus said, in John, Chapter 3, verse 3: *'Truly, truly I say to you, unless one is born again, he cannot see the kingdom of God.'*"

"Amen!"

"'Except a man be born of water and of the spirit, he cannot enter into the kingdom of God'. Hallelujah."

"Hallelujah!"

"And now my friends, those of you who want to be born again and are willing to give yourself into Jesus' hands; receive him into your hearts, and those who wish to reaffirm their faith, come forward to be baptized in the Holy Spirit!"

He made his way off the stage, and stood beside the stone "birdbath".

Prester John waved his hand. "This ancient baptistry I have brought home from the Holy Land and have filled with water from the Jordan River - the same that baptized our Lord and Savior. Now I invite each and every one of you to come forward and be born again in Jesus' name.

"And for those of you who have already given your life to Christ, I invite you to come forward and reaffirm and reinvigorate your conviction." Prester John clasped his hands behind his back and smiled.

Under the direction of ushers, people began to make their way out of the stands, forming a line leading up to the baptistry. Prester John leaned in close and spoke briefly to each supplicant as they stepped up, and then dipped his hand into the water of the baptistry and let a few drops fall from his hand onto the crowns of their heads.

Claire watched the baptism routine for a while until she became weary of the repetition. She stepped out of line when her row was being led down to be baptized, and slipped from the tent into the fresh air of the fair grounds.

Hugging herself against the cooling night air, she gazed upward at the stars, nostalgic for a cigarette, a habit she had quit two years earlier.

The magnificent swath of the Milky Way shone high in the clear sky.

Something about Prester John's Biblical references had made her uneasy. She was pondering the reason when she was startled by a voice behind her.

"You're not staying for the last act?"

Claire spun around, instinctively reaching to the small of her back for her handgun, until she remembered she had decided not to take it to the revival.

"Whoa." The man took a step back. "Didn't mean to scare you."

The height of the man was quite impressive. He was smiling down at her. Claire took him in in one glance: at least six foot six, rangy, wearing a buttoned up black trench coat and pants with matching cowboy boots. His long sable hair was parted in the middle and covered part of his ears. He was leaning on an unfurled umbrella as if were a cane. Dark liquid eyes glinted at her out of a long, clean shaven face with a square jaw. The thought flashed in Claire's head: *Prester John's dark twin brother.*

Claire said, "I've seen enough. Revivals aren't really my cup of tea."

The man laughed, a deep throaty sound. "I understand perfectly."

For a moment the two assessed each other. He looked familiar to Claire. Then she remembered: he was the man that had been standing by the side of the road when she drove into town.

"Have we met before?" she asked.

"I don't believe so. My name is Smith, by the way." Again that wide smile. He held out his hand.

She knew it was rude, but she could not get herself to take the man's hand. It wasn't because he was repulsive - on the contrary, she found Smith quite attractive. He radiated a strong sexual aura. Perhaps that was why Claire found him a little threatening and was wary of having physical contact.

"Claire Brannigan," she said.

Smith lowered his hand, still smiling. If he was offended by Claire's slight, it didn't show. "What, if you don't mind me asking, brings you to the fine town of Testament Hill?"

In response to Claire's surprised expression, he explained, "It's pretty obvious you're not a local."

Claire attempted a smile. "You first."

"We stick out like sore thumbs around here, don't we? I'm a dowser, actually."

Claire took half a step back. "Really? I have to admit, I would have never guessed."

"You probably thought I was a traveling salesman."

"No..." Claire said. "...well, maybe I did."

"I understand. You don't come across a dowser very often." He cocked his head. "Your turn."

"I'm a hydrologist."

"Hydrologist?"

"It's a type of geologist that specializes in the dynamics of water - how it is distributed, how it circulates, things like that."

"So you're in Testament Hill to find out what's going on with the water supply?"

"That's right," Claire said. "The police chief here in town contacted a friend at the university where I teach and do research, and asked for some help. I was intrigued, and frankly, an opportunity for a respite from world of academia sounded great, so I volunteered."

Smith nodded. "I was invited here for the same reason - the water situation."

"To dowse? By who? Chief Childress?"

Smith stared at her blankly for a moment, then answered. "That's right."

Claire said, "I guess he wanted to cover all the bases."

Their conversation was interrupted when people began filing out of the revival tent and out to the parking lot.

"Looks like it's over," Claire remarked.

"Yes."

Claire gestured at Smith's umbrella. "Expecting rain? You know that's been pretty rare around here."

Smith looked up at the sky. "You never know. Don't want to get wet." An odd expression formed on his face for a moment, then he smiled. "Say, I'd go for a cup of coffee. I hear the coffee at the Sunbeam Café is not bad. Would you like to join me? It's a lovely night for a walk."

When Chief Childress asked Edith if she could man the phones at the station Saturday night after the revival, she said yes. She didn't mind. *Just until eleven or so*, the Chief had said. *Revival's supposed to wind up about nine, so if everything's quiet by eleven, we'll probably be okay.*

He would man the phones himself, the Chief told Edith, but his wife's sister and husband were coming to dinner, and he promised Flo he'd be home.

Calls were normally routed to the Highway Patrol after hours since Testament Hill didn't have a full time dispatcher. However, the Chief didn't want to waste the state's time for the idiotic misbehaving that sometimes occurred after a revival. From Chief Childress' experience, revivals and such had a tendency to rile up a certain segment of the populace. Got their adrenaline going or something. Then the usual town idiots would go to the saloon and get more agitated and altercations would ensue. Childress preferred to take care of those issues without involving outsiders.

Edith was happy to oblige. She was going to be in town anyway for the revival and the extra hours would pad her paycheck, and help fill in another lonely night. And then there was the other reason. One she kept to herself: she could listen for the *voices*.

They were hard to hear, just a whispering under the

normal static of an idling dispatch radio.

Of course, Edith didn't tell anyone. They'd think something was wrong with her hearing, or maybe she was getting a little dotty. Then maybe they'd be thinking about replacing her. That wouldn't do. She needed the income. It had been hard to make ends meet since her husband, Harold, was killed two years ago during the corn harvest when he got caught in the thresher trying to clear a jam. (It was a closed casket funeral).

Nighttime, when no one was in the office to make noise, was the best time to listen for the voices on the dispatch radio. Edith found the best frequency to listen to was just a little ahead of the State Highway Patrol channel. And then you had to turn down the 'squelch' knob so that the static wasn't filtered out.

She noticed them around mid-July. At first, it seemed to be just an increase in the usual hissing garble and Edith supposed it was because of radio getting old. Maybe dust and dirt was getting inside, and the wires getting rusty or whatever they did with age.

Lately, however, she could almost make out words. At first, Edith worried it may be just her imagination confabulating. But the more she listened, the more she became convinced it was something real. She had read in a magazine somewhere about sightings of Unidentified Flying Objects, and speculated that maybe she was picking up on their messages to each other.

Or, maybe it was demons preparing for the end times. Or maybe angels. Edith was frightened of the voices but also eager to find out their meaning. She was beginning to believe that the messages were specifically for her - a warning or some call to action. And they were becoming more urgent in tone. Pressing more and more into her brain. If she could just figure out what they were trying to tell her.

So that night, she sat very still with the dispatch radio hissing in one ear, listening, reading passages out of her Bible, and occasionally stealing a little nip out of the Chief's bottle she knew he kept hidden in the bottom drawer of his desk.

It helped with her headaches, which had become worse lately.

"You don't believe in dowsing, do you?" Smith stirred his coffee idly and looked up at Claire. They sat in a corner booth at the Sunrise Café, deserted except for a teenage couple sharing a sundae at the counter.

"Frankly, no." Claire waved her hand. "There's no scientific evidence that it is effective."

Smith's eyes narrowed a fraction. "Is that so? Have you ever tried it yourself?"

"No, I haven't."

"Maybe you should, you might be surprised. Of course, it doesn't work for everyone."

"Of course." Claire smiled. "Did you know that Martin Luther once forbade dowsing, or water witching, way back in 1495. He felt it was the devil's work."

"Interesting tidbit," Smith took the spoon out of his coffee and set it carefully down on his napkin. "Dowsing is a simple process, really," he said. "An object is held loosely in the hands, traditionally a Y-shaped branch from a willow or witch hazel." Smith pretended to be holding a branch in his hands. "Actually, all kinds of things can be used, such as a pair of L-shaped metal rods. The dowser simply walks the area to be searched and when the stick dips, or the rods cross, there probably is water below."

Smith noticed Claire's expression. "I can see that you are a skeptic. You're aware, I'm sure, that plain ol' H_2O has some very special properties."

"Indeed it does." Claire tested her coffee and poured in a little cream. "Water: let's see… first of all, it covers seven-eighths of the Earth, which means it plays a very significant role in things like the weather, geography, geology and of course, biology." She paused, thinking.

"Water generally occurs on Earth in the temperature range where it is in a liquid or vapor phase," she continued. "which allows for the free movement of dissolved and suspended molecules making the perfect medium for life to begin and evolve. Also - the water cycle of evaporation and condensation moves water around on the surface though rainfall and flowing creeks and rivers, which in turn, helps spread life-giving nutrients."

Smith raised his eyebrows. "And...?"

Claire took a breath and went on. "The anomalous fact that it expands rather than contracts when it turns into a solid causes ice to float. Solid water is lighter than liquid water. That keeps lakes from freezing bottom up and allows for the seasonal turnover of water, and keeps it oxygenated so that water breathing creatures can live."

Smith said. "Impressive."

"Let's see," Claire tapped the table with a fingertip. "Its high specific heat - the ability to store a lot of energy - helps moderate the temperature of the Earth's surface, so we don't have extreme hot and cold as the Earth rotates daily from light to dark and the angles of incidental solar light changes through the seasons... I could go on."

"Please do."

"Water is also a dipole molecule."

"So...?"

"As you may know," Claire explained, "water molecules are made up of two hydrogen atoms connected to an oxygen atom, arranged in unique angles to each other, giving the water molecule an unbalanced electrical charge, so that it has an attraction to itself, which allows for surface tension and capillary action which draws water up inside narrow tubes, as in the phylum of plants. Without which we would have no plants as we know them. Also the capillary action wicks water from wet areas such as wetlands into dry areas."

"Fascinating." Smith said.

"Yes, it is," Claire agreed. "There's more: water's unique dipole structure, when linked up with other molecules such as nitrogen and carbon, in a process that's not yet clearly understood, form very complex molecules that fold up into *proteins,* which are the basis of life. Our bodies are basically skin bags carrying around a chemical factory creating proteins in a solution of water."

"A delightful analogy," Smith rubbed his chin.

"Sorry, I didn't mean to bore you with a lecture. It's the teacher in me, I'm afraid."

Smith smiled. "No, not at all. I enjoy learning how science is figuring out how Creation works… So, we agree: water is a very special substance. It has many anomalous properties. Who's to say that water dowsing is not possible? That there exists some special relationship between life and water that science cannot explain?"

"I think you might be stretching it a bit."

"It's the connection of water to life that makes dowsing possible," Smith argued. "A sub-conscious connection to a dimension of reality that is not apparent to the everyday five senses. That's what dowsing is: using a sixth sense."

"A little too mumbo-jumbo for me," Claire said. "what exactly is the sixth sense?"

Smith pyramided his hands on the table. "*There are more things in Heaven or Earth, Horatio, than are dreamt of in your philosophy.*"

Claire said, "*Hamlet.*"

Smith turned his head towards the outside window of the café. "You should come out and see me work, Claire. Get a demonstration. I'm going out to Amos Doyle's farm tomorrow to dowse."

Claire recalled the vision of Smith standing by the side of the road the morning she drove into town, and was tempted to ask how he intended to get to Doyle's. "It just so happens I'm also going to be there in the morning with my assistant do some testing," she said.

"Then I will see you there, and we can compare methods."

"I look forward to it." Claire finished off her coffee. She noticed Smith had not touched his. "Coffee's no good?"

"Actually, I don't drink coffee. Getting coffee was just an excuse to talk to you."

For a moment their eyes met, and Claire felt as if some

force or energy had passed between them. It was exciting and frightening at the same time. Looking into Smith's eyes was like staring into dark, endless space.

Smith glanced downward. For a second, Claire thought he was staring at her cleavage.

He leaned towards her. "That amulet you're wearing…where, if you don't mind me asking, did you get it?

Claire's hand reflexively clutched the necklace. "I found it actually."

A shadow passed across Smith's face. "Would you mind if I take a closer look?"

Chapter 11

Sunday morning

Around 9 o'clock, Claire stopped at the police station before meeting Wilson at Doyle's farm. She was hoping Chief Childress would be there so she could inform him about the use of explosives for the seismic survey. When she walked in, Chief Childress was in earnest conversation with a man wearing a crisp blue uniform. She hesitated at the doorway.

Childress smiled and waved her in. "Come on in, Doctor Brannigan. Help yourself to a cup of coffee. I'll be with you in a minute."

While Claire poured half a cup of the thick brew into a mug that she first surreptitiously wiped with a paper napkin, she heard the two men talking about the missing trooper. From what Claire could pick up, the trooper apparently went to investigate the complaint of someone setting off fireworks off Highway 23.

"Excuse me gentlemen," she interrupted. "I apologize, but I couldn't help but hear. I saw a Highway Patrol car on Highway 23 on Friday morning when I came into town."

"What time would that have been, miss?" the man in the uniform turned to her. He had a bland, clean-shaven face with a long jaw and small rodent-like eyes. His salt-and-pepper hair was cut in a military style flattop.

"I guess about 7 a.m.. It was just before the Sinclair gas station. The patrol car went by heading west, flasher going."

"Is that so?" the man said. He blinked at her. "And who might you be?"

Chief Childress stepped between the two. "Captain Bob Norris, this is Doctor Claire Brannigan, she's a geologist from the university who has come to investigate our well water problem. Claire, this is Captain Norris, from the Highway Patrol."

"Nice to meet you, Claire Brannigan." The man attempted a smile. "You say the car was headed east on 23 about 7 a.m.?"

"Yes. It was shortly after I heard a booming sound and saw a flash in the sky. I thought it was lighting and thunder."

"Well, thank you for the information, Miss Brannigan." The captain turned to Childress. "Let us know, Chief, if you find out anything else that may be important."

"Of course."

Captain Norris nodded curtly to Claire, spun on his heel and went out the door into the street.

Childress poured himself some coffee and sat down at his desk. Claire waited while he thoughtfully stirred it with a pencil. Finally he looked up at Claire and waved her to a seat across from the desk. "So, is there something I can help you with, Doctor Brannigan?"

"Please, just Claire is fine."

"Fine. then… Claire, what brings you here this morning?"

"I just wanted to let you know that my assistant and I are going out back to Amos Doyle's place, and we are going to do some ground surveys."

"Okay… So..?"

"Just wanted to warn you, we're going to be using some explosives."

"Explosives?"

"Yes, just some small charges of dynamite we will be setting off in bore holes to send vibrations into the ground. We'll place seismic sensors in arrays around the explosions. By the timing of the reflections of the shock waves picked up by the sensors we can get some idea of the nature of the underlying strata."

"Sounds kind of like radar."

"That's right, Chief. I thought I'd let you know in case you get any reports of explosions out that way."

"I appreciate that," Childress said. "When do you think you will be done making a racket?"

"I hope to be done late in the afternoon."

"Okay. Good luck." Childress waved his pencil. "Let me

know what you find."

Claire got up to leave. She went to the front door and turned. "And by the way, that dowser you sent for - he's going to be out there too."

"Who?"

"The man that calls himself Smith."

"Never heard of him," Childress said. "I never contacted a dowser. Don't believe in that bullshit, pardon the expression. Amos Doyle probably sent for him."

Claire frowned for a second then smiled. "Maybe I misunderstood."

On the way back to her car, Claire recognized Edith walking down the sidewalk. She was wearing a grey woolen shawl and had a large purse clutched tightly to her bosom. Her eyes were downcast, so at first she didn't notice Claire.

"Hello again, Edith."

Edith stopped and looked up. "Oh...good morning, Doctor Brannigan."

"How are you, today?"

For a moment, Edith didn't respond. She frowned, then brightened. "I'm fine, thanks. On my way home from church. How are you?"

"Good, thank you."

Edith hesitated then took a step closer to Claire. Her voice lowered. "Are you going back to Amos Doyle's farm today? Because if you are, be very careful."

"What do you mean?"

"I mean the curse of Testament Hill, Claire, if I may call you that."

"Certainly," Claire said. "Now, about this 'curse'..?"

Edith stepped closer. "No one talks about it. They think if no one mentions it, it doesn't exist, or it will leave us alone."

"Can you tell me about it?"

Edith glanced around as if to see if anyone might be close enough to overhear their conversation. "Come by the house tonight for a drink, and I'll give you the whole story," she said. "Down the road from the Doyle place, going east - there's a corner store and gas station. Next to it is a building with four small apartments. I live in number 4. Moved there a year or so after my Harold passed and I had to sell the farm. Any time after six, I'll be home."

"I appreciate the offer." Claire hesitated. "But I have a lot of work to do and only limited time here."

"...I'll tell you about the other time we had a drought."

Claire considered for a moment. "I'd like that. Provided I don't get delayed at Doyle's, I'll be there."

"Good." Edith's eyes narrowed. "What are you planning to do at Amos's place?"

"Today? Just a survey, a look around." Claire decided not to mention the seismic tests.

"Well, then, see you tonight. Goodbye." Edith lowered her head and hurried off.

Smith arrived at Doyle's farm ahead of Claire and Wilson. The dowser walked up from the road to the house. There was no one around. A penciled note was pinned to the side door. In a careful hand, it informed the reader that Amos Doyle had taken the tractor up to the back twenty and would return at eleven.

Smith strode over to the old abandoned well that had attracted Claire's attention the day before. For a long while he stared down into the stone filled pit, then he raised his hands and looked up at the sky.

In a soft but strong voice, he spoke in a language that had not been heard for eight thousand years. It was a singsong language, full of long melodic vowels, with a hypnotic rhythm. An expert in the history of human tongues might have been able to discern similarities to ancient tongues such as Egyptian, Sanskrit, Greek and Celtic.

When he finished, Smith brought his arms down and bent over the well. Faint electric currents began to swirl in his brain.

The stones in the well began to vibrate, as if they were on a sifting table. The motion became more energetic, and the stones separated and levitated, rising up a few inches and hovering. A bright blue fountain of glitter rose up from the well's depth and filled the spaces between the stones. As Smith leaned over the well, his face felt bathed in a tingling warmth. He held his eyes wide open, taking in the light.

Soon, he thought, *very soon, my fathers. Our time is coming.*

He stood perfectly still, until after a minute or so, the light faded and the well went dark. Smith blinked hard. The stones collapsed back into a pile. He rotated his head on his shoulders a few times then stepped back from the well. The eddies in his brain slowed and stopped.

A John Deere Model D appeared over a rise behind the barn, its intermittent engine ignition giving it a distinctive sound and the nickname "Johnny Poppers". An old man was at the wheel. Smith moved away from the well to the driveway.

At the same time, the sound of tires on gravel got Smith's attention. A Jeep turned up the drive from the road. In the back was mounted a crane-like mechanism. Smith recognized Claire from the sun reflecting off her red hair in the passenger seat. A young, goateed man sat behind the wheel. They pulled up and jumped out.

Claire was smiling. "Smith, this Mike Wilson, my post-doctoral assistant from the university. Mike, this is Smith, the dowser I was telling you about."

The two men tentatively shook hands and said nothing.

"I guess we can get started," Claire said, watching the tractor pull into the barn. "I'll just have a word with the owner, and make sure he's okay with our plan." She walked to the barn and met Amos Doyle as he came out.

While Claire and Doyle engaged in conversation, Wilson and Smith stood in awkward silence.

"So," Wilson said finally, "you're a dowser?"

Smith looked him straight in the eyes. "That's right."

"You know, as a geologist, I find the concept very intriguing."

Smith put his hands in his pockets and rocked back and forth in his pointy black cowboy boots. "Is that so? Why's that?"

"Actually, I don't see how it could work. In a scientific sense, I mean. But I haven't totally dismissed the idea. When Claire told me you would be here today, I was excited. Would you mind if I observed you? I won't get in your way."

"No problem." Smith's said, his voice flat. "You're welcome to watch... and I would be very interested in the techniques the modern hydrologists use."

"Sure. I'm sure Claire wouldn't mind. Who goes first?"

"If there's no objection, I would like to, before you disturb the ground with your explosions."

"You know about those?"

"I just assumed that's what you would be doing - trying to figure out where the underground water is by seismic exploration." Smith looked over towards Wilson's car. "So that's your gear mounted in the back?"

"Yep." Wilson glanced at the Jeep. "It's kind of a miniature cable tool setup. It will drill a two inch hole. It can only go down as far as thirty feet or so, but it will be enough for our survey."

"I see."

"And where's your gear?" Wilson asked.

Smith reached inside his long frock coat and pulled out two L-shaped objects. "This is all I need."

"No willow branches?"

"I use copper rods. It's a personal preference. It's the dowser that makes the process work. The rods or sticks react to changes in the dowser's nervous system as it is affected by the physical presence of water."

"Sure, I get it." Wilson said. "Just because science can't as yet explain how it works, doesn't mean it's bogus. There are a whole lot of phenomena that scientists scratch their heads over."

Smith smiled thinly. "Precisely."

Claire and Amos Doyle walked up.

"So I think we're all set," Claire said. "What have you guys come up with?"

"If it's okay with you, Claire," Wilson said. "Smith here is going to do his dowsing thing first, before we smack the ground."

"Sounds good. How long do you need?" Claire looked at Smith.

For a moment, Smith said nothing. He was staring intently at the ground.

"Just a few minutes," he answered finally. "I just ask that while I am working I have no distractions."

"Of course." Claire nodded to Amos Doyle and Wilson, and the three walked back to the farmhouse. Claire and Wilson sat on the back porch steps while Doyle stood up on the porch leaning up against the railing.

"Where's your beautiful granddaughter today?" Claire asked Doyle, casually making conversation.

"She's out back picking apples with Raven."

"How nice."

The three watched silently as Smith methodically made his way back and forth across the farm yard, with one L-shaped rod in each hand, held close together, pointing out away from his body.

Claire was surprised that instead of looking at the ground at his feet, Smith was staring out at the distant horizon. She wondered if he was in some kind of trance. "How does he keep from tripping, the way he is not paying attention to where his feet are?" she remarked.

Wilson turned to Claire. "Speaking about tripping - maybe he's high. Smoked a little Mary Jane before coming here."

"Wilson!" Claire admonished.

He waved his hand. "There's a whole world out there besides rocks and water. All kinds of cool metaphysical stuff like clairvoyance, telekinesis, UFOs, levitation by meditation... "

"You're joking, right?" Claire said. "There's a lot of crazy stuff, you mean."

Wilson stared at her for a moment. He moved his mouth as if he was going to reply, but either thought better of it, or couldn't think of anything to say.

Claire half expected him to go "Aw shucks" and kick his toe in the dirt like a child. Of course, Claire reminded herself, he was just a man-child. She resisted the impulse to reach out and tousle his hair.

"You're such an innocent," she said.

Wilson snorted good-naturedly.

Smith had apparently finished surveying one patch of ground, and moved higher up towards the barn.

"Devil's work," Amos Doyle mumbled. He was watching Smith with tightened eyes. He reached into a pocket of his overalls pulled out a red bandana and wiped his nose vigorously.

Claire turned to him. "What do you mean?"

Doyle pointed a bony finger towards Smith. "Dowsing... it's witchery, if you ask me."

Claire was confused. "But I thought maybe you sent for him."

Doyle shook his head. "Not me, Doctor Brannigan. I figured you asked him here."

Smith traversed the ground around the barn, came back down and moved around the front of the house, working his way towards the road. Finally, his tucked his rods back into his coat and strode back up the driveway to the porch in quick strides.

"No luck, Mr. Doyle," he called out. "If there's any water, it's deep under the rocks. I could be wrong, but my experience tells me there's no use drilling in this area." Smith raised his long arm and pointed eastward down the fence line following the road, where the rolling land settled into a bowl-like depression. "My guess is to try down there apiece."

"What good's a well down there?" Doyle said under his breath.

"So much for dowsing," Wilson added.

Claire stood up. "Let's see what we can find," she said

quietly. She turned to Wilson. "Ready to drill?"

Amos Doyle watched their preparation from a rocking chair on the porch, his face set. Smith, his face expressing of mild amusement, followed the pair around.

Using the small cable drill mounted to the Jeep, Claire and Wilson bored a two-inch diameter shot hole in each corner of a square thirty feet to a side, half way between Doyle's well house and the windmill. Two adjacent holes went ten feet down and the other pair went down twenty feet. Next, Wilson delicately lowered a quarter stick of dynamite in each hole, labeled the fuse wires and ran the wires to the Jeep. Then he and Claire evenly staked twelve Mark 4 Delta geophones, in two strings of six, in the ground running in parallel lines along opposite sides of the drill square. Claire hooked each geophone up to a channel of a paper strip recorder on the hood of the Jeep while Wilson secured each fuse wire to a blasting box.

As a last step, Wilson went around re-checking shot holes. He got down on his knees and peered into each one. He got to the last hole.

"Whoa!" He leapt to his feet.

"What is it?" Claire asked anxiously.

"I saw a flicker of blue light in the hole and thought the charge was about to blow my head off." Wilson said, staring down at the ground. "My whole life flashed before my eyes."

"Are you okay?"

"Yeah, must have been my imagination." He waved his hand. "We're all set."

The three gathered around the Jeep.

"This is all very fascinating," Smith said.

Wilson smiled. "It is cool, man. See…" he explained with obvious enthusiasm, "It's a lot like radar, but instead of electromagnetic waves, the survey uses the sound waves caused by the explosion to penetrate the ground. We have these geophones, which are basically microphones, placed a little bit in the ground, to pick up sound waves from the explosions. The waves reflect off whatever's down there like an echo." Wilson pointed to the strip recorder on the hood. "We simultaneously record those echoes on the strip recorder, one trace above the other, all lined up. By correlating the returns, we get a picture, so to speak, of the composition of the underlying strata."

Smith's expression darkened. "How far down does it penetrate?"

Claire answered. "Pretty far. Even here, with the charges relatively shallow, we can get a picture a couple of hundred feet down. There's a lot of variables, but that would be the average."

Smith said, "What's next?"

"First, I turn on the recorder, that has a channel for each geophone." Wilson reached down and there was a sharp click. The roll of chart paper on the recorder started creeping under the twelve tiny pens, at the moment tracing out straight lines. He pointed to the box connecting all the fuse wires. "Then, I flip that green safety switch on that blasting box, screw in the red T-handle, and slam it down."

"Why not just another button?" Smith asked.

"Good question," Wilson said. "The T-handle is a relic from the days when pushing down the handle forced a magnet through a coil, generating an electric pulse that fired the blasting caps. Having to screw it in acts as a kind of safety, preventing unintended ignition. Now we use batteries and capacitors to generate our electric pulse. The T-handle just closes a switch. They kept the same style, I guess, so there would be no confusion."

"Confusion when using dynamite is not a good thing," Smith said blandly.

"Exactly," Wilson chuckled. He turned to Claire who was casually leaning with one hand on the hood of the Jeep. "Are we a go?" he asked.

"Go," Claire said.

Wilson's head swiveled, scanning the area, making sure he knew where everyone was. Amos was still at a safe distance watching from the porch. Smith, arms crossed, was behind the Jeep.

"Fire in the hole!" Wilson yelled. After waiting five seconds, he flipped the green toggle, turned the T-handle ninety degrees to unlock it and pushed it down in one firm smooth motion.

Nothing happened.

Wilson cursed.

Claire said, "What's going on?"

"Hang on," Wilson said impatiently. He fiddled for a moment with the wires on the ignition box.

"Fire in the hole!" He raised the T-handle and brought it back down again.

The air was so still, Claire imagined for an instant that time had stopped. In the distance, a crow cawed.

"Son of a bitch!" Wilson said through clenched teeth. "This crap equipment we have to use because the university is so dammed cheap." He turned to Claire. "I had this same problem before. Something probably worn out with the electrical contacts in the box. I'll have to take it apart and check it out later." He picked up the box and shook it violently.

Claire winced. "Jesus! Careful, Wilson."

"What? Are you afraid it's going to set off the explosives?" he said sarcastically and then grinned at her. He put the box back down and raised the handle again.

"Fire in the hole!" He slammed the handle down.

There was a deep thumping as the charges of dynamite exploded, accompanied by a tremor in the ground, like a heavy truck passing nearby. The needles on each channel of the recorder traced out a series of sharp waves, peaking, then diminishing back to a flat line.

"I think that was all four," Claire said. "That's good. No duds to worry about. Good work Wilson."

"Thanks." Wilson was bent over, peering intently at the strip recorder. He frowned. "This is just preliminary..." he said without looking up. "We'll have to take these back to the No-tell Motel to study...but it looks like we have an anomaly here, people."

Chapter 12

Claude Wiggins felt particularly fidgety. His sleep the night before had been restless. He had tossed and turned, trying to ease the aches and pains of old age, and then, when he did finally fall asleep, he was tormented by nightmares.

In the morning, he awoke with a cold dampness on his forehead. Wiggins could not remember the specifics of the nightmares, only that they left him uneasy like portentous gusts of wind through the tree tops before a storm.

After spending the morning puttering aimlessly around the house, Wiggins gave up, and he lay down to nap on the sofa.

At two o'clock, he aroused groggily and decided to go down to his shop and work on the deputy's cruiser. It would keep his mind busy.

The walk led him past the silo.

Wiggins usually avoided going close to the silo by taking the long way around the barn. That day, he chose to make his way directly to the shop. When he got close to the silo, his nerve failed him and he pressed his eyes shut. After decades of routine, Wiggins could find the way around his barnyard blindfolded.

As he passed the silo, (he could tell he was close from the change in ambient sound) he felt suddenly warm, as if he had just stepped from the shadow into the bright sunshine. An almost physical force was pulling him toward the silo door.

"No!" he yelled. He opened his eyes and the world started to spin. He willed his legs to run, but they were wrapped in sheets of lead. His boots were being held to the ground by thick tar.

Wiggins gasped. "God help me!"

The air grew warmer, then became hot and thick. Sweat poured from his face and his eyes bulged. He looked up into the sky and prayed:

Our father, who art in heaven, Hallowed be thy name.

And lead us not into temptation, but deliver us from evil...

The sky overhead was rotating like a kaleidoscope.

"Ohh..ahh..h," Wiggins swooned.

A dark shadow flew across his field of vision.

The air suddenly cooled. Wiggins was able to lift his foot. With a supreme effort, he managed a step. The terrible weight on his legs lightened. His next step was easier. The next easier still. He inched forward.

He had passed the silo and was now shielded by the corner of the barn.

"Thank you, Jesus!" Wiggins called out in relief.

He quickly cleared the barn and made his way to the shop. After anxiously fumbling with the rusted lock, Wiggins opened the door and stepped inside. He flicked on the shop lights and leaned against his work bench, breathing heavily.

Coming out of the gloom, his cat jumped up on the bench.

"Jumping Jehoshaphat!" Wiggins jerked back. "You gave me a turn, Wally!"

The cat rubbed against his arm.

Wiggins took a deep breath. "It's okay, you're a good boy." He patted the cat affectionately on the back.

The cat stared at him for a moment, then turned his head towards the rear of the garage. Wiggins followed his gaze.

Deputy Hooper's shiny Plymouth Savoy shimmered in the stark blue-white illumination of the bare overhead fluorescent bulbs. Wiggins had parked the car in the shop the day before when the Chief and the deputy dropped it off.

The cruiser's gaudy grill grinned menacingly. With its angled body work over the headlights and its large clunky grill, it looked like an angry shark. Wiggins tried to ignore the eerie countenance of the Plymouth as he walked over and turned on his air compressor, waited a few minutes for it to build up pressure, then used the hydraulics to raise the cruiser on up on the lift.

He knew what he had to do now. It was all very clear.

From his tool cabinet, he picked out a small file from the top drawer. His movements were methodical, unhurried. Anyone watching might have called his actions robotic, as if he was sleep-walking. Whistling an old children's lullaby, Claude Wiggins stood under the chassis of the Plymouth and raised the file to the brake lines.

After they had recovered the geophones, reeled up the cables and filled in the shot holes on Amos Doyle's property, Claire and Wilson offered Smith a ride back to town.

"I'll find my way back. Thanks." His guarded tone discouraged any questions. "And Claire - I'll see you this evening, then."

Wilson did a double take at Claire. She smiled and said nothing.

Back in town, after a quick dinner of burgers and fries at the café, Claire left Wilson in his motel room with the strip recordings. "You're better at analysis then I am," she told him. Actually, Claire found the process of lining up and correlating the recorder data repetitious and tedious. Maybe the devil was in the details, but she was more interested in the big picture.

"Besides I've got a date this evening with Edith the dispatcher from the police station," she told Wilson on her way out the door.

"Is that so?"

"Yeah, she promised to tell me about another time of drought and all about the Curse of Testament Hill."

"Oouu." Wilson shook in mock fright.

"Could be interesting. By the way, Smith is coming with me. I told him about meeting with Edith, and he asked to come along. He's also staying here at the motel."

"I was wondering what he meant back at the farm." Wilson said, his head bent over the recording data. "Well, just be careful...there's something creepy about that guy."

Claire pulled her car in front of room seven and tapped her horn. Smith came out and gave her a slight wave.

Claire noticed he had changed his long coat to a leather bomber jacket. He was wearing Levis held up with a wide belt sporting a large silver buckle with the head of some creature that, in the fading late afternoon light, she couldn't quite identify. The bottom of his pants draped over cowboy boots. His long wavy black hair was pulled back and held in place with a silver ring.

He walked around the hood of her Volvo and climbed into the passenger seat.

"Thanks for bringing me along." His smile reminded Claire of a used car salesman. "It should be interesting."

"No problem. Happy for the company." Claire glanced around. "Where's your car?"

Smith waved his hand dismissively. "That old clunker broke down on me on the way here. It's being repaired at a gas station outside of town. Who knows when it will be fixed. They told me that they had to send to Fort Dodge for parts."

Claire pulled out of the lot, subconsciously checking to see if the creepy deputy's car was lurking in the shadows. She headed down the road towards Doyle's farm.

She could sense Smith's eyes upon her. "Edith told me her place is just a little ways down the road from Amos Doyle's," she told him.

"Oh, that's convenient."

Claire glanced at her passenger. She was relieved to see Smith had turned away and now appeared intent on the darkening farmland as it rolled by. She squinted at his short ponytail.

"If you don't mind me asking, are you a member of one of the native tribes around here?"

Smith turned back to her, his expression stony. Claire immediately regretted her comment.

"I'm sorry. I didn't mean..."

Smith's face relaxed, and he managed a thin smile. "No, no. Quite alright...you could say I have tribal connections...going way back."

"Oh? One of the local tribes? The Osage? The Missouri?" Claire said. "The Oweyu?"

Smith paused before answering. "It's a mixed heritage."

Even though he seemed to be making light of their conversation, Claire detected an edgy undertone. For a while, they didn't speak.

"My grandmother used to tell me I had Indian blood in my veins," Claire said, making conversation.

Smith gave her a sharp look. "Oh, really? Is your family from around here?"

"Well, I actually grew up in Chicago," Claire said. "Moved to Missouri when I was a teenager. But apparently some of my ancestors came from this area."

"Interesting."

"My great, great grandfather, who was a Jesuit priest, came to Missouri in the early 1800's to set up a mission. He ended up fathering several children, one of whom was my great grandmother. It was all quite scandalous."

Smith sniffed. "The Jesuits came out of the goodness of their hearts, I'm sure. To save the natives' souls."

"Why else go through all the hardship and danger?" Claire asked.

"I can't think of any other reason."

A gust of wind sent a horde of brown and orange leaves skittering across the road ahead.

"Was there something else that brought Jesuits here?" Claire thought out loud.

Smith, staring straight ahead, said, "Like gold or something?"

Claire waved her hand. "I don't know. Maybe they were searching for something."

"The past holds many secrets," Smith said, his voice almost a whisper.

The car rounded a corner.

"There's Doyle's farm," Smith inclined his head.

Claire was happy to change the subject. "Okay, Edith's place should be down at the next intersection."

A minute later, she spotted the apartment building. "Oh… my."

She wasn't expecting a penthouse, but the four unit complex was dingy and forlorn. It stood next to an boarded up corner store with a rotted porch leading up to a broken glass door. Faded Camel and Chesterfield cigarette posters were peeling from the windows. The apartment building was on the same gravel lot. One unit had a rusting '51 Chevy Bellaire by the front door. It was missing a left front wheel and leaning on a jack. Parked in front of the end unit was a pristine military blue Chrysler Windsor that Claire guessed was from the early 1940s.

Claire pointed. "That's got to be Edith's car, I bet."

She parked the Volvo beside the Chrysler and she and Smith got out of the car and walked up to the end unit. On the stoop were two wilted white carnations in clay pots. A narrow trellis was crudely nailed next to the entrance, laced through with ivy. Strung at the top of the trellis Claire spotted some small whitish bulbs. *Onions?* she thought. *Garlic?*

She exchanged glances with Smith, then opened the creaking screen and gently knocked twice on the inner door.

From inside, Claire could just make out Edith's voice. "Just a minute."

Seconds later, the door swung open. Edith was standing in the entrance in a long flowered house dress. She had on a waist apron and fuzzy pink slippers.

"Claire. I'm so glad you came by. I don't get many visitors. I just set the kettle for tea."

Edith held open the door, and caught sight of Smith who was standing off to the side. "Oh, she said, "I see you brought a friend." She eyed Smith up and down. An expression of concern crossed her face, quickly replaced with a tight smile.

"I hope it's okay. Smith and I are…working together on the water shortage problem," Claire explained. "When I told him about our conversation, he asked to come along. He also has an interest in local history."

"Yes, yes, of course." Edith waved them in. "Come in, please."

Claire wiped her feet on the rope rug and stepped inside

with Smith in tow.

"Edith, this is Smith." Claire made a split second decision not to mention her companion's occupation. "Smith, this is Edith Brown."

"Well, please, have a seat." Edith motioned to a threadbare red velvet sofa in the tiny living room. "Would you like some nice Earl Grey tea?"

"That would be very nice," Smith murmured, as he carefully eased his long body into the sofa and clasped his hands together in his lap.

"Milk and sugar?"

"Just black, please."

Edith looked at Claire, who was still standing by the door.

"I think I'll pass," Claire said. "Not much of a tea drinker, I'm afraid."

Edith winked. "Neither am I. How about a bourbon? On the rocks, or with a splash? It does a person good to have a nip now and then."

"Well, I..."

"Join me, I don't like to drink alone. Although that doesn't stop me. And please, sit down, dear."

"Bourbon sounds good," Claire said. "With just some ice please." As she settled on the other end of the sofa, Claire turned to Smith. "Want to change your mind, and join us?"

"No, I'm good, thanks."

Edith shuffled off into the kitchen, and there were noises of cupboards opening and shutting and clinking glasses.

Claire took the opportunity to check out the apartment. In front of the sofa was an oak coffee table covered with the circle stains of drink glasses. The sofa faced a window that opened to the parking lot. Under the window was a cedar chest. A small T.V. sat on top with wildly bent rabbit ears. Besides the sofa, there was a battered captain's chair in one corner, next to it was an end table, with a fringed shaded lamp. An upholstered rocker covered with a gaudy afghan was placed at a right angle to the sofa.

Claire noticed that the living room looked clean, even

though it was cluttered with an eclectic mix of whatnots: cheap ceramic figurines of cats and dogs sitting on sagging shelves, a couple of snow globes, a vase with faded plastic daisies. On the walls was a reproduction of a Cezanne, a velvet portrait of Elvis, and a print of Warner Sallman's iconic *Head of Christ.*

Edith reappeared, carrying Smith's tea cup and saucer in one hand, two whiskey glasses with cubes of ice held in the other, and a bottle tucked under her arm. Claire recognized the orange label of Four Roses bourbon.

She handed the cup and saucer to Smith. "Here's your tea, Mr. Smith."

Edith put the glasses down on the coffee table and poured generous portions of whiskey into the glasses. She picked one up and holding it expertly in her hand, plunked down with a satisfied smile onto the rocker. "Ahhh." Edith took a swig of her drink, swished it in her mouth for a second and swallowed. She smacked her lips and grinned. "Now that's the ticket."

Claire and Smith took the cue and each reached for their drinks.

Claire took a nip from her glass. The warmth of the Kentucky whiskey descended down her throat. A glow rose in her stomach. "That certainty hits the spot," she said.

Edith leaned back in the rocker and smiled at each of her visitors in turn. "Now, I know you came to hear the story of the Curse of Testament Hill."

Claire smiled, "Yes, please."

"As far back as people can remember," Edith began, "strange things have been happening around Testament Hill: sightings of phantoms flitting to and fro in dark alleyways at night; curious blue lights on the ground; calves born with extra legs; apples in the shape of human heads; tree fungus with the faces of demons."

Claire was disappointed. Edith's account of oddities seemed to be superstitious interpretations of aberrations that normally occurred in nature.

"...children born deficient, and some with special gifts."

Edith's last remark got Claire's attention. She couldn't help but think of Ivy Doyle. And the strange boy in the diner - *Gilbert*, she remembered.

Smith reached down for his tea cup in the saucer. He cleared his throat. "Just old wives' tales I suspect,"

Edith nipped at her whiskey demurely, then looked up. "Then there was Rachel Doyle."

Claire said, "Ivy's mother?"

Edith leaned forward. "Yes. It was horrible. They found her body in a well at their farm after she'd gone missing for three months or so. May the dear girl rest in peace."

"Was she *murdered*?" Claire asked.

"Coroner's report said she had killed herself." Edith met Claire's eyes. "I ask you: who in their right mind would commit suicide by jumping into a well?"

Claire thought: *Who in their right mind commits suicide, period?* Then she nodded sympathetically. "It does seem very odd."

Edith shook her head. "Maybe it was suicide, but she was driven to it."

Claire said, "What do you mean?"

"By the evil presence that infects Testament Hill."

Smith blinked. "Evil presence?"

"The Dark One that dwells in Testament Hill," Edith explained. "I think he comes up from the ground, from under our fields, under our town. I saw him myself one night, when I was a child. Out my bedroom window. My mother told me I was just having a nightmare. He was tall, dressed in all black with...." Edith stopped in midsentence and glanced at Smith, then quickly turned back to Claire. "Have you seen the blue lights yet?"

Claire flashed back to the light she saw when looking down the old well at Doyle's farm and Wilson's vision while setting the dynamite. She considered mentioning it, but then told herself that the lights had some perfectly natural explanation.

"No. I haven't," Claire said.

Edith wagged a finger. "Well, I believe that marks his

presence. That's what makes people crazy around here. Been happening for years." Edith finished off her whiskey, downing it without a flinch. "It is the root of the Curse of Testament Hill."

Claire was unsure how to react to Edith's narrative. She was pretty certain the old woman was dotty, but something about her account was troubling. It seemed as if there were clues in it, pieces to the puzzle that when solved, would explain what was happening around Testament Hill.

"So," Claire said gently, turning the conversation, "you mentioned something about the other drought...?"

"Oh, yes, of course." Edith smiled. "I've forgotten - that's why you came to town in the first place." She raised her hand. "So in 1952, we had a bad drought too. Actually, it was more like this one, not so much a true drought. Yes, rainfall was a little scarce, but not *that* scarce. Not enough, I believe, to cause the wells to go dry. Just like now. Lasted for a couple years, then things pretty much went back to normal. Until now, of course."

Edith appeared to be thinking for a moment. "I want to warn you to be very careful with whatever you are doing out at Amos Doyle's farm." She caught Claire's eye. "I wouldn't disturb the ground there, if I were you."

Claire was about to explain the need to do just that when Smith coughed, and she saw him slightly shake his head.

"Well, Edith," Claire said. "It's been fascinating. Thank you for filling us in. We'll keep what you've told us in mind. And..." Claire raised her glass, and placed it on the table. "Thank you for the drink."

"And the tea." Smith said, getting up from the sofa.

"Oh, but you just got here," Edith said. "and Mr. Smith, you haven't had any of your tea. Is it not to your liking?"

"It's fine," Smith said. "It's just my stomach's been a little delicate lately."

Edith followed them to the front door and just before Claire turned to step outside, Edith said, "I was meaning to ask you, Doctor Brannigan, if you don't mind," She pointed to the amulet that Claire was wearing outside her blouse.

"Where did you get that usual cross?" Edith reached out and pulled her hand away just short of touching it.

"It's more like it found me," Claire answered.

"Well, it certainly is unusual." Edith leaned in and peered closely at the cross for a second. She looked up at Claire, then at Smith.

"Good-night then," she said.

"You don't believe in that stuff about an evil curse, do you?" Smith said as Claire drove them back to the motel.

"A curse? No." Claire glanced at him. "But I know that there is *evil*. I've witnessed it firsthand."

Smith rubbed his forehead. "So you believe there actually is some kind of evil force or being?"

"You mean like the Devil?"

"If you want to call it that. The Devil, Satan."

Claire absently touched the amulet at her throat. "Logically, scientifically, I'd have to say no. But there are times that I wonder. I think we all can imagine demons, it's in our blood, in our history, in our racial memory as a species." She turned to Smith. "Don't you agree?"

"Evil exists only in the mind of humans." Smith waved his long-fingered hand towards the window of the Volvo. "Look at nature: There's no evil. I admit, it's 'red in tooth and claw', as Tennyson wrote, but there's no animosity; no revenge taking; no cruelty for cruelty's sake; no pleasure taken in the pain and suffering of others. Only people do that."

"I am tempted to agree." Claire said. She gazed out at the horizon as the last rays of sun withdrew into the dusk. "Sometimes I think it's as if some people become *infected* with an evil that makes them do awful things."

"Evil caused by germs?" Smith looked at her, and smiled his teeth shiny in the falling light.

"I mean, perhaps some kind of force or external influence." The idea brought into Claire's mind the enigmatic luminosities out at Doyle's farm. She shivered involuntarily.

She steered the Volvo around a corner and the Sleep-Tite Motel came into sight.

"Well, I doubt that," Smith said.

Claire braked the car to a stop. For a brief moment her eyes met Smith's. "Well, good night then."

Smith opened the passenger door, stepped out, and then leaned back in. "Thank you for inviting me, Claire. It was an interesting evening."

Before Claire could reply, he gently shut the car door and walked briskly towards his motel room.

Chapter 13

Owen Childress poured himself a shot of Old Crow, scooted back in his chair and put his feet up on his desk.

There had been reports of a prowler along the south edge of town by the railroad tracks. Deputy Hooper was out on his usual five p.m. to one a.m. patrol. Chief Childress had asked him to do an extra sweep in the area. Hooper seemed happy to comply.

It was after 9 o'clock Sunday evening. Childress didn't need to be in the office. If there was a problem, Hooper could call him at home.

But Childress was restless. His wife Flo had gone to bed early, complaining of her headaches. He watched *The Virginian* on the television, hoping to get sleepy, but it didn't work. He decided to drive over to the office, maybe catch up on some paperwork. Childress polished off his whiskey and sighed. He was thankful not to be out patrolling at night.

He would never tell anyone, not even his wife, but he had become increasingly uneasy going out after dark, especially in isolated areas.

The beginning of his *affliction,* as he secretly referred to it, could be traced to an event on Christmas Eve, 1952.

Recalling that night, Childress freshened his whiskey from a new bottle.

He had parked his cruiser in the lot of Norquist's drug store, facing the crossroads of town and had just poured a cup of coffee from his Sportking vacuum bottle. It was around midnight.

He was doing extra patrols because B and E's usually increased during that time of year. Childress figured it was due to people being down and out and desperate to bring home something to put under the tree or on the dinner table. The presence of the patrol car around town might discourage temptation.

It was just a shadow in the night, maybe even a trick of

the street lamps and the wavering of bushes. But it had chilled him to the bone. He told himself over and over that's all it was, but in his heart, he knew that what he saw was an abomination.

It had caught the corner of his eye: moving from the grey sandstone front of Union State Bank and disappearing around the corner. He remembered blinking hard, thinking it was just some rheum floating on his eyeball.

Childress started the cruiser's engine and, headlights off, slowly idled out of the parking lot. He turned at the corner so that he could see the side of the bank. Just as his line of sight cleared the edge of the building, he saw it again, and this time, there definitely was *something* moving towards the rear of the bank.

He had watched awe-struck as the apparition solidified into a man-like shape. It was tall. Childress, trained to identify suspects, pegged its height at least six-six, six-seven.

The figure was wearing what looked to be a long black coat. Childress reached down, turned on his spotlight and adjusted its beam to shine at the bank. The figure stopped and turned to face the light.

He'd never forget the image. It was as if it had been branded onto his visual cortex. It appeared to be a man, or it could have even been a woman. The face was androgynous like a mannequin. It had long dark hair, huge black eyes. Then it grinned at him and Childress gasped. It was like a mad dog baring its teeth.

Childress squeezed his eyes closed to block the terrible vision, and when he had reopened them, the creature was gone.

Since that Christmas Eve night, Chief Childress could never be sure if he saw the apparition again. There were a couple of fear-filled moments on night patrol where he might have caught a glimpse of it slipping into the shadows around the buildings downtown or in backyards of neighborhood homes. But no more clear visuals.

He often wondered if what he had seen was just a dream: perhaps he had fallen asleep in his cruiser that night, and dreamt the whole thing, and the monster was just a waking nightmare. He wasn't under the influence at the time, but it had been a period when he was hitting the bottle heavier than usual. It could have been some sort of delirium caused by alcohol poisoning. He tried to convince himself that was the case. Sometimes he almost believed it.

However, for Owen Childress, the night would never be the same.

He shook his head, trying to clear the dark thoughts. He distracted himself by admiring his well-worn M1943 combat boots propped on the desk. They were out of style, even for the military, which had switched over from the russet-colored boots to all black in the mid-fifties. But the M1943s had served him well through two wars, and as long as he could still get them from army surplus, he'd wear them to his grave.

Plus, Childress mused, they were a good luck charm. He wore M1943s all through the Big One and Korea, and he came home in one piece.

On the other hand, his buddy, PFC Al Koski, who wore the new black M1948 boots, wasn't so lucky.

The nature of Koski's death still haunted Childress Chief. His squad, part of the 25th infantry division, was executing mop up operations against bypassed North Korean enemy elements around Seoul in October 1950.

The poor son-of-a-bitch Koski was walking one step behind and to Childress's left as the squad moved up to a crossroads of a tiny Korean village, Donsan-ni, or something - Childress could never quite remember.

A bullet from a North Korean sniper's Mosin-Nagant rifle slapped the edge of Childress's helmet and ricocheted towards Koski. It entered Koski's forehead above the left eye. Childress remembered the sound like it was yesterday, the ringing clang, the soft thud, and then Koski's surprised "Oh!" like he used to joke whenever he farted.

Koski toppled face up into the road and lay perfectly still with an astonished expression and dime-sized ruby hole in his forehead. The bullet had lost power by careening off

Childress's helmet. There was no gaping exit wound common with head shots. Just a little blood oozing out from the hole. The bullet had tumbled around inside Koski's skull, shredding his brain. Death was instantaneous.

The sheer random nature of Koski's death had shaken Childress' faith in a fair, just God. To compensate for the loss of that psychological crutch, the then Corporal Childress began to lean on some typical military superstitious routines: never stepping into a vehicle starting with his left foot; never shaving before a mission; tucking an ace of spades into the band of his helmet.

That was when Childress latched on to the notion that his boots were a good luck charm. In the twisted logic of superstition, he wondered if Koski's new style boots had caused the PFC's bad fortune. Better safe than sorry, Childress figured.

His mind returned to the present.

Superstitions or not, he reflected, there was a certain comfort in tradition - things that had proven their worth over time. Why change something that works?

Childress reached down and tapped his .38 Police Special. *Like this baby.*

It was a dependable, reasonably accurate firearm. It virtually never jammed because its revolver action was elegantly simple. He grunted thinking of those new automatic handguns being touted by some manufacturers. Sure, the old model 1911 Colt .45 automatic was pretty reliable and had good stopping power, but it was heavy and bulky. The .45 required more care than the revolver, and its safety arrangement, which necessitated a round to be chambered before firing, was awkward. Getting that first shot off in time was a doubtful proposition. A delay could have fatal consequences.

Officer to armed criminal: "Now, hold still while I get my gun ready to shoot."

After falling to the ground after being shot by the criminal: " No fair! I wasn't ready!"

Childress's .38 revolver, on the other hand, had six rounds already chambered in the cylinder. Its double-action rotated the bullet into position, cocked the hammer and fired, all by squeezing the trigger.

It was always ready.

I'll stick with the simple, tried and true, Childress nodded to himself. *Life often deals unpleasant surprises when you least expect it. Shit is bound to hit the fan. And when it does, it is good to be prepared with gear you can count on.*

He downed a generous slug of whiskey. He didn't have to worry about drinking on duty, because he wasn't: Deputy Hooper was.

It was Hooper's birthday.

He couldn't wait to get out on the streets that night. The Chief's request to give the rail yard extra attention was perfect timing.

Hooper walked briskly across the station's lot to the Plymouth cruiser recently returned from the shop. He was anxious to get going.

He had made up his mind to give himself a very special present.

Hooper got in the Plymouth, settled back in the seat and took a deep breath. This night was his night. No one would be giving him anything. No one probably even realized it was his birthday, and even if they did, likely wouldn't give a damn. Nobody ever really cared about him. Shit, one time his own parents forgot his birthday.

Hooper lowered the cruiser's window and spat.

His parents - what a couple of losers.

His father was killed working for the county road crew when Hooper was twelve. A chain securing two massive concrete drain pipes to a flatbed broke loose while his father was following in a county pickup truck. The pipes tumbled off the bed and steamrolled up the hood of the pickup, through the windshield into the cab. The police told Hooper's mother that her husband was killed instantly.

During the wake, where beer and whiskey flowed freely,

the son overhead a county worker telling another that Hooper's father had been weaving in and out and tailgating the flatbed, at one point getting so close that he rammed into the back, and that's when the pipes broke loose. The worker lowered his voice and said the elder Hooper probably had been drinking on the job again, and the son of a bitch probably deserved what he got. Young Hooper had to check himself from saying "Amen!" and turn his face so no one would see him smirk.

Deputy Hooper missed his mother about as much as he missed his father. She went to her grave three years ago when the coffin nails she smoked for fifty years caught up to her and she died struggling for a last breath.

May they both burn in hell.

He didn't go to his mother's funeral service. He only visited her once in the hospital when she lay dying. She begged him for a cigarette, and he was perversely glad to slip her a few.

He had come to the hospital to gloat.

His father had abused him and his mother had chosen to ignore it. Hooper usually managed to push the memories of it far back in the recesses of his mind. All he had left was the hate. And the feeling of being cheated out of a normal life, of being punished for things he never did, and the terrible vacuum of never being loved.

Lately, though, it seemed that the simmering anger had been fading more and more into the background of his mind. A sense of peace had come over him. He felt more comfortable with himself; who he was; the things that he did; his little proclivities.

Happy birthday, Hooper. Enjoy your present to yourself.

He was excited. As he pulled out onto the street, he reached under his seat, checking one more time. There was the cool smoothness of the wine bottle. He swore as he pricked his finger on the point of the cork screw he had taped to the bottle. He thought about bringing a couple of wine glasses, but decided that would be a little over the top.

Ida Wagner was certain to have some glasses they could use. He hoped she did have proper wine glasses though. It would make it more romantic.

Everything had been carefully thought out: Hooper had played it out many times in his mind. *I bet I smoked a whole pack of Pall Malls planning tonight.*

Instead of driving his cruiser by the railroad tracks behind Ida Wagner's house, Hooper decided to leave it concealed on the other side of the tracks, at the mill, wedged in a dark area between the grain silo and storage building. That way, if the plan went south, he could just slink back unseen to the mill and leisurely drive out, instead of hurriedly taking off in the damningly conspicuous cruiser.

The assailant would never be found.

Assailant. Hooper rolled the word around in his mouth. He hoped it wouldn't come to that.

He parked the car precisely at 9:45. While keeping on the lookout for anybody that might be watching, he grabbed the wine bottle and walked across the tracks to Ida Wagner's backyard. The sound of his boots crunching on the gravel echoed off the grain silos. He tried to lighten his step. With his heart thumping wildly in his chest, Hooper fingered the pack of cigarettes in his shirt pocket, desperate for a smoke, but forced himself to ignore the craving. The glow of a cigarette would be too eye-catching in the dark.

Ida Wagner had a small metal shed at the back of the yard where she stored her mower and yard tools. It was old and rusted and the door had long since come off its hinges. The doorway faced the back of the house. Hooper slipped inside and crouched down. The shed smelled of old grass clippings and gasoline.

It was the perfect spot.

Hooper stared at the back of the house. There was a dim light coming from the rear kitchen window, as if filtering in from the living room at the front. He could just make out the outline of the bathroom window. The glass was black. Bringing his wristwatch close to his face, Hooper tried to make out the time. He rotated his wrist trying to catch a stray reflection on the dial so he could see the position of the hands. It was useless. He counted to three hundred twice, trying to ignore the ache building in his calves and thighs.

"Damn it," He whispered.

He was just about to give up and sneak out of the shed when the bathroom light snapped on. Hooper could actually hear the sound of the light switch. The sudden realization that he had never been this close caused his heart to beat even faster. From the cruiser, he had been maybe seventy-five feet from the window. From his vantage point in the shed, he was only twenty-five away.

He waited, eyes riveted to the window. Even in the cool October air, beads of perspiration began to form on his forehead. Shadows moved along the wall inside the bathroom. Hooper licked his lips. His mouth was dry.

Then the shades came down in the window and there was nothing to be seen but the slight wavering of the yellowed shade as air moved around in the bathroom.

"Son of a bitch!" Hooper startled himself by speaking aloud. He peered cautiously around the edge of the shed into the darkened yard. Nothing.

His body tensed. He would go with the plan and act out his fantasy: wait until he figured Ida Wagner would be undressed for her bath, go up to the front door and knock.

Then Hooper's shoulders slumped. The wine bottle slipped from his grasp and landed on the soft dirt with a dull thump.

It was just a fantasy. He wasn't really going to do anything. He was just getting a thrill out of playing pretend, making it a little more real by getting a little closer - getting out of his car, creeping into the yard, going all the way to the shed.

But now the deputy was in a quandary. Seeing Ida nude from the closeness of the shed would have been gratifying enough. That would have worked for him. He could take it all in and then skulk away to his car have a smoke or two and add the adventure to his store of fantasy memoirs.

Now he felt like a parched man led to a cool stream but unable to drink. The anticipation had wound him up into a twisted spring.

He needed to release the tension.

I'm going to do it.

Hooper snatched up the wine, crept out from the shed and slouched towards the house. His legs felt rubbery and he was light-headed as if he had skipped a meal and his blood sugar was low. Pausing in the middle of the yard, he bowed his head and took a few deep breaths. The ground at his feet was illuminated by an eerie blue light. He looked skyward and saw the full moon shining through fluorescing clouds.

A few more steps and he came to the back porch.

He climbed the steps. With his mind strangely blank, he reached out, fingers quivering, grasped the door knob and twisted. His sweaty hand slipped over its smooth brass surface. He wiped his palm on his pants and tried again, and was shocked when the door clicked open. His heart thumped in his chest with a mix of excitement and raw fear. He felt short of breath again, and took a gulp of air.

The door made a loud squeak when he pushed it open. He froze and peered inside. The door opened into a tiny mud room which led into the kitchen. The pale yellow light of a street lamp glimmered through the window over the sink. He could barely make out the outlines of the kitchen.

Hooper counted. *One one-thousand, two one-thousand...* When he got to sixty, and there was no response to the squeak, he stepped into the kitchen and closed the door very gently.

He stood in the dark, slowly turning his head, holding his eyes as wide as possible to enhance his night vision. Weak slivers of light shimmered here and there along the counters and walls, off a chrome toaster, an empty glass by the sink, and a rack of kitchen knives.

On impulse, Hopper tip-toed over and slid out the first knife his hand came to. It was a six inch long serrated paring knife. He absently ran his thumb along the blade while he stood stooped over, trying to minimize his profile in the darkness. He put the wine bottle carefully on the counter.

A light flashed on in the hallway that led to the bedroom.

"Hello? Hello? Is anyone there?"

He recognized Ida Wagner's voice.

In spite of his paralyzing fear of being caught, Hooper couldn't help but think: *No. Nobody here but us murderers and rapists, you stupid bitch.*

"I'm armed, and I will shoot to kill." Ida's voice was quavering, but resolute.

Hooper grimaced. *Fuck, I'm outta here.*

He hurriedly tip-toed back to the door, opened it, and slipped out on to porch. He jumped down the steps and jogged across the grass.

The back door swung open and a porch light flooded the yard. Hooper spun around to face the light.

A voice called out. "Oh my God! It's you Deputy Hooper."

For a second, Hooper debated running for it, but realized it was too late.

"Mrs. Wagner..." he said. He realized he was still holding the paring knife from the kitchen. He put his hand behind his back and slipped it into his belt.

"I'm so glad you're here," the silhouette in the door said. "I think someone was trying to *break* into my house!"

Hooper blinked into the light. "Yes...I...was patrolling in the area and saw a prowler..." He paused, trying to collect his wits. "He disappeared into your backyard...I decided to pursue him on foot."

He walked towards the light. Ida Wagner standing in the door frame, one hand holding her robe closed and in the other, a dark L-shaped object. Hooper took a few more steps towards the porch. Ida was smiling down at him. Close up, she didn't look as attractive as in his imagination, but as Hooper eyed her up and down, with her curves showing through her thin white satin robe, he found her to be very desirable. Then he sucked in his breath.

The L-shaped object Ida was holding was a Colt .45 Model 1911. It looked huge in her small hand.

Ida must have seen his expression. She laughed, and waved the gun. "This was my husband's old army sidearm. He forced me to learn how to shoot it. I thought it was silly at the time. But now, I'm glad I have it."

Hooper nodded numbly.

"I'm actually an excellent shot, deputy. That prowler would have been in for a big surprise if I'd caught him coming in, let me tell you."

Hooper swallowed trying to wet his dry throat and unconsciously crossed himself. "Did you get a look at the prowler?" He said, with his hand on the catch on his holster.

"Too dark," Ida said. She let her hand slide down on the fold of her robe so that a generous amount of her ample cleavage was exposed. "I think we must have scared him away. You came at just the right time."

She cocked her head at Hooper. "Would you like a cup of coffee, deputy? It's the least I can do for one of Testament Hill's finest."

"Well...."

Ida hand slipped further down on her robe. "A nice hot cup of coffee?"

Hooper took a few steps closer towards the house, his heart racing again. The earth spun beneath his feet. He forced himself to stop, close his eyes and take a deep breath. *Jesus,* he thought, *don't go fainting on me, you jackass.* He opened his eyes. Everything had taken on a surreal aspect. The air felt especially crisp on his face, the scent of the late blooming wild roses along the porch was as strong as if he had them pressed to his nose. The grass blades of the lawn took on a clarity he had never seen. He could make out the tiny pebbles and grains of sand in the ground. And the ground at his feet glowed with a filigree of pale blue light.

Hooper blinked rapidly. The light brightened. He felt compelled to step into its boundary. There was a prickly sensation that started at his feet and rose up through his body. He stood still over the spot.

"Deputy?" he could hear Ida calling to him. There was a slight tone of annoyance in her voice. "Are you coming, or not?"

The light faded then was gone. Deputy Hooper walked up to the porch and grinned at Ida Wagner. "You talked me into it."

Chapter 14

Monday morning

Claire waited until the sunshine slipping past the curtain edge crossed her face before she roused herself. She slid upright in the bed and she gazed around her room.

In the soft light of dawn, the room was reminiscent of her dorm room at college: cramped, with cheap functional furniture and drab walls. At least, thank God, Claire mused, she didn't have to share her motel room with Betsy Norton. Her roommate at college had been such a prissy. Claire immediately regretted that thought. *Poor Betsy, she didn't deserve what happened to her.*

Claire threw off her blankets, swung her feet over the bed and stood up. She caught the image of her nude body in the mirror on the bathroom door.

Once Claire had tried sleeping in the raw, she found she enjoyed the comfort and sense of freedom. Sometimes she fantasized about traveling to some South Sea island and spending the whole time going around in her birthday suit.

Maybe when I get old, I'll wear pajamas or a nightgown or something.

Besides, she thought, as she twirled in the mirror, *why cover up this great body?* She posed and turned, liking what she saw. She felt unusually sensual. Tempting. Desirable.

Claire often felt that way when she first started seeing Ben Trask. Then, their liaisons were fresh and daring.

Lately, though, they had been slipping into a predicable routine. While Ben seemed to have settled comfortably into their stable, if uninspired relationship, Claire found herself growing bored and dissatisfied. The relationship had gone from hot to warm to lukewarm.

At first, she tried to ignore the urgings of her unfulfilled desires and channel her restlessness into the activities of her profession.

But now, coming to Testament Hill, Claire felt like she had entered into another universe, far from the conservative restraint of university life. It felt liberating and also a little scary. An adventure, for certain.

She'd met two men, Preston and Smith, both mysterious and with auras of power and self-confidence. That was, she had to admit, quite alluring. She chuckled to herself as she turned and headed into the bathroom. Her reactions were so stereotypical, maybe even juvenile.

Screw it, she thought. It was arousing, refreshing, and made her feel years younger. *What could be wrong with that?*

She took a quick shower and got dressed. She was going to meet Wilson at the Sunbeam Café. He had called her late the night before, excited to tell her about what he had discovered from the geophone recorder data.

On her way out, Claire took her Smith & Wesson from the nightstand drawer and placed it in her purse. Just before tucking it away, she did her usual inspection, making sure the safety was on and the hammer rested on the empty cylinder. She stopped in front of the mirror, checking her appearance, for a second staring into her own eyes.

"Just who are you, Doctor Brannigan?" she said softly.

Half an hour later, when Claire arrived at the diner, Wilson sitting in a booth staring intently at the seismic recorder roll held flat on the table with two coffee mugs.

"Hey." Claire said.

He looked up and smiled. "Hi Claire."

He waved to the spot next to him in the booth. "You might want to sit on this side, so we can look at this together."

Claire slid in next to Wilson. Their hips were touching through their almost matching khakis. Wilson shifted slightly, but Claire noticed his move did not break contact.

"I thought you might want to look at this before we eat." Wilson pointed to the roll of paper.

A young waitress with her wavy blond hair in a ponytail appeared at their table, holding an order pad. She smiled at Claire. "May I get you something, ma'am?" she asked.

"Just a cup of coffee for now, please."

The waitresses' sparkling green eyes flicked down to the paper on the table. She had a scattering of freckles across the bridge of her nose and on her upper lip.

"We're here testing the ground for water," Claire explained, noticing the girl's curiosity. "Are you interested in science?"

"Well, yes… a little, I guess."

"Don't be embarrassed. Science makes the world go around. We need the curiosity and vision of young people like you."

The girl blushed. "Thank you, ma'am."

Claire peered at the waitress's name tag. "And I'll take that coffee black, Audrey."

"Oh, of course, right away, ma'am." The girl turned and hurried away.

"Cute." Wilson said, looking after her.

Claire nodded. "Kind of reminds me of myself. I used to wait tables at a diner after school."

"Really?" Wilson stared at her, and Claire imagined him trying to visualize her in a ponytail and apron. She pointed at the table top. "So, what do we have here?"

Wilson rubbed his eyes with the tips of his fingers and looked down at the paper roll. "Some very interesting stuff. I was right with my first reaction: There are indications of anomalies in the ground under Doyle's property."

"Like what?"

Wilson took a pencil out of his shirt pocket and traced it along some of the squiggly lines of the report. "See these discontinuities in the sound reflections from the explosives?"

"I see them. There is a definite differential in reflectivity, the density is much lower." Claire looked at Wilson. "Loose sand? Porous rock?"

"Much less dense." Wilson tapped his pencil on the recording. "It's air. There's a network of caves."

Claire frowned. "Looks like about eighty feet down. Below the water table. If there are caves, they should be filled with water, in which case, the reflections wouldn't be like these."

"That's the thing," Wilson nodded. "They should be. But these results show them to be voids. The caves are dry."

Claire bent her head over the table. "Do you think this could be a malfunction of the seismometer?"

"It's possible, but everything else appears normal. The recordings indicate the expected strata above and below the voids. If the machine was malfunctioning I think we'd see more garbage."

"Does this relate to the failures of water wells?"

Wilson pursed his lips. "Not sure. Perhaps some seismic event opened up some deep crevasses, causing the groundwater levels to temporarily drop."

"That's what I'm thinking," Claire said. "I wonder..." she was remembering the boom and the flash she witnessed on the way into town.

Just then the young waitress returned with the coffee. Claire looked up. "Thank you, Audrey."

"Would you like to order now?" Audrey asked them.

Wilson grinned up at her. "Sure thing, babe. I'd like the breakfast special, eggs over easy, Canadian bacon, rye toast."

Audrey blinked.

"Don't mind him," Claire told her. "He's a city slicker, got no manners. I'll have buttermilk pancakes and an orange juice, please."

"Coming right up," Audrey smiled shyly. "I couldn't help but overhear... were you guys talking about caves?"

"Why do you ask?" Claire said.

"Well, because - I probably shouldn't tell - but some of us found a cave just east of town, on the side of that round hill on Amos Doyle's property."

"Well, this part of Missouri has lots of caves," Wilson said. "It's called karst landscape - with thousands of caves, sinkholes, and underground streams. It's caused by the groundwater dissolving the underlying soft rock like limestone."

"Yeah…" Audrey hesitated. "But what's really odd is it didn't used to be there."

Claire and Wilson exchanged glances.

Claire put her coffee cup down without taking her eyes from Audrey. "Are you sure?"

Audrey's blush deepened. "Well, some of us, I mean, couples, we'd sneak into this long ditch on the side of the mound with blankets, to you know, for romance. It was private-like. And it's kind of hidden by some juniper brushes."

Claire reached out and patted the girl gently on the hand. "Your secret is safe with us, Audrey."

"There was no cave," Audrey explained, "then, there was. Weird. My boyfriend said he thought it might be a sinkhole. What do you think?"

Claire smiled reassuringly. "Hard to say, Audrey. Do you think you can draw us a map of where it is? We'd like to check it out."

"I'll try. I'll work on a map, and bring it back with your meal."

After Claire and Wilson had eagerly devoured breakfast, they studied Audrey's map.

Claire said, "She did a nice job, this map is pretty good."

"I don't know," Wilson said, squinting at the scribbles on the back of a place mat. "The cave is probably just some coyote burrow."

"Could be," Claire said. "It looks to be at the base of Testament hill."

Wilson frowned. "What do you mean? The town's probably six or so miles away."

"I'm talking about the original Testament hill - it's a big mound right about here…" Claire tapped her finger on the sketch. "The original town was founded at the bottom. Chief Childress told me the story. It was abandoned and relocated to its present site after some disaster."

"What kind of disaster?"

"Unclear," Claire said. "The Chief told me there were several different tales of what really happened. But - here's something I'm sure you'll find fascinating: the event occurred right around the time of the New Madrid earthquakes."

Wilson's eyes went wide. He rubbed his forehead. "1811 thru 1812," he said. "a series of the biggest quakes ever to hit the United States, up to 8.0 on the Richter scale. Luckily, the epicenter, around New Madrid, Missouri, was sparsely populated at the time, so damage and injures were minimal. It was felt as far away as New York, Washington, D.C. and Charleston, South Carolina. If it happened today, it would be a national catastrophe."

Claire spread her arms, "Here, in Testament Hill, being that we're only say, fifty miles from the epicenter, the quake would have been very strong indeed."

Wilson chewed on a thumbnail. "Do you think the town's abandonment is connected to the 1811 event?"

"Certainly a possibility, Claire said. "Something else that's curious: I think the original Testament Hill is probably man-made. Its profile is way too symmetrical."

"Could that be related to the New Madrid incident?"

"I don't see how. The mound was probably made by Paleo-Indians long before the quake." Claire picked up the map, folded it neatly, and tucked it into her purse. "I'll keep this sketch of Audrey's just in case we get bored and want to check out her cave story."

She gulped the last of her coffee and put the cup down on the table. For a moment she contemplated the pattern of grounds that had settled in the bottom. She imagined they formed odd elongated figures with their arms extended and hands locked, dancing in a circle. The shape of the figures looked vaguely familiar.

"Wilson," Claire said, keeping her head bent over the cup. "Have you ever heard of the Nephilim?"

"Sure."

Claire looked up. "Tell me about them."

Wilson raised his eyebrows. "Why do you ask? It's not a word that one hears very often."

"Preston - I mean Prester John - he talked about them

during the revival I went to Friday night."

"You're not turning religious on me, are you?"

Claire laughed. "No. Just curious, is all."

"Well, the Nephilim are mysterious beings mentioned in the Old Testament. They are only mentioned directly once, or twice, depending on the translation." Wilson leaned forward, warming to the subject.

"The first is in Genesis, Chapter 6. This is just before the story of Noah, when God decided to destroy all life on Earth with a flood because it was corrupt and filled with violence. In the Bible, it goes something like this:

'The Nephilim were on the earth in those days; and so after that, sons of God came in unto the daughters of men, and they bear children to them, the same became mighty men which were of old, men of renown.'

As she had many times in the past, Claire was impressed by Wilson's knowledge of the arcane.

"I'm familiar with that part of Genesis," she said. "Doesn't it say there were *giants* in the earth in those days?"

"Well, there's some confusion and disagreement about translations," Wilson explained. "I was quoting from the Hebrew Bible - the Torah - which is a much older source than the Standard King James Christian Bible. There are also other references about giants in the Bible: people variously referred to as the Anakim, Rephaim, Zuzim, Emin and Annunki. Another direct mention is in Numbers, chapter thirteen, I believe:

The people we saw in the land are of great height. There we saw the Nephilim, and we seemed to ourselves like grasshoppers.

Claire pushed her cup away. "Well, it seems as if you have done some research on these Nephilim."

"The Bible's got lots of interesting and curious stuff." Wilson grinned.

"But, correct me if I'm wrong - weren't the Nephilim

destroyed in the Flood, you know, the Noah's Ark thing?"

"Good question, Claire. Maybe a few Nephilim, or perhaps their offspring, survived. Some say that Goliath of Gath, the giant that David slew, was descended from the Nephilim. In Deuteronomy, a ruler called Og, killed by the Israelites, is described as the last of the remnant of giants. His bed was said to be nine cubits in length."

Claire said, "Refresh my memory. A cubit is how long?"

Wilson laughed. "It's the average length from the tip of the middle finger to the elbow, about eighteen inches, a foot and a half."

"So, this Og character's bed was..." Claire closed her eyes for a moment. "Over thirteen feet long... He was a big guy."

"Right," Wilson smiled. "Even owing to exaggeration, and problems with translation, there does seem to be evidence that there once was a race of people that could be judged as giants."

"So, the Nephilim were supposed to be hybrids, essentially, of humans and...?"

"The Bible calls them 'sons of God.'

"Or angels? Fallen Angels?" Claire said. "I think that's what Prester John was saying."

Wilson sat back and rubbed his beard. "Or maybe these Fallen Angels are actually aliens."

"Aliens?"

"Yeah, extra-terrestrials, Claire."

"That's ridiculous."

"Have you ever read Ezekiel, the book in the Old Testament?"

"Can't say I have."

"Well, you should check it out." Wilson's eyes shone. "Ezekiel was a Hebrew prophet from around 600 B.C. His description of his vision calling him to be a prophet sounds like it could be a primitive person's interpretation of a spacecraft coming down to Earth. It's really quite amazing. It makes you think."

Claire frowned. "Where's the evidence? I mean, how

about some kind of irrefutable artifact? Something ancient that could not have come from any existing technology? Or, say, a simple bone from one of these giants? We find bones of dinosaurs sixty million years old, but nothing of these giants."

"Well, first of all," Wilson countered, "there were hundreds of thousands of dinosaurs, existing for millions of years. No comparison to something like a Bigfoot or extraterrestrial whose "footprint" would have been relatively miniscule." Wilson leaned back in his chair. "Let me put it this way, Claire: thousands of deer live in the wild, right?"

"So?"

"How many deer bones have you come across in the wild, with all your field time in geology, discounting road kills?"

"I don't know... twice, that I can remember."

"And suppose these creatures, say, Bigfoot or extraterrestrials, purposefully hid the remains of their dead in order to remain elusive for the purpose of survival. Let's say they incinerate them."

"Then we wouldn't find any remains."

Claire turned to look out the window. Large cumulus clouds were beginning to form on the horizon. She watched them for a moment, then said, " Occam's razor: the simplest explanation is the most likely. Conclusion: giants, Nephilim, aliens, Fallen Angels, whatever - they don't exist. It's a myth," Claire said with finality.

"Whatever." Wilson wiped the last little bit of egg off his plate with a piece of toast. "To change the subject: what's the plan for this morning, boss?"

Claire took a deep breath and switched gears. "We'll have to go back to Doyle's farm. We could fire off some more shot holes to double check, but I got a gut feeling that would be a waste of time."

"I've got an idea," Wilson said.

"What is it?"

"We can use my homemade remote camera. Drill a bigger, deeper hole, into the cave, or whatever, and send the camera down to take pictures. I brought my developing equipment."

"Yes, we could do that." Claire picked up the check from the table and slipped a generous tip under the edge of her plate for Audrey. "It would verify that there are caves below."

"So if the caves are dry..." Wilson knitted his brows. "then what?"

"Good question," Claire said. "Let's wait and see what we find. I'll ask Chief Childress for the name of a reliable well-drilling outfit to drill the deeper and wider hole for the camera to get down to the caves."

Chapter 15

It had a peculiar smell.

Gilbert Beamer, blind since birth, had developed a very keen sense of smell. He could detect the presence of another person, and very often their identity, by the pheromones in the air long before they drew close enough for a sighted person to notice them.

That much was true. But sometimes people thought his extraordinary olfactory sense was augmented by something else entirely. Karl Beamer suspected his son possessed a sixth sense: an ability to detect things that were outside the realm of the five senses. Once, during one of the rare occasions when he opened up about himself, Gilbert had spoken of it to his father.

"Well, Pa, it's kind of like I can just smell it. It's not really smelling though. It's kind of like hearing, but not really hearing... I just know."

And now, Gilbert took a deep breath... there it was, stronger now.

He sat in his favorite spot, a crook in an old twisted chestnut tree at the far end of his family's property.

It came from the west, across an old field that his father, Karl, had left fallow in the years since taking up well-drilling full time. From the direction of Amos Doyle's farm and the mound called Testament hill.

Gilbert couldn't see the landscape, but since exploring the area as a child, hand in hand with his father, then on his own when he was older, he had developed an internal map of the countryside.

What he was sensing that evening had an urgency to it, an almost gravitational pull. And a sweet promise in it too, as if he was an insect being subtly drawn to a newly blossomed flower.

Gilbert slid down the tree trunk, picked up his walking staff and moved confidently in the direction of the beckoning.

He reached the ridge that separated his family's property from Amos Doyle's and climbed to the top. The breeze blew stronger there, and the summoning was more urgent. Ahead and below, was a ten acre fallow pasture on Doyle's property that ran up to the Testament hill mound.

Somewhere near the base of the mound was the attraction.

Gilbert moved confidently down the ridge and strode into the field. After a couple of minutes, he could feel the coolness of the mound's shadow. His steps took him up a slight incline.

He was at the place of beckoning.

He swung his staff before him, exploring the ground. There was some foliage. There was the unmistakable tang of juniper berries. Past the juniper, the ground dipped. He probed it, building a picture in his mind.

It was a shallow depression leading into the mound, maybe five feet wide. Gilbert got down on his knees and traced his staff along the bottom. The depression gradually deepened.

He tried to imagine its origin. It didn't seem natural. The only thing he could think that could have caused it would be water flow, as from a small creek or run. But the ground here was too high for anything like that. Something had made it; perhaps a man with a shovel or some kind of machine. Gilbert stepped carefully down into the trench and crouched so that he could run his hand along its surface. It angled downward and was carpeted with wild grasses like the rest of the field. His hand grasped the sapling of a tree, then an even larger tree he guessed was around ten years old.

So the trench had been there for a while.

He turned his head left and right. In the center of his hearing, down ahead in the trench, was a *gap*. A blank in the soundscape. It reminded him of standing in front of the wagon doorway of a big barn.

There was the metallic whiff of cold damp stone.

Gilbert hesitated, wary of the unknown before him.

He again became aware of the beckoning, the alluring pull that he had first felt sitting in tree. Its origin was ahead, coming from the blankness.

Gilbert stood and walked further down the depression. He could sense the mound loom up before him. He stopped. The blankness was directly ahead. He reached forward and moved his arms around. There was a large opening in the side of the mound, maybe seven feet wide and five feet high, roughly ellipsoid, leading deeper into the earth. An entrance to a cave. Gilbert ducked his head and took a step inside.

Cool, dank air drifted by.

Gilbert was confused. No one had ever mentioned anything about a cave on the property.

"Hello?"

"*Hello?*" A faint echo returned, eerily distorted as if it was another voice answering from the depths of the cave.

Gilbert was pondering his next move when the urging became stronger, and he felt an almost physical push into the cave.

Instead of becoming afraid, calm settled over him. He heard a soothing voice begin in his head. At first it was at the edge of his perception, then grew in intensity and divided into a multitude of voices. It was like the relaxed, hushed murmuring of an audience before a curtain rise. Gilbert took a few steps further into the cave.

There was a soft fluttering on his neck. Then another on top of his head, and on his forehead. Gilbert froze.

Something heavy landed on his right shoulder and held on with a strong sharp grip. It hurt.

Gilbert lost his nerve. He whimpered and flapped his arms wildly. His hands closed around something rough and scaly with large talons that dug into his flesh. His first thought was that some demon had seized his shoulder, but as he reached higher, he touched feathers.

It was a bird.

The bird remained still while Gilbert ran his hands over its body. He felt the wide, flat face, the sharp hooked beak;

the huge eyes of the creature blinking as his fingertips drew across them.

An owl.

Gilbert jumped as a second bird landed on his left shoulder.

Now the voices merged into one voice that bloomed inside his head, filling his brain. A filigree of invisible threads like neurons connected him to the consciousness of a multitude of beings.

You are ours now, they told him.

Gilbert reached out to them with his mind.

And you are mine.

When she came back from the restaurant meeting with Wilson, Claire spent the afternoon making phone calls to arrange for a well driller to meet her at Doyle's in the morning.

Karl Beamer, the well driller recommended by Chief Childress, was not enthusiastic about working on such short notice. Claire told him that the geology department would pay extra. He agreed to come out.

Next Claire called Amos Doyle. He also sounded less than thrilled with the plan, but grudgingly agreed when Claire explained that she and Wilson had limited time and would have to return to the university soon.

After making all the arrangements and feeling restless, Claire decided to go for a walk to burn off some nervous energy. Turning the corner at the center of town to head back to her motel room, she almost collided with the police dispatcher.

"Edith." Claire said, holding her hands up. "I'm sorry."

"That's okay, dear." Edith smiled and tightened her scarf around her neck. "Actually, I was hoping I might see you. There's some more to the story of Testament Hill, I thought you would find interesting."

"Really?"

"I think you need to know something about Ivy and a

young man named Gilbert." Edith said, lowering her voice.

"Gilbert? A young blind boy?"

"Why yes. Have you met him?"

"Not exactly. We crossed paths at the Sunbeam Café. We had a brief conversation."

Edith nodded. "Karl Beamer, the well driller, it's his son. Adopted son, mind you." Edith's voice was almost a whisper. "Ivy and Gilbert, they're brother and sister. Twins."

"I don't understand."

"Rachel was their mother. And that no good husband of hers that ran off, Clyde - he's not the father."

Claire blinked uncomprehendingly at Edith.

"You see," Edith explained, "I used to be a midwife around here, before they built the new hospital in West Grange. The town doc was awfully busy, so I helped bring a lot of children into the world."

Edith leaned in closer. "It was a difficult birth. We had no idea it was going to be twins. I asked Rachel if she had any twins in the family, you know, because it can run every other generation. She said no, and blurted out that Clyde wasn't the father."

"I see."

For a long moment Edith closed her eyes and said nothing. Her eyes opened a slit. Her voice was distant, recalling a memory from the past. "It all seemed like a dream to Rachel," she said slowly. "She told me the whole story, and swore me to secrecy. But she's gone now, many years, and I think the time has come for the truth to come out."

"Yes," Claire said gently, not wanting to discourage the revelation.

Rachel had met the man at the country fair, Edith recounted. Her husband, Clyde, was off on one of his "sales" trips to Ames. He sold some kind of gizmo that was supposed to get you better gas mileage. Edith was sure it was a scam.

Rachel confided in Edith she didn't miss her husband. In fact, she was glad when Clyde went away. At first, when they were newly married, and Clyde was gone on business, their tiny rental seemed empty. But now, Rachel said, it was a relief when his brooding presence wasn't swaggering drunkenly around their cramped three room flat.

Clyde Deacon had always been an "enthusiastic" drinker, Edith told Claire. Rachel, in her young innocence, thought it was just something young men did. Have a beer or two and maybe a shot of whiskey after a hard day. But eventually Rachel became aware that Clyde had a problem. His drinking was getting out of control. He would unpredictably alternate between sullen passivity and rage. A few times he even struck her.

One day Rachel roused her husband from a drunken stupor on the sofa by sticking a twelve gauge under his chin and told him if he ever hit her again, he would go to sleep and never wake up.

"Good for her," Claire said.

Edith nodded. "He never hit her again, that bastard."

After that - Edith continued with her story - Clyde's sales trips became longer and more frequent. Which was fine with Rachel.

Then Rachel met a man at the county fair who was very tall, with black eyes and long, dark hair. Rachel told Edith she thought he looked like a Hollywood movie star.

And unlike her husband, the man was gentle. When he first touched her - a brief caress of her cheek, Rachel was shocked and her instinct was to pull away. After all, she was a married woman.

But it felt so good. So unlike her husband's rough, selfish animal moves. The word *rutting*, Rachel told Edith, came to mind whenever she thought of Clyde's lovemaking. Clyde would take care of his needs in a rush and then immediately sit up on the edge of the bed, pull on his baggy briefs and shuffle off to the kitchen to get himself another beer. Sex with Clyde, Rachel confided, had become an unpleasant, almost unbearable chore.

The tall man took her back to his motel room and the rest of the evening was a blur of the man's gentle caresses becoming more urgent and her body responding like she had never before imagined. Rachel later drove home in a daze.

"The next morning," Edith told Claire, "Rachel told me that she sat by the kitchen window of her flat, drinking tea, thinking about what had happened. She felt guilty about the previous evening, but as the memories ran through her head, she couldn't help but smile.

"Then, somewhere in the core of her body there was a fluttering, the lightest stirring. It was impossible of course, it had only been - Rachel remembered glancing up at the wall clock, a mere eight hours. But she knew with a certainty what had begun."

"The twins." Claire breathed.

"Yes," Edith nodded. "Born eight months later. Premature. Ivy was the runt, so to speak. She was such a tiny little thing when she was born, like a baby china angel. Full head of raven black hair, though. Beautiful."

Claire said, "Yes, she is.

"Gilbert was always tall," Edith went on. "Even at birth he was an abnormally long baby. Freakish, I dare say. Rachel found out soon after he was born that something was wrong. His eyes would constantly move side to side, and he would have seizures. The doctors suspected he had some rare disease, and told her there was no cure. The disease caused blindness."

Claire said, "Sounds like de Morsier's syndrome."

"Yes," Edith said. "I think that's what they called it."

Claire frowned. "But if I remember correctly, it usually causes stunted growth."

"I don't know about that. Gilbert grew like a weed, looking much taller than you would expect for his age."

"Maybe he was misdiagnosed," Claire suggested.

"And folks around here think he's a healer."

"A healer?"

"Yes. They believe his touch can cure. Some say it's a gift from God." Edith knitted her brows. "I'm not sure about that, but it's true that he has a talent."

Claire frowned, processing this new information. "I understand that they must be fraternal twins, because of the different sex," she said, "but I'd never guess that Gilbert and Ivy are brother and sister. They seem so different."

"Yes, they certainly are." Edith cocked an eyebrow. "What are you thinking Claire?"

"Nothing, really, just making an observation."

"I have my suspicions, too." Edith tightened her scarf as if she had a sudden chill. "I wasn't going to mention this, but Rachel had the oddest dream the night after her liaison."

"Yes..?"

"Well, mind you it was just a dream, I expect, but she said she had a vision of someone, like a ghost or something visited her in the night and had congress with her."

"Congress?"

"Well, you know...intercourse."

"Oh."

"Just a dream. But she said it was so realistic."

"Might it just be a aftereffect of her time with the stranger?"

"That's what I said too. But Rachel insisted it was not. She said the visitor was a *being full of light*. That's was how she put it."

"A dream, surely."

Edith shrugged. "Anyway, Clyde, Rachel's no good husband, left for good right after the births, and Rachel couldn't handle caring for two new babies. She suffered from melancholy, you know. Now, the Beamers had always wanted a child, so Ivy and Gilbert were separated soon after birth, and the Beamers took Gilbert as their own, and Rachel kept Ivy and moved in with her parents, Amos and Fern Doyle. No one else needed to know." Edith looked Claire in the eyes. "I'm telling you this in confidence, you understand."

"Of course." Claire was wondering why Edith felt compelled to share this information.

Edith tightened her scarf around her neck. "Well, then, good day." She turned suddenly and quickly walked away.

"But..." Claire called out.

Edith disappeared around the corner.

Claire walked slowly back to her motel room, her mind troubled. Ever since she had arrived, as she learned more about Testament Hill, it was like a shade was being slowly pulled down over the town, blocking the light, making it darker and darker.

Around five, Wilson rang her, asking about her dinner plans. Claire told him she was bushed and was going eat a snack in her room, work on some lecture notes for the next semester, shower and fall into bed early.

Actually, she was planning on going to Duggan's. She was hoping to see John Preston/Prester John again. And three would be a crowd.

Coming out of the shower, Claire opened her suitcase on the bed, and standing with her hands on her hips, scrutinized its contents: two identical white linen blouses, a black and white checked flannel shirt, tan dungarees, black dungarees, denim jeans worn out at the knees, and assorted underwear.

"Jesus," she said to herself. "Sexy stuff you got there, Claire."

Well, maybe the jeans. They were pretty tight fitting.

Pathetic.

Then she remembered. It was still probably in the car - she was a procrastinator about putting stuff back its proper place - the outfit she had worn to the staff retirement party for old Professor Clark. She had taken it to the cleaners afterwards and thrown it in the trunk of the Volvo. It was a snug satin red shift with a low neckline. She wore it because she thought it might excite Ben, but he had barely noticed it and not until she gave him some hints. The high heels were probably still in the trunk too. It was probably over the top for Duggan's. And she didn't have any nylons.

To hell with it. She'd wear the dress to the pub. And the heels. Go barelegged. Besides, she hated wearing nylons.

John Preston was wondering why he came to Duggan's

in the first place. He spun his beer mug on the bar as he looked around. The place was pleasant enough. It was humming with a mix of couples and groups that were obviously families. Everyone was chatting, laughing, stuffing their faces.

He had hoped, with his long hair stuffed up into his cowboy hat, he wouldn't be recognized and it seemed to be working. At least nobody was paying him any notice.

A familiar pang welled up. He pushed the emotion away. Feeling lonely was a waste of time, he told himself for the millionth time. I've done just fine by myself. Real fine.

He turned back and idly watched the bubbles rising in his drink, reflecting about his past. His thoughts turned to the day Wesley Clapp's troupe showed up at the town of Marjorie.

As the town's deputy, Preston had been assigned security detail for Clapp's revival meeting. Clapp recognized him right away as the young man who had worked for him years earlier. Clapp convinced Preston to come back for a drink when he got off duty. They sat around a campfire in a circle of trailers the troupe traveled in. The two reminisced and laughed about old times. Around midnight, Clapp got up to urinate and never came back. Preston didn't give it a second thought, being as they had been hitting the bottle pretty hard.

A rabbit hunter found Wesley Clapp's body the next day in a nearby dry gulch. The county coroner said Clapp's head had been bashed in, probably by hitting his head on a boulder after he fell. Being that it was a dark night and Clapp had been drinking, his death was ruled accidental.

Preston took Clapp's death as an opportunity to return to what he realized was his true calling. He quit his deputy job, rejoined the troupe and swiftly moved to take Clapp's position as the main attraction. Preston took the moniker *Prester John*, after the semi-mythical priest king of the Middle Ages, supposedly descended from the Magi.

As "Prester John", Preston worked shrewdly to improve

the performance of the revivals. He taught himself the Bible, memorizing dozens of verses so that he could use them as tools when the right time presented itself. He altered his appearance: he grew his blond hair long so that it rested over his collar and bleached it so that it was almost white. He took to wearing long black frock coats that he bought at used clothing stores, then eventually had them tailor made. With his tall stature, his appearance presented an air of authority and solemn wisdom.

He also changed the approach of the revivals, abandoning the *healing* aspect of the performance, which was a dicey proposition at best and liable to disastrous backfires.

Instead, "Prester John" decided to emphasize being reborn through dramatic baptism or re-baptism rituals conducted during the revival meetings. After the crowd's religious zeal had been sufficiently stirred up, donations would flow in to support his proselytizing mission.

By the time he was 28, five years after Clapp's demise, John Preston, alias Prester John, had a lucrative tent revival troupe that traveled extensively in the South and Midwest. His name became well known in Baptist and Pentecostal circles, and some representatives from one of the television networks in New York had met with him several times about the possibility of a television show based on his ministry.

By investing in blue chip stocks like IBM and AT&T and promising new companies such as Hewlett Packard and Fairchild Semiconductor, Preston had accumulated considerable wealth by the time he was thirty.

He had sworn to escape the hand to mouth existence he and his father had lived, traveling from one crummy oil town to another. And now, Preston mused, taking a satisfying sip of his beer, he would never go hungry again, never again have to scrounge and scrimp. He could retire anytime and live in luxury.

But he chose to continue his ministries. He told himself it was to keep the cash rolling in. However, every once in a while, as in a moment of introspection while shaving in the mirror, Preston suspected he actually did have some kind of calling.

His thoughts turned to the revival in Testament Hill. Everything had gone well. The take was satisfactory. The troupe would soon be moving on to another town.

Preston took a deep breath. For a moment his shoulders slumped. He was exhausted. Ten shows in two weeks. He wasn't getting any younger: thirty-four wasn't an old geezer, but he wasn't the same tireless twenty-three year old that he was when he began preaching.

Besides, he hadn't been sleeping well lately. Dark dreams disturbed his sleep. The same dreams over and over: nightmares of falling through frigid emptiness and being chased by fleeting shadows, dark spirits that, as they got close, changed into giant bat-like creatures. Sometimes, in a dream, he would be walking naked down a long murky corridor, heading towards a light at the end, but he could never quite reach the light. He would awaken with a jolt, his body damp with cold sweat, his jaw aching from grinding his teeth.

At first, Preston tried to ignore the nightmares, but when the same ones returned night after night, he began to question their meaning. While researching dreams, he found the writings of Sigmund Freud's former student, Carl Jung, the most intriguing. Especially Jung's idea that dreams were caused by the unconscious communicating with the conscious, and how it tied into the idea of a collective consciousness and the concept of archetypes.

Preston learned that Jung defined archetypes as primordial themes and images imprinted on the human psyche. For example, there was the Demon, the Angel, the Serpent, the Mother and the Sage. Archetypes also included events and places, such as the Flood, Fire from the Sky, Heaven and the Underworld. Jung believed these innate, mythic motifs were common to all humanity. There was a theory that they were an evolutionary development based on actual events from the dawn of human history.

The skeptical, coolly logical side of Preston believed it

to be all nonsense, but his instincts were raising an alarm. He needed to discover the threat his dreams were foretelling.

Preston, alias Prester John, was struck by an ominous feeling that, here and now in Testament Hill, his life was about to be transformed.

When Claire stepped through the door of Duggan's, there he was, sitting alone on the same bar stool. A little thrill went up through her body.

She stood in the foyer for a moment, hoping he would notice. She realized she was striking a pose.

John Preston turned and his eyes were immediately upon her. He smiled broadly and raised his glass. Allowing herself a little extra sway to her step, Claire walked up to him. His eyes never left her.

"Are you waiting for company?" she said.

"I didn't think so...until I saw you come in." Preston waved his hand at the stool next to his. "Please, it would be my pleasure."

Claire slid into the stool, crossed her legs, put her elbows on the bar and cupped her hand in her chin. "Haven't I seen you around these parts before, pardner?"

He leaned in close and raised a finger to his lips. "Our little secret."

She laughed. "I won't tell if you won't."

"Deal."

Preston caught the barmaid's attention and turned back to Claire. "What are you having, Miss?"

"Hmm." Claire glanced up.

The barmaid had appeared in front of them. Sherrie was smiling. Apparently, she had dropped her snarky attitude. *Maybe because it was clear that Preston was only interested in me*, Claire mused, *and they were no longer rivals.*

"Tonight, I think I'll have a martini, dry and dirty, please. Gordon's gin if you have it, please, Sherrie."

Preston added, "And a refill for me, please."

The two watched in silent anticipation as the barmaid

prepared their drinks.

"I went to your revival," Claire said after her drink arrived.

"I know. I saw you in the audience."

Claire ran her finger along the rim of her glass. "Nothing else in this town to do."

"You're right about that. So what did you think?"

Claire wagged her head. "Well, Prester John, I thought you were very effective."

"Well, thank you. *Effective?* I don't know if I should take that as a compliment or not." Preston said. "Anyway, I don't work off a script, but I have a pretty good idea beforehand how the night is going to go."

Claire sipped her drink. "I see."

"I've been doing this for a few years, and frankly, between you and me, the whole performance is canned, so to speak. I take into consideration my audience, what they expect, and deliver."

"That sounds so cynical."

"My experience in the real world has made me who I am."

"And who is that exactly?"

Preston looked into Claire's eyes and said nothing for a moment. "Damned if I know," he said finally. "Do any of us know for sure who we really are?"

Claire raised her glass. "Isn't that what's life's about? Discovering who we are, why we are on this Earth?"

Preston grunted good-naturedly. "Life should be so simple."

"Maybe it can be, if we can cut through all the bullshit." Claire met his gaze again. "Really, I found your presentation quite interesting. I was a little confused about the message, truthfully. All the references to the flood, etc."

"Me too."

"I didn't understand the point."

Preston nodded. "I'm not sure even I know. The whole thing about the Deluge and the Fallen Angels and the Nephilim. I wasn't intending to talk about that."

"I see."

Preston rubbed his forehead for a moment. "Hell, there's something about this place, something in the air."

"Here? In Testament Hill?"

Preston glanced around the bar. "Since I've come to this town, my intuition has been setting off little alarm bells. Like just before the townspeople are going to run me out on a rail."

"This town kind of gives me the creeps too." Claire smiled at him. "You'll give me fair warning when you figure out what's going on?"

"I promise." Preston gazed into his drink. "Well, maybe something is going on in this bar, a chance meeting of two people." He looked up. "What do you think?"

"You're quite a charmer, John Preston. Of course, that's your profession after all."

Preston reached out and lightly put his hand on Claire's bare knee. Normally, Claire would have offended by the action, but it felt good. His fingers traced a delicate circle. An electric-like tingle ran up her thigh. For a second their eyes met again. Then his hand withdrew.

Claire resumed breathing. "So, do you believe in it?"

Preston shook his head. "Believe what?"

"The story about the flood in the Bible."

Preston frowned. "Everything in the Bible is gospel, Claire," he said in a serious voice.

Claire was taken aback. "Well, I'm sorry. I didn't mean to disrespect…"

She stopped when Preston chuckled.

"Just pulling your chain, Claire." He glanced down at Claire's legs. Her dress had ridden up when she crossed her legs on the bar stool, exposing a long swatch of smooth ivory thigh, peppered with pale freckles. Preston seemed enthralled by the vision. Claire was amused by his reaction. She hoped he might reach out and touch her again, but after a second he lifted his eyes.

"Sorry," said Preston awkwardly.

"Why, I do believe you're blushing, Mr. Preston." Claire

laughed and reached for her drink.

"I don't usually get flustered like a school boy. I'm actually quite suave and debonair."

"I'm sure you are, sir."

Preston smiled. "So, Claire, to answer your question: I'm not sure what I believe. It depends on what day you ask me."

Claire nodded. "I know exactly what you mean. I generally think of myself a realist, being a scientist and all that." She shifted on her stool, "But coming into this town, talking to people, things that I've seen…"

"Like what?"

"Well, for instance: Ivy Doyle. She's Amos Doyle's orphaned granddaughter. She seems to have this telepathic connection to a pet crow. And there's this boy, Gilbert…" Claire decided not to mention his relationship with Ivy, told to her in confidence. "He's blind, but I swear, he has some kind of ESP thing going on. And apparently townspeople think he had curative powers. Then the police dispatcher, Edith. She's been telling me about all kinds of strange things that have been going on in Testament Hill."

"Such as?"

Claire ignored his question "…And then there's this weird bluish flashing light…"

Preston stiffened. "Flashing blue light you say?"

"Yeah. I first saw it driving into town. Then again, looking down an old well out at Doyle's place."

Preston shut his eyes for a moment.

"What is it, Preston?"

He opened his eyes and shook his head. "Nothing. Just when you said blue light, it triggered something, but I can't quite remember. Something that happened a long time ago."

"Really? I wish you could recall."

"I will let you know if I remember," Preston said.

"I hope you are inferring we'll see each other again."

"I'd like that." Preston smiled. "Should we order something to eat? I'm ravenous."

"So am I."

Chapter 16

Tuesday morning

The bullet grey sky hung low that morning and a cold wind whipped the dry leaves into vortexes along the ground. Claire pulled the collar higher on her denim coat. She and Wilson were standing around his Jeep at the bottom of the Amos Doyle's drive, peering down the road to town.

Wilson pulled his beret down tighter on his head. "Fuck it, I'm waiting in the car."

"Watch your language," Claire said half-seriously as Wilson climbed into his Jeep. "The people around here are not used to such vulgarity."

"Bullshit," came back Wilson's mumbled reply.

They were waiting for drillers to show up. They were twenty minutes late.

Chief Childress had told Claire that Acme Well & Pump, owed by Karl Beamer, was the best driller in the area. Beamer knew his business, the Chief assured her, and was reasonable.

Claire was beginning to wonder if he left out *prompt and reliable* for a reason. She looked into the Jeep. Wilson's head was bent over a newspaper spread in his lap.

"Anything worth reading?" she asked.

"Jesus." Wilson tapped the newspaper. "There's a story here about our government setting off a thermonuclear bomb above some island in the South Pacific last July. The light from the explosion lit up the sky in Hawaii *eight hundred* miles away, and caused electromagnetic disturbances that took out street lights on the Islands; set off burglar alarms and stuff."

"That's exciting."

Wilson looked up at Claire. "Well, I don't know if you know, but in 1959 and 1960, there was a voluntary moratorium on above ground nuclear testing."

"So?"

"Well, France broke the moratorium in 1960. The Russians responded by resuming testing. In 1961, they exploded the largest bomb in history, called the 'Czar Bomba'."

"That's a crazy name."

"Yeah." Wilson lifted a finger in the air. "I was talking to a friend of mine who works for the University of California at the Lawrence Livermore laboratory. They do nuclear weapon stuff for the government. He said the Czar Bomba's yield was fifty megatons. That's the equivalent to blowing up fifty million tons of TNT. My friend said that would be a solid cube of TNT with edges a thousand feet long. That's like…" Wilson hesitated, calculating, "…stacking around eighteen football fields with TNT a hundred stories high, and exploding it all at once. The Czar Bomba *broke* window panes over four hundred miles away."

"Scary."

"Scary is an understatement. Right after the Russkies resumed testing, the U.S. started testing again, too. There's been hundreds of tests in the last couple of years."

"That's insane."

Wilson folded the newspaper and tossed it in the back seat. "Yeah, well get this -" His voice took on a conspiratorial tone. "In July, there was an underground nuclear test in Nevada called *Storax Sedan* that sent a radioactive cloud across the U.S. My friend was on the team that went out and took samples from around the country. Now, this is secret stuff: guess where the prevailing winds took the highest concentration of fallout?"

"Pray tell."

Wilson put his arm out the window and pointed to the sky. "Right here in the Midwest, just a few months ago. Yesiree."

"Really? How much radiation are we talking about?"

"In some counties, up to one hundred and forty thousand Nanocuries the day after the explosion."

"Is that bad?"

"Well, normal is probably around eighteen."

"Eighteen? That's, what…" Claire closed her eyes for a moment, doing her own calculation. "Eight thousand times higher than normal?"

"Yep."

"Are people getting sick?"

Wilson made at face. "It's the long term effects that we need to worry about. There are over a hundred different kinds of radionuclides produced by a nuclear explosion. Some are more damaging than others. Stronium-90, for example, gets into our teeth and bones masquerading as calcium. We may not pay the price for fifty years until we eventually get cancer from the radiation. It's a ticking time bomb, Claire. I bet by the year 2000 most people in the U.S. will meet their end by cancer. "

"That is a horrible price to pay."

Wilson shook his head. "I'll tell you, we're setting loose the devil."

A screen door banged. Claire looked up towards the house to see Ivy trotting down the drive with the adolescent lope of a young filly getting used to its long legs.

Ivy was beaming. "Hello, again, Miss Doctor Claire." Ivy stopped, breathless, and looked up at Claire, her eyes round. "Grandpa said you were coming today to work with the well drillers."

"That's right, Ivy."

Ivy clapped her hands together. "What fun. I am happy to see you again, Doctor Claire."

"And I you, Ivy. And you can call me just Claire." Claire craned her head to the sky. "And where is Raven today?"

Ivy smiled mischievously. "Oh, you know, doing crow things I expect, Just Claire."

Claire bent down to look Ivy in the eyes. "No, I really don't know. What kind of things do crows do?"

Ivy turned her palms up.

There was a rustling in the air, and Claire took a step back as the big black bird swooped in and settled gently on Ivy's outstretched hand.

"Mr. Beamer is just over the hill," Ivy said.

Claire looked down the road. At first there was nothing,

then after a couple seconds, a yellow drilling truck appeared over a hump in the road.

Claire turned back to Ivy. "How do you do that?"

Ivy shrugged. "I don't do anything. Raven just lets me know."

The Jeep's door opened. "Here they are," Wilson grumbled. "About time."

The big truck pulled up behind the Jeep. Karl Beamer climbed out. He walked over and shook hands in turn with Wilson and Claire as they introduced themselves.

Beamer pointed at the truck. "I got my son Gilbert with me today." He spread his arms. "Where do you suggest we drill, Doctor Brannigan?"

Claire pointed over her shoulder. "We discovered some anomalies during our testing that seem centered near the old well, about eighty feet down."

Beamer whistled. "That's a ways down. Should be below the water table, into the bedrock."

"That's the thing, Mr. Beamer. Our testing indicates that there are voids in the rock."

"Voids you say? Do you mean caves?"

"Exactly." Wilson answered. "And they seem to be dry."

Beamer shook his head. "I'd expect them to be filled with water. I know we've had a drought lately, but that far down…should be water."

"We're kind of mystified ourselves," Claire said. "That's why we want to drill down and take a look."

Beamer pointed to the ground. "How are you going to see anything through a little drill hole?"

"We have a miniature camera that can be lowered into the hole and take pictures," Wilson explained.

"I'd like to see that," Beamer said.

Claire said, "You're welcome to watch."

Beamer motioned to his rig. "I'll move the truck and get set up."

Amos Doyle came out of the barn and walked over. "Good morning to you, Miss Brannigan… Mr. Wilson."

Claire smiled. "Good morning, Mr. Doyle."

Doyle nodded to Beamer. "Karl. How have you been? How's the missus?"

"She's well, Amos."

"Good to hear." Doyle turned back to Claire. His eyes flicked down at Claire's throat, and widened. "Pardon me, that charm around your neck, miss - if you don't mind me asking, where did you get it?"

"It's a curious story," Claire told him. "When I first drove into Testament Hill, I stopped at the gas station at the edge of town to buy a soda…"

"…and you found it in the vending machine." Doyle finished her sentence.

"Yes… How did you know?"

For a moment, the old man did not speak. His face was solemn.

"That belonged to my daughter Rachel, Ivy's mother," he said. "I was there, ten years ago, when she lost it. At the Sinclair station to get gas for the tractor. Rachel came along with Ivy. Ivy was just a toddler then."

"Oh, my gosh. What a coincidence."

Doyle rubbed his hand across the stubble on his chin. "Rachel had a craving for a soda, and wanted to get out of the house for a while. She had little Ivy in her arms." He stared at the amulet. "I remember she had it around her neck."

Claire said, "She lost it in the machine."

"Well, we weren't sure where it went." Doyle told her. "Rachel noticed it was missing when we were driving back to the farm. She remembered Ivy tried to reach up and pull at it. It meant a lot to Rachel, so we drove back to the station. We figured she lost it while she was buying her soda, but couldn't find it to save our lives."

Claire nodded. "It got caught in the machine and I found it when I was trying to clear a jam."

Doyle shook his head. "It's like it was waiting for you to find it."

Claire turned the amulet over in her hand.

Doyle said, "Rachel found it when she heard rumbling

one morning here at the farm and went outside to investigate. She walked around and spotted it at the top of the old Testament Hill when the charm glimmered in the light of the rising sun. It was just lying in the grass."

"How long ago was that?"

"Let's see...Rachel only had it for a little while before she lost it. Maybe a couple of months, so that would be in 'fifty-two."

Claire held the amulet up. "This 'VRS' engraved along the rim? It seems vaguely familiar to me, but I can't quite place it. Do you have any idea what it means?"

"Can't help you there."

"And the crystal?" Claire ran her finger gently over it. She felt a barely noticeable electric-like prickle.

Doyle said, "I wouldn't know anything about that, either, miss. Like I said, Rachel herself just found it by happenchance."

Claire began lifting the necklace over her head. "Now you should have it back."

Doyle waved his hand. "No, you better keep it. Perhaps it was fate that you found it. You may need it for protection. Like a charm."

Claire let go of her necklace, and it fell back onto her throat. "Are you sure?"

"I am."

Back at the Sleep-Tite Motel, the dowser Smith stood by the pool, gazing into the water. A burning rose up from the nape of his neck to back of his skull. The voices began in his head. He closed his eyes and listened. In the distance was the rumble of a truck on the state road. Smith's eyes popped open and he took a deep breath as if testing the air. He needed to return - *They* needed his help.

After conferring with Claire and maneuvering the drilling rig into position, Karl Beamer set the stabilizing jacks, raised the cable tower and locked it in place. He set the casing shoe in the ground and started up the deck engine that would crank the spudding beam up and down.

When the engine coughed into life, the truck door opened and a gangly boy wearing dark glasses got out and walked over to Claire and Wilson. He was using a long knarled staff to guide his way. He appeared to be staring directly at Claire. Claire recognized him as the boy from the café.

"How are you again, Miss Brannigan?" he asked.

"Hello...Gilbert." Claire cleared her throat. "On my left is Mike Wilson. We're here from the university to see if we can help determine why the wells have been drying up around Testament Hill."

"Yes, my father told me about you." Gilbert reached into his shirt pocket, and took out a pack of Camels and a Zippo lighter. He tapped out a cigarette, lit it, took a long drag and let the smoke out slowly thorough his nostrils.

Claire and Wilson exchanged surprised looks

"Well, don't you think it's just because of the drought?" Gilbert said.

"It could account for some of it," Wilson answered. "But the rate at which the water table is falling is extraordinary, so we're trying to find other explanations."

Gilbert took another drag on his cigarette then held it out as if he was examining its tip. "What other explanations could there be, I wonder?"

"That's what we're doing here today," Wilson told him. "Drilling a bore hole to see what's going on."

"How far down do you intend to go?"

"Around eighty to a hundred feet."

Gilbert tilted his head upward and blew out several perfect smoke rings. "Why go that deep?" he asked. "Around here, wells have never had to go more than thirty to forty feet."

"Our seismic survey indicated that there may be a cave system beneath us," Claire explained.

Gilbert's snapped his head towards her. "I don't think you should go there."

She said, "Why on Earth not?"

Gilbert took another puff of his cigarette and said nothing.

Just then, Karl Beamer came over.

"We're just about ready to start drilling," Beamer told them. His glance shifted from Claire to Gilbert and back to Claire. "Something wrong here?"

"Gilbert thinks we shouldn't be drilling that far down." Claire replied.

"Is that so?" Beamer kicked at the dirt with the toe of his boot. He hesitated and glanced at Gilbert, who had stepped away and whose attention now seemed focused on the drilling rig.

"Gilbert has what you might call a special gift," Beamer said softly. "My son can sense things we normally can't. Just like some animals. You know..." his eyes met Clare's, "I once had a ewe that every time a bad storm was coming, would run circles around the water trough. At the old folks' home in Ames, where my pappy stayed, they had a dog that would go by and sit by someone's room, and the next day, that person would have passed. Gilbert's gift is no different. A natural gift."

Wilson was nodding his head. "I've heard of things like that."

"Well, it could just be that one of their five senses is just better than ours," Claire observed. "I mean, lots of animals can see better than us."

She suddenly realized that Gilbert had turned back to them and was listening in on the conversation. Claire was immediately embarrassed at her faux pas. "I mean..."

"That's okay, Doctor Brannigan," Gilbert told her, his expression unreadable. "Science has its uses, and its limitations. '*There are more things in Heaven or Earth, Horatio, than are dreamt of in your philosophy.*'"

For a second, Claire's vision blurred and she felt light headed. The ground felt as if it had shifted under her feet, and she spread her stance to keep her balance. She blinked at Gilbert. "I guess...that's true."

"You okay, Claire?" Wilson asked, noticing her expression.

"I think we're ready to go here," Karl Beamer was saying.

Claire and Wilson watched the percussive drilling process for a while. The walking beam, driven by the four-cylinder Continental deck engine, raised and dropped the fifteen hundred pound stem and chisel-like drill bit about forty times a minute by alternately pulling and releasing a cable looped through a pulley at the top of the derrick. With each cycle, the bit dug and chipped a little deeper into the earth.

After a half hour or so, Wilson, apparently bored, drifted back to the Jeep and got in the driver's seat. Claire noticed his head bow and he appeared to be dozing. Ivy stood by Claire a little longer, then wandered off to the barn, Raven perched on her shoulder.

The initial fascination soon wore off for Claire too, but for some reason she felt compelled to stay close while Beamer ran the rig. The noise of the operation discouraged casual conversation. She was content to sip coffee from a thermos while leaning up against the fender of the truck.

She estimated that the rig got down about twenty feet in the first hour. Under the watchful eyes of Karl Beamer, Claire occasionally checked the slurry coming out of the bailer by squeezing it through her fingers. She could tell that the drill was going through a thick layer of silt, then sedimentary rock, as expected. Based on what she and Wilson saw in the seismic readouts, she anticipated reaching the void at about thirty feet.

Claire walked over to the Jeep to check on Wilson.

"How's it going?" he mumbled, his eyes half opening.

"Nothing unusual yet. You can go back to sleep."

Wilson nodded and closed his eyes.

Claire was halfway back to the rig when Beamer let go of the cable, slammed the engine lever, and jumped back.

"Whoa!" he said.

Gilbert, who had been sitting in the cab with the door

open working a yo-yo, jumped down from the passenger side.

"What's wrong?" Claire said.

"I think we broke into that cave you were talking about, Miss Claire," Beamer said.

Claire turned to the Jeep. "Wilson! Get the camera gear. I think we're ready to get some pictures."

After his usual stop at Cagney's bar for a pack of smokes, Deputy Hooper tucked the cruiser behind the thick white cedar across from the Sinclair gas station. While the Plymouth was in the shop, Hooper was temporarily driving the Ford Interceptor that the Chief usually drove.

Hooper sighed and checked his watch: it was five-thirty in the afternoon.

The spot was one of his favorite locations for a speed trap because it was just past the sign that reduced the speed limit coming into town from 50 mph to 30 mph. Hooper had measured out the distance from the sign to the Sinclair driveway, and using a stopwatch, got an good estimate of a car's speed as it approached. It was a rough calculation, but it was enough for Malcolm Cramer, the local justice of the peace.

It was a mild evening for the season, and the last glow of sunset was fading in the west. Hooper had his windows half-way down to let in some fresh air while he smoked. A few crickets chirped in the yellowing vetch and wild parsnip at the curb. He yawned and rubbed his eyes. A pair of headlights approaching perked him up. He flicked his cigarette out and when the car passed the speed limit sign, clicked the stop watch taped to the dash. The car, a '55 Chevy Bellaire, cleared the gas station driveway and Hooper clicked the watch again. Six seconds to travel two hundred feet. Not even close to over the limit.

The deputy eased back in the seat, and lit another cigarette. His thoughts kept returning to the night he was invited into Ida Wagner's house, so he was trying to distract himself by focusing on his job. But it wasn't working.

He vividly remembered walking up to the house, Ida standing in her doorway, smiling. Stepping across the threshold.

Then his brain hit a blank wall. It was like going out and drinking too much at Cagney's and the next morning not remembering how or when he got home. What happened at Ida Wagner's after he went inside the house was blacked out. All that was left was a suspicion that something terrible had taken place. He did have a hazy impression of sitting at Ida Wagner's kitchen table drinking wine, Ida laughing and flirting with him, the front of her robe slowly opening. Then the vague recollection of a blinding light, and terrific pain inside his head.

Then nothing. Just the nagging sense that he had done something bad. He half expected that at any moment his mother would return from the dead with her switch to beat him for what he had done. Hooper looked uneasily over his shoulder into the darkness of the woods behind him.

Voices by the road caught his attention, and a moment later he observed a young couple walk into the gas station. They were holding hands. Hooper watched idly as they bought a couple of sodas from the vending machine. The boy leaned up against the machine, put his arm around the girl and drew her close. Hooper could hear her giggle.

Hooper had a girlfriend once. It was back in high school, his senior year. Her name was Charlotte Hamm. She was a junior assigned to be his lab partner in science class. If it hadn't been for the necessity of them working as a team, they would have not gotten together. Hooper was too shy, and Charlotte probably would have never noticed the skinny kid with sad eyes and worn, passed down clothes who had a habit of picking his nose.

Charlotte was no beauty. Her body was on the pudgy side and her face was round and flat and marred by acne, so that the phrase *pizza pie* often came to Hooper's mind when he looked at her. Plus, her eyeballs bugged out.

However, Charlotte had long, blond hair that was always clean and shiny, a fetching smile and a bubbly personality that made her popular at the school. Hooper would daydream about seeing her naked and running his hands all over her baby smooth skin.

Charlotte reluctantly agreed to go out with him. Hooper figured it was because he was one of the few boys at school that had a car. His uncle had passed down a beat-up '40 Ford coupe to him after his cataracts had left his vision too cloudy to drive. The Ford wasn't fancy, but it ran.

The pair's tentative relationship ended when Hooper, tanked-up on some pilfered corn liquor, tried to grope Charlotte after driving her home from a school basketball game.

His moves were so awkward and clueless, that instead of being aroused, Charlotte became annoyed, and when he persisted, she pushed him away in disgust. She jumped out of the car and ran into her house. Hooper squealed away in the coupe, fearful that Charlotte's father would come charging out, pull him out of the car and beat the crap out of him.

After that incident, Charlotte refused to answer Hooper's phone calls, and if they passed each other in school, she turned her head. One day Hooper overheard Charlotte and some of her friends chatting in a stairwell. Charlotte would say something and the other girls would giggle. He couldn't hear clearly, but made out his name, and a few words like "clod" and "repulsive".

He felt his face flush with shame and stalked away unnoticed.

He never spoke to Charlotte again, or for that matter, had any significant conversation with any girl in high school.

Hooper tried to convince himself that he didn't like girls anymore. He decided that they were frivolous, conceited and cruel - just like his mother. It was just as well that he didn't have anything to do with them.

On the other hand, he was urged by sexual desire towards women, and the two conflicting states of mind often troubled him.

When he finished high school, Hooper got a job picking up merchandise at a wholesaler in Cape Girardeau for the Testament Hill Hardware store. While in the city, he would often buy girlie magazines, and occasionally would drive the store's '46 Dodge panel truck up to St. Louis to go to a burlesque show. One time, after having too many shots of bad whiskey in a murky saloon down by the rail yard in St. Louis, Hooper took up the offer of a prostitute who had sidled up to him.

At first he was excited with the prospect, but as they made their way to her seedy hotel room and he got a look at the hooker in the street light, his ardor waned. She looked close to fifty, with frizzy bleached hair. Her lipstick ran messily all around her mouth, and when she turned to grin at him while pulling him along, the condition of her teeth disgusted him.

Then he just wanted to get away, but he had already stupidly given her the ten dollars, so he went along. She unlocked the door to her second floor room and he followed her in. It was lit by a dim bulb hanging from the ceiling. There was nothing in the room but a single iron-posted bed sagging in the middle and covered with a thin, stained sheet. The hooker unceremoniously dropped his hand, and with practiced ease, kicked off her heels, pulled off her fake cashmere sweater and stepped out of her skirt. She was wearing nothing underneath.

She stuck a pose, her hip trust out, her hands clasped over her head.

"So, are you ready to play, farm boy?"

Hooper looked down at the floor. He had never seen a naked woman before except in a girlie magazine, and those pictures were often blurry. He was afraid but curious, and when he finally raised his eyes to look at the nude woman before him, he was repulsed by the vision. It was not all as he had fantasized.

The hooker stepped up to him. "What's a matter, Slim? A little nervous are ya?" She reached out, undid his belt, unsnapped his trousers and jammed her hand down his boxers.

"Need a little help getting going?" She leaned in and whispered into his ear, all the while trying to get a reaction with her manipulations.

After a moment, she grunted, withdrew her hand and stepped back. She got down on her knees, loosened Hooper's belt and jerked down his pants. "I have an idea that might get you ready."

Startled, Hooper stepped back, and pulled up his clothes. "No!" he said.

The woman got up. She wasn't grinning anymore. She sneered at him.

"What's a matter? You don't like girls?" Cupping her hands under her sagging breasts, she pushed them out and wagged them around. "Hoochee, goochee, goochee," she said.

What happened next was muddled like a bad dream. Hooper remembered how his hand stung as it smashed into the hooker's face. She went down without a sound, crumpled in an obscene heap on the floor, her head cocked sideways, her eyes open as if she was looking for a lost earing along the baseboard. Blood, looking like black oil in the gloom, began to ooze out of her broad nose and mouth.

"Hey." He prodded at her rounded, loosely fleshed belly with the toe of his boot. "Hey."

There was no response. He crouched down and forced himself to bend in close to her face. He thought he detected faint whiskey-tinged breathing.

Hooper straightened up, and moving urgently, picked up the purse she had left beside the grubby bed and rifled through it until he found his ten dollar bill. He dropped the purse, stuffed the bill in his pocket, and went to the door.

He opened it a few inches, stuck his head out and looked both ways down the hall. There was no one around. He stepped out of the room. Just before quietly shutting the door behind him, he peeked back in.

"Bitch," he hissed.

Chapter 17

Gilbert Beamer favored laying on of hands in the evening. Usually his father would drive him to the person's house, or in some cases, an old folk's home or a hospital.

Gilbert would go in alone. Karl Beamer used to accompany his son, but when he got to be twelve or so, Gilbert asked to perform his healings by himself.

Karl was relieved not to have to watch the ritual. It always made him uneasy. From the time seven year old Gilbert had first cured a woman of debilitating headaches when he impulsively placed his hands on her temples, the father had felt that there was something not quite right about it. He knew that, in the Bible, Jesus himself had performed healings, but Karl had a nagging doubt about the goodness of Gilbert's acts. Sometimes he worried that it might be the work of the Devil.

Most people around Testament Hill believed Gilbert's powers were a blessing. On the surface, it seemed that only good came from his touch. But Karl Beamer knew his son better than anyone, except perhaps his mother, who, if she did have any suspicions, chose to keep them to herself.

Beamer perceived a subtle pattern after witnessing dozens of healings: there was a price to pay.

A couple of years earlier, Tommy Parker, the town barber, had acquired a wicked cough that just wouldn't go away. Beamer reluctantly consented when Tommy asked for Gilbert's help, even though he doubted that the consequences of Parker's thirty year, two-pack-a-day cigarette habit could be so easily purged. After Gilbert's laying on of hands, Tommy Parker's cough eased and the barber continued to puff away as always.

A month or so later, Tommy Parker fell asleep while smoking in bed. They found the charred remains of his body embedded in the burnt mattress after what was left of his bungalow had cooled down enough for investigators to comb through the ruins.

Then there was the time when Elise Petersen and her husband came to Beamer for a cure for her barrenness. They had been married for six years and were desperate for children. After Gilbert's laying on of hands, the Petersens were thrilled when she became pregnant with twins.

The first girl emerged healthy and pink, but her sister was a kneeling breech. Because of her position, the baby's umbilical cord became crimped during the birthing, cutting off the mother's oxygenated blood to her brain. As a result, the child developed severe palsy.

There were other unfortunate "coincidences" that followed Gilbert's healings, but Beamer chose not to think about them.

He was sitting in his pickup parked in front of the Widow Wheeler's place, waiting for Gilbert to come out. He checked his wristwatch and glanced at the front door, figured the healing would be over soon. Beamer rested his head back on the seat and closed his eyes.

People would always go to the father first to request a healing, then Beamer would confer with his son. Gilbert always agreed. Except one time.

The pastor from the Methodist church requested a healing for relief of his gout. Gilbert declined to help, at first saying he was not feeling well. Beamer knew his son was faking an illness. Gilbert later explained that he just didn't like the pastor. He thought the humorless, stiff old man was creepy. Beamer didn't press the issue, since he agreed with his son's assessment, although he couldn't tell him. After that one time, Gilbert hadn't refused any more healing requests.

That evening, Beamer had conferred with Thelma Wheeler's sister, Mavis, on the front stoop while Gilbert waited in the truck. Mavis said that Thelma had taken to getting up late and laying on the sofa in the living room all day, watching soaps on the television. Thelma complained of a pain in her abdomen that she said was only made bearable if she was still and reclined. A trip to the doctor and tests at the county hospital discovered no cause for her discomfort. The doctor had discreetly suggested to Mavis that perhaps her sister's condition was more a mental than physical nature. Mavis told Karl Beamer that she was hoping that a visit from his son Gilbert might raise her sister out of her malaise.

Beamer went back to his truck and spoke with Gilbert. His son agreed he would go in to see Thelma, who was at the time laying in her bed. Karl Beamer would wait outside.

After thirty minutes, Beamer was beginning to regret that last cup of coffee before leaving home when the front door opened and Mavis Wheeler came dashing out, her face pale.

"Hurry!"

"What is it?" Beamer said as he climbed out of the truck and rushed up the walk.

"Hurry!" Mavis repeated.

Beamer followed her into a bedroom at the rear of the house. Inside the room, Gilbert was sitting on a rocking chair in the corner with his ankles crossed and his hands clasped behind his head. He was swaying back and forth. A cigarette dangled from his mouth.

Beamer looked to the bed. It was empty.

"She's in the bathroom." Mavis answered his unspoken question.

The pair headed to the bathroom. Thelma was leaning over the sink putting on a heavy layer of mascara. She had the mascara brush in one hand and a lit cigarette in the other. Beamer was shocked to see that Thelma was wearing only red lace panties and matching bra that were obviously many sizes too small.

Thelma turned to them and smiled, her teeth stained with lipstick. "I haven't worn this get up in ages. I bought it for my honeymoon." She laughed and took a puff of her cigarette. "But now I think: why not wear it anyway?" She giggled. "Close your mouths you two, you look like morons."

"Thelma!" Mavis said, aghast. "Cover yourself!"

"Oh, don't be such a prude." Thelma put down her mascara brush and stepped up close to Beamer with a hand on her hip. "I'm sure Karl doesn't mind seeing me like this." She swept her hand across her body with a flourish. "Not bad for an old gal, eh, Karl?"

"Yes...I...well..." Beamer stammered.

Mavis grabbed a robe off the hook on the bathroom door and used it to block Beamer's view. "Shame on you, Karl Beamer!" She glared at her sister, who had turned back to the mirror and was now busy applying bright clown-like circles of rouge to her cheeks.

"Just what in God's name do you think you are doing, Thelma?" Mavis voice rose hysterically.

"I thought I'd go out tonight," Thelma sniffed. "Maybe over to Cagney's pub for a drink." She lifted her eyes to the ceiling. "What I'd really like to do is go to that new nightclub in Dansville, except I don't have a car." She looked at Beamer expectantly. "How about it, Karl, would you like to take me? We could have a good time." She winked.

Karl Beamer cleared his throat. "I don't think that would be a good idea, Thelma."

Mavis pushed Beamer back out of the doorway into the hall and closed the bathroom door behind them. "Karl." she whispered fiercely "What has Gilbert done?"

From the other side of the door Thelma was saying: "Well, I guess I'll just thumb a ride to Dansville."

Deputy Hooper shook out of his reverie, straightened up in the cruiser's seat. As he watched, the young couple at the gas station disengaged and walked off holding hands, disappearing into the darkness like specters.

He lit up another Pall Mall.

Ida Wagner - yeah, she turned out to be a bitch too.

Dark pictures now flickered through Hooper's memory, like an old-fashioned picture show. He squeezed his eyes tight, reached up and massaged them, hoping the images would fade away. A great surge of guilt and dread washed across his brain.

He cringed, as if waiting for the switch across his bare

buttocks. He could imagine his mother's voice, her breath hot and wet in his ear as if it was just yesterday.

"The devil has shone his evil light upon you!" Prudence Hooper was screeching. "I found Mrs. Ketchum's mouser, Caesar, hanging in the woods beyond the shed. That old tom be skinned naked, eyes gouged out. You think I don't know who done it?"

"Ma…" young Frank Hooper wailed. He was leaning up against the kitchen wall, his palms flat. His drawers were dropped down to his knees. He started to turn his head.

"Don't you eyeball me boy!" His mother's arm swung forward, the birch switch whistling in the air. It snapped across eleven year old Hooper's skinny buttocks.

It felt as if someone ran a lit blowtorch across his behind.

"I'll whip the devil right out of you, God as my witness!"

Another blaze of fire. Then another. Hooper bit down on his lip, hard, knowing from experience that his cries only incensed his mother to inflict more punishment.

Then, for a moment there was nothing.

Hooper remembered hearing the scuff of his mother's slippers across the kitchen floor, the scratching of a match, the sound of Prudence Hooper inhaling deeply and exhaling, the smell of burning tobacco.

"You can pull up your britches now," she told him.

The memories used to give Hooper instant stabbing headaches, but tonight they had little effect. *Doesn't mean nothing*, he thought.

Hooper opened his eyes. The moon had come up, its pale silver light casting wavering black shadows along the road. The pressing weight of remorse and dread lifted from him, replaced by an icy calm.

Everything's clear now.

Deputy Hooper smiled to himself, his teeth gleaming in the stark light.

Claire and Wilson walked down the street from the motel to Duggan's for an early dinner. Wilson had developed the photographs taken from the drill-hole camera in his room with a portable film processing kit he had brought from the university. Claire suggested that they study them over their meal.

"Boy, do I have a craving for a greasy burger and a mound of fries," Claire said as they sat down into a booth.

"Not me, I'm having the corned beef and cabbage." Wilson grinned. "Just like Mom used to make." He placed the envelope containing the photos on the table. "Let's eat before looking at these."

"Okay." Claire was studying the menu. "You really having corned beef and cabbage?"

"Yep. But not really like my mom used to make." Wilson scrunched up his face. "My mom was a pretty lousy cook, God bless her. She couldn't make a tasty meal to save her life."

Claire looked up. "Wilson, you're talking about your own mother."

Wilson lifted his shoulders. "We all made fun of her cooking. It was a running joke. It was all in good fun. She was a good sport about it."

Claire said, "Of course, nobody else volunteered to do the cooking."

"Of course," Wilson laughed. "My family and I loved her bunches. She had a heart of gold. My mom could see the good in the most pathetic bum on the street. She always had some change to spare so they could get a bite to eat, maybe get a fresh start. I always figured they'd use the money to buy a bottle of cheap wine."

"Well," Claire said, "I guess the world is what we make of it. If we think the world is bad, we will see evil everywhere, if we think it is good, the earth is a glorious place."

"What's your position, Claire?"

Claire put down her menu. "The jury's still out on that one."

"Well, I think it's both," Wilson said. "I think that's what makes the world go around, the struggle between good and evil, the yin and the yang, the light and the dark. Basically, you could call me a Manichean."

Claire smiled. "I see. I thought this month you were a Zen Buddhist."

"That was last month," Wilson said making fun of himself. "Now it's the philosophy of Mani."

The waitress took their orders and brought them coffee.

"I'm sure you are going to explain it all to me," Claire said after the waitress left.

"Of course,"

Claire watched incredulously as Wilson dumped four heaping teaspoons of sugar in his coffee.

"See," he began, "Mani was this guy who was born in Babylonia, in present day Iraq, around 200 AD. He was raised in a Judeo-Christian household, and was likely exposed to the Gnostic and Zoroastrian ideas floating around at the time. Also, he supposedly traveled to India and Afghanistan, where he probably was further influenced by the ideas of Hinduism and Buddhism."

Wilson took a sip from his cup and then continued. "Mani went on to develop his own theory about how things worked, which he believed succeeded and surpassed earlier teachings. He claimed to be the Paraclete, the last prophet of a line of prophets including Buddha, Zoroaster and Jesus."

"And his theory was…?" Claire prompted.

Wilson formed a small circle with his thumb and forefinger. "In a nutshell, Mani taught that the Earth is a battleground between the forces of Good and Evil, locked in an eternal struggle for dominance."

"Interesting," Claire said. "Where does God fit into this picture?"

Wilson leaned forward. "See, that's the thing: according to Manichaeism, God is *not* omnipotent, not an all-powerful being. Therefore, God isn't responsible for the bad things that happen. The bad power - Satan, if you will, is responsible."

Claire waved her spoon. "Well, that solves the problem of Evil, how bad things can happen to good, innocent people."

"Exactly. To me, it's intellectually tidy."

"I'm happy for you, Wilson. But I think it may not be that simple."

"Well, it's ultimately a mystery, I guess. Perhaps resolved by faith."

Claire reached into her blouse pocket, pulled out a piece of paper and placed it on the table. "Speaking of mysteries, take a look at this note I found slipped under my motel room door this morning."

Wilson reached out and unfolded it. It was printed in a neat cursive. He read it aloud:

Skander Grey Wolf
13 Standing Rock Trail

Ask about the Taima.

Regards,
Edith

Wilson cocked his head at Claire. "What are you going to do about it?"

"Probably nothing. Edith's a little eccentric."

"Cool. But maybe you should check it out."

"We'll see," Claire said doubtfully. "It might be interesting to pay this Skander guy a visit. Also, I was thinking of dropping by the Testament Hill library and doing some research through the newspaper archives about past droughts. It might give some us perspective on what's going on around here."

Wilson shrugged. "That would be cool too, I guess."

"Would you like to come?"

"Where?"

"To the library."

"Sounds just too exciting for me." Wilson smiled.

"However, I wouldn't mind going to see this Skander guy with you."

Claire shook her head. "I think it might be better if just I go. Two people might be a little too...intrusive. He may not be forthcoming. I'll just go myself."

Wilson made a mock pouting face.

"Before we start checking out the photos," Claire said, changing the subject, "did you notice that, from the seismic tests, the underground system at Doyle's generally went from northwest to southeast?"

"Not really."

Claire reached into her jacket, pulled out a large piece of paper. She unfolded it on the table and rotated it for Wilson to see.

"It's one of the USGS topographic maps of the area you brought," she explained. "See, here's Highway 23, and here," Claire tapped the map, "are the wells on Doyle's property." Claire traced her finger along the map. "And this would be the general track of the anomaly we discovered."

Wilson nodded. "Towards the Testament Hill mound."

"And if you continue along this line..."

"It goes towards where Audrey's sketch shows the location of the cave on the side of the mound."

Claire met Wilson's eyes. "I think it could be a connected system."

Wilson grinned. "It would be a gas to check out Audrey's cave. Maybe it's an opening to a huge system, like the Mammoth Cave in Kentucky."

"Maybe later." Claire moved her hand over the map and pointed to the area representing Doyle's property. "But remember, we're here to figure out why the wells are drying up."

Wilson drummed his fingers thoughtfully on the table. "Yeah, but the cave system could be related."

"I don't see how, exactly," Claire said. "Those caves have probably been there for thousands of years. Unless something is happening down there."

"Like what, Claire?"

"Beats me. Maybe it has to do with the heating of the motel pool."

"Some tectonic activity? The gates of hell opening up?" Wilson shook his head. "The owners are just pulling your leg about the pool."

The waitress came to their table with plates of food. Claire reached for her fork. "Let's eat, then take a look at those photos from down in the drill hole."

"You bet."

"Do they show anything interesting?"

"Very interesting indeed," he mumbled through a mouthful corned beef.

Chapter 18

After dinner with Wilson, Claire decided to take a brief shower and go right to bed. Before climbing into the tub, she touched necklace around her neck with the intention of removing it, but was distracted when she went back into the room to grab her shampoo.

While rinsing her hair, she looked down. The amulet was lying across the drain in a puddle of water. Apparently it had become free of the necklace during her shower. The water was gradually rising in tub. When she reached down and picked up the amulet, the drain gurgled and the water ran down.

Claire frowned. It seemed strange that the amulet dammed the water. It wasn't big enough to cover the strainer. On impulse, she placed it back down on the drain, and the water immediately began building up again. Alarmed, she snatched the amulet up, and again, the water rushed down the drain.

Claire hesitated. Caught between curiosity and fear, she started to lower it back down and then stopped, pulled the shower curtain back, leaned out and quickly placed the amulet on the sink.

It's just blocking the drain, she told herself, *nothing more.*

She shut her eyes, lowered her head so that the shower spray beat down on the back of her neck. After a minute, she turned off the water, stepped out of the tub and vigorously toweled herself dry. She pulled on a long T-shirt and slipped the amulet back over her head. Then she turned down all the lights and carried a chair up to the room window. She opened the curtains and sat down with her knees up to her chin and her long toes gripping the sill.

It had begun to drizzle outside. For a while, Claire mindlessly watched the play of the traffic lights reflecting off the droplets on the window pane.

Against her will, her thoughts turned to the phenomenon

of the water drain and the amulet. It didn't make any sense. There's no way the amulet could affect the water, she decided. It had to be an illusion. Perhaps the real cause was her moving her weight in the tub, which somehow changed the way it drained, maybe by slightly warping the bottom of the tub. Yeah, Claire nodded to herself, something like that. She pushed the issue to the back of her mind.

She tried instead to focus over what the down-the-hole photographs had shown.

The photographs from Wilson's contraption were dark and fuzzy but verified their suspicions: there was definitely a cave system under Doyle's property. And what's more, as far as they could tell from the images, it appeared to be dry, which by itself was not unusual. But since the water table was at a considerably higher level than the caves, as evidenced by the well history, they should be flooded. Water would have percolated through porous limestone rock and filled them.

Then Claire noticed something in the images that might provide an explanation. However, it only presented another, even more perplexing mystery: the walls of the cave in the picture looked to be vitreous - the surface was smooth and shiny as if the rock had been fused by being exposed to great heat and had basically turned into a glass. The only natural way to produce that kind of heat was through volcanic activity. Activity that would have occurred, of course, after the caves had been formed. Since Missouri hadn't had any volcanic events for a billion years or so, and the caves were most likely younger than two million years, the cave walls had to have been heated by some other event.

But what? Claire couldn't even guess.

Okay, so - she thought - *there's no water percolating into the caves because the walls have somehow been sealed by turning into glass.*

That answers one question. But now, another mystery: how did the walls become fused?

Claire chewed on a thumbnail. Then, an idea: what if it wasn't natural? What if it was purposely engineered to be kept dry? And what significance, if any, did it have to the lowering of the water table and the drying up of the wells?

She let her mind wander. Events replayed in random slices: The discovery of the cave; Gilbert's warning; Edith's story about the curse; the strange story of the amulet. There was a pattern somewhere in it, but Claire couldn't make it out. One thing was clear: It was all a little unnerving.

A cool wisp of air brushed the back of her neck and Claire turned to check the room. It was dark, but there was enough light coming in the windows to see there was nothing moving.

Tonight, even her room was subtly forbidding. Claire realized it brought to mind her dorm room back in college.

And that awful night ten years ago.

Claire got up, went over to the night table and pulled open the drawer. She grabbed her .38, went back and sat at the window, the revolver nestled in her lap. While idly running her fingers over its cool, slightly oily surface, she appreciated its precisely machined functionality; its stark singularity of purpose. It was a *weapon*, and she controlled it.

It gave her comfort.

She took a deep breath. She didn't want to replay the event of a decade ago, but at times, the recollection came back to her unbidden, often after a long day, when she was tired, alone and in a quiet place. The replay didn't do any good. Nothing could change what had happened. But still the memories would return like unwanted and frightening guests.

John Brannigan had been a detective in South Chicago. After years of experiencing firsthand the horrible things that people did to each other, Claire's father eventually turned into a misanthrope, viewing people with mistrust and disdain. He once said that he truly believed the world be a far better place without any human beings on the planet. His disillusionment and frustration left him sullen, argumentative and cranky. He started drinking to escape.

Claire's mother, witnessing what the job was doing to

her husband, convinced him to make a change. John Brannigan consented and after a few months of job hunting, he was hired to be a detective for the police department of a small college town in Missouri.

Claire was twelve when her family moved. Her parents bought a tidy white frame house two miles from the police station. It was also within walking distance of the college, where Claire eventually attended for her first two years of undergraduate work.

John Brannigan stopped drinking when he started the new job and soon became much like his old self, although he still retained a general distrust and wariness of people.

He insisted that all his children know how to defend themselves, and as part of his mentoring, would take them to a firing range to practice handling a firearm. Claire's two younger brothers had little interest in guns, and when they grew old enough to stand on their own, declined to go anymore to the range.

To her initial surprise, Claire found she enjoyed firing a gun. She liked the feeling of empowerment that came holding a weapon and the competition of target shooting.

The biggest draw for Claire though, was the chance to spend time alone with her father. It gave the two an opportunity to do something without the rest of the family diverting her father's attention. They developed a routine: shooting at the range and then going for chocolate fudge sundaes afterwards, which was their little "secret".

Claire eventually bought her own firearm, a single shot Beretta target pistol which she kept in a nice leather-bound case.

She had it with her that night, June 18, 1952.

It was just a few days before summer break at the university where Claire had gone away to complete her baccalaureate in geology. She had one more final to take before moving out of the dorm and going back home for the summer. Her last exam was for Psych 101, an easy requirement class. Claire felt confident about taking the exam, and decided to go to a gun range the evening before the test day to relax and fire off a few rounds.

On the way back to her dorm, Claire stopped at a corner store to pick up a few sundries, a bag of chips and some Royal Crown Cola.

She and her roommate, Mary, had planned on snacking while watching the new TV series called *Death Valley Days*.

Their dorm room was on the first floor of one of the oldest dormitories, Adams Hall. It was built in the 1920s for male students. When a new dorm was put up for the men, the hall was allocated for nursing students, which, at the time were exclusively female. Eventually Adams Hall became general housing for any female student.

The dorm was a dreary, chocolate brown brick structure with wood framed windows that were often difficult to open due to broken mechanisms and warped frames. As the days grew longer and hotter, students had the habit of leaving their windows wide open to allow outside air to circulate in the cramped rooms.

The campus police never determined how the assailant gotten into Claire and Mary's room. He may have crawled in through an open window, or just entered when the door was left unlocked.

He was waiting for Claire's roommate when she returned to her room that evening after taking a shower in the communal bathroom down the hall. Mary was wearing a bathrobe and had her towel in one hand and her soap and shampoo in the other. Interviewed later by the police detective, she couldn't recall if she had left their room door unlocked.

When she got into her room and turned to close the door, Mary told the police, her assailant came out of the shadows, grabbed her around the neck with one arm and held a knife to her throat with another.

"Scream and I'll cut you," he whispered, his breath moist against her ear. "I've been watching you, on campus, Mary. You've always ignored me. But I was meant to have you."

Mary fainted. As she collapsed she apparently caught the man off guard. She vaguely recalled slipping from his grasp to the floor and the assailant's knife nicking her throat. A tiny trickle of blood ran down her neck and was wicked up by the collar of her terrycloth robe.

When Mary regained consciousness, the man had dragged her to the bed, and was leaning over her, his breathing heavy and fast. He smelled of cigarettes and alcohol. He reached down, and with shaking hands undid the belt to her robe and tore it open.

"What...what's...happening?" Mary asked him.

The man climbed on to the bed and straddled her. He struggled with his belt buckle, cursing as it caught on the belt loops. He finally got it undone, unzipped his pants and was in the act of yanking them down when the dorm room opened.

Claire stood in the doorway, squinting into the dark dorm room, waiting for her eyes to adjust. Intuition told her something was not right. She could hear heavy breathing. It didn't sound at all like Mary's.

Then she heard Mary moan.

"Mary?" Claire said. "Mary, are you okay?"

There was a barely audible squeak.

Claire knelt on the floor, popped open her gun case and took out the Beretta. With practiced motion, she quickly chambered a round, reached up and clawed at the light switch on the wall.

The scene illuminated like a frame from a horror movie.

Claire took it all in with one look. "Get off her now, you bastard." she hissed.

The man twisted to face her. For a moment he froze, his eyes wide, hands still holding on to his waistband.

Claire leveled her gun at the man's chest. "Now!"

The man scrambled off the bed holding up his pants.

"Claire..." Mary sat up and pulled her robe across her body. "Help me!"

Claire brought her Beretta up and centered the sight between the assailant's eyes. The man's hands went up in the air. His pants slid down to his knees exposing yellowed briefs with a ragged waistband.

"I'm going to blow you away like a varmint," Claire said between clenched teeth.

Tears welled up in the man's eyes and ran down his cheeks. "Please..."

Claire had seen the man before - around campus, emptying trash bins and mowing the lawn. He was mid-thirties, unshaven, his hair matted and greasy looking. He was wearing a red and black flannel shirt. She remembered especially his eyes: under dark heavy eyebrows, black as obsidian, wet from tears.

"Please..." he repeated. He reached down with shaking hands and pulled up his pants.

Claire squeezed down on the trigger of the Beretta, steading herself for the recoil.

"Just let me go." The man's voice cracked like a teenager. "I swear I'll never do anything like this again. I don't know what got into me. I just have been a little mixed up lately."

"Claire..." Mary was saying. "...don't."

Tears dripped off the man's chin and splattered onto the floor.

Claire's gun lowered an inch.

The man took a deep breath and inched his way to the open window. "I was weak. I'll get help. I'll confess to my priest."

Claire wavered. For one split second the would-be rapist reminded her of her younger brother, the one who was always getting into minor scrapes with the law, constantly disappointing their parents, always giving pathetic excuses, always getting another chance.

Claire lowered her gun a couple more inches.

Seeing his chance, the man dove headfirst through the window.

"Oh shit!" Claire rushed to the window and pointed her

gun out.

With his arms and legs flailing wildly, the man was running through the gloom to the tree line at the edge of the field behind the dorm.

Claire took steady aim at the shadowy figure and fired.

The Beretta barked in her hand and the burning residue of the round's powder flared from the muzzle into the dusk.

The shadow kept running and disappeared into the trees.

A fog began to rise across the parking lot in front of the Sleep-Tite Motel. While she gazed through her motel room window into the mist, Claire could almost imagine the figure of Mary's attacker fleeing into the darkness. She raised her hand holding the .38 and aimed it out the window.

"Bang," She whispered.

She blinked. Then blinked again.

Something *was* moving in the field. A pure black silhouette of a man framed in a barely discernible bluish aura. Tall and wearing an impossibly large hat. No wait - maybe holding an umbrella.

Moving instinctively, Claire slipped out of her chair onto the floor so that she was below the level of the window. She crawled over to her purse, took out her compact, and staying low, crept back to the corner of the window. She opened the compact and raised it carefully, angling its mirror so that it reflected back to her eyes the image out the window.

But the mirror was too small and the image it returned was just black and grey blurs with yellowish blotches from the street lights.

Claire turned her head and looked back into her room. The only illumination was the feeble light coming in from the street.

Always make sure that you are against a darker background than your opponent, her had father told her. *Then you can see them and they can't see you.*

She pulled back from the window to make sure no stray light from the outside would fall upon her, and raised her head just enough to peek over the sill.

There were still bizarre black shapes in the field across the road, and if Claire fixed her eyes on one long enough, one would appear to move or shimmer, but she knew that was just her eyes playing tricks on her. Nothing that looked like a person. She fixed her eyes straight ahead in their sockets and moved her head side to side to scan the terrain. After a minute, Claire had convinced herself that what she thought was a person was her imagination working on a dark collage of tree trunks and bushes.

Nevertheless, she pulled the blinds closed before getting up off the floor and rechecking her door lock.

That night Claire slept with her revolver under her pillow.

Chapter 19

Wednesday morning

Edith got up early and drove to the Sunshine Café. It was her day off, and she was anxious for the Testament Hill public library to open and was too fidgety to sit around waiting in her apartment. She decided to stop at the café and have a cup of tea and an English muffin to kill time.

While she sipped her tea, keeping an eye on the wall clock advertising Nesbit's Orange Soda, she wondered if Doctor Brannigan had gotten the note she left at the motel. She was starting to have second thoughts about it, but of course, it was too late now. Claire Brannigan had probably already read it.

Edith nodded to herself. It was the right thing to do. She had a notion that the geologist needed to know the whole story. Destiny had brought the young woman to Testament Hill. And there was something in Claire's eyes that had impressed Edith: a certain strength, plus a wisdom that belied the her age.

Edith reviewed her plan.

She would ask Dorothy, the librarian, for copies of all the Testament Hill Citizen Newspapers from 1950 to 1953. That was her best guess where she might find the articles she was searching for.

The first article would be about the infamous Christmas train wreck. Edith couldn't recall the exact year, but she remembered it was right before the holiday. If she asked Dorothy, she would probably know. But Edith wanted to keep her research a secret. She didn't want to arouse suspicions.

At nine o'clock, Edith got up, paid her bill and walked the block down Main Street to the library. For a few minutes, she made small talk with Dorothy. Then, feigning a casual tone, she asked the librarian if she could take a look at some newspaper archives, explaining she wanted to research an old obituary.

Dorothy raised her eyebrows but was too polite to question Edith's request, and in minutes, Edith was sitting at a table with a pile of bound, archived *Testament Hill Citizen* newspapers.

She found the issues for the weeks following Christmas 1950. Christmas was on a Monday that year. *The Testament Hill Citizen* came out once a week on Wednesday. There was nothing in the December 27th paper about the train wreck. Then she shuffled flipped to the next issue published on January 3rd, 1951.

Edith's skin pricked. There it was on the front page, in bold 144 point block letters:

HELL COMES TO TESTAMENT HILL
34 DEAD
Train Wreck Causes Huge Blast
Dozens Injured

Edith scanned the article. The Milwaukee Road Hiawatha came into town at 7:10 p.m. on Christmas Eve. The express train consisted of two diesel-electric locomotive units pulling six coaches and was passing through Testament Hill on the way from St. Louis to Little Rock. It was sleeting heavily and the sleet was reflecting back the locomotive's headlights into the cab, limiting visibility to one hundred feet. The signal lights were all green. The engineer kept the throttle steady at sixty-five MPH, in spite of the poor conditions. He was running late.

He either did not see the switch flag, or wasn't paying attention. Otherwise, he would have noticed that the switch was turned to direct the train onto a spur that ran by the mill.

The three hundred thousand pound locomotive thundered down the spur, smashed through the bumper stop and hurtled across the mill's parking lot. Behind it, the unmanned B engine unit uncoupled from the rest of the train, twisted onto its side and slid through the gravel, angling across the lot until it was stopped by a grain silo's thick concrete walls.

The lead locomotive continued upright, plowing across the lot. The passenger coaches uncoupled from the engines and careened along behind the lead unit.

The engineer and fireman probably stared out the cab in paralyzed horror as the locomotive shot irrevocably toward a liquid propane storage tank. The massive impact of the locomotive split the one thousand gallon container in half. Freed from its pressurized confinement, the propane instantly vaporized. A second later, the cloud of gas detonated.

The explosion blew out windows on homes a mile away.

The engineer and fireman in the cab were killed along with all thirty-two passengers in the first coach, whose momentum had carried it into the inferno. The other five coaches veered off at the last second and were spared the brunt of the explosion and fire. Many passengers in those coaches were seriously injured but no one was killed.

Some survivors reported seeing a strange flash of blue light through the windows seconds before the crash.

There was no determination as to how the track had been switched to direct the main traffic into the spur. The spur had last been used three days earlier to load some grain cars from the mill. After that, three trains had passed safely through on the main, the last on December 21.

It was believed that someone had either mistakenly or maliciously switched the spur back onto the main sometime between the last through train and the evening of the accident. The person responsible was never identified.

On the front page of the newspaper there was a picture of the aftermath of the disaster: a crowd of onlookers standing in the sleet. Edith picked herself out, standing in the background. She had come into town that evening to attend Christmas Eve mass.

Edith bent closer and peered intently at the photograph.

And there he was.

Just as she remembered after all this time: a tall man in

dark clothing. He was standing apart from the other onlookers, one arm held behind his back, the other holding a large black umbrella. She pulled her magnifying glass out of her purse and held it over the picture. The face of the man was indistinct.

Edith could feel the throb of blood in the veins in her neck. Her hands shaking, she reached back to the pile of archives and located the issue for June 3rd, 1953.

It was the most painful day in her life: the day they lost Harold Jr., their precious six year old son.

He was killed while riding the bus home from school.

Edith took a deep breath and opened the paper.

The article was brief:

A Stearman Kaydet biplane was spraying pesticides over a nearby potato field at tree top level. The pilot wasn't aware of the newly strung power lines running along the road, or perhaps had been distracted by something on the ground. The lines sheared off the tail, and the plane cartwheeled into the side of the school bus which, as fate would have it, was passing by.

The plane's wings were fabric-covered wood and broke apart and scattered around the bus. But the five hundred pound radial engine bolted to a welded steel airframe tore through the side of the bus, taking her Harold Jr. and two other students to be with the Lord.

Edith looked down. She squeezed her eyes shut then slowly opened them and forced herself to examine the photograph taken at the crash site. The image threatened to inflame the old heartache that was always with her. She mentally pushed the rising anguish away and studied the picture.

There was the tangled mess of the collision, a fire engine, an ambulance, the Chief's car and a Highway Patrol car. A few people were visible standing at the scene. Edith recognized a young-looking Chief Childress. There was John Wheeler from the fire department. There were a couple other males she could not identify.

But none of them were the tall dark man.

Edith turned to the next page of the paper and there was

a modest article about the graveyard memorial service for Harold Jr. and the two other children killed in the accident, accompanied by a picture.

And there standing in the background, a grainy image:

The dark man. Towering above the others.

The hard, dull ache in the back of Edith's head began to push its way across her skull to her forehead. She reached for her purse and dug around for her migraine pills.

She must warn Claire.

Chapter 20

Chief Childress walked to the station that morning, and was thankful to see the Plymouth back in the lot. Claude Wiggins must have finished working on it and dropped it off.

Good. Deputy Hooper had his car back, and the Chief his.

Instead of going into the office, Childress climbed into the Ford Interceptor parked next to the Plymouth and drove off. He took the highway out of town. The crimson tops of the maples and oaks that sat high on the ridge lines glowed in the rising sun. He settled back into his seat.

He wasn't quite ready to face the day - dealing with Edith's chatter; getting the shift report from Deputy Hooper; working on next year's budget; calling Captain Norris, as he'd promised, about any developments in the case of the missing trooper.

He rolled down the window and took a deep breath. The cool air was tinged with the musky scent of fallen leaves. "Now, this is the way to start the day." he said to the crows perched on the telephone lines following the highway.

His reverie was interrupted by the crack of static from his two-way police radio.

"Chief Childress, are you there? Over." It was the State Highway dispatch. They handled Testament Hill's calls on Edith's day off.

Damn.

He grabbed his mike and pressed the transmit button. "Childress. Go ahead. Over."

"Got something you might want to check out, Chief, over."

"What is it? over," Childress growled. *Cat stuck up in a tree?*

"Ralph Jackson, the newspaper boy, called in this morning and said Mrs. Wagner hasn't picked up her papers off her porch for a couple of days, over."

"Maybe she's away. On a trip or something, over."

The radio chirped and buzzed. "...says she always tells him if she's going out of town, over."

Childress sighed, slowed his car and made a slow U-turn. "I'm on my way. Over and out."

Claire was on the phone that morning with Benjamin Trask. She had been studying the photographs taken down in the bore holes, and for the life of her, could not come up with any explanation for the glass-like walls. So she sent copies to Ben and was hoping he might have a suggestion for the cause.

"Well, first of all, thank you for sending me the photographs," he said.

"Thank you, Ben, for taking a look at them."

"No problem." Claire could hear him clear his throat, like he always did before launching into one of his "lectures". Normally, she found it kind of endearing, but this morning, it struck her as irritating in its predictability and officiousness.

"First of all, I concur that it certainly appears that the walls of the cave have been subjected to extreme heat," he said.

"Yes, Ben, but what kind of volcanism are we talking about?"

Trask cleared his throat again, and Claire grimaced. "That's the thing," he said. "I don't believe this is a result of volcanic processes."

"I understand, Ben, but what else could it be? What else but magma could produce enough heat to literally melt the walls of the cave?"

"Frankly, Claire, I am at a loss," Trask said. "The heat that causes volcanism, the release of molten magma, as you know, is ultimately caused by nuclear reactions taking place deep in the core, or trapped from the energy of Earth's original formation when it was being constantly struck by cosmic debris. There has been no volcanism in that area for at least a billion years. Any evidence of it, such as your melted rock, would be long gone."

Claire tried to hide her impatience at the lecture in freshman geology.

"Ben, if it's not a geologic phenomenon, are you saying that the vitrification was not natural? Man-made?"

"Well...no, I can't think of anything artificial that could do that. It would take an enormous amount of energy...almost nuclear."

The word *nuclear* triggered a memory in Claire. "Ben, what about an Oklo event?" she said excitedly. "A naturally occurring nuclear reactor?" She was recalling reading about a discovery in East Africa.

For a moment there was silence at the other end of the line.

"Claire, that seems highly unlikely." Trask said finally. "As you know, the Oklo site in East Africa is the only known occurrence where enough uranium ore accumulated in sufficient purity to create a natural nuclear reactor."

"I know, Ben, but it's the only *known* example. There could be more as yet undiscovered."

"The odds..."

"I can't think of any other explanation for the heat source that caused the walls to turn virtually into glass." Claire interrupted.

Ben Trask clicked his tongue, and Claire was thankful not be talking to him in person, because she was sure she would have swatted him.

"Claire, note that the Oklo natural reactor was operating at least 1.5 billion years ago when the natural concentration of fissile uranium was high enough to support a chain reaction. Plus, the site had just the right combination of groundwater to moderate or slow the neutrons down enough to sustain a reaction."

"What about graphite as a moderator?" Claire asked.

"Of course. It's used in commercial reactors. How is that pertinent?"

"What about coal? There are some seams around here in Missouri."

Trask sighed. "Claire, you're stretching credibility. Forget about that idea. I don't know...maybe there was some kind of factory or smelting operation at one time around there and they dumped molten waste into the caves."

"Well, Ben, now you're the one stretching credibility. Damn it, something odd is going on here."

For a moment the neither spoke. The hissing static of the open phone line increased in intensity, and began to congeal into a series of more harmonious groupings. To Claire it almost sounded like the murmur of a distant crowd.

"Claire..." Benjamin Trask said, hesitation in his voice, "When are you coming back? ...I miss you."

There was another moment of silence.

"Soon, Ben. I just need to figure out what's going on here in Testament Hill. It's quite a curious situation."

"I understand. It's just that I can't wait to have you sitting across from me at Alejandra's Bistro sharing a bottle of Chianti."

Claire guessed that Ben probably thought that was a romantic suggestion. That had been their routine for the last two years or so. Now, it seemed to her so mundane. And boring.

She said, "Maybe we could do something different for a change. You know, something a little more exciting."

"Exciting?" A tone of sarcasm crept into Ben's voice.

"Ben, it's not that I don't enjoy our time together. It's just that... perhaps our relationship had gotten a little stale."

"Jesus, Claire. What's gotten into you in Testament Hill? What the hell is going on up there?"

"Nothing, just trying to clear up a geological mystery."

"Okay." Ben sounded resigned. "How about I send you a Geiger counter. If you find high radioactivity in your caves, then we'll revisit your nuclear reactor theory."

"I was hoping you'd say that. You're a prince, Ben. Oh, and one more thing..."

Another sigh. "Yes?"

"Can you send it next day delivery?"

After her conversation with Ben, Claire drove to the town library. She wanted to see if there were any materials there that might shed some light on what was going on at Testament Hill.

The library was housed in a small blue clapboard building on a side street on the edge of town. When Claire walked in, the place was deserted except for a diminutive blue-haired woman behind the desk wearing a pair of pince-nez spectacles. She looked up as Claire walked in and beamed.

"Well, good morning to you, Doctor Brannigan."

Claire stopped in her tracks.

"It's a small town, Miss Claire," the librarian explained.

Claire went up to the desk. "Of course."

"I'm Dorothy, by the way," the woman said, sweeping off her spectacles, and still beaming. "How may I be of assistance?"

It occurred to Claire that the librarian was probably thrilled to have a visit from someone outside of town.

"I was wondering if you might have some material related to the history of the area," Claire said.

Librarian Dorothy pursed her lips. "Of course. But I'm afraid we don't have much. We're a small operation, you know. I'm afraid you will disappointed. Is there anything in particular you're interested in?"

"Early history, the first settlement, anything about the native tribes, any early geological studies."

Dorothy studied the top of her desk as if she might find an answer written there. She shook her head slowly. "Not that I can think of. I'm sorry. We don't have much reference or historical material, unfortunately." The librarian waved her hand at the book shelves. "Fiction, mostly. Classics and a few more modern works - Hemingway, Faulkner and such."

"I see. Well, thank you." Claire turned to leave.

"Doctor Brannigan?" Dorothy's voice was guarded.

"Yes?"

"I do have something I think you might be interested in."

Claire stepped back to the desk. "Please, call me Claire."

"Of course...Claire, then it is." Dorothy smiled shyly. "Anyway, I feel in my bones that fate has brought you to Testament Hill."

"I see..." Claire said, puzzled by Dorothy's remark, "I'm here to see why the wells are running dry."

"Of course you are, dear, no doubt about that." Dorothy reached under her desk and brought out a small, tattered, leather-bound book and held it out to Claire. "I think you might want to take a look at this. You can return it whenever you're ready."

Claire reached out and took the book. Close up, the leather binding appeared to be hand stitched. It was secured with a small tarnished brass clasp. A musty odor wafted off it. Claire began to release the clasp.

"Please, don't open it now," the librarian said. "Take it with you. You'll need to take your time studying it. I hope you can figure it out, I haven't had much luck. Just bring it back when you are through. I'm sure you will take good care of it."

"What is it?"

"I think it might be a journal. It's handwritten in ink, looks like it was probably done with a quill pen. The first page is in English. After that, I can make out dated entries, but the rest is gibberish. "

"How did you get it, if you don't mind me asking?"

"It's been in my family for years. My grandfather found it in 1900, in an old root cellar he unearthed on his farm. It was originally wrapped in copper, I guess to protect it."

The journal felt suddenly heavy in Claire's hands. She gripped it tighter. "Why, thank you, Dorothy, for letting me take a look at it. I'll be certain to tell you what I find out, and return it in original condition."

"No hurry," Dorothy assured her. "It's been sitting around here for years, just gathering dust."

As soon as she got back into her car, Claire set the book in her lap, released the clasp and opened to the first page. It was blank. She took a corner between her forefinger and thumb and gently rubbed it. It felt velvety and dense to the touch. The page wasn't paper. She bent her head closer to examine it. There was a very faint pattern in the medium.

Vellum, Claire said aloud.

The page was made from animal skin, probably from a calf. The pattern was left from the imprint of tiny veins. She carefully turned to the next page. Penned in an elegant calligraphy at the top:

> *Journal of Uaine Fionn, Soldier of Army of Christ and Protectors of the Truth, year of our Lord, 1811*

Grace and Peace unto you,

Account of quest to the New World from County Mayo, Eire.

With her heart racing in anticipation, Claire turned to the next page. As Dorothy had described, at the top was an entry:

December 15, 1811.

Claire's eyes dropped down the page. It was filled with carefully wrought script. She quickly flipped through the rest of the journal.

Her heart sank.

It was all in the same unreadable script. At first glance it looked like random letters, but as Claire scanned the pages, she sensed that there was a pattern. It was a code of some kind, she was sure of it.

Whoever this Uaine Fionn was, he did not want just anyone reading his journal.

Claire closed the journal, re-clasped it, put it on the passenger seat and started the Volvo.

Maybe Wilson can make sense of it, she thought.

The phone jangled her awake with a start.

With one hand, Claire reached under her pillow for her gun, and with the other picked up the receiver. She glanced at the alarm clock: it was 5 p.m.

"Hello?" she said, her voice raspy from sleep.

"It's me. Are you okay Claire, you sound funny?"

"I was just taking a nap."

Wilson voice was excited. "I got it."

For a moment Claire said nothing, clearing the cobwebs from her mind. Then she sat upright. "You figured out the code."

"Yep. Come down to my room to see."

"Wilson..."

"Come on," Wilson insisted, "I've spent a solid four hours figuring this out. It's the least you can do."

"Give me five minutes."

The pair sat on the edge of the bed in Wilson's motel room. Claire studied some hastily scribbled sheets of paper in her lap. "How did you manage to decode it?"

Wilson was obviously pleased with himself. "By the way, it's more properly called 'encryption' and 'decryption'. From the Greek word *kryptos*, meaning 'hidden'."

"Okay, got it, Wilson, thanks. Now: what do you have?"

"It wasn't hard, once I had the inspiration."

"And that was...?"

"I was thinking of ancient techniques for encrypting messages while studying the manuscript," Wilson recounted. "Then it hit me - wham."

"Yes...?"

"*Scytale.*"

"Scytale?"

"Yep." Wilson spelled the word out. "It rhymes with 'Italy'. It's ingenious, simple, but very practical. It was used in ancient times for military communication because it was fast and not prone to mistakes. The word 'scytale' comes from the Greek meaning 'baton'. I recalled reading about it in my ancient history class."

Wilson was relishing revealing his discovery, so even though Claire was anxious to get to the translation of the manuscript, she forced herself to be patient, letting him enjoy the moment. "Go on," she said.

Wilson grinned. "Okay. Scytale is a type of transposition cipher, where letters are shifted around to make the message unintelligible." He made a shuffling motion with his hands. "The key is the scytale itself: a baton, usually a wooden cylinder. A strip of paper is wound around the cylinder. The message is written in a straight line across the axis of the cylinder. When the strip of paper is unwound, the letters appear as a random jumble. Only if it is rewound around a cylinder of the same diameter does the *plaintext* appear."

"Very clever," Claire nodded. "So if you know the diameter of the scytale, you can figure out the spacing of the letters to convert back to plaintext."

"Exactly." Wilson pointed to the papers in Claire's hand. "Once I hypothesized the encryption method, I guessed the wrap parameter pretty quickly: it's six. So to read the message, you start with the first letter, first word; skip five letters; write down the sixth, and so on, assembling words. It was really tedious, so I made myself a scytale."

With a flourish, Wilson pulled out a cardboard tube from beside the bed. "I was carrying maps in this," he explained. "I tried making a couple of cylinders from scrap paper, without much luck, then on an impulse, used this. It worked perfectly, the circumference happened to be correct."

"Great, so what have got?"

"The journal made sense…sort of."

"What do you mean, sort of?"

Wilson lifted his shoulders. "How's your Latin?"

"You read Latin, Wilson?"

"Nope."

"Then how would you determine the wrap parameter?"

"Most European languages have a similar occurrence and relative placement of consonants and vowels," Wilson explained. "So even if you don't know the language, something like 'dorele' is much more likely to be a correct decryption then 'hfvklk'."

Claire looked down at Wilson's transcription. "I took a Latin course in college." She furrowed her brow. "I can make out some words, like *Saluto Pluriman Dicit:* it means basically 'Many Greetings'."

After a moment, she shook her head. "I can't remember enough Latin to read all of this."

Wilson said, "I have a professor friend at Harvard who is an expert in Latin."

Claire looked up. "Send it today."

Claire and John Preston had arranged to meet at Duggan's at seven for drinks and dinner. Instead of sitting at the bar, they settled down at a corner table and were enjoying a couple of cocktails before eating.

Claire was anticipating a possibly romantic evening when Wilson walked into the bar. Tucked under his arm was a globe of the earth. He immediately spotted the pair and hurriedly walked over.

"Shit," Claire said under her breath.

"Hey, you two," Wilson said cheerfully as he got to their table.

Claire lifted her hand. "Mike Wilson, meet John Preston, he's the evangelist heading up the revival at the fairgrounds. John, this is Mike Wilson, my associate from the university."

Claire thought she detected a shadow of disappointment crossing Preston's face. He looked up at Wilson. "Pleased to meet you."

"I'll just be a minute." Wilson settled on the edge of a chair. "I don't want to interrupt your evening."

Claire said, "We're just having a drink together."

"Of course." Wilson looked at Preston. "I'm Claire's graduate assistant. You know - a gofer and minion."

Claire shook her head. "You're much more than that, Wilson. You're a valuable asset."

Wilson ignored her remark. "Claire is a brilliant geologist, Preston. She's done some groundbreaking research. Had many papers published. I'm lucky for the opportunity to work for her."

"I don't doubt that," Preston said.

"Well, then," Claire said, "if we are done with our mutual admirations, Wilson, why on earth are you carrying a globe into a bar?"

Wilson laughed. "Sounds like the beginning lines of a joke: 'A pretty geologist and an evangelist are sitting in a bar, and a handsome young man walks in carrying a globe…"

"Harr, harr," Claire said. "Seriously, what's with the prop?"

Wilson held the globe out. "I just had this flash and had to tell somebody. This little beauty was graciously lent to me by Mr. B at the motel."

Claire could tell that Wilson was eager to reveal his idea. He was constantly coming up with crazy notions. Admittedly, as often as not, he would be on to something.

"Tell me what you got " she said.

"I've been thinking of our conversation about the Biblical flood, Claire," Wilson began. "Question: if a worldwide flood did happen, what could have caused it?"

Wilson waited for a reaction. Claire and Preston were looking at him expectantly. He shrugged and held up the globe.

"Let's suppose, first of all, there *was* a flood - the deluge described in the Old Testament. As you may know, tales a devastating flood are common in the recorded myths of the ancient world. Besides the story of the flood in the Bible, there is mention of it in older Sumerian tales such as the *Epic of Gilgamesh*. Even in North America, many native tribes have stories of a flood."

Wilson pointed to the western hemisphere. "The Pawnee have a tradition that the first people on earth were big and strong and did not believe in Ti-ra-wa, the Creator. Ti-ra-wa became angry and caused a flood that caused the giants to sink into the earth."

"Interesting," Preston rubbed his chin.

Wilson tapped the globe with his finger. "Now, there is a theory that the stories of a great flood may have originated from catastrophic releases of trapped water from the melting of glaciers from the last ice age."

Claire said, "Glacial lake outbursts."

Preston looked questioningly at her.

"It's what happens when water built up behind melting glacial ice is released suddenly," she explained. "For example, the Missoula floods were caused by the breaching of ice dams in Montana at the end of the last ice age, releasing an immense quantity of water from glacial Lake Missoula."

"We're talking about a huge flood," Wilson piped in. "Consider this: Lake Missoula was the size of one of the Great Lakes. Think of that emptying in *hours*. The flow is estimated to have been ten times the flow of all the present rivers in the world combined. Peak rates of sixty *cubic kilometers* of water flowing every hour, moving at up to eighty miles per hour. The raging waters created the scablands of eastern Washington state, washing away the soil, scouring the rock and creating deep channels for hundreds of miles."

Preston's eyebrows went up. "Wow."

"Yeah, we're talking about a *flood*." Wilson bounced the globe in his hand. "And, they're also pretty sure that the English Channel was carved out by another glacial outburst, hundreds of thousands of years ago during an earlier ice age. One or more of these floods could be the inspiration for the deluge stories."

Claire said, "But there are some caveats with associating a glacial outburst with the Biblical flood."

"What would they be?" Preston asked.

"First of all, the timing is wrong," Claire said. "The last glacial outbursts occurred around twelve to eight thousand years ago. A little early to account for estimates of the Biblical flood."

Preston held up a forefinger. "Not necessarily. The date of the Flood could possibly be that far back. Traditional dates calculated from the Bible would place the flood roughly four to five thousand years ago. But eight is not out of the question, historically."

"But there's another problem," Wilson countered. "Because the Biblical event wasn't just a flood."

Preston closed his eyes for a moment. Then he opened them and tapped his temple. "The deluge. The forty days and nights of *rain*."

"Exactly," Wilson nodded enthusiastically. "The outpouring due to a glacial flood would not cause the heavy rainfall as described in the Bible. Of course, the number forty may be symbolic. For example, the Israelites wandered in the wilderness for forty years after the exodus from Egypt; Moses was up on Mount Sinai for forty days; Jesus fasted in the desert for forty days before his temptation by the Devil."

"The Deluge..." Preston closed his eyes and recited from memory: " '*The fountains of the deep were broken up, and the windows of heaven were opened. And the rain was upon the earth forty days and forty nights.*' "

"And that brings me to my last point," Wilson looked at Claire and back to Preston. "Question: what event could cause the fountains of the earth to open up and bring on a torrential downpour that lasts days or weeks?"

For a moment, Claire and Preston stared blankly at Wilson. Then Claire sat back in her chair and snapped her fingers. "An *impact event*."

Preston turned to her. "A what?"

"Bingo." Wilson spun the globe in his hands and then jabbed his finger at it. "A collision between Earth and a celestial object. Like the one that caused the Barringer Crater in Arizona."

"I've actually been there," Preston said, "on one of my cross-country revivals. It's quite amazing."

"Indeed," Claire said. "However, the Barringer asteroid was relatively small. If we look at the moon, or even Mars, we see impact craters from objects *miles* in diameter. The Earth's had its share of big collisions, too. We don't see most scars of past collisions on the Earth because they have been obliterated by thousands, even millions of years of erosion from water, wind, and tectonic activity."

"Right," Wilson brought the globe forward. "Now suppose an asteroid, about a quarter of a mile in diameter, hit the Earth. Say in came down the Atlantic. Say it happened around ten thousand years ago. Consider what effects that would have."

"A cataclysmic pulse of water, causing wide spread tsunamis." Claire answered. "And then…" she paused for effect. "torrential rain from the tremendous amount of water vapor that would have been blasted into the atmosphere from the heat of impact."

"Dig it, Preston," Wilson said, "With a rock that big, traveling through the atmosphere doesn't slow it down much. It heats up from friction with the air to become incandescent, but it arrives almost at full speed, which is going to be ten miles a second. That's around thirty-six thousand miles an hour."

"Unbelievable." Preston shook his head.

Wilson bobbed his head. "Yes, it's definitely burning rubber. It punches through to the sea bottom. Normally large asteroids are estimated to penetrate about as deep as their diameter before exploding. Figure this bullet from space drives in a quarter of a mile before it stops. Think of the momentum the asteroid has, with its mass of say, roughly ten million tons, going ten miles a second."

"It's basic physics, Preston," Claire added. "This rock is traveling thirty times the speed of a rifle bullet. And a bullet weighing millions of tons. All that energy is released when the asteroid bullet is stopped. Equivalent to how many atomic bombs…?" Claire looked at Wilson.

Wilson scrunched up his eyes. "Let's see…the yield of the Hiroshima bomb was around six Tera joules…say the asteroid has a mass of nine hundred million kilograms with a velocity of ah…16,000 meters per second…the kinetic energy is of course, one-half the mass times the velocity squared…" Wilson blinked hard a couple of times. "Roughly thirty thousand Hiroshima A-bombs."

"Thank you sir." Claire bowed to Wilson and turned to Preston. "Now most of that energy would be converted to heat, vaporizing a tremendous volume of water and sending it into the atmosphere. As the water cooled and condensed, the result would be a torrential global-wide rain that could continue for weeks, months. Coupled with the tsunamis generated by its impact, we have something that would fit the historical description of the Flood."

"So," Preston leaned forward, "something like an asteroid hitting Earth caused the flood of the Bible? That's your theory?"

"Yep," Wilson said. "I believe that the deluge of Genesis could be an account of an actual historical event that describes the destruction caused by an impact event." Wilson ran his hand across the globe. "Much of human settlement back then was around bodies of water, and for that matter, still is, for obvious reasons. Water is not only used for drinking, but for irrigation, sources of food and transportation."

"So humans would be especially susceptible to the impact effects because of our natural inclination to settle near large bodies of water," Preston concluded.

"Exactly," Claire said. "The coastal civilizations bordering the Atlantic Ocean would be swept away, and huge tidal waves would rush hundreds of miles up the rivers. "

"A random strike from outer space..." Preston mused, finishing off his cocktail. He looked in turn at Wilson and Claire. "...or perhaps not so accidental."

"What are you saying, Preston?" Claire asked.

"One could interpret the deluge in Genesis as God's way of destroying the corruption brought by the offspring of the Fallen Angels, the Nephilim."

Claire studied his face for a moment. "So, Preston, God caused an asteroid to strike the Earth to destroy the Nephilim and corrupted mankind?"

"...and cast Samyaza and the rest of the Fallen, into the bowels of the Earth," Preston added.

"Do you really believe that?"

"God works in mysterious ways," Preston was smiling, but Claire got the impression he was dead serious.

Chapter 21

Thursday morning

Claire couldn't wait to get back to Doyle's farm after she received the Geiger counter sent by Ben Trask. Over Wilson's objections, the pair skipped breakfast and headed out in his Jeep.

At nine-thirty a.m. they arrived at the farm and explained to Amos Doyle their plan. With some reluctance he consented, and told them he could be found back by the chicken coops if they needed him.

Wilson quickly rigged an extension cable to the Geiger counter so that they could lower the sensor tube into the bore hole they had used for the camera while the meter stayed above ground. As they were preparing to lower the tube, a screen door slammed. Claire looked over to see Ivy bounding down the porch stairs.

"Hey, you guys!" She waved and ran towards them.

Claire waved back. "Hey yourself, Ivy,"

Ivy stopped short, eyeing the Geiger counter in Wilson's hand. "What's that?" she asked. "A Geiger counter? I've never seen one in real life before, only in a magazine. That's neato."

Wilson grinned at Ivy. "It is. Do you want to see it work?"

"Yes, please."

"Okay." Wilson crouched down so Ivy could see. "In this yellow metal box," he explained, "is the power and an amplifier to boost up the signal from the Geiger-Muller tube."

"And that's a volt meter." Ivy pointed to the dial with a needle and gradation marks.

"Yeah, pretty much. It's a read-out that gives us a visual of how much radiation is getting into the tube."

"It also clicks to tell you radiation is present."

Wilson was obviously impressed. "That's right."

"I read about it in some magazine at the library," Ivy explained.

Claire was listening to the exchange. "Well, I think it's really cool that a little girl like you has such an interest in science," she said.

Ivy eyes widened. "What does being a girl have to do with it?"

"You got me there, miss." Claire smiled and looked into Ivy's huge dark eyes which seemed to be glowing from an inward fire.

"I just think it's really nice how science can find out how stuff in the world works," Ivy said.

"Yes," Claire said, "Science helps us find the truth."

Ivy giggled.

"What's funny about that?" Claire asked.

"But does it tell you *why*?"

"What do you mean, Ivy?"

"Why flowers are beautiful." Ivy turned her palms up. "Why chocolate cookies are so delicious. Why my grandpa loves me and I love him."

Claire was momentarily left speechless by the profundity of the young girl's question.

"Well...I..."

"She's got you there." Wilson laughed. He was down on his knees slowly lowering the probe down the bore hole. After a couple of minutes of playing out the cable, he stood up. "I think we're in the cave."

Claire watched expectantly while he picked up the meter box and twirled some knobs. It immediately began clicking.

"I'll be damned, Claire," Wilson said, staring at the meter. "You were right: there's a high level of radioactivity down there. Way more than any normal natural occurrence."

Claire looked over his shoulder. "Enough to be the residue of a nuclear reaction that melted the walls of the cave?"

Wilson shrugged. "I don't know. I'm not a nuclear physicist. It seems like it would take a hell of a lot of reacting to do that. The melting temperature of limestone is what? 2,500 degrees?"

Claire nodded. "There's a lot a variables, but yeah, I think we have to be looking at something that high that to vitrify the cave walls."

"Well, it's obviously not that hot now. It would have vaporized the equipment we sent down." Wilson tapped the meter on the Geiger counter.

Ivy, who had been watching the procedure, apparently lost interest and skipped off towards the house.

"See you later, Ivy," Wilson called after her.

Ivy waved a hand over her head. "For sure."

Claire crossed her arms and thoughtfully rubbed her boot in the dry dirt. "I need to go down and take a look," she announced.

Wilson gave her a quizzical look.

Claire pointed to the barn. "Down the old hand dug well under the windmill: I saw something there the other day."

"What did you see?"

"Possibly an opening into the cave system. At the bottom of the well there was a black area on the wall. It looked like it could be a passage."

"That's crazy, Claire." Wilson stood up and began reeling in the Geiger tube from the test hole. "We don't know the condition of the old well's wall. The masonry is probably deteriorated. The wall could collapse with the slightest disturbance, and you'd be trapped. And what about the radiation? It's just not a good idea."

"Just a few minutes is all I'll need," Claire persisted. "I've made up my mind. There's something very odd going on around here, and if I can get into the cave system, it might give us valuable information. Do you have your rock climbing equipment with you?"

"This is good gear, it should keep you safe." Wilson was tugging at the straps of the harness around Claire's shoulders. "I always keep it in the vehicle in case I spot a good opportunity to conquer another rock."

The pair had driven up to the well under the windmill. Wilson attached his climbing harness rope to a powered winch bolted on the front bumper of the Jeep.

"Let's do it." Claire lifted up a leg and straddled the stone lip of the well.

"Got everything?" Wilson said, patting her backpack. "Flashlight, rock pick, sample bag? Don't forget to use the Geiger counter, we need to monitor the radiation."

"Jeez, you're clucking around like an old hen," Claire chided him. "Just lower me down."

"Okay." Wilson walked back to his Jeep "I'll give you enough slack to get you over the edge, then start lowering you. Let me know when you're ready."

There was a brief exciting moment during the descent when the rope got hung up on a piece of masonry, but Claire cleared it easily and continued down into the dank black pit. She bent her head so that the beam of the flashlight rigged to her hard hat was aimed at the bottom. The well was an eerie tunnel shrinking to a black circle below.

"We're good, keep going," she called up, making an effort to sound upbeat, while fighting off increasing apprehension and a growing sense of claustrophobia.

As she got down fifteen feet, Claire could make out details of the bottom. It was sandy with a few small rocks strewn about. "Almost there." She called. And then her feet touched bottom. "Stop."

Wilson's head appeared in a circle of daylight above. "You okay?"

"Get me a couple more feet, and lock it down."

The rope slackened. Claire was relieved when the ground held her weight. She was worried she might sink into a quagmire. She let go of the rope, took out a large flashlight from her pack and jammed it into a crack in the well wall. Then she checked the Geiger counter clipped on her belt. Its reading was only slightly above normal. Good. She pulled out the flashlight and examined her surroundings.

She was disappointed. The black void she noticed when checking out the well with Amos Doyle turned out to be just a shallow depression that traveled horizontally a couple of feet into the earth and stopped.

"Crap."

"What did you say?" Wilson called down from above.

"It's just a damn well."

Claire patted the bottom of the well with her foot. After a few pats, there was a sucking sound as the alternating pressure of her boot wicked moisture to the surface. Moving her boot, she bent to get a closer look at the small puddle that had formed at her feet.

At that moment, her necklace unclasped and the amulet plopped into the puddle.

"Shit! Not again!"

When it splashed into the water, it seemed as if the garnet-like crystal in its center pulsed with a golden light before it disappeared in the puddle. Claire figured it was just a reflection of the flashlight beam. She reached down to retrieve the amulet but jerked up when she saw see that the puddle had grown dramatically. *That's odd.*

Her surprise turned to alarm when the puddle continued to get bigger. In seconds it was covering the bottom of the well and starting to rise over her boots.

"Wilson!"

There was no response from above.

"Wilson!" she called louder. Her voice was lost echoing in the tunnel above. The water was now over the top of her boots soaking her socks and the hem of her dungarees.

She sucked in breath in preparation for a scream and grabbed wildly on the rope and tried to pull herself up.

"What?" came Wilson's voice.

"Pull me up! Now!" Claire's voice was unrecognizable to herself in its hysteria.

"What?"

"Get me out of here!"

To her immense relief, the rope attached to her harness went taut. At the last second, Claire managed to plunge her arm into the water and snare the necklace with the amulet before she was lifted into the air.

After a minute that seemed like an eternity, she felt Wilson's hands grab under her arms and pull her up over the edge of the well. She scrambled over and fell to the dirt when her knees gave out.

"Shit, Claire." Wilson extended his hand. "What happened down there?"

Claire jumped to her feet, undid her harness and went to the edge of the well. She took the flashlight off her helmet and pointed it downward. "The well was filling up with water. Fast!"

"Really?" Wilson joined her at the edge and they both peered down.

"I thought I was going to drown."

"Are you sure it wasn't just a little seepage caused by your weight on the mud?"

"Are you kidding?" Claire waved her flashlight around. The beam glinted off the water at the bottom of the well. "See... look at that..." Her voice trailed off.

Wilson peered down the hole. "Well, maybe there's a little water down there. From your hollering I thought you were drowning."

There was a small puddle shining at the bottom of the well. Seconds later it disappeared as it was absorbed by the ground.

"What?...I...don't..." Claire stared at Wilson. "I swear, the water was coming in like crazy."

Wilson looked sideways at her.

Claire pointed to her soaked boots and pants. "Then how do you explain this?" she said defiantly.

"Son of a bitch," Wilson was saying.

But Claire wasn't paying attention. She was holding the amulet in her palm and frowning.

They were packing their equipment back into the Jeep when Ivy returned. As Claire watched her approach, she was startled. It seemed that every time Ivy took a step, the dirt at her feet briefly lit up with a gold light. Claire blinked.

"Do you see that?" Claire whispered to Wilson.

"What?"

Claire pointed. "Look! Quick. At Ivy's feet."

"I don't see…" Wilson said. He craned his head forward. "What the hell…?"

Just then the light faded and was gone.

Claire turned to Wilson. "You did see that, right?"

"Maybe. I don't know, some kind of glow at her feet." Wilson rubbed his eyes. "Must be some weird illusion - like a mirage or something." He looked up into the sky. "Something about the sunlight through the clouds…"

"Bullshit."

"Some kind of illusion, Claire," Wilson insisted. "What else could it be? An optical illusion, that's all."

Ivy came up, "Hey, guys. I want to show you something."

Wilson rubbed his goatee. "Is it more exciting than a real Geiger counter?"

Ivy glanced dramatically over her shoulders. "Way more. Only if you can keep a secret, though."

"Can't promise you that Ivy," Claire said. "Until we see what you are talking about. If it's dangerous or something grownups need to know, we might not be able to keep it a secret. We'll try to if we can."

"Hm-m-m." Ivy pursed her lips, wrinkled her brow, then smiled. "Okay. Follow me." She took off running towards the barn.

Claire looked at Wilson who inclined his head after Ivy. "Let's go," he said.

They trailed after the young girl as she rounded the barn and trotted across the field towards the Testament Hill Mound.

"Boy," Wilson said, sucking in air, "She's quick like a fox. It's hard to keep up."

Claire passed him. "That's what you get for your bad habits," she called back.

Ivy reached the hill and bounded to the summit. She stood at the summit, hands on her hips. "Come on, you guys!"

"Hold on, Ivy!" Claire struggled to the top and was joined by Wilson seconds later. Claire was panting and made a promise to herself to start some kind exercise routine.

"Okay, Ivy," she said, "what is it you wanted to show us?"

Wilson was bent over, hands on his knees, catching his breath. He looked around. "This place gives me the creeps somehow."

"Yep, that's what my grandpa says," Ivy said. "He tells me to steer clear, but I think it's a neat place. I come up here to sit and think. Me and Raven. Sometimes I imagine that the wind up here..." Ivy waved her hand, "whispers to me, telling me things. But I can't quite make out the words. Maybe when I get older, I'll understand."

Claire thought she detected a slight tingling at her feet as if there was some large machine humming away below.

"Yes," Wilson thumped his foot on the ground. "Who knows what secrets this mound holds?"

Ivy winked at him. "I know one secret. That's what I want to show you." Ivy pointed to something out of sight down the far side of the hill. "Down here. I found it when a storm washed some of the hill away last spring." She disappeared down the hill.

Claire and Wilson followed, and saw Ivy was using her hands to part a jumble of Queen Anne's lace that had sprung up in a small washout gully on the side of the hill. "Come look. My grandpa never saw it because he has no reason to come up here. It's a secret."

"Let's see what you have found..." Claire crouched down beside Ivy and peered into the gully.

She sprang to her feet as if she had received an electric shock. "Oh my god!" She stared wide-eyed at Wilson.

He rushed to her side. "What is it?" he said, alarmed at her reaction.

In a low voice, Claire said, "It's a skull, Wilson, a human skull. At least that's what I think it is."

Wilson got on his knees, pushed away the weeds and

was motionless for several seconds. He bent closer and stared down, saying nothing. He reached carefully into the weeds and moved his hands around. Then he looked up, his normally mischievous expression solemn.

"It's..." he shook his head. "...it's some kind of human, but from the size it must have been a giant!" He glanced over at Ivy, whose smile had vanished and whose eyes began to well up with tears.

"I thought you'd like it," her voice quivered.

Claire stood and put her hand on Ivy's shoulder. "Well, we're very glad you showed it to us. It's very special. It's just that it's... a surprise to see it for the first time. Why did you keep it a secret?"

Ivy looked down at her feet. "Because Raven told me it was a secret."

"It must have been buried here and the weather finally exposed it," Wilson was saying. "From the looks of it, mind you I'm no archeologist, but it could be hundreds of years old. The bone is very clean of any kind of tissue, and discolored by age. But the size - this being must have been at least seven, eight feet tall."

"Giants in the earth," Claire murmured softly.

"Holy Moses!" Wilson said, standing up. "Claire take a look, this skull has double rows of teeth!"

Claire forced herself to get back down and examine the remains. The skull was positioned face up in the ground, its jaw dropped open so that it appeared to be grinning, its teeth bared. Holding her breath, she bent to get a closer look. "Wilson, it's ghastly."

"Claire," Wilson said, "I've read about finds like this, back in the 1800s and early 1900s, when settlers were clearing the land or digging wells. Reports of discovering huge human skeletons. Some with double rows of teeth."

Claire rose up, stepped away from the remains and brushed her hands vigorously on her jeans, as if she was trying to rub off some stubborn dirt. "I'm sorry, Ivy," she said, "but we are going to have to tell people about this."

Chapter 22

Chief Childress pulled up in front of Ida Wagner's house and sat for a moment staring at the front door. Three rolled up newspapers were scattered around the base of the porch. He recognized her car in the drive.

That was sort of odd, he had to admit, but certainly there was a mundane explanation. Ida probably went away for a few days to visit her sister, who, if Childress remembered correctly, had moved to St. Paul. Just walked to the train station. It was only a block away.

He sighed. It was going to be awkward, seeing Ida if she was home. He generally tried to avoid crossing paths with her in town, and if he did, their meeting was kept to a polite "How are you?"

Seven summers ago they had a brief fling. Ida had a problem with some hobos from the train setting up camp at the back of her yard. Childress volunteered to spend a couple nights on her property to make sure the tramps got the message to move on down the line. At first he just sat in his cruiser parked in the shadows, but after an uncomfortable night, took up Ida's offer to stay in the house, keeping surveillance by watching out the back kitchen window.

They had known each other since high school. Childress and Ida's future husband had played on the same football team. They had even double-dated a couple of times.

Ida's husband had been taken by leukemia the previous year, and Childress and his wife were going through a rough patch. One thing had led to another, and Ida and the Chief had ended up taking solace in each other's arms. After a few months, the unsustainability of their situation became more and more apparent, and they ended the relationship by mutual agreement.

Childress reluctantly put his mug in the holder, opened the door to the cruiser and stepped out. He half expected the front door to open and Ida to come strolling down the sidewalk to greet him, but nothing happened. The air was very still. Childress stared at the house. A shadow passed over it, as if a cloud had drifted across the sun. He looked up. It was a clear, crisp late September morning. The sky was flawlessly clear. He tried to shake off a dread that descended over him. Now he saw that the mailbox was stuffed with flyers. Walking up to the porch, Childress casually unsnapped his holster. He rapped on the front door and waited.

A gentle breeze blew across the front of the house, carrying with it the unmistakable odor of death.

Drawing his service revolver, Childress put his shoulder to the door and grabbed the handle, expecting to force it. But as he turned the handle, the door swung open and he almost fell inward as it gave way.

"Oh my god!" He gagged as the full intensity of the smell of decaying flesh enveloped him. Holding his gun ready in one hand, and his nose in the other, Childress lurched from one room of the house to the other.

"Ida!"

The front room and kitchen were empty. Everything looked tidy and in place. A half pot of coffee sat on the stove. Childress stepped down the hall to the bedroom. The bed was unmade, the sheets pulled back and piled in a bundle on the floor.

Childress turned. The door to the bathroom was partially closed.

"Please God..." Childress squeezed his eyes shut and pushed the door. He blinked.

The bathroom was empty. For a split second, he felt a sense of relief. Maybe something just got into the crawl space, like a raccoon or something, and died, and Ida moved out because of the odor.

Then he saw the blood.

There wasn't a lot. Just a smear on the floor by the sink. As he moved to examine it more closely, he spotted a line of droplets across the bottom of the mirror over the faucets.

"Jesus."

There was one room left. Childress charged into the back mud room.

It was empty. Dirty footprints led in and out of the back door. Man-sized boot prints.

Probably just the gas company guy coming to check the meter.

But the blood. And the smell.

In his mind's eye, Childress visualized the rotting body of a huge raccoon in the crawl space beneath the house, trying by force of will to make that a reality. He had been down there once to fix a leaky drain. It was a shallow crawl just two feet deep, dank and pitch black.

He ran outside to the trapdoor that opened up into the crawl space, fell to his knees and clawed it open. The stench hit him like a slap in the face. He turned his head away and gagged, struggling to keep down his stomach contents. Childress stood up, and on wobbling knees, trotted to the cruiser and brought back a long, four cell flashlight.

Taking a deep breath, he turned on the flashlight and knelt back down to the crawl opening. He held the flashlight in his outstretched arm as he squirmed halfway into the crawl space. He swept the beam of the flashlight across the dirt.

And howled.

When the State Highway Patrol arrived with the forensics team and the coroner's van, Chief Childress was seated in his cruiser, bent over, the door open. Near his foot was a small pool of vomit that he had half-heartedly tried to cover with kicked dirt. Childress watched as the team walked up. He was desperate for a drink, but knew he'd have to wait until the horrible ordeal was over.

"Around the back," he croaked when they approached. "The body's in the crawl."

"You going to be okay?" It was Captain Norris. He lightly touched the Chief's shoulder and bent down. "You two were friends, right?"

Childress looked up, his eyes glistening. "Yeah, thanks, Bob. I just need a minute."

"No problem, Owen. Take your time." The captain

straightened up and turned to move away.

"Bob, just to warn you…"

The captain looked back at him.

"Her face…" Childress' voice wavered. "It's gone. It's been cut off."

"Are you sure it's Ida?" Norris asked gently.

"Yeah," Childress said. "I'm sure. I recognized a birthmark on her body. She's nude"

Captain Norris nodded grimly, turned and headed up to the house.

And one more thing, Childress was going to say, but changed his mind. *There was some kind of blue light coming out of the ground under the crawl space. It blinked out right after I went in.*

Chapter 23

Claire spotted the road sign through the sun's glare on the Volvo's windshield: *Big Rock Trail.*

She turned the wheel and bumped down the rutted dirt road edged with prickly ash and flaming orange sumac. The road passed into a forest of basswood and black locust, their leaves yellow with autumn. The canopy became denser, and the bright day turned into golden-tinged twilight.

Claire began to have doubts about her decision to find Skander Grey Wolf. But she had the rest of the day free and if she was going to find the man mentioned in Edith's note it might be her only opportunity.

A peculiar object came into view, hanging over the road from the overhead branches. Claire stopped the Volvo and stuck her head out the window to get a better look. It appeared to be some kind of charm constructed out of various twigs and bits of fur and feathers bound with leather thongs. Its configuration reminded her of the amulet around her neck. She wondered if was meant as a warning or as protection.

Claire rolled up her window, clicked down the door locks and continued bumping down the trail. After creeping along for a mile or so, she gave up and searched for a spot to turn around. Then she spotted a cabin up on a wooded rise to her left, and stopped.

For a couple of minutes Claire sat in the car watching. There was no movement around the cabin. A blue jay cackled noisily in the tree.

Claire let out a little yelp and jumped in her seat when there was a tap on the passenger window. It was an old man with dark, deeply creased skin and long silver hair tied in a ponytail. He bent down and made the motion of rolling down the window.

With some trepidation, Clair reached across and lowered the window two inches.

"I'm Skander Grey Wolf," the old man spoke through

the crack. "Who comes to visit me?"

"My name is Claire Brannigan. I am visiting Testament Hill to see why the wells are drying up."

The man closed his eyes for a moment, then said, "You found more than you bargained for, I think."

"Well... yes. I got your name from a friend." Claire brought her window down. "I hope you don't mind. I don't mean to trespass."

The man seemed to consider this for a moment. "Please, come up to my cabin, I have coffee brewing. We will talk."

"Thank you."

Claire locked up her car and followed the old man up the path to his primitive but sturdy looking cabin. He walked briskly with surprising agility. They reached the cabin and he gestured for her to take a seat on one of the pair of bent branch chairs on the covered porch. As she stepped onto the porch, Claire glanced up. Above the cabin door, spread out and pinned with nails, was the preserved carcass of a large bird.

"Is that an owl?" Claire pointed.

"Yes," Skander Grey Wolf said. "To ward off evil."

"Is that a tribal tradition?"

The old man shrugged. "Let me get us some coffee." He disappeared into the cabin. Claire noticed that a rusted horseshoe was spiked onto the inside of the door.

A minute later, the two were sitting on the beautifully crafted chairs. Homemade wind chimes hung from the side of the porch roof clinked softly in the light breeze. Claire took an sample taste from the large mug the old man had handed to her. The liquid was steaming hot and rich. She detected some exotic flavors - perhaps roasted chicory and acorn? It crossed her mind that he might have put something less benign in the brew, but then decided she was being too paranoid.

Skander Grey Wolf watched with a wry smile while Claire sampled the coffee.

"Very good, Mr. Grey Wolf," Claire said, thinking he was waiting for a reaction.

"I think so," the old man said. "My friends call me Grey Wolf, but you can call me Skander." He paused for effect then chuckled. " Skander is my white man's name, from my mother's side. It's derived from the name Alexander."

"I see."

He smiled mischievously. "I was just pulling your leg. My friends actually call me Skander, as you may too. Please. I rather like the name. Grey Wolf is so predictable."

He sat back in his chair with a satisfied expression. "The owl, to answer your question, is not one of my people's traditions."

"I see."

"We respect all of nature's creatures."

Claire was confused. "Then...?"

"It's insurance," Skander explained. "My grandmother was European, from a country called Albania. You have heard of it?"

"Yes."

"I actually know nothing of it, except her people had a belief that owls were creatures of the underworld, harbingers of death. Apparently, it is not an unusual belief. For example, the Romans would nail owl carcasses over doors as a warning to ward off evil in a household."

Skander pointed at the stuffed owl over the door. "I figure, it can't hurt. Part of me is abhorred at its presence, but I grew up with one above my parents' lodge, so it is also, paradoxically, a comfort."

"So you feel the need to protect yourself from evil." Claire waved her hand towards the woods and glanced around. "But it seems so peaceful here." As she peered into the shadows in the forest, she shivered and suddenly appreciated the owl totem.

Skander blew on his coffee. "You have come to ask about the time of the Great Taima, the earth cracking open."

Seeing Claire's perplexed expression, Skander explained. "You call it the New Madrid earthquake, I believe. We called it Taima because it means thunder."

Claire was taken aback. "How did you know?"

"Knowing things, that's what I do," Skander said blandly. "Now, about the earthquake: there is a story passed down from my grandfather's grandfather, then to me. So it would not be forgotten." He stopped and stared into Claire's eyes. She felt that he was somehow judging her.

Skander set his coffee by his feet. "My people believe that long ago, in the time of the First Grandfathers, giant demons, called the Anuk, came down from the sky and walked the earth, spreading their evil ways - ways that went against the harmony of the world..." Skander leaned towards Claire and lowered his voice. "...including the practice of cannibalism and bestiality."

Claire made a face.

"The Great Spirit caused a terrible storm and flood to come across the land to destroy the Anuk and those human beings that followed their ways," Skander went on. "The Anuk fled under the earth to escape. Then Spirit Warriors came down and built a sacred mound, you call 'Testament Hill', above their sanctuary so that its power would keep the Anuk trapped. And so it was for thousands of moons.

"Then in 1811, a great new star appeared in the heavens and its emanations caused the great shaking and cracking of the Earth, which is also known as the New Madrid earthquake."

Claire said, "Why, yes, there was a famous comet that appeared in the sky that year."

"Do you think I am making this up?" Skander asked, with a twinkle in his eye.

"I didn't mean..."

Skander waved his hand. "Anyway, to continue: the ground moved under our people's village. Trees toppled, lightning flashed in the dark sky, and the earth split open like broken pottery and smoke and sand blew from the cracks."

"Yes, that sounds very similar to accounts that I have read about the quake."

"I am glad of that." Skander said drolly. Then his voice became somber. "At first, the people were very afraid, and cowered in their tents, but then their Seer, Migumi, called out to the warriors and set them around their camp to protect them. He had been forewarned that the quake signaled the coming of a great evil in a dream."

To Claire's surprise, Skander reached in his pocket and pulled out a pack of Camels, holding the pack out to her. She gently shook her head.

He carefully lit up and took a languid drag. "Stuff will kill a person. But it helps an old man to think, to remember."

Skander settled back in his chair. "After the shaking stopped," he went on, "the smoke cleared, and for a while the land became very still. The warriors gripped their weapons tightly in their hands and looked all about, but nothing happened. Some began to wonder if the Seer was wrong. A few even went back to their campfires."

"Then what happened?" Claire leaned forward.

"Then all Hell broke loose." Skander paused dramatically. "And I mean *Hell*. The giant Anuk emerged from the earth. They rushed into the village like a herd of buffalo, brandishing flaming swords."

Claire was taken aback. "My god."

"The Oweyu warriors fought with great bravery, and helped by the magical powers of their Seer, many of the Anuk were destroyed, and the rest driven back into the ground, and the Anuk were again sealed in the bowels of the Earth."

Skander took a few puffs of his cigarette. "However, a high price was paid. Many of the warriors were killed. All that was left of the tribe were mostly the old and women and children, one of which was my grandfather's grandfather. Survivors dispersed and were absorbed by the other tribes, the Osage, the Missouri, and the Chickasaw. The Oweyu people were no more. History has forgotten us."

Skander fell silent. Claire waited.

He peered at her. "Let me ask you this, Doctor: have you seen any colors?"

Claire stiffened. "What do you mean, *colors*?"

"I think you know what I mean. And from your reaction, I see you have. Now this is important: what colors did you see?"

"Blue. Like electricity."

"Where, exactly?"

"Down in a well. Out at Doyle's."

"Yes. Anywhere else?"

"No..." Claire thought for a moment. "Well, I did see a bluish flash in the sky when I first came into town at daybreak. Towards the north."

Skander's face was grave. "Anywhere else? Please think carefully."

"This is probably nothing. Just my imagination, I suspect. Out in the wooded field, across from the Sleep-Tite Motel where I am staying. I saw a silhouette surrounded by a dim blue halo. Also, Wilson, my doctoral assistant, has seen it. On the ground out at Doyle's."

Skander reached down for his coffee mug. "Any other colors?"

"I saw a gold glow on the ground around the feet of Doyle's granddaughter. Just one time, when she was walking towards me. Wilson saw it too.

"Ivy?" Skander's head shot up. "Are you sure? It wasn't just your eyes playing tricks?"

"Wilson was with me. He saw it too."

Skander looked up towards the ceiling. "Very curious," he said, his voice strangely flat.

Claire took a deep breath. "Skander, how much of the Great Taima tale do you think was true? I mean, what *really* happened back in 1811 and is not just an allegorical myth?"

"All of it is true, of course." Skander raised his cigarette to his lips, took a long drag and exhaled slowly through his nostrils. "And I sense that there is a new stirring in the earth. There is trouble coming again to Testament Hill." He stood up. "Now, please finish your coffee. You must leave me."

Claire shifted in her chair. "But Mr. Grey Wolf..."

The old man waved his hand dismissively. "Please. Go

now. We will talk again."

Claire and Wilson went to Duggan's for an early dinner. On the way they stopped at the Testament Hill post office to send the giant skull recovered from the mound to the university for analysis.

By unspoken agreement, they kept their conversation light. After a meal of shepherd's pie, they decided to have one more drink before calling it a night. Wilson's opted for an Old Bushmills, neat, and Claire her usual martini.

"How's your drink?" Claire asked.

Wilson closed his eyes for a second and took a deep breath. "Excellent." He nodded at Claire's glass. "Yours?"

Claire shrugged. "I've had better. But it's not bad. A really good martini is tricky to mix. Just a little too much vermouth, and it's a goner. Too little, and you just have some gin. And it has to be super cold."

"How much vermouth is supposed to go in?"

"Well, there's a lot debate about that," Claire said, swirling her little finger in her drink. "Five parts gin to one part vermouth is considered normal, I guess. But sometimes it could be a little as one part vermouth to fifteen parts gin."

"Huh."

"FDR liked his one part vermouth to 2 parts gin." Claire pointed out. "Vice President LBJ supposedly makes his by pouring vermouth in a glass, emptying it out and then filling it with gin. Calls it 'the in-and-out martini'."

"Funny."

Claire pointed at Wilson's glass. "Your Irish whiskey: What makes Irish whiskey 'Irish'?"

Wilson savored another nip before answering. "Scotch whisky, which by the way, is usually spelled without the 'e', is distilled twice. Irish whiskey is distilled three times. Makes it smoother. And Irish whiskey is made from half malted and half unmalted barley, that makes it a bit more 'citrusy' than all malted. That started to save money because the British only taxed malted barley."

"So, what exactly is malting?" Claire asked with a

slightly feigned interest, trying to keep the conversation casual.

"Malting is allowing the barley seed to sprout, then heating it to stop the germination process," Wilson explained. "Malting develops certain sugars and enzymes that aid the process of fermentation. Scotch is traditionally made with malt dried from the heat of burning peat, which gives Scotch whisky the smoky flavor. Whiskey, you understand, is essentially distilled beer."

"I'm impressed. You know your whiskey."

Wilson nodded. "I like to know what I'm drinking."

"Okay, let's see what else you know," Claire said. She paused and stirred her martini. "This time about geology. Back to business. What is your opinion as to what's happening around here?"

Wilson held his glass up to the light. "Let's see... Wells drying up: indicates water table has lowered."

"Because?"

"Perhaps some kind of fissure occurred and the water has been draining into the caves we discovered."

"But the caves are dry."

"Right. As far as we can tell. But the system could be enormous, and the water going even deeper."

Claire nodded over her drink. "That's probably what's happening: some tectonic event opened up fissures so the water is flowing into the previously blocked caves. Eventually, the voids will fill, and the water table will return to normal."

"Well, then we've resolved the situation here in Testament Hill." Wilson clinked his glass on Claire's. "We can blow this crazy pop-stand."

"Not so fast," Claire said. "We shouldn't be too hasty in our conclusions. Remember, the caves we've detected are dry. We really have no reason to suspect there are more caves deeper. Perhaps there is some other mechanism causing the water to be drawn down."

"Maybe it's settling down to a normal level, whereas in the past it was unnaturally high for some reason," Wilson speculated. "Perhaps, historically, the wells around here were being regenerated by artesian pressure - being fed by a higher water table. Topographic maps show the area is in a slight depression."

Claire considered what Wilson was saying. "So something happened to this water level causing it to drop, something that wouldn't be obvious locally?"

"What else could it be?" Wilson wondered.

The images of the startling water backup of the shower drain and the rise of water in the old well came into Claire's mind. But because she couldn't make a reasonable connection, she decided not to mention it. Plus, she just as soon put those disturbing episodes out of her mind.

"We need more information. There are still too many questions." Claire rotated her martini glass on the condensation that had run onto the bar top. "But why now? What started the whole thing? And what about the radiation? And the vitreous rock?"

Wilson shrugged. "I'm thinking some kind of seismic event opened up new passageways, and exposed some natural uranium deposits."

"And the melted walls?"

"You got me there. But I'm sure there's some logical explanation."

For a moment, the pair quietly nursed their drinks.

"And what the hell is up with the skull?" Wilson said perking up. He rubbed his hands together. "I can't wait to hear from the anthropology department, and maybe get a radiocarbon date on that baby. I wonder if anything like it has been discovered before."

Back at the motel, after walking Wilson to his room, Claire wandered over to the pool. She wasn't quite ready for bed. Her body felt charged. The night air was unusually warm. Leaning on the wrought iron fence that surrounded the pool, she watched while the light danced on the surface of the water. It had a slightly blue tinge.

I'm imagining that color everywhere.

She looked around, searching for the source. In the east, looking like a dull gold coin, a full moon was rising. She looked back at the pool.

The complex patterns of light on the pool surface were hypnotic. Claire imagined seeing all kinds of fantastic shapes moving haphazardly across it. The light became more intense. It was almost as if the pool lights had come on, but Mr. B never turned them on. Then it faded and was gone. Claire looked back up at the moon, which was now shrouded by a cloud.

Is it all my imagination, this glowing light stuff? She wondered. Then: *But Wilson's seen it too.*

The pool was inviting. Claire felt drawn to it. She looked around. All the room lights were out. The evening was quiet except for a warm breeze rustling the leaves. There was no traffic on the road. She walked quietly to her room and a couple minutes later snuck back out with a towel wrapped around her naked body.

After one more look around, Claire took off her towel and placed it by the edge of the pool. She paused for a moment, then lifted the necklace with amulet over her head and placed it carefully on the towel. She padded down to the shallow end, enjoying the sensual feel of the open air around her body; the subtle thrill of being naked in a public space. She stepped into the pool and slipped into the water. At first it felt too cold, but after she swam a couple of lazy laps, the temperature felt perfect. She rolled over, floating on her back, and let herself drift.

Her thoughts wandered for a few minutes. The image of her roommate from college appeared in her mind. She tried to push it out of her consciousness, as she usually did when that happened, but tonight Mary's image was especially vivid.

I'm sorry, Mary. I'm so sorry.
I should have killed him when I had the chance.

As they had done countless times before, the events of the night of Mary's death replayed in Claire's head as she floated motionless on the surface.

Claire heard it first over the car radio. She was back home for summer break and was driving her dad's Buick station wagon to the library. A local station playing mostly country music with the likes of Merle Haggard and Marty Robbins, interspersed with the odd rock and roll song by Elvis or the Everly Brothers. A break in the music for a news flash:

The body of a young female college student has been found by a utility worker in a drain pipe near the university student parking lot. Preliminary examination indicates she had been stabbed to death. Police suspect the identity of the assailant to be the same as the person that had attacked her last month in her dorm room, before being interrupted by the woman's roommate. Police are carrying out a state-wide dragnet in search of the suspect.

Claire knew the regret would never go away. She should have shot the monster right in the room before he got away that night. But she had hesitated. Just for a moment. The pleading look on the man's face, the expression of desperate sadness and pain like an animal caught in a trap, had caused her pause. Perhaps he had been driven to do evil by uncontrollable forces. Maybe he wasn't totally responsible for his actions. Maybe he could be redeemed.

I wish I'd killed the bastard right then and there. Put a bullet through his sick brain, Claire thought. *I was so naïve. He was a truly evil person.*

Never again, Claire had sworn to herself, would she hesitate for a second in the face of such evil.

She read later in the newspaper that the killer had been shot to death by police when he was cornered in some dark alley in Ames. He had threatened the officers with a butcher knife.

Claire had felt relief that he was dead. May he burn in Hell.

But it was too late for Mary.

She drifted to the side of the pool, and pushed away with her toes.

There was the sound of shoes on the pavement. Claire rotated to her feet and waded towards the cover of the pool's edge.

It was Smith. His head was down and he was dressed in his standard all-black outfit. He apparently hadn't noticed her and went past, heading for his room.

"You're out late," Claire called out, before she could help herself.

Smith stopped in his tracks, and turned his head slowly in her direction.

"Hello, Claire." Smith took a couple steps towards the pool.

"The water looked so inviting, I thought I'd sneak in for a skinny dip." Claire couldn't believe what she was saying.

"I see." Smith took another couple steps closer. Claire could see his teeth shinning as he smiled.

"Join me?" She smiled back.

Smith was now at the edge of the pool gazing down at her. Claire knew that he would now be able to see her full nakedness. She shamelessly pushed away from the edge, and waved her arms gently back and forth, treading water in place.

Smith crouched down at the rim and reached out to the water as if he was going to test it with his fingers, but then pulled away. "I think not," he said.

"Chicken." Claire slapped the water with the palm of her hand, sending a few drops towards Smith.

He turned his head sharply with a grunt and sprang to his feet, vigorously rubbing his sleeve across his forehead.

Claire was surprised at his reaction. "Sorry."

A wave of anger passed over Smith's face and then was gone. He smiled thinly. "It's okay, you just startled me, that's all."

Claire was suddenly embarrassed and confused about her own behavior. She moved discreetly back to the cover at the edge of the pool.

"Maybe another time." He touched his hand to his forehead, "Goodnight, Claire." He turned and walked off.

Claire waited until she heard Smith's door open and close. She scrambled out of the pool, hastily wrapped her body in the towel and hurried to her room.

Chapter 24

Friday morning

It was an unusually warm morning. Wilson had buzzed Claire's room and asked her if she would join him poolside for coffee and bagels he had picked up at the café.

"Sounds great," Claire told him. "Give me a couple minutes to get dressed, and I'll meet you there."

A few minutes later they were making small talk while enjoying the surprisingly delicious bagels and strong brew.

"So," Wilson said, his voice garbled by a mouthful of bagel, "Did you ever go see that Grey Wolf guy from Edith's note?"

"Yes. It was interesting. He told me about an Oweyu legend that probably is related to the New Madrid earthquake."

"Yeah?"

"Something about giants called the 'Anuk', demons that live underground. They came out of the earth during the quake, and there was a battle between the Anuk and the tribe's warriors."

Wilson almost choked on his mouthful of bagel. "Holy shit!" he exclaimed. "That's the origin of the skull I bet. It's one of the demons killed in battle with the Oweyu."

"Well, let's not jump to conclusions." Claire picked up her coffee cup. "Let's wait to see what comes back on the tests."

"Right."

Claire swallowed the last morsel of her bagel. "Speaking of strange things: there's something curious about Smith."

"What's that, beside the fact that he's a dowser, really tall, dresses in all black and has really weird eyes?"

"Besides that," Claire laughed. "You know, at first, I had the impression that Chief Childress had sent for him. But when I asked the Chief, he told me he hadn't. He guessed Doyle had sent for him."

"So?"

"When I asked Doyle, he said he thought dowsing was the devil's work. He would have never sent for Smith."

Wilson tapped his fingers on the table. "*That* is curious. I also had the feeling, Claire, that Smith's dowsing was a red herring."

"I did too. It seemed to me that he was deliberately trying to lead us away from the area of the caves, suggesting that we drill down in that meadow."

"Why would he do that?"

"I think it's obvious, Wilson," Claire said. "I think he was trying to keep the caves a secret."

"Why?"

Claire took a deep breath. "If we had the answer to that question, we might have an answer to what's going on around Testament Hill." She brushed away bagel crumbs from her lap. "In the meantime I think we should find the cave opening Audrey was talking about."

"Hey, Claire, that's what I said before."

"Okay, Let's check it out. Maybe this afternoon."

"Man, why don't we go this now?"

"I have other plans."

Wilson smirked. "Date with the preacher?"

"None of your business."

"All right. I'll study the topographic maps and figure out exactly where the entrance might be."

Claire reached out and briefly touched Wilson's hand. "We'll go together. Don't you go out there exploring on your own. You know the dangers of spelunking alone."

Wilson grinned. "Yes, Mother."

Edith couldn't wait to get to the office that morning. In her purse, she had pages secretly torn from the newspaper archives at the library. She was convinced they revealed an evil presence that had once stalked the town of Testament Hill.

And it had returned.

The dark man. The one that came with Claire to her apartment.

Her first impulse was to show Chief Childress. After all, he was the head of police. Who better to handle the situation?

But as Edith made coffee and waited for the Chief to show up, she debated with herself. How would the Chief react? Would he just brush off her discovery as some insignificant coincidence? The crazy theory of a senile old woman? And if he did suspect something evil was going on, what could he do? Of course, Owen could handle everyday civil disturbances and common criminals. But this was a totally different kettle of fish. Perhaps he could call in the State Highway Patrol.

Then a thought: what if the Chief was in on it?

No, that was crazy. She'd known Owen most of his life, except when he went in the army to fight the Germans in the big war, and then away again to that terrible fight in Korea.

That did seem to change him. Of course it would. But Edith was sure Owen Childress, in his heart, was the same down-to-earth kid she knew when he used to help out at the farm during summer breaks.

Or was he?

Edith sat down at the dispatcher's desk and sighed.

She knew the Chief had a secret drinking problem. Working with him day to day at the police station, it was hard not to notice. She recognized the signs. Her Harold had also come home from the war with the urge to take to the bottle.

Edith made up her mind. She would confide instead to Doctor Brannigan, the geologist from the university. From the moment Edith met Claire, she had felt a connection. Providence had brought the young woman to Testament Hill. After work, she would go to the Sleep-Tite Motel and show Claire the newspaper articles.

After breakfast by the motel pool with Wilson, Claire waited in her room for ten minutes. Peeking first out the door to make sure no one was around, she walked back down to the pool carrying the necklace with the amulet in her palm.

If it had come to her in a dream, or if the idea had just been quietly fermenting in the back of her mind, Claire couldn't recall, but she woke up inspired to try an experiment. She knelt down by the pool, glanced over her shoulder, and dangled the amulet by its chain a foot from the surface of the water. When nothing happened after a minute, she slowly lowered it until the amulet was just touching the water.

Nothing.

Feeling foolish, Claire checked again to make sure no one was looking.

What am I expecting, really? she thought, *A demonstration of magic that defies the laws of physics? Laws that have never been proven wrong? Laws upon which hinge all of Creation?*

This is bullcrap. I'm letting this place get to me.

As Claire started to get up off her knees, her free hand slipped on the damp patio stones and she lurched forward over the pool. She quickly recovered, but not before the amulet dipped completely into the water. When she went to pull it up it resisted, as if weighted down.

What the...?

Claire tugged on the necklace, but the amulet was stubbornly stuck in the pool, as if the water had turned viscous, like cold molasses. She was afraid of pulling any harder for fear of breaking the chain. Getting down on her stomach to brace herself, she reached out with her other hand to cup it underneath the amulet. As her hand got closer, the water felt thicker and thicker as if it was hardening glue. A sharp tingling began at her fingertips and flowed up her arm into her shoulder and neck. With a supreme effort, Claire got her hand around the amulet and jerked upward, almost pulling her arm out of the socket.

"Shit!"

The amulet broke free of the surface, trailing a column of water like a small vortex, which thinned and collapsed back to the surface.

Claire got up and stared in astonishment at the object grasped tightly in her hand. The gemstone at its center flashed with a golden light a couple of times then went dark. Claire closed her eyes, put the necklace back around her neck, and waited, her body tensed. Nothing happened.

She didn't expect anything. After all, she'd been wearing the necklace and amulet for a while without any effect. Apparently it had to be surrounded by moisture to 'turn on'. Luckily, contact with her skin's dampness wasn't enough to trigger a reaction.

Claire had her suspicion confirmed. The amulet, once activated, somehow *drew* water to it, like iron filings to a magnet. That was certain. And it was a very powerful force. She could hardly wait to show Wilson her discovery.

When Claire went back to her room, she found a note taped to her door. It was in her assistant's neat, immature print. It informed her that he was going to drive into Dansville to pick up some supplies, and he would get together with her that afternoon. She thought the message a little odd, but didn't give it a second thought.

Claire sat down on her bed and rubbed her temples. She realized she had a pounding headache. The gravity of what she witnessed with the amulet was beginning to sink in. It was, scientifically, pretty much impossible. But she saw it with her own eyes. She hit the mattress with her fists.

Nothing was making sense around here. Her faith in the impartiality and objectivity of reason was being tested since coming to Testament Hill. Maybe there was something else going on. Something even deeper and more profound than science. After all, science and math were analytic tools, they can tell you how but not why. Ivy's remarks came back to Claire like a voice in her skull: Why are flowers beautiful? Why my grandpa loves me and I love him?

Claire stretched out on the bed, closed her eyes and drifted off to sleep. After a couple hours, she awoke with a start. She shook her head and stood up.

She needed to talk to Skander Grey Wolf. She had a lot more questions.

Chapter 25

On the road to Standing Rock Trail, Claire spotted a dark haired young girl in a white dress walking along the shoulder. It was Ivy. She was carrying a lunch box in one hand and some books tucked under her arm.

Claire pulled up beside her. "Are you coming home from school, Ivy?"

Ivy stopped and turned her head slowly towards Claire. "Yes, I missed the bus, Miss Doctor Claire," she smiled broadly. "I'll just walk."

"I can give you a ride home, if you like."

"No thanks, Miss Claire. It's not much farther, and it is a beautiful day for walking."

"Well, you be careful then." Claire waved and drove off, glancing now and then in the rear view mirror until Ivy's shrinking figure appeared as a tiny porcelain doll on the horizon then disappeared.

Smith was lying fully dressed on his motel room bed, the sun shut out behind the curtains. He was mulling over his impression of Ivy. He was quite certain she was the One. The One always comes when the Masters are about to rise.

She would have to be dealt with.

A flash of light began in the center of his brain and radiated outwards. It was a signal of alarm. Smith got up and went outside. There was an old Nash Rambler parked at the far corner of the motel parking lot, partially hidden by overgrown weeds. He had spotted it earlier and made a mental note. It was strewn with fallen leaves and its tires were slightly flat. It was obvious it hadn't been driven for a while. Smith hoped it still had some gas and enough juice in the battery to turn it over.

Ten minutes later, with his left arm casually hanging out the driver's side window, Smith was cruising north on State Road 23, limiting himself to the speed limit. He was anxious to get to the cave, but didn't want any trouble.

An intruder was close by and the Masters were concerned.

Claire parked in front of Skander Grey Wolf's cabin. While she sat in the driver's seat vacillating, she half expected him to materialize at her window again. After a couple minutes, she got out of the car and walked up to the porch. There was a sweet smell of burning hickory in the air. Claire knocked lightly on the door. Nothing. She tried knocking again, this time a little louder. Still no response. Disappointed, she turned and was headed back to her car when she heard it: a man's voice in the distance, back in the woods. It was singsong, and repeating some phrase she couldn't make out.

She realized it was Skander Grey Wolf, and he was chanting.

Claire stood and listened. The chant was unintelligible but enthralling. It resonated with something deep within her subconscious, like a distant memory she couldn't quite put her finger on.

A warning squawk from a blue jay nearby jolted her back to the present. She gazed into the woods, and thought see could just make out the silhouette of Skander Grey Wolf through the smoke of a campfire. His hands were raised to the sky.

Suddenly he turned and appeared to be looking right at her. He waved. "Hello again, Claire," he called out.

Claire waved back. "Hello, Mr. Grey Wolf. I hope you don't mind me coming around again."

Skander came out of the woods and walked up. He placed his hand on the fender of the Volvo and smiled. "Nonsense. I enjoy company once in a while. Especially if it is a pretty young lady."

Claire pulled the amulet out from under her shirt.

Skander nodded solemnly. "You have it. I suspected as much."

Claire held it up. "It looks like an apostles' cross. Except for this yellow gemstone in the center."

Skander shook his head. "The stone is a piece of the spirit stone. And the design is not an apostles' cross."

Claire frowned. "What do you mean?"

"It's a representation of an Anuk, the creatures that I told you about. The circle around it is a magic circle meant to contain them."

"Really?" Claire said. "I thought it was a crudely made cross."

"It's a figure, like a stick figure." Skander traced his finger above the amulet. "See, here's the body, the head, the arms raised to the heavens."

Claire stared down at the amulet. "Yes, I can see that now, like a child's drawing."

"It's no child's work," Skander said. "It's serious business. It was forged by Oweyu Seer with the help of a Jesuit priest who was ministering to the tribe."

"Then I shall give it to you."

Skander shook his head slowly. "No. There is a reason that you have found it. Keep it close. Now: please leave."

"But.." Claire protested, "I have more questions about it. It has an amazing property."

"Go." Skander said gently. "We both have work to do. Goodbye for now." He turned and walked away.

When she returned to the motel, Claire checked the parking lot. Wilson's Jeep was still gone from its spot in front of his room.

Maybe he got delayed in Dansville.

By five p.m., she was getting irritated and a little worried.

Wilson wasn't always prompt, but he was reliable. He wouldn't have forgotten their plans to locate the cave Audrey had told them about.

Claire made her way to the motel office. Mrs. B. was in the foyer, banging around the floor with an old Hoover vacuum cleaner. Claire waited until she was noticed. Mrs. B. reached down and shut the machine off and gave her a friendly smile. "Can I help you, Doctor Brannigan?"

"I was wondering if Mr. Wilson, my colleague, has left any messages for me."

Mrs. B.'s eyes lifted to the ceiling. "No, I don't believe so. But let me check that he didn't leave a note with the Mister."

She shuffled behind the reception desk and flipped through some papers. "Nothing from Mr. Wilson, but this package did arrive for him. The postman dropped it off earlier. I couldn't help but notice it's from Harvard, Department of the Classics." She pulled out a manila envelope.

Claire extended her hand. "I'll be sure he gets it."

Mrs. B hesitated for a moment then and handed it to Claire. "I guess it's okay, you two being colleagues and all."

"Thank you." Claire went to the window and looked out at the parking lot, hoping that she would catch Wilson's Jeep pulling up

Mrs. B looked up. "Something wrong?"

"No... well, I'm not sure. We had planned to meet earlier to do some exploring..."

"You know, I did see him earlier, and he was asking about some of the roads around Amos Doyle's farm."

"We were planning on heading out that way together this afternoon," Claire said. "Would you happen to know anything about a cave around Doyle's farm?"

Mrs. B shook her head. "Can't say that I do."

"Well, if you see Wilson, I'd appreciate if you'd tell him I'm looking for him." Claire headed for the door."

"Of course." For a second, Mrs. B stared blankly at Claire. Then she lightly slapped her forehead and reached under the front desk, and pulled out an envelope. "Oh, tarnation, I almost forgot – something else - a telegram came for you today."

As Claire headed back to her room with the package from Harvard tucked under her arm, she hurriedly tore open the telegram.

university anthropology dept.
dr steven gold director

claire brannigan

>thank you

>we were very excited upon opening the package from you

>the specimen appears mutation homo sapiens or giant hominid such as recent discoveries in Java of a proposed new species of hominid Megantropes

>its unprecedented size and unorthodox jaw structure suggest strongly that it belongs to a previously unknown species, perhaps some kind of cross-species hybrid.

>further investigation urgently recommended to resolve contrary evidence

>regards steven

Claire stared at the telegram.

Maybe Wilson was right: the skull was the remains of one of the giants- the Anuk - destroyed in the battle with the Oweyu one hundred and fifty years ago.

She folded the note back up, and slipped it into the pocket of her khakis.

Once in her room, Claire sat down on the edge of the bed and hurriedly opened the package from Harvard. Inside, was the tattered journal the librarian had lent her and a sheaf of typewritten papers held together with a paper clip. Claire slipped off the clip, and after taking a deep breath, she began to read from the first page:

Dear Michael,

I have done my best to translate this. This is a fascinating document. Someday you must tell me the story behind it.

FYI: "Uaine Fionn" is a Gaelic spelling of an Irish name that we would translate to "Owen Flynn."

The text, as you recognized, is in Latin, but a particular type called *Hisperic Latin,* a version used by Irish monks starting around the tenth century. It was an amalgamation that, besides Latin words, included odd and obscure words in Hebrew and Greek, along with a peppering of Celtic.

None-the-less, in spite of this complication, I believe my interpretation is a fairly accurate representation. (I am now patting myself on the back.)

PS- I have inserted some paragraph breaks to facilitate understanding. Also, a few comments of my own are indicated by parenthesis. Note that I have taken the freedom to 'Americanize' the translation for readability.

Here's the text:

I have been sent by the Father General on a quest to locate and secure the Tzohar. I have in my procession a copy of the map contained in the secret tract, History of Magog, which was carried from ancient Scythia to Erie (Ireland) by Magog, son of Japheth, son of Noah, in antiquity. The manuscript has been kept secret by our sect of Jesuit monks on the isle of Aran for hundreds of years.

The History of Magog recounts the story of a magical gemstone called the Tzohar. It was given to Adam by the archangel Raziel. The Tzohar was passed through Adam's descendants to Noah. Noah used the Tzohar to bring light to the Ark during the darkness of the Deluge.

When the waters began to recede, Magog, Noah's grandson, was instructed by the Archangel Raziel to place the Tzohar above the spot where the Fallen Ones - the Angels that had turned away from God - had descended into the Earth to escape the Deluge. The Tzohar would keep the Fallen trapped by keeping the waters high in order to trap them in their refuge. Magog was given a map in order to locate their refuge and traveled across the world, braving great hardships and danger, to carry out the Archangel's bidding. On completion of his task, Magog returned to Erie.

I have been tasked by our Father Provincial to locate the Tzohar, to prove the greatness of the Lord, and the truth of the Bible. Using a copy of the map from the History of Magog to guide me in my quest, I have sailed to the New World and embarked on a voyage up a majestic river called the Misizibi (sic) by the natives.

December 10:

After voyaging northward for three weeks in a fur traders' boat up the river from the port of La Nouvelle Orleans, I encountered a band of natives, who call themselves the Owyu. The Owyu live in a small village on a rocky bluff overlooking the river, and had spied us coming. A group of four natives, paddling a canoe, rendezvoused with our boat. I was at first afraid for our lives. But our captain, a veteran of the frontier, assured me that they were a friendly type. A native who appeared to be the leader spoke the language of the French since he had learned it from fur trappers. When I told him about my mission, he became very animated and insisted that I go to their village.

After mooring our boat, and leaving several stout men behind to secure it, I walked with the captain to the village. There, after presenting the chief with a gift of woolen cloth, I informed him of my quest for the stone of Tzohar. The chief immediately took me to the tribe's shaman, a man called Mihigun.

The shaman led me to a large earthen mound, whose top was marked by a row of half-buried boulders in the form of a cross. He told me his people had a legend that powerful spirits, called the Anuc, lay asleep deep under the mound and would rise again on the day the ground trembled. I believe that these spirits may be the Fallen Ones.

The tribe shunned the mound, but a religious sect from France, calling themselves the Nouveau-ne, (new born) had recently settled at the base of the mound and built a small village. They considered the mound, with its Christian-like cross, to be a holy place.

I was very anxious to begin my search for the Tzohar, but Mihigun insisted that I return to the village to meet with the tribal elders. I felt it prudent to agree.

December 11: The map from the Historie of Magog indicated the placement of the Tzohar in a mound marked with a cross, thus I concluded the mound to be the location of the Tzohar. I secretly began to dig for its location the next morning, taking care to be out of sight of the settlement of

Nouveau-ne.

Mihigun soon discovered my activity. He understood what I was looking for and told me that the shiny stone was no longer there but had been taken away by some of the Nouveau-ne settlers, who believed it a pagan artifact, and had broken it in pieces and threw them in a nearby bog. This caused me much alarm, and I endeavored find traces of it, but was unsuccessful.

After retiring for the night in a lean-to, I was awakened by terrific shaking of the ground and deafening roar. I feared that what the Owyu myth predicted had begun. I was anxious that the shaking would arouse the Fallen Ones, and since the Tzohar was not present to neutralize them with its heavenly power, they would send forth their Anuc.

The Owyu were also most alarmed, and their warriors and shaman armed themselves and prepared for the onslaught. I spent the evening in prayer.

December 12: A terrible day. The earth has cracked open near the mound and the Anuc have emerged from it. They are gigantic men of fierce countenance, wielding flaming swords, who look as all to be from the same mother.

The Nouveau-ne mistook the giants for harbinger angels of the Rapture, and went rejoicing and singing to meet them. They all fell before the Anuc's terrible swords. Men, women and children were all slain, and their settlement set afire. The Anuc then attacked the Owyu village. A great battle ensued. The Owyu warriors have fought bravely, but suffered many losses. In their rampage, the Anuc violated some of the Owyu women.

We survivors hid ourselves in a nearby bog.

The Anuc seemed loathe to follow. Mihigun has told me that his vision had shown him that they fear the touch of water.

December 13: The earth still rumbles, though not as severely. My prayers have been answered, as an Owyu child has found a fragment of the Tzohar on the river bank by the bog where we hide. An amulet was quickly forged of copper under the instruction of the shaman, Mihigun, using his magic alchemy, and the fragment of Tzohar was embedded in it. Even though I felt I was treading close to idolatry, I myself prayed over it. We hope with the combined magickal (sic) powers will be successful in sending the Anuc back to whence they had come.

Claire felt suddenly very cold. She put the translation down on the bed. With trembling hands she pulled out her necklace and stared numbly at the amulet.

My God, this is it.

She closed her eyes for a moment and tried to quiet her thumping heart. After a few seconds, she opened her eyes, picked up the translation and continued reading.

December 14: At sunrise, accompanied by a group of warriors, Mihigun and I emerged from the bog, and walked to the mound and climbed to the top. The shaman held the amulet before him, and I was at his side, giving prayers and holding high my crucifix. The Anuc appeared out of the morning mist, holding flaming swords, and with a terrifying countenance. I began to waver in my resolve. Then, upon spying the amulet, whose fragment of Tzohar had begun to glow with a bright golden light, the giants stopped their advance. At that moment, the earth shook again and cracked open the maw of Hell. The Anuc plummeted back into the abyss with the most dreadful screams. And the earth again trembled and the mouth of Hades slammed shut.

Praise be to the Lord.

The amulet with the fragment of the Tzohar was returned to the top of the mound and buried in order to contain the power of the Fallen Ones for eternity.

These last days, whilst preparing to depart the Owyu Village to return down the river to Nouveau Orleans, I have fallen ill with an ague and a fever. I fear for my life. I have encased my journal in copper and pleaded for Mihigun to secrete it away as a record of these miraculous events. He assures me that he will hide it in a sacred place used by the First People.

Soldier of Christ,

Uaine Fionn

(Mike- this is the end of the text.)

Regards,

Henry

Claire slid the pages back in the envelope and placed them on the bedside table.

Her mind raced.

Too agitated to wait in her room for Wilson to show up, Claire walked down to the café and back, mulling over the contents of the translation and the telegram. It was all beginning to form a picture. The drought, the vitrified caves, the appearance of Smith, the local tales of evil giants, the bones of a giant on Doyle's property. And now the Jesuit manuscript.

If Wilson's theory about a celestial impact causing a world-wide deluge was correct…

My god, what if it's true? Claire thought. *Fallen Angels taking refuge from the Deluge in a cave in Missouri?*

Right here in Testament Hill?

Claire's could feel her pulse thumping in the hollow of her neck.

That was just crazy, she thought fiercely. *There's no such thing as angels, or Anuk or even Wilson's aliens. There's a scientific logical cause for what is happening.*

Claire's felt her certainty crumbling.

What if something has aroused them, as did the New Madrid quake?

She had to find Wilson.

Chapter 26

The Jeep was parked off the road. Smith drove a quarter mile further until he found a farm tractor path that led around a grove of jack pines. He turned unto the path, parked the Rambler behind the trees and got out. Then he walked back to Wilson's Jeep and climbed to a spot on an adjacent hill which gave him a good view of the mound and the surrounding area.

Wilson was close. Smith could sense his presence.

He had to prevent Wilson from entering the cave and learning its secret, but as he waited for Wilson to appear, a different plan formed in Smith's mind.

Wilson was young and naïve. His mind, though clever and intelligent, was still immature.

Malleable.

He could be useful.

As soon as Smith finished his thought about Wilson, the bearded young man appeared, hiking up from the road, carrying a flashlight and wearing a small backpack. Smith crouched down and watched as Wilson entered the field below and headed for the Testament Hill mound. About half way across the field Wilson stopped, lifted a hand to shield his eyes from the sun and craned his head forward. Then he took off at a jog toward a grouping of large juniper bushes near the base of the hill.

Wilson reached the junipers and bent down, appearing to be examining something on the ground. Then he stood up, stepped forward and pushed into the shrubbery.

Just before he disappeared, Smith fixed his eyes on the back of Wilson's head and whispered something in an ancient, long forgotten language.

The cave entrance was obvious once Wilson waded through the junipers. It was quite large. *I could drive my jeep through it,* he thought. A curious five foot wide semicircular swallow trough ran along ground directly to the entrance, getting deeper as it went. Wilson stepped down into it and walked to the entrance. It seemed to him that the trough was like an artificial path to the cave, but its curved sides didn't make sense.

When he reached the cave mouth he noticed that, unlike the trough, which was quite overgrown, the opening looked raw. There was no undergrowth and the exposed rock was clear of any weeds, lichen or moss. It looked new. Wilson recalled Audrey's remark: *it didn't used to be there*.

He stepped into the mouth of the cave, and turned on his flashlight. He moved cautiously into the interior, following the narrow beam of his small flashlight along the floor. The trough became shallower then all but disappeared. The temperature began to drop. Wilson suppressed a shiver. Somewhere ahead was a steady drip of water. The feeble light coming from the entrance faded as he went, until everything beyond the beam of his flashlight was cloaked in blackness. Wilson began to question the wisdom of embarking on a solo exploration. Each step further into the cave took a little more will power.

He turned to head back.

There was a whirring sound.

Wilson swung his flashlight in its direction. Two large blurred shapes materialized in the air out of the depths of the cave and dove at his head. Wilson lifted his arms, let out an animal-like yelp, and stumbled further into the cave, frantic to escape the attack. As he plunged on through the darkness, an astounding realization came that his attackers were two great horned owls .

Wilson glanced backward. The owls had banked and were diving towards him, the light-gathering ability of their enormous eyes easily penetrating the gloom.

In a flash they were on him, their wings beating against his face. Wilson screamed, his hands flailing uselessly as hooked beaks tore at his neck. Blood spewed from his torn carotid arteries, spattering down his shirt and on to the dirt. He took a few wavering steps, then blacked out from oxygen loss to his brain and fell face down to the cave floor. For a few seconds, Wilson's limbs jerked spasmodically. Then he went still.

The birds alighted on either side of him. One owl lifted a leg, and with talons extended, prodded the body. It bent its head down, the huge blank disks of it eyes peering closely into Wilson's face. It prodded him again.

Then the pair simultaneously leapt upward, beat back out the cave entrance and burst into the open air.

Smith, from his vantage point on the hill, watched them fly away, his lips slightly curved upward, stretching the pale skin on his face. In the distance, a pair of crows were exchanging angry caws.

Smith shut his eyes and began to murmur.

A few drops of icy water broke loose from the cave roof and splattered on Wilson's neck, mixing with the blood and running down in tiny rivulets.

His body, sprawled on the damp cave floor, began to shudder. Wilson slowly got to his knees, his head hanging down. He stayed in that position for a long moment, and then got unsteadily to his feet. He took a few jerky steps in a random circle, lurched towards the entrance of the cave, and stepped through into the sunlight. Smith was standing in full view on the hill, watching. Wilson, his face ashen, his eyes wide and expression blank, looked up and cocked his head at Smith.

Smith lifted up his arm as if saluting.

Wilson appeared to nod. He turned and shuffled towards his Jeep. On the way, he reached to the ground and picked up a pointy fist-sized rock. He climbed into the Jeep, placed the rock on the dash and started the engine. After a few seconds, he jammed the transmission into gear, turned the Jeep around, and headed back out to the road.

After the Jeep had gone, Smith walked down to the cave and disappeared into the entrance. He would stand guard for the Masters. He knew more intruders would be coming.

Edith drove directly to the motel after work. Mrs. B. informed her that Dr. Brannigan had driven off in her funny-looking foreign car.

"Is everything alright, Edith?" Mrs. B. asked, moving a vacuum cleaner cord to a different outlet. "You seem a little flustered."

"I'm fine." Edith turned toward the office window and looked out. "How long ago did she leave?"

"I guess about fifteen minutes."

"Do you have any idea where she was headed?"

"She was going to look for her associate, Mr. Wilson. He's gone missing."

"Mercy."

Mrs. B. pulled on an ear. "She did ask me if I knew anything about a cave on Amos Doyle's property. Around Testament Hill."

Edith turned back to Mrs. B. "A cave? I've never heard anything about that, and I've lived here all my life."

"Funny thing, Deputy Hooper was in here earlier asking the same questions." Mrs. B. shook his head. "Mighty peculiar things have been happening around here lately." She switched on the vacuum cleaner and started moving it back and forth across the lobby carpet.

Edith watched her in exasperation until she realized Mrs. B was finished with their conversation. Edith raised her voice. "Thank you. And good day."

When she got back into her car, Edith mulled over her options: she could wait until Claire got back, or drive out to Doyle's property and try to locate her. Claire's car was unusual, so if Edith spotted the model, it would have to be Claire's.

Edith headed out to the highway.

Claire drove first by the café and then Duggan's bar, hoping to spot Wilson's Jeep parked out front, speculating that he might have stopped at either place on his way back from Dansville. No luck. Now she was becoming truly alarmed. She was sure now that Wilson, in spite of her instructions, had gone to the cave alone. And her gut told her something was wrong.

Next she drove to the police station. She saw that the Chief's car was gone and Deputy Hooper's cruiser was parked out front.

Great.

Claire sat for a moment, considering not going in. The thought of dealing with that jackass Hooper was revolting. But she had to do something.

She got out of her car and stalked into the office. Hooper was sitting at the Chief's desk, his legs propped on the table, cowboy-booted feet crossed at the ankle. He was holding his automatic handgun up, wiping it with a rag. The only thing missing from the scene was a stem of prairie grass dangling from his mouth.

The deputy pretended not to notice her.

"I need to talk to the Chief," Claire announced.

The deputy turned slowly, regarding her through half-closed eyes. "Not here," he said.

"When do you expect him?"

"Well, miss, he's out on a very important case. Don't know when he'll be back."

"Can you contact him on your radio for me…please?" Claire pointed at Edith's desk and the dispatch radio.

The deputy knew he was revealing information he shouldn't but couldn't resist. "He's investigating a murder, a grisly one, I may add. He should be back here in a little bit, if you care to wait."

Claire's heart went up to her throat. "It's not…it's not my assistant from the university, is it? Mike Wilson?"

Deputy Hooper was obviously enjoying her angst. He silently counted to five before answering. "No ma'am. I can't divulge the victim's name, of course, but I can assure you it was not Mr. Wilson."

Claire let out her breath. "Thank God." She stared at the deputy. "My colleague is missing. Can you help?"

"Is he injured?"

"I don't know. If I knew that, deputy, I'd know where he was."

Hooper uncrossed and re-crossed his legs. "Well, maybe we should just wait a bit before launching a full scale *in-ves-ti-ga-tion*. Mr. Wilson's a big boy, I'm sure he can take care of himself."

The deputy brought his legs down, stood up and made a show of sliding his pistol in his holster. "Now if you don't mind, I have some *important* police work to do," he said, his voice dripping with sarcasm. "You're welcome to wait here for the Chief. I'm sure he wouldn't mind, since you two are close and all."

Claire threw up her hands, scowled at Hooper, and stomped out into the street, slamming the door behind her.

"Bitch," Hooper said. He stepped to the window, hoping to catch sight of her walking away.

Something caught his eye: a flare of light that silhouetted the buildings on Main Street.

That damn blue light again. For a moment the deputy was held spellbound. The light flowed into the station, through his eyes and filled his skull. It hurt, but he couldn't look away. It was as if fingers were inside his brain clawing along its lobes. He winced and groaned.

Go away.

Then, as suddenly as it had come, the light and the clawing stopped.

As if in a trance, Hooper slowly got up from behind the desk and went over to the small refrigerator in the corner of the office where they kept sodas and lunches. He opened it and pulled out a folded paper bag labeled 'Deputy's' in large sloppy script. He swore softly as some red-tinted liquid dripped from the bottom onto the floor. He spread it around with his boot until it wasn't noticeable. Then he waited a few minutes to make sure Doctor Geologist was gone, and followed her out.

Claire parked her car a block down from the police station and sat waiting for Chief Childress's car to appear. There was no way she was going to sit in the office keeping company with the obnoxious deputy. She looked over at Norquist's Drugs and imagined going in and buying a pack of smokes and enjoying a few puffs while she sat. But the temptation was never going to be stronger than her resolve not to smoke again. She settled back in the seat, preparing for a long wait.

She was surprised when not five minutes later, Deputy Hooper stepped out of the station clutching a paper bag. He headed straight to his patrol car without noticing her presence. He got in, cranked the engine, gunned it a couple of times, and took off quickly, his tires chirping on the asphalt.

The Jeep pulled up to a stop where Ivy was walking at the side of the road. From behind the wheel, Wilson leaned towards the open passenger window.

He coughed, then in a hoarse voice called out, "Hey, Ivy! Need a ride? I'm headed towards your farm."

Ivy looked over at Wilson. "Oh, I don't think so...".

Wilson didn't look so good to Ivy, like he had been sick or something. His skin sagged and had a yucky grey-green coloring. There were deep dark circles under his eyes. He had a scarf tightly wrapped around his neck. His shirt was painted with what looked like blood.

Ivy frowned at him. "Say...where are your glasses, Mr. Wilson?

"What?" Wilson's blinked and twitched his head.

"Your glasses," Ivy repeated. "Don't you need them to drive?"

"Come on," Wilson urged, ignoring her question. He coughed again. "Have you ever ridden in a real Jeep before?"

"Well," Ivy looked up and down the empty road.

"I might even let you drive it," Wilson said as he casually reached for the rock on the dash and tucked it under his knee.

About a mile from Doyle's property, Edith spotted a red

smudge on the highway. As she drove closer, she saw that it was an old tractor parked sideways across the road.

"As I live and breathe, that looks like Claude Wiggins' Farmall," she said aloud.

She slowed the Chrysler and brought it to a stop at the side of the road about twenty feet from the tractor. There was no one in the seat, but she could hear the engine idling.

"What in tarnation?" She turned off her ignition, pulled on the parking brake and sat. Something about the situation bothered her. After a minute, Edith got out of the car, impulsively grabbing the dog-eared leather-bound Bible that she always kept on the dash. She walked cautiously toward the tractor, looking around as she went.

"Claude? Is that you, Claude?"

She stopped and listened. There was only the sound of the idling Farmall and a bumblebee buzzing near some chicory flowers along the side of the road.

The weeds rustled behind her and Edith spun around to see Claude Wiggins standing with a rusty harvesting sickle in his hand. He was dressed in bib overalls with the legs partly tucked into muck boots. Long, oily hair fell across his forehead and his beard sprung in wild grey clumps from his face.

"'Afternoon, Miss Edith," he said. His bloodshot eyes looked briefly up at her, then cast down to his feet, as if he was embarrassed to be caught doing something bad.

Edith's first thought was that he had been drinking, but when he took a step towards her, his gait was strong and steady.

Edith began to be afraid.

"Why, Claude, how have you been?" Edith tried to make her voice sound chirpy. "Haven't seen you at church in a coon's age."

"Yes, ma'am."

"Is everything alright?"

"No, ma'am." Claude's eyes remained fixed on the ground.

Edith had a bad premonition. She grabbed her Bible with

both hands and held it in front of her like a shield. "Claude, you know, God always answers our prayers when we're in need or hurting."

Claude's head came up and he glared at her, his eyes wide. He raised the sickle.

"I'm sorry, Miss Edith…" he mumbled.

Edith pushed down a scream erupting from her throat. Somehow she knew that would just propel Claude further into his madness. She forced herself to smile, and raised the bible higher.

"The Bible teaches us how to pray, Claude," she said, her voice now strident and clear. "Pray with me now:

The Lord is my shepherd; I shall not want…

The sickle went up higher.

Edith flinched but persisted. "Claude! Pray with me now. Let's pray together."

Wiggins squeezed his eyes tight.

"Claude," Edith said, her voice very calm. "Pray with me:

He maketh me to lie down in green pastures: he leadeth me beside the still waters.

Edith stopped and waited. Claude said nothing. Edith raised her eyes to the sky. It was a clear and brilliant blue. Edith imagined angels in flowing robes descending down towards them.

"Claude," she said again, "pray with me:

He restoreth my soul: he leadeth me in the paths of righteousness for his name's sake.

The sickle lowered a couple inches. Claude's mouth worked. At first nothing came out. When he spoke, his voice a croak:

He restoreth my soul: he leadeth me in the paths of righteousness for his name's sake.

"Yes!" Edith said. "Yes. Now let's go on:"

Now, haltingly, they spoke in unison:

Yea, though I walk through the valley of the shadow of death, I will fear no evil: for thou art with me; thy rod and thy staff they comfort me.

Thou preparest a table before me in the presence of mine enemies: thou anointest my head with oil; my cup runneth over.
Surely goodness and mercy shall follow me all the days of my life: and I will dwell in the house of the Lord forever.
Amen.

Claude brought his arm down and the sickle fell from his gasp. It rang loudly as it struck the asphalt of the road. He dropped to his knees.

"I...I", he stammered. Tears rolled down his cheeks and drool gathered at the corners of his mouth and dripped to the pavement.

Edith reached down, gently grabbed the collar of his shirt and pulled upward. "Get up, Claude. You're free now."

Wiggins rose sluggishly. Without a word, he turned and walked towards his tractor, at first shuffling, then his steps becoming quicker and firm. When he got to his Farmall, he practically leapt up into the seat. As Edith watched, he threw it in gear, and turned it so that it was facing homeward to his farm. He rolled by Edith and held up his hand.

Edith waited until Wiggins disappeared over a hill and then got back in her car.

"Thank you, Lord," she whispered, putting her Bible back on the dash and starting her car. "Stay with me," she added. She pulled back onto the road and pressed down hard on the accelerator.

Edith's fear was confirmed: she was sure now that the evil that had been sleeping and waiting at Testament Hill was arising. She had to find Claire and warn her. And warn her about that man, Smith. He certainly was its vanguard.

Down the road, Edith recognized the long rise that would take her to the north edge of Doyle's farm. She breathed a sigh of relief, and crossed herself. Even though it was a Catholic custom and Edith considered herself basically a Baptist, she got comfort from making the sign and felt it was, after all, a Christian gesture.

A police cruiser appeared at the crest of the hill, coming from the opposite direction and sped towards her. Edith knew it was Deputy Hooper because he always drove the newer of the town's two cruisers. Chief Childress preferred driving the older Ford instead of the shiny new Plymouth.

She contemplated trying to flag him down and warn him about what was going on, then she realized that he would certainly mock her. Edith never did care for Deputy Hooper. Even though he didn't openly ridiculed her religious proclivities, she always sensed he regarded them with contempt.

As the deputy's car drew closer, Edith was shocked when she saw that Hooper had moved to the opposite side of the road and was now heading directly toward her. She was confused about what he was doing. Perhaps he was distracted by something, maybe the radio, and hadn't noticed he had strayed over. She was sure that any second he would look up and see that he had drifted and jerk the cruiser back into its proper lane.

But he didn't. As the two vehicles closed in, Edith could make out the face of the driver. Her mouth dropped open: it looked like Ida Wagner.

Edith squinted hard as the cars closed in. It was Ida Wagner's face, but it was gray and monstrously distorted.

Edith opened her mouth to scream, but her voice box was frozen and she only managed to hiss.

As she held down her car horn and swerved wildly to escape the certain collision, the truth came to her: the deputy was wearing Ida's face. Like a Halloween mask from Hell.

Her Chrysler spun out of control and plunged head-on into a drainage ditch. The narrow ditch trapped the car's front end and it somersaulted onto its roof, flattening it and blowing out the windows.

Edith was spared being crushed because she was thrown out the window as the car tumbled. She flipped through the air and was impaled upright on a cedar fence post. Except for the blood dripping from her gaping mouth and the top of the post protruding out the back of her neck, it looked as though she was resting against the fence, taking a moment to enjoy the bucolic countryside.

Down the road, the deputy's car slowed to a stop, did a U-turn and idled by the crash scene.

"Why, good afternoon to you, Miss Edith." Deputy Hooper said as he went by, his voice distorted by his veil of human flesh. "You have a blessed day!"

Claire sat in her car pondering her options. She decided to wait a while longer for Chief Childress to return. She opened her glove box and did a quick check of her revolver.

A car door slammed. Claire looked up to see Childress had pulled up to the station. He was hitching up his trousers and heading for the door. She jumped out of her car.

"Chief Childress!"

He stopped and turned. "What can I do for you, Doctor?" he asked somewhat irritably.

"I need your help."

"Well, then, come into the office."

He opened the door to the station and waited until Claire stepped in, then brushed past her and went to his desk. He pulled out a bottle of whiskey from his drawer and poured a generous amount into his coffee cup.

Claire said, "I'm sorry to bother you."

Childress plunked down with a grunt into the chair. "It's been a hell of a day." He took a swig from his mug and looked at Claire, who was standing with her hands behind her back. His voice softened a little. "So... Claire, what can I do for you?"

"My colleague Mike Wilson is missing."

"What makes you think he's missing, exactly?"

"He was supposed to meet me this afternoon and we were going together to investigate a cave on Amos Doyle's property."

"A cave, eh?"

"Yes, we suspect it might have to do with the lowering of the water table." Claire wasn't going to mention her more sinister suspicions.

Childress ran his hands through his thinning hair. "Where's this cave supposed to be?"

"We heard it's on Doyle's property. Right off Route 23."

"Do you think it's possible he decided to explore the cave himself?"

"I do."

"That's not too bright. Hopefully he hasn't got himself lost or hurt."

Claire raised her hands. "Chief, can't we organize a search party or something?"

"Right now I've got my plate full," Childress told her, voice rising. "I got a murder, Deputy Hooper is AWOL, and my dispatcher, Edith, is missing." He threw up his hands. "I don't know what's going on, but things have gone to shit since you guys arrived from the university."

Claire made a face. "I hope you're not implying..."

"I'm not implying anything." Childress closed his eyes for a moment, then he sighed. "I'll do what I can, Doctor Brannigan. Understand that my resources are limited..." he hesitated, then said gravely, "Amos Doyle called me. He was very worried."

Claire's heart went to her throat.

"His granddaughter's missing. Ivy never came home after school this afternoon."

Claire covered her mouth with her hand.

Childress took a deep breath. "I got a bad feeling about all of this."

Claire stepped closer to the Chief's desk. "You must let me help you find her."

Childress shook his head. "I'm going to ask for help from the Highway Patrol, especially now since I can't find Hooper. You focus on finding your friend, Wilson."

That reminded Claire. "I don't know if this means anything, but Mrs. B. at the motel told me Deputy Hooper was asking about the cave."

Childress nodded and finished off his whiskey. He stared thoughtfully at Claire for a moment "Don't go alone to find

Wilson," he cautioned. "Do you have anyone you can ask to help you search until I get some more help around here?"

Claire swept her hair off her forehead. "Possibly, yes."

"Good luck, then."

After Doctor Brannigan left, Childress got on the phone to Captain Norris, informing him of the new developments. Norris agreed to meet at the station with some of his troopers in ninety minutes to organize the search for the little girl. They would postpone the investigation of Ida Wagner's death until they located Ivy.

After hanging up, Childress paced impatiently in his office for a couple of minutes, then decided to use the hour and a half to scout around in his cruiser for Ivy.

He briefly contemplated stopping home to grab a sandwich, but wasn't ready to face what was sure to be his wife's insistent questions and harping about the hazards of his job. She'd also probably nag him about retirement so he could spend more time with her, helping around the house. Maybe even go on that cruise they'd been talking about for years, blah, blah, blah. It would turn out to be more about her in the end.

Instead, Childress pulled into Norquist's Drugs and bought a fresh pint of Old Granddad. He was thankful old man Norquist wasn't behind the counter. The young clerk, who only looked slightly familiar, didn't blink an eye at his purchase and didn't try to make conversation.

Childress planned to drive out towards Amos Doyle's farm and retrace what should have been Ivy's route from school. There were a few abandoned buildings and two-track roads along the way that he figured should be checked out. He could still get back in town in time to meet with the Highway Patrol.

He poured a generous slug of bourdon in his mug and swung his cruiser on to Highway 23, letting the draft from the windows wash over his face, as if it could take away the troubles of the day.

His radio crackled and a voice said:

"Do you copy, Chief Childress? This is Sergeant Carson from the state crime lab, over."

Childress snatched up his mike. "Go ahead, Sergeant. This is Chief Childress."

He could hear a voice clearing on the other end, then:

"Captain Norris wanted me to call you right away, over."

"Go ahead." Childress was impatient.

"Got a couple things to report. Both not good."

"Give it to me, damn it."

The radio crackled. "First: Thelma Wheeler. Somebody out running their hounds discovered her body off the side of the road near Dansville. Looks like a hit and run. She was torn up pretty bad."

"Jesus Christ! What was she doing out on the road?"

For a moment the speaker was silent. "And the second thing, Chief Childress...We got lab results from fingerprints on the kitchen cleaver that appears to be the murder weapon in the Ida Wagner case."

"Tell me."

"They belong to Deputy Frank Hooper, sir."

"Son of a bitch!"

Childress didn't bother signing off. He dropped the mike and pressed the cruiser's accelerator to the floor.

The cave Hooper was asking about was supposed to be just down the road.

Claire decided to reach out to John Preston.

She drove to the fairground and found the nicest looking trailer, a shiny new twenty-eight foot Airstream Traveler and knocked on the door. She was relieved when John Preston answered.

He stood in the doorway with a bottle of beer in his hand, shirtless, wearing a pair of worn blue jeans that hung low on his waist. His blond hair cascaded over his bare shoulders. A gold cross hung from a chain on his muscular, tanned chest. In spite of the seriousness of her business, Claire felt her heart skip a beat.

"Hello, Claire. What a pleasant surprise." He pointed at himself. "I'm sorry - I wasn't expecting any visitors."

Claire forced her voice to be cool. "Pardon me for bothering you, Preston. I'm afraid something bad has happened."

"Of course." He waved his hand. "Please come in. Just give me a second to get decent."

"No, that's okay. I'll just wait out here."

"Sure. I'll be right out."

Claire sat down on his door step. A minute later, Preston appeared at the screen door, now wearing a denim shirt. "Beer?" he said.

Claire started shaking her head then changed her mind. "Sure."

She could hear the two pops of the caps coming off. Preston came out, sat down next to her and handed over a cold bottle.

He waited until she took a long pull.

"So...?" Preston looked expectantly at Claire.

"Wilson's missing. The police can't help because apparently Ivy's missing too."

"Ivy?"

"Amos Doyle's granddaughter. Remember I told you about her pet crow? Amos told the Chief she never showed up from school today." Claire's voice cracked. "She's only twelve years old."

"My God."

"Of course, the police are busy looking for Ivy. I understand that. So they can't help me to find Wilson. Wilson and I were supposed to meet this afternoon. But I haven't seen or heard from him." Claire glanced anxiously at her wristwatch. "And now it's after 6 p.m....Crap, I'm worried that something's happened to him, too."

"Like an accident?"

"No...yes...maybe. I don't know. He's a little reckless sometimes. Impulsive."

"He's a kid."

Claire rubbed her forehead. "I can't help but think the

two are related: Wilson and Ivy's disappearance."

"Would you like my help?"

"Please."

Preston put his beer down. "Okay, do you have an idea where to look for your colleague?"

"Wilson and I were planning to locate a cave we heard about from Audrey, a waitress at the café, near Amos Doyle's farm. Maybe he decided to head out there alone to check it out."

"A cave?" Preston stood up. "Let's go." He reached down, gently took Claire's beer from her grasp and helped her up. "Do you know where it might be?"

"I've got a map in the car, same one Wilson had. He's meticulous about such things - always gets two in case one gets misplaced."

Chapter 27

Ten minutes later, Claire and Preston were in her Volvo racing down the road toward Doyle's farm. Preston volunteered to drive, so that Claire could navigate using the map and keep an eye out for Wilson and Ivy.

Claire chewed on her lip. She initiated conversation to ease the stress. "Your pamphlet - the one handed out at the revival. How much of it really happened?"

"You mean the part about stumbling out of a brothel, the white light, falling down in the dirt, the bearded figure?"

"Yes. Is any of it true?"

"All of it." Preston laughed. "Actually, it's *somewhat* true. It's an edited version. Compressed and dramatized."

"I guessed that."

"I did have an epiphany of sorts, and it did lead me back to preaching." Preston glanced at Claire. "I had been drinking one night, and it was in Texas. It was probably just too much alcohol. I fell down in the street, thought I saw a light glowing around me and heard a voice telling me I had a mission in life."

"A voice? God? An angel?"

"Naw. Probably just my subconscious talking to me. About something I'd been ignoring." Preston rubbed the back of his neck. "When I was young, I joined a revival troupe... you know, doing odd jobs to earn my keep, learning the business, so to speak."

"I see."

"Anyway, I caught on to the ins and outs of the business fast. Became a real asset to the organization. Eventually, I felt I was ready for a bigger piece of the pie. But my ideas were ignored, and I felt I wasn't getting the respect I deserved."

"So?."

"So I left. Did a stint in the military, got out and bounced around the country working oil fields. That's when I had my inspiration to get into the preaching business again."

"You started your own revival troupe."

"Well, not right away. Actually, I got a job as a deputy sheriff in a town called Marjorie in Texas. The vision that I had was still stuck in my mind, but I wasn't sure how to act on it. Then, by happenstance, the revival troupe I used to work for came into town. When their leader died in an accident, I rejoined the troupe and ended up taking over."

"That's quite a story," Claire said.

"I guess." Preston said. "Life's strange that way. Of course, I was drawn by the financial rewards, but I did have that weird experience. I still wonder about it even to this day."

"What about the people you preach to? Is it all bullshit?"

"If you had asked me that six months ago, I'd say mostly yes. But now I'm not so sure. I keep going back to that night in Texas. Maybe it really did mean something."

"You are the only one who can answer..." Claire stopped in midsentence. "Wait!" She pointed out the windshield to the road ahead. "Is that Wilson's Jeep?"

"Where? I don't see anything."

Claire strained her eyes. "I guess it's nothing. For a second, I thought I saw something disappear over that hill up ahead."

Preston gave Claire a sympathetic look. "Don't worry, we'll find your assistant."

Claire ran a hand through her hair. "I also wanted to ask you: what do you believe about the story of the Fallen Angels and the Nephilim?"

For a moment, Preston said nothing, his eyes fixed on the road ahead. Claire thought maybe he didn't hear her through the wind noise.

"You mentioned them in your sermon," Claire prompted.

"I did. I really don't know what inspired me to bring them up." He shook his head slightly. "The evidence is sketchy," Preston said. "There are various references to them in the Bible and other ancient documents such as the Apocrypha."

"Apocrypha?"

"Yes. 'Apocrypha' comes from Greek, meaning, roughly, obscure or hidden. The Apocrypha are ancient writings that were not officially included as 'canon', or accepted, when the 'official' Bible was being compiled by the Catholic Church. The Book of Enoch is part of the Apocrypha. It describes beings called the 'Watchers'- rebellious angels led by Samyaza. They supposedly came down to the Earth and fathered children with human females. The giant offspring were called the Nephilim, as I mentioned in my sermon."

Preston glanced at Claire. "I suspect there may be something to it."

"That God caused the world to flood, in order to kill the Nephilim and drive the Fallen Angels underground?"

"Perhaps those stories are interpretations inspired by actual historical events, like Wilson's comet theory, that's all," Preston said. "As I said, I wasn't planning on mentioning them. It just came out."

Preston guided the car around a sharp curve. The rush of air coming in the window pushed his hair across his forehead. He took his hand off the wheel and flicked it away. "Claire...I've been having these dreams lately, disturbing dreams."

"Yes...?"

"About, I think, Fallen Angels."

Claire turned to him, eyes intense. "Preston, something really scary is going on here."

"Maybe it's just all in our imagination."

"Wilson and Ivy missing is not in our imagination."

"Of course not."

"There's something else." Claire pulled the amulet out from under her shirt and held up it up for Preston to see. "I found this by accident. It originally belonged to Rachel Doyle, Ivy's mother."

"That's quite a coincidence."

"I've been developing a hypothesis about it. I had a conversation with an old Indian that Edith had referred me to - Skander Grey Wolf. He lives alone in a cabin in the woods outside of town. It turns out he is one of the last living descendants from the Oweyu tribe."

"And?"

"He told me an Oweyu legend about demon spirits that dwell under the Testament Hill mound. During the New Madrid earthquake in 1811, these spirits, called the Anuk by the tribe, arose out of the ground and attacked his tribe. The Oweyu warriors managed to fight them off in a battle that decimated the tribe."

Preston shook his head. "That's a disturbing story, Claire."

"And get this: the Oweyu used a magical object that had the power to keep the demons imprisoned." Claire tapped the amulet. "I believe this is it, and I have an idea of how it works - I first noticed something strange about the amulet when I was in the shower "

"I would have liked to see that."

"I bet you would." Claire managed a smile. "Seriously- the amulet stopped the water from going down the drain when I accidently dropped it in the tub. Then, while I was checking out a well that had dried up, I almost drowned when the well started filling after the amulet fell in a puddle at the bottom."

"That's pretty incredible."

"And scary. Get this: I did an experiment with the pool water at the Sleep-tite Motel. When I just touched the amulet to the surface, nothing happened. But when I totally immersed it in the water, there was an amazing reaction. It *drew* the water in around it. It was a very strong force."

Preston took his eyes off the road for a second and gave Claire a puzzled look.

Claire pointed at the amulet. "It attracts water and causes it to coalesce around it like a wick or maybe more like a seed crystal. It's hard to describe."

Preston took a long breath. "Think about what you're proposing, Claire. It's really far-fetched."

"It all connects," Claire argued. "Whatever is down in the caves must be hydrophobic, fearing contact with water.

The Jesuit Manuscript mentioned something about the Anuk's abhorrence of water."

"Jesuit Manuscript?"

Claire told Preston the story of the journal - how the Jesuit priest came looking for the Tzohar in 1811. How he discovered that French settlers had removed the stone from its place on the mound above the caves, broke it, and threw the fragments in the river. Then came the New Madrid earthquake. The Anuk were roused, and with the Tzohar gone, the water table quickly dropped and they were freed. That's when they emerged and attacked the settlers and the Oweyu.

To protect the survivors, the Jesuit priest and the Oweyu medicine man constructed the "magical" amulet, using a recovered fragment of the Tzohar. They used it to ward off the Anuk and send them back to their cave.

Preston whistled. "So you're think that there might be a connection between the Anuk and the Fallen Angels of the Bible?"

"It's crazy, I know. But it all fits, in a way."

Preston swept his hand towards the windshield. "We'll get it sorted out. For now, we should just concentrate on finding Wilson."

"Right. Let's find that cave."

Testament Hill mound came into view.

Claire pointed. "The cave that Audrey, the waitress, mentioned should be somewhere on that side of the hill."

"Let's go." Preston pulled the car to the side of the road and parked.

They jumped out and Claire grabbed the backpack from the rear seat containing a flashlight and the Geiger counter. While Preston attention was diverted, she covertly patted the .38 she had tucked in the small of her back to make sure it was secure and still hidden by her blouse.

The wild rye crunched loudly under their feet as they crossed the parched field. Somewhere out of sight a squirrel chattered a warning.

"Look..." Claire motioned with her hand. "See, tracks in

the grass, where someone has driven a vehicle. They're recent."

Preston's gaze followed her finger. "Yeah, I see them. Good catch."

They followed the trace of pressed prairie grass across a large field.

Claire saw it first, hidden behind a huge spreading dogwood. "Preston, look!"

It was a State Highway Patrol cruiser.

They circled the bush. The cruiser's driver door was open.

"Hello?" Preston called out. "Hello…anybody here?"

Claire rested her hand behind her back next to bulge of the .38. They cautiously went up and bent to look into the car. Claire was relieved to see it was unoccupied. The handset from the police radio was lying on the seat.

In the back of Claire's mind, a little alarm was going off. She stepped back from the car and scanned the area. The two bands of flattened grass led from the back of the car out to the highway, tracing out the path the trooper had driven.

Preston straightened up, and following Claire's lead, glanced around, "He must have been looking for something."

"I bet this is the car that sped by me the morning I was driving into town," Claire said. "It was right after I saw a flash of light and heard a boom."

She paused and met Preston's eyes. "Chief Childress and the Highway Patrol captain were talking about a missing trooper at the station. The trooper was apparently checking out a possible explosion. It happened just before I saw Smith standing by the side…" Claire's voice trailed off.

"*Claire.*" Preston's voice was strained. He was staring at something on the ground.

"What?"

He motioned.

"Here…it's not good."

Claire walked over and stooped over the spot where Preston was pointing.

There was a dark brown stain on the grass.
"Is that...?" she asked.
"Blood? I think so, Claire."

Claire waited vigilantly by the trooper's car, her hand resting on the butt of her Smith & Wesson while Preston spiraled out, scanning the underbrush. After about ten minutes, he stopped short, knelt down for a moment in some tall weeds then stood back up, his face ashen.

"What?" Claire said. Her voice wavered. "It's not..."

"It's the trooper."

Claire took a few steps towards Preston.

Preston held up his hand. "Claire... don't... He's dead. All cut up. It's not pretty. There's some large feathers scattered around the body. What or whoever attacked him went after his throat and face." Preston rubbed his forehead. "Try to get hold of somebody on the car radio while I look around some more."

"Right."

Claire hurried back to the cruiser and slid into the driver's seat. After fumbling with the radio controls for a few frustrating minutes, she decided that something was wrong with it. She pulled gently on the microphone cable. The other end came free. It had been shredded as if it had been chewed. She examined the ragged cable and decided there was no way it could be repaired.

"The radio's been sabotaged," Claire called out to Preston. She climbed out of the car holding up the ragged microphone cable.

Preston came over and examined the cable. "What the hell...?"

"We still need to look for Wilson, "Claire said. "I bet he didn't spot the trooper's car and went to find the cave. We need to find it."

"Say, where's his Jeep?" Preston wondered aloud.

"I don't know, but I'm sure he was around here looking for the cave." Claire looked at the mound. "Audrey, the waitress at the café mentioned something about a clearing hidden by bushes."

Preston pointed. "See those junipers next to the hill? I bet that's what she was talking about."

They ran to the mound. Preston got there first and elbowed his way through the branches. "Claire, it's the cave!" he called out. "There's a ditch here, so be careful."

A minute later, Claire had joined him. She shook her head. "It's a big opening. I wondered why it wasn't common knowledge."

A long depression in the ground leading out from the front of the cave as if someone had once done some excavation, although it had long since overgrown. Claire pondered the furrow for a moment. Perhaps it was dug to make it easier to enter the cave. As Claire crouched down to take a closer look, something else on the ground a couple feet away caught her eye.

She cried out and looked up at Preston. "It's Wilson's beret, and it's covered in blood. I'm sure something's bad happened to him!"

"Let's not jump to conclusions, Claire." Preston reached out and put his hand lightly on her forearm. "Maybe he just bumped his head on the cave roof or something."

"I hope to God you're right, but just in case..." Claire reached behind her back and pulled out her .38.

Preston eyes went wide.

"Long story." Claire said. "If somebody's hurt Wilson, I'm going to deal swift justice, right here and now."

Claire was looking at the ground in front of the cave entrance. "These rocks have been disturbed recently.

"How recent is 'recently'?"

"Just weeks or days. "It doesn't take long for Mother Nature to go to work. The way these rocks around the entrance are strewn about...almost as if it was caused by an explosion." Claire bent down and ran her fingers along one of the rocks. "I wonder if it has to do with what I witnessed when I first drove into Testament Hill. I figured it was just lightning and a loud thunderclap..." She put her hand to her mouth. "Preston, what if something came out of the cave and attacked the trooper?"

Preston swung his arm at the entrance. "Shall we?"

Claire took a deep breath. "I don't think we have a choice but to go in."

With Claire at point with the .38, Preston followed one step behind, lighting the path with the flashlight.

As they made their way into the cave, a dank breeze tinged with something sulfurous wafted past them. It made an eerie moaning sound as it reverberated from the depths.

"This theory of yours about the Fallen Angels -" Preston mused aloud as they warily made their way deeper in the cave, "what are the odds that of all places on Earth, they would seek shelter here in Missouri? It's doesn't seem very Biblical, if you know what I mean."

"Pretty good odds, if you think about it," Clare said, keeping her voice down. "We're not far from the geological center of the United States. It's somewhere around Lebanon, Kansas. Not far from here."

"How did anybody figure that out?"

"It was done very ingeniously, back in 1918," Claire explained. "They cut out a cardboard outline of the US and balanced on a pencil point. If you think about it, it makes sense. Of course, it's been measured more accurately since then, but the original estimate was good within twenty miles or so."

"Clever," Preston said. "Okay, then, what's the significance of the geographic center in relation to your theory?"

"Consider: What better place to avoid the aftermath of the impact that Wilson proposed?"

"Away from the oceans."

"There you go. The geographic center of the U.S is as far from the oceans as you can get, and it's in a seismically quiet area," Claire explained. "You certainly wouldn't want to be in an area like Yellowstone, the San Andreas fault or the Cascades when the asteroid struck. The enormous impact on the Earth's crust could activate quakes and volcanos in those seismically volatile areas."

Preston thought about what Claire was saying for a minute. "What about the New Madrid quake?"

"I don't have all the answers," Claire admitted. "Perhaps they didn't know about the New Madrid fault."

"But there's certainly other safe areas on the planet..."

"Like the Mongolian Desert?" Claire suggested.

"Yeah."

"Hell, who knows - maybe there are some Fallen Angels lying in wait there, too."

"That's a scary thought," Preston said. "Ok, another question: how did these Fallen Angels know they needed to find a sanctuary?"

"Hey, you're the religion guy. They're supernatural beings, right? Maybe they got super knowledge." Claire glanced at Preston. "Seriously though, maybe they had an advanced knowledge of astronomy. They knew what was coming." Claire ducked her head to clear a low spot in the cave roof. "Watch out, Preston," she warned.

Preston didn't reply. He stopped and was looking down on the floor of the cave. "You know, this trough... you can still see its trace here. It's as if something careened into here like a giant bullet."

Claire noticed the expression on Preston's face. "What is it?"

"I think I might know what caused it," he answered, his voice suddenly hoarse. "It's just too incredible."

"Tell me."

"Wait."

Preston swept the flashlight beam across the ground. Up ahead, the trough abruptly curved 180 degrees, as if whatever had plowed in and skidded around before coming to a stop. Partially buried at the end of the curve was a black egg-shaped object. It was about ten feet long and five feet in diameter. Its round blunt end faced the cave entrance. The opposite, narrower end was fitted with square fins arranged like an open ended box. Along the top of the "egg" was a jagged half-inch wide crack as if the casing had split.

Preston sucked in his breath. "My God! There it is. I

can't believe it!"

"There's what?" Claire asked, alarmed. "It looks like a bomb."

Preston stepped up to the object. He ran his finger along its side. "There's faded lettering here: *"Close is good enough for government work."*

He stepped back, lifted his hands and laughed. There was a hint of hysteria in it that Claire found slightly frightening.

"It is a *bomb*, Claire, an atomic bomb - a Mark IV, to be exact. It ended up here after being jettisoned by a B-36 Peacemaker bomber in 1952."

Claire went to his side and tried to discern his expression in the dim light. "How would you know that?"

"Because I was the one who dropped it."

Standing in the gloom of the dank cave, Preston told Claire the story of Air Force flight 2122: how the aircraft had engine trouble and it was decided to jettison the bombs. "I was the bombardier. My name was John Preskovics back then," Preston explained. "I legally changed it when I started preaching and set up a corporation for tax purposes. An English sounding name opens more doors."

"I see." Claire blinked, trying to process Preston's revelation.

"I had heard rumors that they never found the second bomb, and after a couple months, the government gave up the search," Preston continued. "I can see why they never found it: it must have come in horizontally because of the low altitude from which it was dropped and plowed across the ground. By some unbelievable coincidence, it broke into this cave system."

"It *is* an unbelievable coincidence," Claire said, circling around the bomb. She pointed at the crack. "Could this be what's causing the higher than normal radioactivity we detected with the Geiger counter down the well?"

"Possibly." Preston swept the flashlight beam around the

bomb. "The plutonium core hasn't been breached, I'm sure - the radioactivity would have been off the charts. Probably just cracked the outer shielding."

"Would that contamination go all the way to the well at Doyle's?" Claire was thinking about the glassy walls in the cave, and her theory that nuclear energy was used to melt them.

"Who knows? I guess air circulation in the cave could move radioactive particles around."

"But..."Claire was thinking out loud. "It wouldn't generate any heat."

"Not at all," Preston said. "We've probably not even been exposed to enough radiation to be harmful."

"What amount of radioactivity isn't harmful?" Claire made a face and took Preston's hand. "Let's get out of here." She pulled him towards the entrance. A minute later they were back out to the sunlight and fresh air.

For a few seconds the two looked blankly at each other.

"What are we going to do, Preston?" Claire said. "About the dead Highway Patrol Trooper and the discovery of the bomb? What about Wilson? I think he might be still in the cave somewhere, maybe hurt or lost. He maybe didn't notice the bomb in the darkness, and went right past it."

"Well, we need to let somebody know, of course," Preston said. "You drive back to town and tell the Chief. I'll stay here and look around some more."

Claire shook her head. "How about I stay here in case Wilson shows up hurt or something, and you go back in to town. I think you might have more credibility with the authorities at this point."

"I'm not sure leaving you here alone is a good idea."

Claire pointed the muzzle of her revolver at the ground, flipped it open to check the cylinders and closed it with an expert snap of her wrist.

"Don't worry about me," she said.

Preston managed a grin. "Right." He handed Claire the flashlight and started walking back to the road. He called over his shoulder. "I'll be back as soon as I can with some help. And stay out of the cave for now."

Childress spotted the Chrysler Windsor lying upside down in the ditch. He choked on his coffee. "Son of a bitch!"

As he pulled over to the shoulder, he saw Edith.

In spite of the grotesque illusion that she was merely leaning against the fence post, he could see immediately that she was dead. A cold fury rose up in his chest.

Movement on the road ahead caught his eye. It was Deputy Hooper's Plymouth cruiser, disappearing behind a swirling veil of dust. It was about half a mile ahead, moving towards Doyle's farm.

Childress squealed out on to the highway, the tires of his '56 Ford Interceptor yelping as they hit the asphalt. As he roared after the deputy's car, Childress noticed Wilson's Jeep at the side of the road as he flashed by. It barely registered to him that someone was slouched down in it as if taking a nap.

He pressed the cruiser's accelerator to the floor and the Interceptor's Y-8 engine responded with a snarl and throaty growl from the exhaust.

By the time Hooper noticed he was being chased, Childress was up on his bumper. Using tactics learned from State Highway Patrol pursuit training, Childress angled his car into the left rear fender of the Plymouth and turned sharply into it, pushing the deputy's car sideways.

Immediately getting off the gas pedal and tapping the brakes, Childress backed off and watched as Hooper's Plymouth began a slow motion spin that spiraled across the highway and into a field of corn stalks. Its wheels dug into the dirt and the car tipped sideways, threatening to overturn, then it righted itself.

Childress pulled to the side of the road and waited. After a few seconds, the Plymouth's rear tires spun in the dirt and the car lurched across the corn rows, back onto the highway and sped off, tires smoking.

"Damn it!" Childress yanked frantically at the wheel of

the Ford and tore back onto the road.

Deputy Hooper's car, with its more powerful 383 cubic inch engine sucking fuel from its 4-barrel carburetor, was gaining on him. Childress ground the Ford's gas pedal and willed his aging cruiser to go faster.

"Shit!" he yelled into the wind as the deputy's car continued to widen the gap. The Ford's speedometer crept excruciatingly up to one hundred and ten miles per hour, then started vibrating wildly and refused to go higher. Childress knew it would take a miracle for him to catch the deputy now.

Up ahead, the Plymouth started into a sharp curve. Its brake lights blinked on for a second then off. Then back on, and off. Then back on for a few seconds. Childress' Ford began to close in as the deputy's car slowed, disappeared behind some spruce trees then reappeared as the Ford swung around the curve.

Claude Wiggins materialized, standing at the side of the road. He held up a hand as Childress zoomed by.

"Whoa!" Childress took his foot off the accelerator as the curve sharpened, and gently applied the brake. His tires squealed and he felt them losing traction. He turned slightly away from the curve until they regained a grip on the road. Ahead, the Plymouth's brake lights were rapidly flashing on and off, but the car did not slow. It began to fishtail. Some liquid was coming down from the Plymouth's undercarriage onto the road. It was squirting out in spurts, and it took a moment for Childress to connect the jetting of the fluid to the timing of the Plymouth's brake lights.

"Mary, mother of Jesus!" he said aloud. "Hooper's ruptured a brake line!"

The brake lights came on again, and this time, he could clearly see that there were two steams of fluid coming from under the Plymouth.

"Sweet Jesus! He's busted both lines!"

Seconds later, the Plymouth left the road at high speed, plunged into a field, and flipped violently three times before ending up on its roof.

Childress drove his car to the shoulder and jumped out, hastily yanking his service revolver from its holster. He stood fifteen feet away from the upturned car and waited. A cloud of fine dust slowly settled to the ground while the Plymouth's spinning front tires whirled to a stop.

He leveled his gun at the driver's door.

"God damn it, Hooper, get out of the car, hands up!"

For a minute there was no response, and Childress wondered if the deputy had been injured. He didn't relish the idea of having to go up to the car and look inside.

The door flew open and Hooper's head appeared. His hair was disheveled and his face ashen. A rivulet of blood ran down his forehead to the corner of his mouth. His tongue came out and licked it away.

"Chief," Hooper coughed. "What are you doing?"

Childress drew a bead on the center of Hooper's forehead. He didn't want to kill the man, but would if he was forced to.

Childress had killed before. The first certain time was in 1943, in Sicily. He was a soldier in Patton's army during the Allied invasion.

Childress had read somewhere that it took on average of ten thousand bullets to kill a soldier in WWII. That was easy to believe. During the war he had often fired rounds in the general direction of the enemy, maybe to get lucky and take down a bad guy or to suppress incoming fire. In rare instances, you could be sure you had struck a human being with your bullets - you'd see the target thrown back by the force of the impact and fall. To Childress, a hit was more like bad luck for the enemy soldier rather than the result of his marksmanship.

His first definite kill happened as he turned a corner in the town of Messina, leading his squad on a clearing patrol. Then Corporal Owen Childress came face to face with a German soldier wearing the black uniform and insignia of a Panzer division. The slight, blond soldier couldn't have been more than eighteen, and was as surprised at the encounter as Childress. For a split second they both froze, staring wide eyed at each other, their rifle muzzles in each other's faces.

"Okay, here's the deal," Childress had said. "You step back, and I'll step back, and we'll each go our merry way. *Verstehst du?*"

Childress had the feeling, as he looked at the German's pale blue eyes that he understood. They both took a step back, lowering their weapons.

The German kid, for a reason that Childress could never fathom, and which would forever haunt him, began to raise his rifle again, and Childress instinctively reacted by firing two rounds from his M1 Garand point blank into the man's chest, throwing him backward.

Childress could never wipe from his memory the surprised expression of the German soldier's face as he crumpled to his knees and keeled over sideways on to the flagstone street.

"Why did you do that, you dumb, stupid bastard?" he remembered wailing.

That incident flashed through Childress's mind as he called out. "Throw out your service weapon, Hooper! And get out of the car!"

Deputy Hooper's head disappeared back into the upended car, and moments later reappeared. His arm flung out, and his 9mm automatic pistol arched to the dirt ten feet away. Childress waited with his gun ready while Hooper pushed open his door, struggled out of the car and shakily stood up.

After fishing his handcuffs from the pouch on his belt, Childress tossed them at the deputy. "Put these on behind your back and kneel on the ground!"

Hooper stared at him, unmoving, his eyes blank.

"Now!" Childress gestured with his revolver.

Hooper bent over as if reaching for the handcuffs, but instead fell to the ground, rolled and came up on one knee with his automatic in his hand. He pointed at the Chief and fired.

Childress reflexively closed his eyes, waiting for oblivion.

There was a dull click. And another.

"Son of a bitch!" Hooper was saying.

When Childress opened his eyes, Hooper was desperately fidgeting with his automatic, trying to a clear a jam.

"Drop it, Hooper!"

Hooper looked up at Childress, back down to his jammed pistol.

Fighting back the strong urge to drill the deputy's forehead with his .38 police special, Childress barked "I said drop it. Now!" His finger tightened down on the trigger and he braced his arms for the recoil.

Hooper's hands opened and his automatic thumped into the dirt at his feet.

"Damn it, I said drop the gun!" Childress repeated.

Hooper lifted his hands it the air, a quizzical expression on his face. "Chief, I did."

Childress stared. Hooper's mouth opened into a smirk, the blood running down from his cut forehead staining his teeth.

The ground in front of the deputy's feet lit up as if a ray of sunshine was slipping through a cloud.

The Chief looked up in the sky for a second, taking his eyes off the deputy. Hooper noticed and dove for his gun.

Childress shot wildly. The bullet ricocheted off a small granite boulder in the dirt with a dull ring.

Hooper fell on his face in the dirt and lay still.

Keeping his revolver centered on Hooper's head, Childress walked up and stared down at the limp body. After a few seconds, he warily reached out with his boot, jammed it under the deputy's midsection, and with a grunt flipped the Hooper over on his back. An almost perfectly round stain of blood was growing out from the center of Hooper's uniform shirt. Childress watched, mesmerized, until the spreading stain slowed and stopped. He bent down and lifted one of the deputy's drooping eyelids. There was no dilation of the iris when the daylight hit it.

Childress straightened and strolled over to the Plymouth. He peered inside. The spokes of the steering wheel were bent in towards the dash and the rim pushed down, so just the center of the steering column stuck out. Hooper's chest had no doubt been crushed by the impact. He had been a dead man walking.

Childress looked back at the lifeless body of the deputy. "Damn it Hooper," Childress said dourly as he carefully put his revolver back in its holster, "Haven't I always told you to wear your damn seat belt?"

Chapter 28

While waiting for Preston to return, Claire paced at the entrance of the cave, occasionally squinting across the field at the road back to town. After thirty or so minutes she'd had enough.

"As Wilson would say, *fuck this.*" Claire started back into the cave, lighting her way with the flashlight. She tiptoed by the black hulk of the bomb and moved deeper into the darkness. She pressed her hand on the wall. It felt damp and cool as expected, but as she ventured deeper there was a gradual warming of the surface. The air temperature was also going up.

"Shit," she whispered, remembering the Geiger counter in her backpack. She pulled it out and turned it on.

It immediately began ticking. She checked the meter: 200 CPM or counts per minute. The radiation level was above normal, but could be explained by natural radioactivity, such as radon gas absorbed by coal particles in the rock. As she moved further into the cave, the tick of the Geiger counter became much more rapid. Alarmed, Claire looked down again at the meter. The reading had jumped to 500 CPM.

"Crap! This place is pretty hot."

She went in another fifty yards. A change in the reverberating sound of her footsteps stopped her. She clicked her tongue loudly, listening intently to the echo. Somewhere up ahead, the cave must open up into a large space - the timbre and the timing of her click's echo gave it away. Claire was suddenly thankful for the experience of spelunking forays during her geology studies. She took another step forward.

And fell.

It was like tumbling down a long flight of stairs. She instinctively curled into a fetal position and wrapped her arms around her head. There was nothing to do but close her eyes and wait for it to end. The Geiger counter and flashlight flew from of her hands. After an eternity, her falling stopped.

Claire lay on her back, arms still protectively covering her head. Dazed, she blinked rapidly in the gloom, trying to gain her senses. She cautiously stretched out, flexed her arms and legs, then probed her body for injury.

Just some bumps and bruises. Nothing seemed broken. She was lucky.

The darkness was absolute. Claire got up on her knees, reached behind her back, and breathed a sigh of relief: her Smith & Wesson was still snug in its holster. Then she swept her hands across the stony ground. Her fingers touched something cylindrical, smooth and cool.

The flashlight.

She fumbled with it and discovered the switch was in the "off" position. Mumbling a little prayer, she switched it on and was instantly blinded by the light. She turned the flashlight away from her face and aimed it at the floor. The Geiger counter looked totaled. Claire turned the beam back to where she had fallen.

The bumpy rock formation she had tumbled down looked uncannily like a stairway purposely carved into the rock.

Ascending back up didn't look to be a problem. She relaxed a little.

Since I'm down here, I might as well do a little exploring. Maybe I can find Wilson.

She turned the flashlight forward. She was in a narrow passage about twenty feet long. There was an opening at the far end. She got to her feet, walked to the opening and peeked in. A cavern. Claire stepped into it.

Using the flashlight beam as a probe, she scanned the interior. The cavern was about the volume of a small church chapel. The walls were smooth, uniform and shiny black. They appeared vitrified like the images the camera had taken down the well.

She aimed the beam at the far wall.

Things were hanging from the walls.

The objects were long and ovoid shaped, grey, with a

wet looking sheen. There were nine of them, each about ten feet long, clinging to the rock face like bats.

In spite of her fear, Claire stepped closer. The objects towered above her. Up close, she could see that they were segmented as if built up of metal plates.

Or chitin, like insects, she thought, *as if they were enormous chrysalises.*

She reached out to touch one, but revulsion caused her to pull her hand back at the last second. A vibration began to fill the air and move up and down in frequency like a melody. It reminded Claire of the children's song:

> Three blind mice, three blind mice
> See how they run, see how they run
> They all ran after the farmer's wife
> Who cut off their tails with a carving knife
> Did you ever see such a thing in your life
> As three blind mice?

Claire brought the flashlight up and tapped one of the "chrysalises".

There was a cracking sound. The top of the object split open, revealing the ghastly face of a man. The face was long and grey with black hair hanging down each side. The huge eyes were closed. Claire wanted to run, but couldn't move. She opened her mouth to scream, but nothing came out. She could only stare at the face.

Then the face's eyes popped open, and glared down at her. Claire's heart clenched and she went down on one knee.

She recognized the face.

It was Smith, the dowser.

She flinched as there was another crack. Another chrysalis had opened. The face was the same: Smith.

For a second, Claire was paralyzed by the hypnotic gaze of the faces. Using every ounce of her will, she pulled her eyes away and bolted out of the cavern back into the passageway. She scrambled up the stone staircase and stumbled towards the cave entrance.

Wilson was right, the thought flashed in Claire's mind. *Fantastic and bizarre as it was, the Fallen Angels, or something like them, were sequestered in these caves, protected and hibernating in hideous, gigantic pupas.*

Her left foot caught on a crack. She reached out with her free hand to break her fall, and it came down on to something wet and sticky. There was the unmistakable odor of hot copper, like a teapot heating on the stove.

She swallowed hard and aimed her flashlight at the floor of the cave.

There was a pool of blood. A lot of blood. And laying twisted and broken in the middle was an unmistakable object:

Wilson's tortoise shell, horn-rimmed glasses.

Claire's keen echoed through the cave. Holding her soiled hand in front of her, she got to her feet and lurched towards the entrance.

The flashlight blinked twice and went dark.

She swore fiercely, banging the cylinder with the butt of her hand. The flashlight came on once, very brightly, then winked out.

Darkness enveloped her.

"Thank you for ride, Mr. Wilson," Ivy said, smiling brightly. "And by the way, what happened to your glasses?"

Wilson, behind the wheel of the Jeep, turned slowly towards her, his face white, his eyes empty. "What?"

"I'll be getting out now." Ivy told him.

For a moment Wilson looked blankly at her, then said. "I don't think so, Ivy."

Up ahead, a large orange Farmall tractor appeared around a curve in the road. The driver turned the tractor sharply, blocking the Jeep's path. Streep drainage ditches bracketed the highway.

With nowhere to go, Wilson braked the Jeep to a stop. He started reaching for the rock he had placed on the dash when his body went rigid. His hands came to a rest on the steering wheel while he stared unblinking at Ivy.

Ivy got out of the Jeep, then stuck her head back in through the passenger window.

"Oh, yes," she said gently, "I think I will get out." She raised her left hand towards Wilson. Her finger tips glowed with a golden corona.

Wilson's eyes widened for a second, then closed to slits. His head dropped to his chest and his hands slipped from the steering wheel and fell into his lap.

"Now," Ivy said. "you can rest in peace, Mr. Wilson."

For an agonizing moment, Claire stood frozen in the blackness of the cave. As her eyes adjusted, she could make out the dimly lit oval of the cave entrance.

Then she heard the sound of breathing.

"Sassy..." A voice came out of the void.

Claire hadn't heard that nickname for years. It was one her roommate Mary had given her in college. It was inspired by Claire's casual irreverence for tradition and decorum. No one else had ever called her that.

"Sassy."

The voice was familiar.

"How dare you!" Claire opened her eyes wide and thought she could make out a dark silhouette twenty feet down the passageway towards the stairway. She snatched her revolver from its holster and pointed it towards the silhouette.

"Who's there?" she called out, her voice cracking. She pulled back the hammer of the .38. "Answer or I'll shoot."

There was no response.

"I mean it. I'm armed and feel threatened. I *will* shoot... to kill."

"Claire," the silhouette said. "Claire, I'm sorry it has come to this."

Now Claire recognized the voice: it was Smith's.

"What are you doing here?" she demanded.

"I did so like you. You were a very attractive woman, Claire."

"Were? What do you mean *were*?"

"Of course, we can't let you live. Now that you've discovered our little secret." The silhouette hissed loudly as if it was a giant cobra getting ready to strike.

Claire steadied the .38, exhaled slowly and squeezed the trigger like her father had taught her so long ago. The gun kicked violently in her hand. The bright muzzle flash was blinding, and in the confines of the cave, the sharp bang of the round going off reverberated painfully in her ears. Simultaneously, she heard a dull, hollow crack.

A second later, when Claire's eyes had recovered, she saw that the silhouette was gone.

Could she have missed?

Now there was a faint rustling. A slight movement of the air stirred the hair on top of her head.

Bats?

Whatever it was, Claire knew it couldn't be good. She turned and charged towards the entrance, praying she wouldn't misstep and fall again. She could smell the fresh air wafting in. Almost there.

Claire stopped and looked back. The light coming from the cave opening revealed no movement - nothing coming after her. She bent over and breathed deeply, catching her breath.

Something landed on her left shoulder.

Her first impression was that a hand had come on it, but then there was a soft and downy brushing on her neck. In the weak light all she could see was its large shape.

What the...

Now a weight on her other shoulder. Claire yelled and flailed out at the shapes, imagining bats had landed on her.

There was the unmistakable feel of feathers.

They were birds - large birds.

She cried out in pain as their powerful talons clenched down, slicing into her flesh. She staggered towards the light at the cave entrance, pulling at the birds, trying to dislodge them.

She could see now that they were a pair of great horned

owls.

Horned owls were large but these two were enormous. Her mind reeled. She'd never heard of any owls attacking a human being. Perhaps they were a mated pair and felt she was threatening their nest that was somewhere in the cave. In the back of her panicked mind, Claire recalled reading how the grip of the horned owls' talons could exceed that of a grown man. They were carnivores and would often would take animals as large as skunks or even dogs and rip them to pieces with their scimitar claws.

It felt as though someone was holding a hot iron on each sides of her neck. The owls were stabbing at her with their beaks, trying to cut through her skin.

Claire broke into the open sunlight. She shrieked, dropped to her knees and fell forward, her face grinding into the dirt. Her fall dislodged the birds, and they flew off. Waving her arms frantically, Claire lifted her head.

Gilbert was standing twenty yards away, a cigarette dangling from his lips, his dark sunglasses hiding his eyes. The pair of owls alighted on his shoulders.

Claire screamed at him. "Gilbert…what are you doing?"

At that second, the birds launched from Gilbert's shoulders, their wings beating furiously, and dove at her again.

Claire dropped back to the ground and covered her head. One of the owl's talons slashed across the top of her hand as it flashed by. Claire flipped on her back, simultaneously pulling out her .38 and taking aim at the closest owl as it rose in the sky.

She got off two rounds before they disappeared over the crest of a hill. The sound of the gunshots rolled loudly across the fields. Claire stood, and holding the revolver with two hands, leveled it at the hill, waiting for the owls to come swooping around for another attack.

Shooting at birds in flight with her stub-nosed Smith & Wesson was ridiculous, she knew, but she was frightened and angry and hoping that the discharge might at least ward them off. She took a quick glance back at Gilbert, who was now standing with his arms crossed and a maddening smirk splitting his face.

"Gilbert! For God's sake! Call them off!" she yelled.

He brought his cigarette to his lips, inhaled deeply, then blew out a couple of smoke rings. "I can't do that, Miss Doctor Claire. There are powers at work here beyond you and me."

Claire looked back to the hill crest. Just then, the owls reappeared over the top and dove at her. Claire raised her weapon and fired.

Amazingly, this time, a round hit home. The bird to her left stopped abruptly in mid-air as if it had hit an invisible wall while a patch of feathers blew out of its back. The owl fell like a stone to the ground.

Apparently startled by the demise of its companion, the remaining owl pulled up and veered off.

Claire got to her feet and ran towards Gilbert. She grabbed him by his collar and got in his face.

"Stop this right now!" She resisted the temptation to use her last rounds on the sneering, bespectacled youth.

Gilbert stiffened, but the infuriating smile didn't leave his face. He took the cigarette out of his mouth, flicked it away, and lifted his chin.

Claire got the impression he was looking at something in the sky, above and behind her, even though she knew he was blind.

She spun around. Now *three* owls were bearing down on her. Two rounds were left in the .38. Claire forced herself to breathe, aim and squeeze off a shot at the closest bird. This time there was no effect. They were almost upon her. She fired her last round at the owl now only yards away. The bird spun and fluttered to the ground. The other two braked, bringing their powerful five inch talons forward, aiming for Claire's face.

Dropping the now useless gun, Claire raised her hands to cover her head, and waited for the inescapable strike.

Nothing happened.

The air was suddenly filled with the hissing and bill clacking of the owls mixed with a distinctive cawing.

Claire peeked through her hands to see a dozen or so crows mobbing the owls.

Even though they outweighed the crows by five to one, the owls were overwhelmed by the sheer number and ferocity of the attack by their traditional foes. The crows darted in and out, careening into the big birds as the owls struggled to climb. The tangle of birds rose higher and higher, becoming dancing dots in the sky, and vanishing over the surrounding hills.

Claire turned to Gilbert. The smile was gone from his face.

Claire's voice was fierce. "Did your owls from hell attack my friend Wilson?"

Gilbert said nothing.

"Did they kill that poor trooper?"

Gilbert took a couple steps backward. "You ask too many questions, Miss Doctor Claire. You should have never come here to Testament Hill. *They* have been waiting for ages, and now you come and disrupt their return."

"What are you talking about?"

"The return." Gilbert pointed to the cave entrance with his walking stick. "The return of the nine that escaped the Deluge. Like Prester John said at the revival."

Claire blinked at him. "You're crazy. There is no such thing. Everything that's happened in Testament Hill can be explained by natural events."

"I can hear in the doubt in your voice, Claire." Gilbert waved his stick at her. "You cling to your 'scientific' beliefs, but the façade is crumbling. Isn't that so?"

"What you are doing is evil, Gilbert. Don't you see that? What about the healing that you do, all the good you are capable of?"

Gilbert lifted the cigarette again, took a long inhale and blew it out slowly. "There is always a price, Miss Claire. At first I didn't see that. I thought maybe I could do some good. But it's not that simple. Besides, it was kind of entertaining."

"Entertaining?"

"Of course. Frankly, how things turn out is often quite amusing."

"That's just not right, Gilbert."

"What's right and what's wrong? Who decides?" Gilbert scoffed. "Good and evil go hand in hand. You know that in your heart but refuse to accept the truth. That is the way of things. Right now evil is ascending. I chose to go with the flow."

"Go with the flow? Does that mean killing innocent people?"

"No one is innocent, Doctor."

"But we have a choice, Gilbert. We have a *choice*."

Gilbert was silent for a second. He looked up and pointed. "I think our debate is going to have to wait for another time."

Claire followed Gilbert's finger. Over the hill, the crows had reappeared, heading back towards them. The birds were following a solitary crow that flew several yards ahead of the rest.

A diminutive figure stood on the crest of the hill and raised a hand as if saluting the crows. It was a young girl. The low sun outlined her in a glowing halo. There was no mistaking the flowing black hair that was being whipped about by the breeze: Ivy.

A tall man appeared at her side. His long grey hair was also being tossed by the wind. It was the Oweyu medicine man, Skander Grey Wolf.

The crows were now circling above Claire and Gilbert. The lead bird swooped down and hovered just over their heads, beating its wings to keep position in the wind. Claire extended her hand, and the crow glided down and briefly alighted in her palm.

"Hello, Raven, it's good to see you again."

Claire looked back towards the hill, but Ivy and Skander were gone.

Gilbert was slowly walking backwards towards the cave. The crows circling overhead followed him and swooped down so that their long sharp beaks came inches from the top of his head.

"Goodbye for now, Doctor Claire," Gilbert said. He turned and sprinted to the cave entrance, the crows in pursuit. Gilbert threw himself through the mouth of the cave. At the entrance the birds banked sharply and rose up in the air. Raven leapt off Claire's hand and followed them into the sky.

Claire called out to Gilbert. "Wait! Don't go in there, there's something unspeakable in there!"

But he was gone into the darkness.

Chapter 29

"Let him go."

Claire jumped as a hand fell on her shoulder. She spun around, the .38 in her hand.

"Easy, girl."

It was Chief Childress, and behind him stood Preston.

Preston waved back towards the road. "I met the Chief coming down the highway. He followed me back here."

"Thank God." Claire quickly tucked her revolver behind her back. She pointed to the cave entrance, and said in a rush, "Inside I found Wilson's glasses lying in a big pool of blood. And further in there's some monstrosities hanging in a cavern." She took a deep breath. "And Smith is in there too."

"Now calm down, Doctor Brannigan," Childress said. "We'll sort things out. First, what's happened to your neck? You're bleeding."

Claire ran her fingers over her neck. "I'm okay. I just had an encounter with some owls. Apparently they are guarding the cave."

Preston came to her side. "You say Smith's in the cave?"

"Yes. Gilbert's in there too. He ran in after the crows attacked the owls."

Chief Childress looked anxiously over his shoulders. "What are you talking about? Crows? Owls?"

Claire leaned towards Preston and quickly whispered in his ear. "I shot him - Smith. He threatened to kill me. Pretty sure I hit him, but he disappeared."

She stepped back, and pointed to the ridge. "And I don't think we have to worry about Ivy, Chief. I saw her up there. She waved to me. She's fine."

Preston moved closer, his voice lowered. "Claire, what exactly did you see in the cave?"

"Preston, It's *them*. They're encased in a kind of chrysalis like an insect, suspended from a cavern wall." She looked back towards the cave. "Smith - I think he's their caretaker."

Preston turned to Childress. "We must destroy the cave and everything in it. There's evil dwelling there."

"But Gilbert's in there," Claire protested. "And maybe Wilson."

For a moment, Preston and Childress said nothing. They both were staring at the ground.

"What?" Claire demanded.

The Chief said, "Mr. Wilson's not in the cave, Doctor Brannigan."

"How do you know? Have you found him?"

Preston took Claire's hands into his own. "The Highway Patrol found Wilson in his car when they were searching for Ivy. They radioed the Chief."

Claire's eyes started welling up. She wanted to hold her hands to her ears to block out what she knew was coming.

"He's dead, Claire," Preston said. "They've found his body."

"What are you saying?" Claire choked. "Dead? But how?... Who?"

"We're not sure yet, Miss Brannigan," Chief Childress said. "Could be an accident."

"He was killed, Claire," Preston said softly.

For a moment Claire stood in stunned silence. Then in a carefully controlled voice said, "Well, then, we still need to get Gilbert out of the cave, and do something about what's in there."

Childress looked from Preston to Claire. He raised his voice. "What *is* down there?"

"There's something you need to see, Chief," Preston said. "May I borrow your flashlight?"

Childress frowned. "I'm not sure it's wise to go in there."

"It's just by the entrance. Follow me."

With the flashlight showing the way, Preston led them inside the cave and pointed the beam on the black hulk of the bomb. He glanced at the Chief and waved his hand. "A Mark IV nuclear bomb. It crashed here in 1952. There was an accident."

Chief Childress' jaw dropped. "Sweet Jesus!"

Claire was looking back towards the cave entrance. "I get it. That's what made the trough: the bomb breaking through into the cave. That started a chain of events in 1952." She caught Preston's eye, "My guess is that Rachel Doyle came out to investigate the noise of the bomb burrowing into the ground. I'm sure the impact rattled windows and dishware far and wide. I bet Rachel climbed to the top of the mound. That's when she discovered the amulet. It was probably exposed when the earth shifted from crash. Unknowingly, Rachel removed it from its place over the caverns."

"Hold on." Childress held up his palm. "What amulet?

"It's all in a journal written by a Jesuit priest," Claire told him. "I'll explain later."

Claire pulled out the amulet from under her shirt. "This is that amulet, and this…" she tapped the gemstone set in its center "is the fragment of the Tzohar."

Both Childress and Preston reflexively took a step away from Claire.

"My guess," Claire said, "is that the creatures down there are in a kind of suspended animation, hanging from the cave wall, protected in the chrysalis-like shells I saw."

"Waiting to return," Preston concluded.

Claire nodded. "But the caves they had prepared to protect them from the biblical Flood ironically had become their prison. The caverns were waterproofed, but the power of the amulet kept them surrounded by water-saturated earth. They were trapped… that is, until Rachel removed the amulet and the water table started dropping."

Preston nodded. "That also explains why the wells were drying up."

"Yes," Claire said, "and finally, after the water level dropped enough, Smith, their vanguard, was able to blow open the cave entrance, preparing the way for the Fallen to emerge back into the world. I bet Smith is some kind of an Fallen-human hybrid similar to the Nephilim of the Bible."

Childress rotated his head around his shoulders. "I could use a drink...or two."

Claire stepped forward and put her palm gently on the bomb. "Everything that's happening now seems like fate." She looked back at Preston. Her voice was almost a whisper. "Just what brought you to Testament Hill, Preston?"

"It was just on the itinerary," he said. "I take a look at a map and plot out towns that might be a good choice for a revival. Testament Hill was just an improvised stop on the way between St. Louis and Memphis."

"That's all?"

"Yeah, I guess. Something about the name struck me, I'm not sure why. I do recall thinking to myself: Testament Hill - a curious name. I felt drawn to it."

"Maybe because you remembered it from the bomber flight?" Claire suggested. "Perhaps from a name on a map."

Preston rubbed his chin. "I haven't thought about that incident for years. My whole Air Force experience...it's something I've put behind me." He looked at Claire, his eyes intense. "I don't believe in destiny, Claire, but this gives me second thoughts."

"Maybe you two were meant to be here. At this time," Childress said.

Claire turned to him. "Why would you say that?"

"I've seen a lot of things in my lifetime." Childress's eyes went from Claire to Preston then back to Claire. "I've gone through two wars and spent years as a police officer. I've seen people do amazingly selfless deeds, but also have seen people do unspeakable, evil things." Childress paused. "I swear, evil is like a disease that takes hold of people. It comes over a land like cloud of pestilence. I believe it's here, in Testament Hill." He pushed his police cap off his forehead. "But I think Providence creates a balance. When the Evil comes to a place, so does the Good. I think you two are here to fight on the side of Good. It's not a coincidence."

Preston reached out and took Claire's hand.

At that moment, a chorus of inhuman moaning came

from the cave. The three froze, mesmerized by the sound.

"There're coming!" Claire clapped her hands loudly, breaking the spell. "We have to do something!"

She looked anxiously at Preston. He was staring intently at the bomb. "If we could explode this," he said, "we could stop them for good."

"And wipe out Testament Hill while we're at it," Claire said.

"No, not an *atomic* explosion," Preston told her. "The bomb is missing part of its plutonium core. It is kept separate until the aircraft is close to its target. That's so it can't go nuclear by accident - say if the plane is shot down or has mechanical failure."

"Then... how?" Claire said.

"The bomb has a sphere of five thousand pounds of conventional explosives." Preston explained. "It's used to compress the core to critical mass and start the chain reaction."

"Five thousand pounds..." Claire said. "That will probably do the job."

"It will seal this cave entrance with tons of rock and send a shock wave into it that will rip apart anything in its path." Preston said. "Plus, the radioactive material in the bomb will make the cave system deadly for centuries."

Claire turned her palms over. "What about Gilbert? Have you forgotten he's down in there?"

Preston's expression was stony. "He's made his choice. He's picked his side in this battle."

"Right. Let's do it," Childress growled, stepping up to the bomb. "Now - how do we set it off the explosives?"

Preston blew out a long breath. "That's the tricky part. The explosive is normally triggered electrically by radar, which senses altitude. The bomb is designed to explode high in the air to get maximum destruction at ground zero."

"Is there any way to fool the radar?" Childress asked.

Preston shook his head. "No. Besides, the bomb's been here for ten years. The batteries used to power the radar probably died years ..." He stopped in mid-sentence, then said, "There just might be a way."

He pointed to the front of the bomb. "Those four stubs on the Mark IV's nose, they're fuses, designed to set off the explosives on impact with the ground in case the radar fails." He rapped his knuckles on one of the rusty antenna-like rods.

Claire flinched. "Please don't do that."

Preston smiled humorlessly. "It will take a hell of a lot more than me hitting it with my fist to make it go off."

"Well, then what happened?" Childress pointed at the bomb. "It's already hit the ground."

"I don't know," Preston answered. "Perhaps coming in at such a shallow angle, it just kind of skidded in, and there wasn't enough shock to set off the fuses. Or maybe the fuses are defective."

A peculiar odor drifted towards them.

"My God." Claire waved her hand in front of her nose. "That smell is horrible."

Childress coughed. "It's like a rotting carcass mixed with burning sulfur."

They stared down into the cave. A blue flickering appeared deep inside, like a distant lightning storm.

"We've got to think of something fast." Claire reached out and touched one of the fuses. "Preston, is there some way we can we trigger these?"

"It would take a powerful impact..." Preston looked back at the mouth of the cave, then back at the bomb and then back to the cave opening. "You know, there might be enough clearance."

"All set?" Preston shouted.

He was standing with one leg through the open door on the driver's side of the Volvo, revving the engine. In his right hand he clutched a rope. "I'm going to step out and pull the rope. That will knock the rock off the clutch and the car should take off."

"Let's do it," Claire called out to him. She was sitting in the police cruiser next to Childress. The Chief had turned the cruiser so that it was pointed out to the road, and had his foot poised over the gas pedal.

The plan was for the Volvo to charge unmanned through the cave entrance and crash into the nose of the bomb. Preston calculated, the car's impact could set off the fuses.

He raised his arm. "Now, are you sure about this, Claire? It's your car."

"Yes! The car's old anyway. And be careful!" Claire yelled back, realizing immediately how inane her warning sounded.

"Go!" Preston dropped his arm, pulled his leg out, and yanked on the rope. He took off running for the cruiser. After taking three steps, he looked back to see the car skip forward a few feet, and heard the engine stall.

"Damn it!" Preston ran up to the police car. "The car's just going to keep stalling - letting the clutch out suddenly like that," he said. "I'm going to have to drive it until it's moving, then jump out."

Claire shook her head. "Too dangerous."

"It's the only way." Preston pointed back to the Volvo. "I won't have much time after I bail out. Chief, do you think you can drive next to me so I can jump into your car as you go by?"

"Roger that." Childress gave him a thumbs up.

"This is crazy, Preston." Claire said.

"You got a better idea?" Preston turned and ran back to the Volvo. "Let's just do it."

He got into Claire's car and backed it up, aiming the front again at the cave. He waited until the Chief had circled his cruiser around. The two vehicles would pass going in opposite directions within a few feet of each other.

Preston put his foot down on the Volvo's clutch and set a rock down on the gas pedal. The engine revved. He opened the driver door and signaled to Childress, who started his cruiser forward. Timing Childress's approach, Preston eased the clutch out.

This time the Volvo didn't stall. As it accelerated towards the cave opening, Preston leaned out with both feet braced on the door frame, one hand on the steering wheel, the other gripping the roof post.

When the cruiser passed by, Preston jumped towards it, crashing onto the hood. He clung on to the windshield frame as Childress swerved and raced to the road.

He looked back in time to see the Volvo careen sideways at the last second before entering the cave. Its rear tires churned in the dirt then slowed and stopped. The engine clunked a few times and stalled.

"Shit!" he yelled.

Chief Childress quickly brought the cruiser back around. Preston climbed off the hood and poked his head in the passenger window. "I don't know what else to try," he said, exasperated.

Claire glanced anxiously into the cave. The blue flickering was much closer to the entrance. "Anybody got a plan B?"

"I have an idea," said the Chief.

"You two get in the Volvo, turn it to face the road," Childress said. "And get ready to go."

"What's your plan, Chief?" Preston asked.

"Please, just do as I ask. You'll see."

He waited in the cruiser until the pair got into Claire's car.

Claire stuck her head out the window, and looked back. "Okay, now what, Chief?"

Chief Childress stared straight ahead. He raised his voice "I've cheated death many times, Claire."

"What?"

"When others have died around me, I was spared." Childress' voice was hoarse.

Before either Preston or Claire could react, the cruiser roared off towards the cave entrance.

It was too late to stop him.

"Move." Preston told Claire. "Get us out of here, now!"

Claire hesitated, looking back as the cruiser disappeared through the cave entrance.

"Now, Claire!" Preston ordered.

Claire pressed down on the Volvo's accelerator. The car's wheels ripped at the dirt for a second, then caught traction. She swung the car onto the highway and floored it.

A second later, there was a terrific thundering boom. The ground beneath the car dropped a couple of inches and then rebounded.

Claire and Preston rode in silence as dust and gravel rained down.

Chapter 30

Captain Bob Norris handed a copy of the police report to Claire. They were standing in his office at the state police post Saturday afternoon.

"Please," He motioned at a chair with his hand. "Take whatever time you need." He turned and busied himself at a file cabinet.

Claire sat down, took a deep breath and read the report. It described in cold, precise language how a state trooper discovered Mike Wilson in his Jeep two miles west of Testament Hill on the shoulder of Route 23 Friday evening. His body was slumped over the steering wheel. The scarf and shirt he was wearing were heavily bloodstained.

The preliminary coroner's examination determined he had died from massive blood loss due to jagged incisions in both carotid arteries caused by yet unidentified hook-shaped objects. There was little blood found in the Jeep, which indicated that the injuries had occurred in another location. When asked by the detective preparing the report how a dead man could drive a Jeep, the coroner would not speculate.

Interrogated about her encounter with the deceased, Ivy Doyle explained that after she had been picked up by Wilson, she had jumped from the vehicle when he had slowed the Jeep at an intersection, and run away. The police had no reason to doubt her story. It was an open investigation.

Preston and Claire had agreed to tell the authorities only about the discovery of the bomb, and concocted a story about it accidently going off when the Chief drove too close to the entrance.

As she took one last circuit around town, Claire was surprised to see Skander Grey Wolf strolling towards her. He was wearing a pair of neatly pressed khakis and a bright yellow cardigan. His shiny silver hair was freed of the ponytail and fell across his shoulders like a mantle. He was looking down, appearing to be lost in thought.

He looked up suddenly. "Hello, Doctor Brannigan." He said, walking over and gently taking Claire's hand in his. "I wanted to say goodbye..." He paused and his face broke into a smile. "But not until you buy me a drink at Duggan's."

Claire wasn't sure how to respond.

Skander's eyes twinkled, "The mythology about my people and alcohol is horseshit."

"Of course," Claire nodded. "I am just surprised that..."

"Understand, Claire, mind-altering substances have been used by my people since time immemorial to help contact the infinite."

"Well, I..."

Skander waved his hand. "You take everything too seriously, Doctor Brannigan. Relax. A casual drink between friends."

A few minutes later, the pair was sitting at the bar in Duggan's, sipping bourbon. The odd couple got more than a few curious glances from patrons.

"This is good fire water." Skander held his glass up to the light. "Doctor, do you know how the name 'fire water' came about?"

"Because it burns on the way down?" Claire suggested.

"Nope." Skander smiled slyly. "It was a way to test the alcohol content of the drink: if you could light it on fire, it passed."

"You're pulling my leg."

"Perhaps. It is a good anecdote, you have to admit."

Skander leaned in closer. "Now, seriously, I want to say a proper goodbye, but also talk to you about what happened at the cave."

Claire's shoulders slumped. "It was bad. Chief Childress sacrificed himself for us all."

Skander clicked his tongue. "I have been informed of the incident."

"And that poor boy, Gilbert." Claire's eyes watered up. "I think about that all the time. I feel so guilty that we didn't try harder to rescue him."

Skander caught Claire's eye. "You knew in your heart he was already gone. He was possessed by the evil ones. His soul was taken long before he ever went into the cave."

"I hear what you're saying, Skander, but still..."

"You knew." Skander tapped a finger on the bar. "You never would let the cave be destroyed while Gilbert was inside - unless you sensed with a human intuition as old as mankind that he was processed by evil spirits. It was necessary. And now Smith and the *others* have been stopped."

"Smith." Claire's eyes flared.

"Indeed. He was a creation meant to pass as one of us, a hybrid of Anuk and human, to walk the Earth as a vanguard and protector. He was probably conceived when the Anuk attacked the Oweyu in 1811, and violated one of their women"

"And he's been waiting for over a hundred and fifty years for the Anuk to arise again? "

"Yes."

Claire shivered. "A Nephilim."

"I have read of the Nephilim, in your Old Testament." Skander said. "Smith is an offspring of the Anuk and an Oweyu woman, however, he was not as powerful as the giants of old. The Anuk's powers had been greatly weakened since their entrapment so long ago."

"I think I understand. They were isolated from their source of energy."

"Yes," Skander said. "Energy of pure evil. It can sometimes appear as to us blue sparks or flashes."

"Smith had an aversion to water, and now I know why. It disrupts their energy, as water disperses light."

Skander cocked his head. "That's are very perceptive, young lady. You see, our wise men taught that evil is associated with a certain kind of light. The Anuk draw their life force directly from it. They have a pact with the devil, if you will. Evil works through them. In return, they have access to that energy and attain supernatural power and near-immortality. They sense when the evil energy is plentiful; when it lies strong over the land. They are drawn out of their sanctuary like hungry vultures to carrion."

Claire studied Skander's face. "Why now, Skander? Why are they rising?"

"I suspect what happened in Alamogordo in 1944 probably caught their attention."

"Trinity? The first atomic bomb test in New Mexico?"

"Yes. And then Nagasaki, Hiroshima, and the many nuclear tests since." Skander lowered his voice. "Claire, the world has forgotten what the ancients understood: the need to work within nature, not against it. The knowledge that your modern science unlocks is used with no regard of the need to maintain harmony. This gives opportunity for evil to spread its infection. For instance - white man's atomic weapons - they unleash the energy contained within the elementals of Creation. This power was also known to the ancients. They tapped into it with discipline and proper training and respect. That is how the Oweyu Seer repelled the Anuk they came out from their cave during the Taima in 1811."

Claire was astonished. "They used atomic weapons?"

Skander snorted. "Not bombs, assuredly. The ancients were able to tap into the power in a much more subtle manner - through the *spirit* realm." Skander paused and finished off his drink. "I read in a magazine that it takes thousands of people working with thousands of huge machines to produce the tiny amounts of special materials to make your atomic weapons."

"That's true."

"It is so difficult because your culture assumes the only way to work in the universe is through overwhelming physical effort."

"That is the only way," Claire protested, "to separate the fissionable uranium 238 from the common uranium 235. It is *very* difficult."

"Of course, because manipulating the power of Creation at its basic level is very difficult without delving into the spiritual realm. As it should be, otherwise people would be nuking each other left and right in retaliation for the most minor slight, and we would have wiped all life from the Earth long ago."

"Did the Anuk also have this ability to, as you say, manipulate the elementals?" Claire was again thinking of the mystery of the vitrified cave walls.

"Perhaps. The Anuk are supernatural beings. They've existed even before the foundations of the Earth were laid. They are your peoples' Fallen Angels, tempted by pleasures of the flesh to incarnate and come down to Earth. They became trapped in the flesh when they fled the wrath of the great Father and his warrior angels."

Claire's voice was filled with awe. "The War in Heaven."

Skander sighed. "But enough about that. I have more urgent things to tell you. First…" Skander signaled the barmaid. "You must buy us another round of fire water."

When their drinks arrived, Skander held his glass up to the light and for a few seconds appeared engrossed in the prismatic effects of the ice. "Do you think that you, Wilson and John Preston just happened by chance to arrive in Testament Hill at the same time?" he asked.

"We talked about that." Claire said. "Especially after it turned out that Preston had dropped the bomb here back in 1952. Chief Childress, may he rest in peace, believed it was no coincidence: that we were brought here by forces of Good to help fight the Evil."

"Truly." Skander said.

"I mean it just sounds so ridiculous." Claire said. "This is the twentieth century, dammit. Science is going to explain everything…at least that is what I believed before coming here."

"There are more things, Horatio…"

"Oh my God!" Claire almost spilled her drink. "That's what both Smith and Gilbert Beamer quoted to me."

Skander's eyes burned. "Understand Claire: we are all connected. Connected in ways, that science, as yet, cannot fathom." His voice was almost a whisper. "The seers of my people were very powerful, a discipline going back in the shadows of time, when all kinds of strange beasts and different kinds of men roamed the Earth."

Claire looked at Skander with wonder. *Who was this old man?* She thought.

Skander seemed to read her mind. "Yes, I *am* what you might call a shaman. In truth, my people have no word "shaman". It is a white man's word, originally derived from northern Asia. Neither, for that matter, do we have "medicine men". My people have healers and seers, and men of wisdom. There also are those individual who abuse their knowledge and may be considered sorcerers.

Skander tapped the bar with his finger again. "This is the important part: the Oweyu were at Testament Hill because their destiny was to counteract the evil that was sleeping in the caverns."

"And so," Claire inferred, "When the New Madrid quake opened up a dry passage in 1811 allowing the Anuk to escape..."

"The Oweyu were ready. They had been chosen for this battle. The tribe was almost wiped out, but the Anuk were driven back to the caverns. The Oweyu seer at the time, who just so happens to be my great grandfather, worked with the Jesuit priest. The priest knew about the existence and the power of the Tzohar; my great grandfather was versed in the wisdom of the Old Ones. Together they forged the charm that you wear." Skander pointed. "It was created to imprison the Anuk by surrounding their cave refuge with water-saturated earth."

Clair reached carefully into her blouse and pulled out the amulet. "Is it magic, Skander?"

"I believe it was the great science fiction writer, Arthur Clarke, who said something like: 'magic is just science we don't understand yet.'"

Claire took a moment to absorb the revelations. "And Ivy? I know she's special. How does she fit into this drama?"

"I believe she is the successor to an ancient line of chosen souls to fight the forces of Evil, the *Enah*," Skander said. "The Anuk suspected one would be sent when they arose. They sent a minion after Ivy's mother, Rachel, and despoiled her, to drain her power, thinking she was the Enah because she had a special way about her. Rachel fought back bravely against their evil influence, but she knew she could not hold out much longer."

"So she killed herself."

"Yes. A tragedy." Skander nodded solemnly. "They were deceived. Rachel was the *mother* of the Enah. Ivy is the One, the Enah. She was chosen and given the power of the Good. I had my suspicions and when you told me about the glow of her footsteps, I was certain. The vanguard, Smith, also came to realize the truth and tried to lure Ivy to the caves where the Anuk's energy could be focused and her power counteracted, so that it would be safe for the Anuk to re-emerge. But Ivy's power was too strong."

Claire shook her head slowly. "I don't think I'll ever fully grasp what happened here, Skander." She peered at him. "Thank God, it's all over."

Skander stared down at his hands.

"For now," he said quietly. "Understand, evil is one of the primal forces of creation. It has been pitted in battle with the good for dominance since the beginning of time. These forces are with us always, coming to us as spirits, pulling us one way or the other. Those who are morally weak are especially vulnerable."

"But why?" Claire asked. "Why is it that way?"

Skander shrugged. "The reason for the existence of good and evil is probably beyond our understanding. Perhaps without the struggle, Creation would collapse to nothingness. It is the ultimate mystery."

Chapter 31

Claire finished packing in her motel room, picked up her suitcase and walked to the door. She reached for the handle and stopped. She placed her suitcase back on the floor, stepped over to the phone and dialed. She heard a click at the other end of the line.

"Ben?"

"Claire." Ben cleared his throat a couple of times. " How are you?"

"I'm good, Ben. I know this might not be a good time, but for what I have to say, there's no good time, I guess."

Ben's voice was wary. "Go ahead, Claire."

"I'm not going to marry you."

For five long seconds, there was nothing on the line but a haunting static.

Ben's voice was now clear. "Truthfully, Claire, I've been expecting this call. I can tell something has happened to you in Testament Hill. Something that has changed you."

"I'm sorry, Ben."

"Don't be sorry, Claire. There's nothing to be sorry about. In fact, I appreciate and respect your decision."

"You do?"

"Of course. You have the courage to follow your heart. I certainly wouldn't want you marrying me out of a sense of duty, or simply because it was the next rational step in our relationship. We'd be living a fantasy, and it would never last."

Claire felt a weight lift from her shoulders. "Ben…" she hesitated. "…I have a question for you."

Claire could hear him take a long breath. "Yes?"

"It's a geology question."

"Oh, okay. Shoot." He sounded relieved.

"I know you have studied extra-terrestrial geology. Do you think it's possible to purposely divert a large asteroid and redirect it to strike Earth?"

"That's a strange question, Claire. What brought that

on?"

"Long story... So is it possible?"

Ben sniffed. "In theory, I guess. But we certainly don't have the technology today. Perhaps in the future - a missile or some other force could be directed at it to alter its path."

"So, it's possible?"

"Yes. But it would take something supernatural at this point. Is this somehow related to the situation in Testament Hill?"

"Oh, it's just a discussion we had the other night. It's nothing. The idea just kind of stuck in my head."

"Okay." Ben sounded puzzled.

There was a momentary silence, then Claire spoke. "Ben, thank you so much for understanding."

"Claire, good luck. I mean it. I guess it wasn't in the stars for us to be together."

"Goodbye, Ben."

"Goodbye, Claire."

Claire hung up and left the room. She put her suitcase in the trunk of the Volvo and walked to the motel lobby. She had been dreading the phone call to Ben, worried about how he might react. But now that it was over, she felt confident that she had made the right decision. A sense of freedom buoyed her up.

As she had hoped, Mr. B. was lounging behind the front desk. He was holding a dog-eared paperback in one hand and a smoldering cigarette in the other. She stepped up to the desk.

Mr. B. looked up with an expression of irritation that faded as he recognized Claire.

"How are you this beautiful day, Doctor Claire?"

Claire made a motion as if she was bringing a cigarette to her lips.

Mr. B. grinned, reached into some secret cubby hole, brought out a Marlboro and tossed it to Claire's outstretched hand. "Need a light?"

"I'm good." Claire said. "Thanks."

She turned away and stepped through the door. Mr. B.

called out after her, "It'll stunt your growth."

Claire went over to the pool patio and sat down on one of the lawn chairs. The sky was just beginning to lighten in the east. There was no traffic on the road. It was very quiet. Testament Hill had not yet roused. She twirled the cigarette absently around her fingers while gazing into the mirror calm water of the pool.

It felt like so long ago that she and Wilson had sat there, having a couple of beers, watching the sun set.

And now Wilson was dead.

And Chief Childress. And poor Edith, who wasn't crazy after all. Gilbert was gone too, presumed dead in the explosion of the cave. And then there was Deputy Hooper. Claire doubted he'd be missed.

She felt depression and grief threatening to overcome her.

Claire willed a change of thought.

The events of the last few days had inspired a reassessment of her life. She realized now that she had been living in denial: choosing to play the role of a teacher in a small isolated Midwestern college; planning a comfortable marriage with an established and level-headed professor; herself on the track for tenure with its promise of a stable, secure job.

It was as if she had mentally rolled herself up into a cocoon and set about ignoring the rest of the world, trying to be content in the staid milieu of the collegiate universe.

She could not go back. That world would never satisfy her now. It wasn't real. It was a delusion: the smug conceit of the campus elite believing that they illuminated the masses with their superior intellect and arcane knowledge, blinded by the belief that empirical science tells us all we need to know about Creation.

Fools, Claire thought. *Ignorant, arrogant fools.*

The truth was that the world was a battleground. That the conflict between Good and Evil, as Skander Grey Wolf had explained to her, had been going on since the beginning of time. And that Evil must never be allowed to be victorious, for the world would collapse into hellish chaos. The war was forever.

She held the cigarette up close. The enticing scent of tobacco reached her and she breathed in deeply. She examined the Marlboro for a second then flicked it away onto the parking lot.

"Good for you."

Claire turned. John Preston was standing behind her, grinning. He was wearing a gaudy Hawaiian shirt and a pair of swim shorts.

"You scared the bejesus out of me," she told him.

"Sorry."

"You've cut your hair."

Preston reached up and patted the top of his head. "Yep. Going for a new look. It was time." Preston pointed to the pool. The water was faintly steaming. "Looks tempting. I thought I'd go for a dip. Last chance before we leave."

Claire looked back to the pool. "Now that you mention it, it would feel good. Cleansing, you know?"

"Join me, then."

"Didn't pack a bathing suit."

"Don't need it," Preston said. "There's nobody here but us."

"What about the owner?

"He hardly ever comes out."

Claire looked around. They were alone. "Let's do it, then." She jumped up, undid her jeans and in one quick motion pulled them down along with her panties. She kicked them off her feet. The long sweatshirt she was wearing kept her barely decent. "If I'm going in my birthday suit, so are you."

"Deal," Preston said. "Let me grab some towels from the cabana."

While Preston's back was turned, Claire yanked off her sweatshirt and dove into the pool. She descended until her palms touched bottom and then shot back to the surface, treading water with smooth strokes of her arms and graceful scissors moment of her legs.

She stared mockingly wide-eyed at Preston.

"No fair," he said.

"Come on. The water's great. Actually feels warmer than ever."

"Okay…Okay." Preston put his towel on the back of the chair then hesitated.

"Prude." Claire swam over towards the deep end and began tiptoeing back, the water level dropping around her body. She locked eyes with Preston. First her shoulders were exposed, then slowly the water dropped away until she was at waist level, then to the middle of her thighs.

Preston pulled off his shirt in one motion, then reached to the waistband of his swimsuit.

There was a loud grumble and the earth opened up under him. He shot downward as if he was riding an elevator and disappeared.

"Preston!" Claire flailed at the water, struggling to reach the pool ladder. The water was like molasses holding her back. She heard herself screaming. She reached the ladder and scrambled up, her limbs rubbery from fear and shock. She ran to the spot where Preston had been, grabbing her sweatshirt on the way and tugging it over her head.

A smoking hole, the size of a manhole cover, had materialized where Preston had been standing.

"Oh my God!" She knelt down at the edge of the hole. "Preston!"

Mr. B., hearing her cries, had burst out of the office and came running over. "What's the matter, Doctor Claire?"

He spotted the hole in the ground. "What the…? "

Claire looked up at him, her eyes wide. "He fell. Preston. The earth …*swallowed* him."

Mr. B.'s jaw dropped.

Then it was obvious to Claire. "It leads into the caves! The cave system must run under the pool. That's why the water has stayed warm."

She craned her head down into the hole. "Preston! Can you hear me?"

There was a murmur. She thought it could be his voice.

It sounded weak. "Preston!" she called out again. This time there was no response. She looked up at Mr. B.

"I'll call the Highway Patrol," he said. "They'll bring help." He turned and started back towards the office.

"No, wait. It'll be too late!" she yelled. "Get a ladder!"

The dirt around the hole began to crumble and fall inward. The hole opened like the maw of a giant shark. The ground beneath Claire began to give way. She jerked upright and frantically tried to crabwalk backwards, but the ground melted away and with a muffled cry, she slid helplessly into the abyss.

After a terrifying moment of weightlessness, Claire landed hard on her feet and fell backwards. The earth was cold and damp on her bare legs.

Momentarily stunned, she had the notion that she was in her bed at the motel, waking up from a bad dream.

A dull throbbing in her left ankle brought her back to reality. Bringing her knees up so that her feet rested flat on the ground, she probed the ankle with her fingertips, carefully rotating the joint. A minor sprain. Fortunately, a pile of soft dirt and sod had dropped in before her, cushioning her fall.

Claire got up slowly, making sure the ankle would hold, until she was crouching in the darkness. Then the horror of her situation hit home. She lowered her head and swallowed hard, trying to keep in her stomach contents.

"Preston!" she called out.

There was no response. She glanced around, blinking her eyes, trying to penetrate the darkness.

A gleam of light caught her eye: the gemstone in the amulet hanging from her neck was glowing.

At first it was very faint, and Claire thought it was her imagination. But the light suddenly flared.

"Preston!" She called out again, and stood very still, listening.

"Hello, Claire. Nice to see you again."

Smith's face appeared out of the darkness, illuminated by the golden light from the amulet. He was so close she could feel his hot breath.

His voice was a hoarse whisper. "Are you surprised to see me?"

Claire jerked away. "Smith... I thought you were dead."

He grinned, and bowed his head.

Claire inhaled sharply.

The top of his skull had been blown off. The dura mater, the thin protective membrane surrounding his brain, had been torn, and greenish cerebrospinal fluid oozed from the jagged edges of the wound. The tubular convolutions of his brain were pulsating as if it was an autonomous creature living in the bowl of his skull.

"Do you see what your bullet did to me?" Smith pointed to the top of his head. "I'm not so easy to kill, Claire. I've been around for a long time, and many have tried."

She gaped at him. It was definitely Smith, but he looked transformed. He looked older, his face more angular, more sharp. His skin was like tight parchment over his skull. His hair swept back into two deep widow's peaks.

"But the bomb..." Claire said. "It should have killed you."

"The bomb caused much destruction." Smith laughed humorlessly. "Many poor bats and spiders lost their lives."

Claire scanned the floor of the cave for something she could use as a weapon. It was too dark to see anything.

"The explosion sealed up the cave entrance, and cracked the walls so that water began to seep in." Smith continued. "We were trapped. The only way to go was further and further into the caves. Eventually I heard water dripping, so I followed the sound. I reached the source of the dripping. It had an unusual odor. Then it came to me: it was chlorine. I could hear faint sounds from above. It was traffic from the highway. I realized I was under the swimming pool at the motel. A narrow tunnel led upwards, and I wiggled my way up and clawed away at the dirt. Then the roof collapsed and I was thrown back down."

"That's too bad." Claire said.

"Claire," Smith raised his hands. "Why are you so intent

on destroying me? I thought you and I had a connection. I felt it, and I'm sure you did too."

"Those people - you killed them."

"Claire, we've already had this discussion, as I recall. I killed no one."

"I know who you are."

"Claire…"

"*We?*" Claire snapped. "You said: *We* were trapped. You're with those monstrosities in the cavern."

Smith's face twisted with hostility.

"What's happened to Preston, you bastard?" Claire shouted, her fear replaced by rising fury.

Her sudden wrath took Smith aback. He moved into the darkness, away from the light of the amulet.

Claire looked down at the radiant gemstone. And remembered.

The amulet; the engraved letters "VRS"- she had seen it before on something else.

It had been given to her by her godmother on her confirmation when she was twelve: a simple cross on a gold chain. On the crossbar of the cross, in tiny script, the letters "VRS".

"This will keep you safe from evil." Nana, as Claire called her godmother, told her.

Nana had been Claire's wet nurse when Claire was an infant. When Claire was older, her mother casually mentioned that Nana had Ioway blood.

Claire could vividly recall her godmother whispering in her ear as she tenderly slipped the necklace over her head, "Wear it always, my precious."

Sometime in the next few years, as children are careless with such things, Claire lost the cross, but keep wearing the necklace.

VRS.
Vade Retro Satana.
It was Latin: *Get back Satan.*

"Vade Retro Satana," she whispered the ancient exorcism to ward off evil.

"What?" Smith's face reappeared inches from Claire's. His breath was hot and sulfurous.

This time, Claire's voice was loud and strident.

"Vade Retro Satana!"

"What?"

"Vade Retro Satana!"

Smith's grinned, although his eyes showed alarm. "That bullshit is not going to help you, Claire."

"Vade Retro Satana!" Claire shouted.

Smith hesitated then reached out to grab the amulet.

From the darkness, a hand holding a sharp-edged stone came down on Smith's arm. Claire could hear the crack of bone shattering. Arterial blood spurted from Smith's forearm, looking black in the golden light from the amulet.

"How does that feel, you son of a bitch?"

It was the voice of John Preston.

Smith let out a howl, spun around and vanished into gloom.

Claire felt Preston's arm around her waist. "Come on. We're getting out of here!" he said.

He pulled her backward. A circle of light illuminated the ground at their feet. He got behind her and lifted her up toward the light.

"Reach!" he said.

Claire extended her arms as far as she could. Her hands barely touched the edge of the hole. She clawed at the earth and tried to lift herself up. Preston placed his hands on her bottom and shoved.

Her head was in the open air. Sunlight lit her face. She blinked trying to clear the dirt that had fallen in her eyes.

Mr. B. stood above her, a cigarette dangling from his mouth. He grabbed her wrists, pulled her gently out of the hole, and set her on her knees in the grass.

Claire turned back to the hole and leaned over it. "Preston!" she yelled.

Mr. B. reached down again, and seconds later, Preston was scrambling out of the pit.

He coughed. "Thank you, sir!" he said to Mr. B.

"Couldn't find the gosh darn ladder." Mr. B. shrugged.

Claire took in deep breaths, trying to clear her head. "Are you okay, Preston? Are you hurt?"

"I'm fine. You?"

"Just a slight ankle sprain."

"Here, let me check." Preston moved towards her.

"No. Wait." Claire held up her hand. She was staring intently at the hole. Tendrils of smoke spiraled up from it. It was lit up with arcs of blue light.

"They're going to follow us out!"

"What?" Mr. B. stepped over to the hole. He waved his hand to clear the smoke and looked down.

Claire jumped to her feet. "The dynamite!" she said. She took a few limping steps towards her car parked in the lot, then stopped and turned back to Preston. "Get the dynamite! It's in a red crate in the back seat the Volvo. The detonators and hookup wire are in the glove box!"

Preston squinted at her. "Are you going to blow Smith up?"

"No. Just get the dynamite. And the detonators and spool of wire."

"You got it." Preston took off running.

Mr. B. stepped away from the hole, holding his nose. "What's the plan, Doctor Claire?"

Claire pointed at the pool. "We're going to flood the cave. Water will destroy them."

Mr. B. looked puzzled. "Them?"

"Evil beings, Mr. B. They've been hidden in a cave under Testament Hill, waiting to come out."

Mr. B. shook his head then suddenly his eyes widened. "The curse."

Preston returned holding a box of dynamite, a handful of detonators and the wire.

"You know how to use this stuff?" he asked Claire.

"I think so. I've never done it myself, but I've watched Wilson many times."

"God help us," Mr. B. said.

"Yes, God help us," Preston echoed under his breath.

Claire motioned with her hand. "Preston, we need to blow a path from the pool so it will dump all its water into the hole."

He frowned at her. "I don't get..." then he snapped his fingers. "Of course. Water - just like the flood."

Claire opened the box and took out a handful of dynamite sticks and handed them to Preston. "Okay, we need to place these in a line from the pool to the hole and blast a trench for the water."

"Right. How close together?" Preston asked.

"Shit, I don't know." Claire said. "But we got to hurry before they come."

There was the sound of a matchstick flaring. Claire looked up to see Mr. B. lighting up another Marlboro. "I think I can be of assistance, he said. "I used to help my pappy blow irrigation trenches on our farm as a kid."

"Please do!" Claire said.

Mr. B. took the sticks from Preston's hand. "We need to get them as far in the ground as possible, to maximize the effect," he said. He walked to the pool edge and started jamming dynamite sticks in the ground and attaching the detonators and wiring them up. "We'll stick two in together. We want to make sure we get deep enough to drain the pool."

"What about the concrete pool wall?" Preston asked.

"Don't worry about that. I put a pair in the ground next to it. Water's not compressible, so the shock will shatter the pool wall, no problem." Mr. B. stood up. "All right. Now we just hook up your blasting machine to the wires."

"Blasting machine?" Claire slapped her forehead. She turned to Preston. "It's still in my car!"

Preston sprinted back to the Volvo. Claire could see him frantically searching through the back. "I can't find it!" he shouted. "What am I looking for?"

Claire's voice was shrill. "A box! A box with a red T-handle!"

Just then the ground trembled, and a blue light flooded out of the mouth of the hole. Claire leaned over and looked down into it. What she saw made her skin crawl: it looked like a dozen pairs of yellow eyes staring back at her, growing larger as she watched.

They were ascending.

"We've got to blow it," she yelled. "Now!"

Preston returned, breathing hard, holding the blasting box. "Is this what you need?"

"Yes!" Claire grabbed it and set it down on the ground. She fumbled with the wires, running them through the binding posts and tightening them down. She pulled up on the handle.

"Fire in the hole!"

She ducked her head, squeezed her eyes shut and slammed the handle down. It made a whirring noise like a long zipper being pulled up.

Nothing happened.

She frantically checked the connections and pulled up again on the handle.

"Fire in the hole, dammit!"

The T-handle whirled down.

Nothing.

Claire clenched her fists. "It's not working…again!"

She looked back down the hole. The terrible eyes were almost to the top. Blood was throbbing in her temples. She felt as though she was going to faint.

Suddenly, her father's voice was in her head: what he would tell her when they were practicing shooting at the range:

Steady, girl steady. You must always stay calm. That's what will give you an edge over your opponent.

Then she had an idea.

She pulled her Smith & Wesson .38 out of her holster.

She turned to Mr. B. "Will this work?"

For a second, Mr. B. stared at her, uncomprehending. Then he laughed. "Damned if it might! Never seen it done, but seems a hot bullet might do it."

He came to her side. "We only need to set off one. The rest should blow with the shock. That's how we used to blow trenches."

He placed a stick of dynamite on the surface next to the one furthest from the pool, then looked at Claire. "How good a shot are you?" he asked.

"Good enough."

"Can you hit that stick from a hundred feet? We need to get that far at least, so as not to blow ourselves to kingdom come. Even then, we'll be lucky to survive."

"You bet your ass I can." Claire grabbed Mr. B.'s hand and they sprinted away from the pool. She waved at Preston. "Preston, get back. Run!"

Claire knelt down on one knee and raised her arm.

"Everyone, take cover." Claire yelled.

Preston's eyes went from Claire's raised hand holding the pistol and then to the pool. "Wait!" He sprinted to the pool's edge and reached into his pocket.

"Preston! What are you doing? Get away!"

"Claire - hold on!" Preston pulled out a small vial from his pocket, twisted off its top and emptied its clear liquid contents into the pool. He tossed the empty vial across the lawn and dashed to Claire's side.

"Holy water." He met her eyes. "It really is from the River Jordan."

Claire sighted down the barrel of the .38.

"Stop!" Mr. B. raised his hand. "You all need to get down to the ground to avoid the blast wave. Claire, can you shoot lying prone?"

"No problem." Claire got down on her stomach, set her elbows in the dirt and steadied the gun in both hands. Mr. B. and Preston got down on either side of her.

"Fire in the hole!" she yelled, looking around. She took in a deep breath, blew it out and squeezed slowly on the .38's trigger, immediately ducking her head.

The shock wave from the exploding dynamite slammed her like a body blow from a defensive tackle. Claire pressed her face deep into the grass, covered her head with her arms, and lay still while she was showered with clods of dirt and water.

After a few seconds everything became quiet.

Then, through the ringing in her ears, Claire made out the sound of rushing water. She looked up to see a torrent of water spilling out of the shattered pool wall, through the ragged trench blown out by the dynamite and pouring down into the pit.

Preston got unsteadily to his feet and brushed himself off. He reached down and helped Claire up.

"You okay?" he said.

"I think so."

Mr. B. stood up.

"And you, Mr. B.?" Preston asked.

"I seem to be all in one piece." He nodded at the trench. "I think your plan worked, Doctor Claire."

Claire walked back to the hole. The cascade from the pool was rushing down and disappearing into the darkness below. Mr. B. and Preston joined her and they watched wordlessly as the pool emptied. Wisps of steam rose out of the hole. Claire stood with her revolver ready, half expecting some *thing* to come climbing out. After a couple minutes, she realized that was not going to happen and lowered her .38.

"Nice shot," Preston said.

"Thanks." Claire pointed to the emptying pool. "Do you really think your holy water made any difference?"

"Couldn't hurt." Preston put his hands in his pockets. "You know, I've been carrying that little vial of River Jordan water for years. As kind of a good luck charm, I guess."

Claire turned to Mr. B. "Sorry about your swimming pool."

Mr. B. shrugged. "I've been meaning to shut down this old pool for a while. Too much maintenance. Now I don't have to go to the trouble of draining it."

Chapter 32

There was a flapping sound, and a large crow landed on Claire's shoulder.

"Raven. How are you?"

Acting on impulse, Claire had stopped on her way out of town and climbed to the top of the Testament Hill mound. She was not surprised to have company.

Ivy scrambled up. "Grandpa Doyle drove me. I knew I would find you here. Raven wants to say goodbye, Miss Doctor Claire."

Claire turned her head to the crow. "Goodbye, Raven." The bird let out a quiet mew, lifted off her shoulder and soared into the azure sky.

Ivy was beaming at her.

Claire reached down and briefly touched the young girl's cheek. "And goodbye to you too, Ivy. I'll never forget you. Thank you and Raven for saving me from the owls."

"Skander told me you would need my help. We were keeping watch over you." Ivy said. "We knew you'd be coming to Testament Hill."

Ivy took Claire's hand. They watched as a pair of deer foraged in the field below.

"Grandpa told me what you did to keep us safe," Ivy said.

"He did?"

"Yes. Mr. B. called him on the telephone."

"I see." Claire looked into Ivy's eyes. "What do you think, Ivy? Are we safe?"

For a moment, the young girl said nothing. Ivy looked skyward. She murmured something Claire could not make out.

Claire followed her gaze. Overhead, in the brightening sky, tenuous wisps of clouds had come together at a point directly above them. The clouds began revolving, spiraling out like a giant pinwheel. In the center, a black spot emerged and grew. Through it, stars shimmered like diamonds in black velvet.

Ivy continued her murmuring. One central star grew larger until its brightness overwhelmed the others. Claire thought she saw a beam of golden light emerge from it, come down from the sky, and for a second, illuminate Ivy's face like a warm caress.

Claire blinked and the vision was gone. The beam faded. The hole in the sky closed up and the clouds dispersed.

There was a tug on Claire's sleeve. She bent down to Ivy's upturned face. Ivy whispered to her.

Claire straightened, and closed her eyes for a moment, recalling Skander's words: *the Enah*. She looked back down at Ivy. "I want to give you this." She lifted the necklace with the amulet over her head. "It belongs to you. I've just been its temporary caretaker."

Ivy took the necklace. She winked at Claire, then with the heel of her shoe, she dug a hollow in the dirt and lowered the amulet into it. She brushed the dirt back and patted the soil down. "It belongs here, Miss Doctor Claire," she said when she was done.

Claire could have sworn that, just then, the ground heaved slightly under her, like a deep sigh in the depths of the Earth.

Amos Doyle was calling Ivy's name. He waved to them from the road below. He was leaning up against a rusty Chevy pickup, legs casually crossed. Claire and Ivy made their way back down the hill.

"All packed up, Doctor Claire?" Amos asked.

"Yes I am." Claire looked at Ivy. Raven was perched on her shoulder. "Ivy, you take care of your grandpa."

"I most certainly will." Ivy gave Claire a quick hug then nodded to her grandpa. The pair walked over to the truck and climbed in. Doyle cranked it over and stuck his head out the window. "Enjoy your trip out West, Doctor Brannigan."

Claire watched until the truck disappeared around a curve, then started walking back to her Volvo. Hearing a vehicle approach, she stopped and looked up the road.

A red '59 Cadillac Eldorado with a shiny Airstream in tow came into view. It pulled over to the side of the road and slowed to a stop. The driver's door opened and John Preston stepped out. He jogged up to Claire, grinning.

"Hello, Claire. I thought you might stop here on your way out. I was hoping to say goodbye."

"This certainly is a popular place." Claire smiled.

He waved his hand towards Claire's car. "All set to go on your road trip?"

"Yep. I'm going back to the university to wrap up a few things, put my stuff away in storage, and then I'm off on a sabbatical."

"Where to first?"

Claire pointed. "Going to gas up the old Volvo, get on Route 66, and head west. New Mexico first, then Utah, then on to California. Down the coast, maybe end up in San Francisco."

"Sounds wonderful."

"There's a revolution in thinking happening out that way, and I think it might be a good place for me to re-examine my life."

"I totally understand."

Claire took a long breath. "Preston, my world has been shaken to its foundations. I used to believe that science could explain everything. But it cannot. Science can certainly keep us honest; keep us from going down the wrong path; keep us aimed at the truth. But in the end, perhaps the heart is the best judge"

Preston reached out and took her hand. He seemed to be at a loss for words.

"What's the next stop for the revival?" Claire was making conversation, stalling for time, avoiding the inevitable.

"Chicago. Going to take my message to the big city."

"Well, I'm sure you will inspire a lot of people."

"I like to think so."

For a moment they searched each other's faces.

Preston cleared his throat. "This sounds corny, but I bet we see each other again someday."

"Goodbye, John Preston." Claire let his hand drop out of hers. Preston hesitated. His mouth worked as if he was about to say more, but then he turned and walked to his car. As he pulled out onto the road, he waved.

"I've got a feeling we will," He called out.

Two Years Later

Prester John stepped up to the podium and looked upward. Over the rim of the stadium, the skyline of the great American metropolis glowed in the orange hue of the sunset. He scanned the crowd, as always, looking for that certain face, all the while knowing it was futile. Even if Claire was there, somewhere in the tens of thousands of souls, he probably would not recognize her at that distance.

He gently tapped the microphone.

"The battle is always joined, my friends," he began. "The war is never over. We must be vigilant: evil is with us always, in the shadows, in the hidden dark places - waiting to invade our hearts and minds. We must be steadfast and walk a straight path. The path of righteousness."

He paused, letting his words sink in.

"Evil is real. It seeks to pull our souls to its breast, consume us with its fire. It comes to us in many guises: some are brazen, like the strumpet on the street corner, some are subtle like flood waters slowly rising, unnoticed at first, then engulfing us until it is too late to save ourselves.

The Buddha said: *It is a man's own mind, not his enemy or foe that lures him to evil ways.*'"

Prester John raised his arms and spread them out. "So, my brothers and sisters, what is the lesson here?" His intense amber eyes roamed over the audience.

"It is through your own heart and mind that Satan channels evil. He himself cannot directly do evil, only we, with our free will, can *do* evil. So be on guard. Be on the lookout. You must be the sentry of your soul. You must protect and save yourself."

Prester John paused. A myriad of faces were turned to him, waiting to hear his message, hanging on his every word.

It was a huge responsibility. He chose what he said carefully, inspired by the feelings in his heart.

Some, in their fervor were calling him divine, and would reach out to touch him for comfort and even healing.

Prester John knew better: he was just a man. But he knew things, had seen things, and was driven to share his experience. It was the right thing to do. His eyes roamed over the faces again, but this time there was no more yearning. He smiled. He was at peace.

The rising sun reflecting off the Golden Gate bridge gave it an eerily profound and eternal presence.

It's like the pyramids of Egypt or the ruins of Machu Picchu, Claire reflected. She was sitting cross-legged on a hill overlooking the city that she had come to love and call home. On weekend mornings, she would often ride her bike up from her apartment and just sit quietly for a while. And just *be*.

The wind from the bay swept up the hill and set the branches of the Monterey pine over her head waving and whispering. A crow landed in the grass and strutted around.

"Well, hello…Raven's brother."

Claire closed her eyes.

"The blue light was a bad light, the sign of the devil working."

As it had many times as the months rolled by, what Ivy had whispered to her that last day on Testament Hill replayed in Claire's mind:

"And the golden light was the light of angels. They come to us to help us whenever the evil ones arise.

Claire opened her eyes and stared out over the bay. A cloud passed in front of the sun and dark shadows ran across the water. Claire reached behind her back and felt the cold, hard outline of her .38 Smith & Wesson. She was ready.

On the bike path down the hill, Claire stopped to make way for a young girl with long golden hair walking a huge dog. The dog gently nudged Claire and licked her hand.

"My, what a nice dog." Claire said to the girl. "What is his name?"

The girl looked up with a big smile. "His name is 'Wolf'.

Another novel by Philip Kadwell, <u>The Afterlifer's Tale</u>, is the extraordinary recounting of a man's journey into the afterlife, and returning to reveal its unexpected and surprising secrets.

    The author may be contacted through
    libertystreetpublications@yahoo.com